Praise for *It Takes Two to Tangle*

"A delightful romance. Its intriguing plot, replete with unforeseen twists and coupled with a set of passionate characters, quickly make this a page-turner."

—*RT Book Reviews*, 4 Stars

"Theresa Romain has a rare ability to blend beautiful writing, great characters, delicious banter, and a lovely romance all in one perfect package. Her writing is gorgeous."

—*TBQ's Book Palace*

"Tender romance, passion, witty banter, secrets, healing, forgiveness, and love make this story absolutely delightful."

—*Romance Junkies*

"Romain's ability to draw me into the story that deeply is impressive. If you're a Regency fan who likes unconventional heroines [and] the Tragically Wounded Hero… pick it up."

—*Smart Bitches Trashy Books*

"Romain uses strong characters, witty banter, and Cyrano de Bergerac type situation to bring her story to life…definitely a must-read for Regency fans."

—*Debbie's Book Bag*

"Romain creates two enthralling characters that pull you in right away and keep you glued to the pages until the very end."

—*Book Trib*

"Intriguing...what a great read from a talented Regency author! A must-read!"

—*My Book Addiction Reviews*

"Everything you look for in a Regency...Witty and romantic."

—*Under the Boardwalk*

THERESA ROMAIN

sourcebooks
casablanca

Published by Sourcebooks Casablanca, an imprint of Sourcebooks, Inc.
P.O. Box 4410, Naperville, Illinois 60567-4410
(630) 961-3900
Fax: (630) 961-2168
www.sourcebooks.com

Printed and bound in Canada.
MBP 10 9 8 7 6 5 4 3 2 1

One

June 14, 1816
Lancashire seat of the Duke of Wyverne

"The money is gone, Your Grace."

Finally. After eleven years in Michael's service, his steward had abandoned the vague diplomacy favored by the previous Duke of Wyverne. Michael's father had been offended by bitter truths, preferring them sweetened into a palatable pap.

Michael was never offended by the truth, especially not a truth so obvious.

He wiped his pen and placed it next to the inkwell, almost hidden between ledgers and stacks of correspondence. "Of course the money's gone, Sanders. I have more titles to my name than guineas this year. I must simply borrow more."

He sanded his just-completed letter to the engineer Richard Trevithick. Only a few years before, the man had overcome financial ruin to introduce steam-powered threshing in Cornwall. A brilliant innovator. Michael requested his opinion on whether steam power could be made useful in irrigation.

This year, of all years, his dukedom needed as many brilliant and innovative opinions as Michael could lay hands on.

Sanders cleared his throat, then hesitated. The familiar headache began to prod at Michael's temples.

"Yes?" His voice came out more sharply than he intended. Tidying a stack of papers on the battered leather surface of his desk, Michael ignored the steward's gaze. Sanders's sympathetic manner was a bit too personal, as though the older man knew about the headaches or the slipping control that brought them on.

Another cough from Sanders. "The usual sources of credit have dried up, Your Grace."

Michael's head jerked up. "Impossible. Has every bank in England run out of money?"

As pallid as sand itself, Sanders's only color came from gold bridgework he wore in place of three teeth lost during a youthful altercation. Now his face drained paler than usual, and he looked as pained as if he'd had another tooth knocked out.

"England remains solvent, Your Grace, but… I regret that your financial overextension is now common knowledge. I have been unable to secure further credit on your behalf. In fact, it is likely that demands may be made for a repayment of your existing loans—ah, rather soon."

The headache clamped tight on his temples. Michael sat up straighter. "Dun me for payment, as if I'm a common cit? With whom do they think they are dealing?"

Sanders drew a deep breath. "With a man who has no hope of paying his debts, Your Grace. I believe they have lost trust in your judgment, if you'll forgive the frank speech."

Michael stared. "Yes, do continue."

"As long as the prosperity of the dukedom appeared inevitable, securing credit for your estate improvements was not a problem. But with the unusual climatic circumstances... that is to say, the weather has changed so much that... ah..." Sanders trailed off in a defensive flurry of careful language, his old habit of roundaboutation returning.

"My improvement plans remain unchanged, despite the persistence of winter," Michael said.

The damned winter. Until this year, Michael trusted two things in the world: his own judgment and his land. But this year, spring had never come, and it seemed summer would also fail to make an appearance. For months, the world had lain under a chilly frost. And now Michael couldn't trust the land, and no one else trusted his judgment.

"Exactly, Your Grace. This is what they find worrisome. During an unusual year, there is less tolerance for..." Sanders shifted his feet on the threadbare carpet of Michael's study. "Unusual behavior."

"This is an utterly unreasonable response," Michael muttered. "When infinite credit is extended to fribbles with silk waistcoats and clocked stockings."

"Waistcoats and stockings require a smaller outlay on the part of a creditor than do speculative mechanical constructions, Your Grace."

Michael's mouth twitched. "My speculative

mechanical constructions, as you call them, will be the making of Lancashire." Or should have been—*would* have been.

He had planned so carefully, overseeing every detail himself to make sure it was perfect: plowing moorland into canals; researching steam power. And finally, finally, he had a chance of reclaiming land no one had ever thought would be useful.

If his creditors were reasonable. Or if the world hadn't frozen solid. Now there was nothing to irrigate; all the crops were dead. There was nothing with which to water them; the canals were troughs of icy mud.

His signet ring weighed heavy on his finger; he rubbed at the worn gold band. "Well. Even if I am short of funds, Sanders, I will find a way to fix the situation."

"I can think of one possible way, Your Grace." The steward hesitated.

Michael's eyes flicked to Sanders. "Judging from your overlong pause, I'm not going to like it. Do tell me at once."

"You could marry an heiress." Sanders shaped the words as delicately as if he held glass beads between his precious gold teeth. "An alliance with a wealthy family would restore your creditors' confidence, as well as providing the necessary infusion of cash to restart work on the canals." He paused. "Or even build those steam-powered pumps you are interested in, Your Grace."

"Bribery, Sanders?"

The steward's mouth turned up at the corners. "Good sense, Your Grace."

Michael leaned back in his chair and allowed his

eyes to fall closed. Mentally, he pressed the headache into a ball and threw it to the side of his awareness. What was left?

The facts. The money was gone, and if Sanders were right, no more would be coming. Crops were scarce this year. There was barely anything to feed the tenants, much less their livestock or his own sprawling herds of sheep. The duchy was dying.

Sanders made a fair point; credit depended on appearances. Social power depended on appearances. If a man could maintain the appearance of wealth and power, it didn't matter if he had two sous to rub together.

Michael had little use for false appearances, but the polite world had little use for this eccentricity—so they had avoided one another for the past eleven years.

But if Michael's goal was to save the dukedom, he must get more money. And one day, he must get an heir. The steward's suggestion was perfectly logical: a wife would be simply the latest of Wyverne's improvements.

"Very well. I shall marry." Michael opened his eyes, and the headache roared back into his consciousness. Over its pounding, he said, "Shall we convene a house party, then?"

Now Sanders looked as if the glass beads had been shoved up his posterior. "I regret that that is impossible, Your Grace. I have, as you know, kept in contact with your London household over the years, and I hesitate to inform you that they have come into the possession of certain articles of interest regarding—"

Michael held up a hand. "Speak plainly, if you please."

The steward's gaze darted away. "The *ton* thinks

you're mad, Your Grace. It's a frequent source of amusement in the scandal rags."

"Is it? After all the time I've been away, they still talk about me. How fascinating I am."

A good reply. Such words sounded carefree, belying the headache that now clanged with brutal force, or the queasy pitch of his stomach. Michael could ignore these distractions, could do and say what was needed. But that word, *mad*—he had heard it so often that he had come to hate it.

He had never known he was *mad* as a boy—never, until he was sent off to school. If there had been nothing to do but study, he would have excelled, but the close quarters, the games, the initiations others handled so easily had turned Michael ill and shaking. Always scrambling for solitude, he was eventually sent home. A sin for which his father had never forgiven him; a type of son his father had never accepted. But hard-won solitude had been Michael's, save for a brief interlude in London more than a decade before.

A wholly unsuccessful interlude that revived whispers about the old duke's mad son. Michael had hoped these whispers were silenced after so many years. But no: if the polite world was again questioning his sanity, that was undoubtedly why no more credit was forthcoming. Anyone would loan to a genius, but no one would risk a farthing on the schemes of a madman.

Unfortunate that the line between the two was slim and easily crossed, especially this year. Snow in summer could transform even the most brilliant man into a lunatic.

"If I might make a suggestion," Sanders ventured.

"Go on."

"If you travel to London at once, Your Grace, you may take part in the final weeks of the season. You will find many potential brides there and can determine which lady would suit you best." Sanders's thin, sun-browned face softened under its thatch of grayish hair. "Once they meet you in person, Your Grace, they will surely be charmed, and all scurrilous gossip will be refuted."

"Charmed, Sanders? I haven't charmed anyone since I learned to walk and talk." Except for that brief, bright flash of time in London.

Years ago. Unnecessary even to recall it. At this stage of life, he was as likely to charm a wife as he was to plop a turban on his head and charm a cobra.

"I would be delighted to travel to London in your stead, Your Grace," Sanders said, "but I doubt I should answer the purpose to the young ladies of town."

"Shall I, though?" Michael rubbed a hand over his eyes. "A madman. The mad duke. 'The mad duke's bride hunt.' Why, the scandal-rag headlines almost write themselves."

Sanders shuffled his feet. Michael made a dismissive gesture. "It doesn't matter," he lied. "There is nothing I wouldn't do to save the dukedom."

That much was quite true.

Was it mad to care for one's legacy? To make the well-being of his tenants his purpose in life? To trust his land more than the people who had betrayed him so often, so long ago?

Society thought so, and back into its maw he must go—though his escape last time had been narrow indeed. But to save Wyverne, he would do anything. Even go to London; even sell himself for coin.

He only hoped he would fetch a high price.

July 3
London

"Wyverne has reopened his house in St. James's Square," drawled Andrew, Baron Hart, as he pulled on his breeches. "First time in at least a decade he's come to Town during the season. Should be amusing to see what he gets up to, don't you think?"

Caroline Graves, the widowed Countess of Stratton, paused in twisting her wheat-colored hair into a loose chignon. She stared at Hart's roguish reflection in the shield-shaped glass above her dressing table. "Wyverne? That's impossible. Everyone knows he never leaves Lancashire."

Ignoring the startled thump of her heart, she poked a pin into her coiled locks, then adjusted her expression until it reflected nothing more than mild disbelief and milder amusement.

"Back he is, though," Hart said. "Wonder what drove him here? I've heard his pockets are completely empty nowadays. Might be something to do with that."

"I cannot imagine, Hart," Caroline said in a carefully careless tone, turning her head to check the effect of her upswept hair. "You might be right. He could be seeking investors for… whatever scheme it is he's pursuing nowadays."

It was a system of irrigation canals into moorland,

she knew, though there was no reason she should know such a thing.

"Rather prosy, that. I hope it's something more colorful than a hunt for capital. You once got in a bit of trouble over him, didn't you?"

She shrugged; the cap sleeve of her chemise slipped from one shoulder. "Nothing to speak of. I've since been in far worse trouble over far better men than Wyverne."

The first part was certainly true. The second part—she wasn't sure. She'd never been sure, where Wyverne was concerned, whether his carelessness was the simple arrogance of the aristocracy or whether it cloaked something far deeper.

Maybe it didn't matter. The damage he caused was the same either way.

In the glass, Caroline saw Hart stretch, then approach her. He knew the effect of his person quite well. His torso was lean and muscled, like a sculpture. And just as if it were a sculpture, she stroked his contours with her eyes without being the slightest bit aroused.

But he would expect her to be aroused, would he not? She thought of Wyverne and allowed her cheeks to flush.

Hart grinned. "Can't blame a man for getting into trouble with you, Caro. But Wyverne's mad, isn't he?"

"He's harmless enough," Caroline answered in a voice as smooth and colorless as cream. This was false, though his harm did not come from lack of sanity.

"They're betting at White's that he'll be committed to Bedlam before the season's out."

"Impossible," she said again, turning to face Hart. "He has no close relatives. Who would dare try to have him committed?"

Hart blinked in surprise, and Caroline added swiftly, "One never knows, of course. It's possible he'll create a scandal." *Again.*

Hart looked gratified to have Caroline enter into his game. *Scandal* was one of his favorite words. "Didn't think of him as a ladies' man, Caro. Do you suppose he'll come join your court? Be one of your admirers?" He reached out a questing forefinger, his roguish grin confident and possessive.

Caroline allowed him to stroke her arm, caress her collarbone. Such small intimacies held no true intimacy at all when they were shared among many.

This was protection of a sort. As a wealthy widow, she held as much power as a woman could hold in society. She played her admirers against one another without the smallest intention of letting any of them draw truly close to her.

In a way, Wyverne had made her what she was. And now, after all these years, Wyverne was back.

This time, she was prepared for him.

"I doubt His Grace will concern himself with me." Caroline increased the brightness of her smile until Hart staggered back, dazzled, and sat on the edge of her bed. "And I am certainly not concerned with him. Especially not now."

"What do you mean?"

"Just what you think. Just what you might be hoping." She rose from her seat before the dressing table and sashayed to the bed. With a sweep of her arm, she threw back the green damask bedcovers and the bed sheets.

Hart stared up at her like a child who could not believe he had just been offered another serving of apple tart. "By God, Caro, you're a wonder."

Despite her fast reputation, rare was the man Caroline welcomed to her bed. She chose lovers by toting up the positives and negatives, choosing the man with the most of the former and the fewest of the latter. Hart had won her over with a combination of a handsome face, a fine figure, and indomitable persistence.

And with dark hair and green eyes—ah, she had a weakness for those. Though just why, and of whom Hart reminded her, she hadn't allowed herself to consider for a long time.

Nor would she consider it now. Wyverne had no place in her life anymore. Really, he never had. He had made that clear enough eleven years earlier.

With determined force, Caroline pressed Hart to the bed and drew from him the fleeting oblivion of her own pleasure.

Two

Bump.

In Lady Applewood's crowded ballroom, it was impossible not to jostle others. The slim maiden who had just backed into Michael, giggling and chattering, was the seventh to do so.

And as with the previous six, the smile on her lips disappeared as soon as she saw who was behind her. "Oh. Your Grace? Do pardon me—I didn't—that is..."

Fan aflutter, eyes darting wildly, she skittered away into the crowd. Such was her haste that she left a torn flounce behind.

And they called *him* mad. At least he could complete a sentence.

"Think nothing of it," he muttered. He quashed the urge to shudder off the close contact, the press of so many bodies. A London ballroom was the best hunting ground for a wealthy wife—if only the women didn't scatter like partridges whenever he came near.

This afternoon, he had seen a caricature posted in a printshop window: a wild-eyed hunchback wearing a ducal coronet of gold strawberry leaves. In one hand, the creature held a shovel; in the other, an empty purse. He lunged, slavering, for a lily-pale maiden in court dress.

Nonsense of the lowest order. Michael had never been the sort to lunge for maidens, and his shoulders were perfectly square. And he hadn't dug his land's canals himself—though what would be the harm if he had?

Great harm, evidently. The scandal rags had done their work, and thoroughly: the women of London were convinced of his madness. They wanted a Lancelot or a Galahad, not an eccentric Merlin.

A swat stung his forearm. Michael sucked in an impatient breath, the "it's quite all right" waiting upon his lips.

"I vow, Wyverne, I wasn't sure how you'd turn out, given the talk of... well. Well!"

Someone was actually addressing him. How novel. He looked down at the small, rounded form of his hostess, the Marchioness of Applewood. Once a slender beauty, she had retained her good cheer far better than she had her figure.

With another swat on his forearm, she beamed up at him. "It's lovely to see you after all these years, dear Wyverne."

"Thank you." He tried to draw his arm out of her reach. "For the invitation."

The middle-aged marchioness dimpled, reaching up to pat his cheek. "Of course! As I was your last hostess when you were in London so long ago, I wanted to be your first hostess this time. *Wicked* man!"

Michael flinched—from the unexpected touch or

the mention of that long-ago ball. Or both. Despite the world's whispers, he had never felt truly mad until that single night. After he took Caroline Ward in his arms...

He crushed that thought as he would a walnut shell. No.

"You are the absolute *image* of your father, you are." Lady Applewood flushed rosy under her face paint, and she spoke low beneath the din in the ballroom. "He was a handsome devil too, and he always did have a *tendre* for me. Such a flirt! Only do not tell my husband I said that, I beg you. Applewood is such a jealous creature."

"Ah." Any further reply was made unnecessary when her ladyship batted him on the arm yet again.

"*Such* a wicked man!" She beamed at him. "But I knew you'd understand. Now, we ought to find you someone to dance with, shouldn't we? I would *love* to stand up with you myself, but—"

"Applewood is such a jealous creature," repeated Michael. This earned him another giggle, another bat upon the arm.

"Precisely! Ah, just like your father."

The headache sounded a warning gong in his temples. "I resemble my late father in very little besides appearance," he ground out. Then stopping himself, he tried to formulate a pleasant smile. "This was much to his dismay."

Of all the women in the *ton*, he would have considered Lady Applewood least likely to extend him an invitation. But perhaps she hoped for another serving of gossip, such as he had given rise to at her ball all those years ago. Or maybe her mummified affection for his departed father led her to look on him kindly. Whatever the reason, he needed every scrap of such goodwill until he found his footing in society.

The heat of the ballroom pressed upon him all at once: candle flames, wool coats, and hundreds of bodies. A clamor of laughter and chatter in his ears. Perfume, sweet and cloying over the earthy odor of perspiration.

The headache cracked its figurative knuckles and settled in for a long visit.

No. He must ward it off. Fresh air, that was what he needed. There was a terrace to one side of the ballroom.

"I thank you for your hospitality, Lady Applewood," he blurted, remembering to bow over her hand. "Please excuse me."

Twisting aside to avoid the woman's farewell swat upon the forearm, he threaded through the crowd in the direction of the terrace. Dandies and matrons and maidens drew away from him as he passed, whispering, their wide eyes searching his own for wildness. Looking over his form for evidence of a crooked back, no doubt, or inspecting his hands for the roughness of shocking labor.

His arms were painfully tense from shoulder to fingertips. He hadn't expected the rumors to take root so deeply, to outweigh the lure of his title. Nor had he predicted that the only woman to look on him kindly would do so for his damned father's sake.

At last, he reached the edge of the high-ceilinged ballroom. Making fists of his aching hands, he pushed open a French door and stepped onto the terrace.

He drew a deep breath through his nose, expecting

clean, cool night air to clear the pounding from his head. But London air did not bite and wake him with its crispness, as did the air on the Lancashire moors. Even in this freakish, chill summer, the air hung heavy and oily with coal smoke. It coated Michael's lungs and further fogged his head. It reminded him how far he was from where he ought to be.

Still, the quiet was welcome. And the cheerful marchioness had gone to great effort to make the outside of her London mansion as welcoming as most people found the inside. Hanging lanterns warmed the sweep of stone with mottled light, their glass painted with red and gold scrollwork.

As he should have guessed, the effect was irresistible to couples in search of seclusion. His eyes adjusting from the dazzling ballroom to the starlit sky, he could see several shadowy blobs, each the shape of two bodies pressed tightly together. As silently as he could, he crossed the stone terrace and sank onto a bench away from the sight of would-be lovers.

Another deep breath, and the headache began to loosen its grip. A few more minutes of silence and it would slink away. Then he would decide what to do next.

But the silence ended almost at once. "No, Stratton. I will not allow it."

A woman's voice rang out, cool and formal, much louder than the murmurs of lovers in the twilight.

A deeper, placating rumble, then the ringing female voice again. "It wouldn't be proper, Stratton, and you know how concerned I am with propriety." The voice held a bubble of laughter this time, but it popped abruptly. "Now you must excuse me. I have to return to my friends."

Friends. Fortunate lady. Likely she had a dance lined up, and this fool was keeping her from someone whose company she preferred. Michael shut his eyes and wondered how long it would take for an eligible woman to agree to marry him, or even to agree to speak with him. For how long were caricatures posted in the windows of printers' shops?

The voice was louder now. "Stratton, this is unwise of you. Remember what I did last time you wouldn't release me as I asked."

A pause. "You mistake the matter if you think I am bluffing." The sweet tone had gone steely.

Michael opened his eyes. The woman sounded as though she could take care of herself, but the man was insistent. And no one seemed to hear them except Michael. He squinted back at the bright, whirling ballroom. Indoors was a genteel chaos of music and laughter, heedless of the unfolding drama outside.

Michael deliberated for an instant. He must not do anything that seemed mad, for God's sake. But he could not let a woman be menaced.

He stood and strode forward out of the shadows, allowing his feet to thump on the stone of the terrace. Moving directly under a painted lantern, he leaned on the sturdy balustrade, allowing his presence to become known to the too-persistent man.

From here, he could overlook the great house's gardens. They looked tranquil and still, the darkness broken only by the firefly wink of tiny lanterns.

A hand touched his arm. "Ah, here you are. It is

time for our dance. I've been looking forward to it with such anticipation."

The female voice that had bitten so coldly at the unwanted suitor. Now it was warm, even flirtatious. Michael's skin prickled under the pressure of the slim, gloved hand. He turned his head to the side, to see who had approached him.

"Caroline Ward." His numb lips shaped the name before consulting with his brain. His brain conjured delight and dread, then was unable to decide between the two.

His eyes alone were unbothered, gulping the sight of her. She was still a vision of loveliness, tall and curving and fair-haired, with light eyes and a cherry-ripe smile.

And she was *touching* his *arm*.

Too close. She was *too close*. His muscles went into spasm, painful twitches that yanked at his bones. "I beg your pardon, Miss Wa… madam." Was she married? Surely she had married by now. "You must have mistaken someone else's dance for mine." Michael rolled his forearm in an attempt to remove it from her grasp.

"Nonsense, Wyverne. I could never mistake you." Her voice was sweet and warm, but her gaze remained flinty. Her fingers tightened on his arm as a man drew near them.

Anyone observing her from a small distance would see only the brightness of her smile, the intimacy of her possessive hand. But Michael stood close enough to see the plea in her eyes. Ignorant though he might be of the *ton*'s rules and foibles, this message was clear enough.

She needed his help. That was all. *Wyverne*, she called him. He was used to being Wyverne, to offering help to his tenants. He could help her too.

If only she would stop touching him. The sensation was too unsettling to be borne.

"Of course," Michael choked out. "It would be my honor… ah…"

"Wyverne, I've told you time and again. You absolutely must call me Caroline, or Caro if you like. There's no need for this silly formality of *Lady Stratton* between us."

Clever woman, to supply him with her name so smoothly. "As you wish, Caro." So. She *had* married, and married an aristocrat. He supposed that was what she had always wanted.

Her unwanted companion drew alongside Michael and Caroline. He made an unlikely predator: mild featured, of middling height, with light brown hair that was beginning to race away from his temples and forehead. His clothing was fashionable without being flamboyant.

"Who have you here, Caro?" said the new arrival, a haughty expression sitting oddly on his rounded cheeks. "Another of your little friends?"

Michael lifted his chin. "You may refer to me as the Duke of Wyverne."

Caroline smiled. "Your Grace, might I present the Earl of Stratton? My late husband's great-nephew."

Late husband, she said.

Before Michael could tease out more meaning from her words, the earl was bowing to him. "Earl of Stratton, Your Grace, as Caro said. Well, well. This is a pleasure. I've heard a great deal about you." He smirked his way upright again. "You have just arrived in Town, I think?"

Michael acknowledged the bow with a tilt of his head. "Very recently. Yes."

Stratton seemed unsure whether this was a snub or not. After a pause, his smirk folded into a fair approximation of good cheer. "Well, society stands ready to offer you a welcome. No doubt we will all enjoy your stay. Caro, come inside with me."

"I think not." Caroline fired a gleaming smile at the earl. "Wyverne and I might not dance after all; it is so pleasant out here. I am inclined to stay on the terrace for quite some time. But there is no need for you to wait for me, Stratton. Do go inside and find someone to dance with."

Unmistakable dismissal. Though he glared, the earl had no choice but to slither away. Michael fixed his eyes on the cleverly chased buttons of his own coat sleeve but monitored the sounds of Stratton's retreat. Footsteps decreased in volume as he crossed the terrace; then a burble of voices spilled through the French doors from the ballroom and was muffled when the doors clicked shut again.

At once, Michael shook his arm free from Caroline's grasp.

"What was that ridiculous lie about a dance, madam?" He should not bark at a woman, he knew, but the prickling tension in his arm was about to drive him mad.

No. Not mad. It was just… uncomfortable.

She folded her hands, serene as a saint. "Ought I to

apologize for that? I suppose it wasn't well done of me to put you in such a position, but I needed an excuse to escape Stratton. You needn't worry that I expect you to dance with me. In fact, now that Stratton is gone, you can be on your way as well."

She turned away from him, dismissing him.

And he realized where they stood: on Lady Applewood's terrace, mere feet away from where, as a fool of twenty-one, he had allowed her to tear him so beautifully apart.

"So." His jaw clenched. "You use me as an excuse, then walk away. I see that nothing much has changed about you, *Lady Stratton*." He laid his heaviest stress on these final words.

"As a widow of advanced years, I shall take that as a compliment."

"Take it as you like."

"Oh, I shall. I am accustomed to doing what I like." Slowly, she turned back and met his eye. "But I cannot say you have remained unchanged, Wyverne. I remember you as being much more pleasant."

This startled a laugh from him. "Do you? I wasn't aware I had ever been known for being pleasant." Brusque, yes. Mad, undoubtedly. Pleasant? Never.

"I did not say you had been pleasant, only *more* pleasant. But if you are capable of laughter, perhaps there is hope for you yet." She smiled, this time without the flinty look. "And I do thank you for your help in disposing of Lord Stratton. He is extremely tiresome about trying to convince me to marry him—as if persistence alone would ever change my mind."

"Persistence?" He had not considered this tool for capturing a wife.

"More than persistence, sadly. He's not above using threats. But then again, neither am I. Last time Stratton proposed, I *accidentally* hit him in a sensitive area with my knee."

Michael winced.

"Exactly. He did not soon forget that, but it hasn't kept him from proposing again. He wants the fortune left to me by my late husband. This time, he knew enough to shield his sensitive area when he asked, though my answer was no different. Men can be so single-minded when it comes to retrieving property they regard as rightfully theirs."

He managed a clipped, disinterested voice. "I suppose."

When he had said she hadn't changed at all, that had been untrue. The planes of her face were stronger than he remembered, or maybe memory had softened the hard edges. Now her features were as beautifully constructed as a draftsman's plans—the arc of her brow over tilted eyes, a straight nose, and high cheekbones.

At the age of nineteen, she had been fresh-faced and turbulent, the diamond of her debut season. In her way, as brilliant an engineer as any pioneer of steam power: balancing friendships between the wealthy, the notorious, and the bright. Maintaining a clockwork-perfect state of checks and balances.

Such brilliance had always tugged Michael like a lodestone. But he could not afford to become distracted by fleshly desires. He kept such urges soldered up, for they were ready to vaporize him if given the slightest weakness.

Caroline tossed him a grin, and he felt a rivet pop.

"You suppose," she repeated. "For my part, I *suppose* that you are also seeking a bit of property. If the scandal sheets are to be believed, which they sometimes are, you are in London to find a wife. Perhaps you and Stratton can share ideas, not that he has any that are worthwhile."

"That makes two of us." Ah, he could have bitten his tongue.

But she didn't laugh; she simply looked at him. "You have had no luck yet?"

He did not perceive any pity or mockery in the question, and so he answered it. "Very little luck of any sort this year."

As if to underline his sentence, a blast of chilly wind slapped their faces, then subsided again.

She turned to lean against the balustrade next to him, then tilted her head back, faint moonlight limning her profile. In the breeze, wisps of flaxen hair fluttered around her face. A faint floral scent wrapped around Michael like a scarf. Somehow the air seemed lighter, cooler.

Maybe because, for a few seconds, he had served as Galahad instead of Merlin—though his thoughts were none so pure as those of the fabled knight. He felt Caroline next to him as surely as he'd have felt a fire; heat seemed to prickle up and down his body. His disobedient heart stuttered, speared by a shaft of desire, then resumed pounding all the more quickly.

"The weather is strange this year," she said. "So cold, for so long. It has complicated matters for you, has it not?"

"A man who hangs his fortune on irrigation must have something to irrigate."

"Or another fortune with which to build?"

"Or that."

"I should have known that nothing but business and dire need would draw you back to London." She cut a glance at him, and her lips bowed into a bewitching smile that made him forget his surprise. He forgot everything except the color, plum-dark in the warm lantern light, and their shape. She was a promise and a threat. She gave him a siren's smile, and he would be crushed on the rocks, gladly, for a taste… the mere possibility of a taste.

No.

He would not. He had already been crushed, in the economic sense; that was why he was here in London to begin with. Nothing could come from reckless desire except disaster. Nothing could save him—save his dukedom—except careful thought.

"Business and dire need are among the most worthwhile reasons for visiting a city." True, but even to his own ears, he sounded stuffy.

"I've no doubt of it. I didn't intend to mock you. Those aren't the only reasons one might visit, though." She kept her gaze trained on the moon, now almost obscured by a passing cloud. "You know, you never told me good-bye."

"If you are referring to the last time I was in London, I bade no one good-bye. As my father was in desperate health, I left in a hurry. I was understandably preoccupied with other matters." Still stuffy, but now he sounded annoyed too. That was acceptable. Better she think him annoyed with her than with himself.

Because his father's health had been no more than an excuse. The late duke had been dreadfully ill for a long time, and there was no reason to think he would ever improve, nor any reason to expect that he would suddenly die. No, Michael hadn't left London for his father's sake, but for his own.

His time in London had been an escape, a chance to prove the rumors wrong. But in the end, he had proved them right, and Lancashire was not far enough to flee from this dreadful knowledge.

After a long silence, Caroline spoke. "The reason should hardly signify at this distance in time. I understand that a duke, or even the heir to a dukedom, has many responsibilities. Far too many to grant him space to think of those he leaves behind."

"I left no one of significance behind."

Too harsh—far too harsh. He realized that even before her head snapped back, almost as though he had slapped her.

"I see," she said calmly. "As we are not friends, then, and never were, it only remains for me to thank you for your service tonight in freeing me from Stratton." She dipped into a curtsy. "I shall return to the ballroom now, Your Grace."

Was there a tremor in her voice? Had he wounded her feelings? Michael had no idea how to tell. But he had gone wrong somehow, for she was already walking away.

"Wait, Caro." The words burst from deep within him. "Please."

She stopped but did not turn to him. Her shoulders were squared, held high and confident. They looked far too small to carry all his burdens.

This was a mad idea. Or perhaps it was genius. Or perhaps it was nothing but a frail hope.

"Will you marry me?"

Three

Two ludicrous proposals in less than half an hour. Even for Caroline, this was developing into an unusual evening.

"I beg your pardon." She turned on her heel and faced Wyverne. "You are making me an offer of marriage? After telling me that you have long found me insignificant?"

"I didn't intend to single you out. I referred to everyone I knew in London."

"That does not improve the matter." She suppressed a laugh of disbelief. "Why are you proposing marriage to me, Wyverne?"

His gaze caught hers, then turned back toward the garden of Applewood House. "Just as you suspected. I need a wealthy wife."

He offered to share her life but would not even look at her. Typical Wyverne. There was no comprehending the man.

But Caroline could comprehend his response easily enough. It was what all her suitors would say if they were honest. Usually they gilded their intentions in fine words or sweetened them with lavish gifts, but Caroline knew what lay at their hearts.

Nothing.

For Caroline was wealthy; therein lay her appeal. This was, at least, a change from her debut season, when she had possessed no currency but a flawless face. Even after a near-disastrous brush with scandal, she had parlayed her beauty into a marriage beyond anyone's dreams but her own. In her nine years of marriage, she had earned every farthing of the generous income her late husband had willed to her. Now many men of the *ton* wished to relieve her of it.

She had never expected Wyverne to be among that number. Actually, she had never expected to see him again.

"I'll give you credit for honesty," she said.

Wyverne's mouth flexed. "I owe my future wife nothing less. My dukedom requires funds and quickly. Would you consent to be married quite soon?"

If only the words had been spoken eleven years earlier and in quite a different tone of voice. Caroline was impervious to such an offer now.

He had told her she had not changed much, and on the surface he was correct. She had taken great pains to retain her looks over the quiet years of her marriage and the raucous span of her widowhood. Though she'd recently reached the age of thirty, she could hold her own against any maiden. What the passing seasons had taken in freshness, they had replaced with luster.

The years had treated Wyverne less gently. Oh, he was still a handsome man: his profile cleanly cut, his hair waving and dark. Under the sultry light of a hanging lantern, she could tell the unique shade of his eyes, a dark green touched with brown, like evergreen needles at the end of summer. But time had sharpened his cheekbones, had sunburned faint lines on his forehead and at the corners of his eyes, broadened his shoulders, stretched him taller. He looked large enough to bear any burden, and as careworn as if he carried the troubles of the world.

It suited him, this look of strain. Dewy youth had never laid on him smoothly as a superfine coat, as it did so many young men in London. Now his face matched who he had always been inside.

Even in his frankness, proposing to her for her money, he was different from others. He sought her wealth not for his own gain, but for the sake of his dukedom. It was not any more flattering to Caroline, but it was noble in its way.

"No, Wyverne. Thank you for the honor of your offer, but I will not consent to be married anytime soon."

He looked puzzled. "You wish to wait to be married, then?"

She shook her head slowly. It felt lighter than usual. "I do not wish to be married at all."

"If you marry me"—Wyverne's eyes now focused an inch above hers—"you shall be the most powerful woman in Lancashire."

"Ah, but I like to live in London."

"You will be a duchess; that's more prestigious than a countess."

"I am aware of the order of precedence. However, a widowed countess has freedoms that even a married duchess does not." She raised her chin. "Have you any other arguments, Wyverne?"

"This is not an argument," Wyverne said in a clipped voice. "It is a proposal." At last, he looked her in the eye.

Her skin felt overheated under the cool caress of the night breeze, and her throat caught on something painful.

Drat. She clearly wasn't as prepared for Wyverne as she'd thought. How could she build a defense against him when there was no one like him on whom to practice?

But this was hardly a reason to toss away everything she had worked to gain for herself. If her youthful fascination—if Wyverne himself—could be mastered, then nothing and no one would have a hold on her.

"As I have already told you, Wyverne, I do not accept your proposal," Caroline said. "Instead, I offer you one of my own."

His brows lifted. "An investment? I had not thought of making a financial bargain."

"That is exactly what you *did* think of when you deigned to offer me your hand in exchange for my money. But I am not interested in marriage, especially for financial reasons."

"What do you propose, then, if money is of no interest to you?"

"Money is of great interest to me, but not in relation to you."

"Then we have nothing more to talk about."

"But we do, Wyverne." She was blurting the words almost before she knew what she intended to say, knowing only that she could not let Wyverne dismiss her again. "I could help you with a more personal arrangement. If a fortune is what you desire, I can put you in the way of a few wealthy fools with whom you might gamble."

A hint of a smile; just a slight dent at the corner of his firm mouth. "Fortunately for those fools, I cannot afford the time or risk of gaming tables. No, it must be a sure thing."

She cast about for another idea. "Names, then. The names of a few women you might court. I'm certain I can think of someone who would serve your purpose better than I."

"You are certain of that, are you?" Evergreen eyes caught hers. That was all he said, and as she looked at him, the air seemed to lay sultry over her, like a satin shawl.

"I'm certain, yes. I am not the same woman you knew, Wyverne. And I know more than you realize."

There was something coiled and intense in his stance. Caroline saw his gaze float down her body, then back up to her face, and he swallowed. His fingers began a jittery dance on the balustrade. "I must marry," he said in a strangled voice, "and soon, and for money. I can pursue nothing else."

"I know that too." Some sweet edge within her began to crumble.

He was as unyielding as she remembered. Though awkward, he was completely certain of his own rightness. He was difficult to be around, and perhaps that was why he was so difficult to forget.

As swiftly as Wyverne shook off her touch, slanted

a reluctant glance over her face, Caroline's old fascination had bloomed again. She wanted to caress away those fine lines, tease his troubles off his soul, feel his skin sliding under hers, hot and tight with desire. She wanted to shake up his sense of honor, unsettle him, enchant him.

She had always wanted that.

But she would not let him know. If he cared only for a fortune, any woman with plump pockets might do.

"Names," he said at last, "will do me no good. All the names you might suggest, unless they be yours or Lady Applewood's, belong to people who think me mad and will not speak to me."

"Dear me. And neither of us is available for matrimony at present."

He turned away from her, leaning on his elbows and looking out over the garden.

"Wyverne, this is ridiculous. You're no more mad than..."

"The king?" His voice dropped low, like stones into water.

"Certainly not." The poor king raved and frothed. Wyverne, as Caroline remembered him, simply didn't fit into a neat corner of society. But was that the fault of the man or of the corner into which he didn't fit? "You make a fair point, though. We must not discount the power of reputation."

"We?" He darted a glance at her. It might have been a trick of the feeble light, the deep shadows, but Caroline could have sworn something kindled in his expression.

"Yes, *we*." The idea was sudden but perfect. If she could make him need her, why, he wouldn't be a mystery anymore, or a fascination. He'd be nothing but a man, and one under her power. It would be easy, then, to lift him from her heart and mind. As neatly as a cook coring an apple. "I shall help you, Wyverne. Give me a free hand and five outings in society, and we shall have every woman in London wanting you."

"Every woman?"

Caroline raised her eyes to heaven. "All right, give me *six* outings, then. And give me more than two words by way of reply."

"I don't need to be wanted. I only need to be accepted."

"Ah." So simple, so tragic. Caroline had always needed both. "Well, we can arrange that too."

When he turned away from the starlit garden to regard her again, his attention made her insides swoop. She wanted to reach out a hand, stroke the fine, high planes of his face, but as soon as her hand lifted, she thought better of it. She had felt his tension earlier when she only touched his sleeve.

"Why should you do this for me?" His tone was clipped, suspicious.

"Consider it a token of the friendship we long ago abandoned." *He* abandoned. He would not leave her again, not unless it was on her terms.

"I cannot accept that honor from you."

"Why not?"

"No matter what one desires, I neither expect nor offer something for nothing." His lashes lowered, shadowy crescents on his cheekbones.

"Did you think I would help you for nothing?" Caroline's trill of laughter sounded breezier than she felt. "You give me too much credit for selflessness. Wyverne, if I find you a bride, I shall be the toast of London society. Not to put too fine a point on the matter, but it really will be quite a challenge as long as the caricaturists keep creating their abysmal prints of you. With my aid, though, I am certain you will gain the hand of a suitable bride."

It would be perfect. *Perfect.* The man who had almost destroyed her reputation eleven years earlier would now become the making of it.

"You are certain, you say." His jaw clenched, and Caroline again felt the slippery urge to run a finger over the clean angles of his profile.

"Yes."

In actuality, she was not. Wyverne was not like other men, and for this reason, the world thought him mad. Maybe Caroline was mad too, for she sought to repeat history, even though her plans had gone so far awry the first time.

"Then I would be honored by your assistance. I shall call on you tomorrow." His mouth bent into an awkward shape that approximated a smile. He looked down at his gloved hand, then slowly extended it.

"Oh, for heaven's sake, Wyverne." Caroline covered a swell of glee with briskness. "Don't bother. I know you don't like to shake hands."

At once, his expression relaxed and his hand dropped to his side. Caroline could not resist adding, "Instead, we shall seal our bargain with a kiss. Isn't that what this terrace is for?"

She stepped closer to him, and his chin drew back, his brows furrowing.

"I'm only teasing," Caroline murmured—not that she had truly expected him to step closer instead of away.

"I know," Wyverne replied, soft as a sigh. "I was merely surprised. When I spoke of desires earlier, I referred not to your own responses, but to mine."

His lips twisted, though the expression looked more sad than joyful. He sketched her a bow before excusing himself and withdrawing into the shadows.

He had not touched her at all. And yet, he had.

Four

To Michael's eye, Caroline's house was a tall stucco tooth in the chattering mouth of Albemarle Street. Feet, hooves, and wheels trekked back and forth before it in a constant clatter and tumult. Bright flowers tumbled and spilled from window boxes, heedless of the unusual snap in the summer weather. The effect was, Michael supposed, convivial and lovely.

It was entirely wasted on him.

Oh, not because of scorn for its appearance. His own London seat, Wyverne House, was a drafty, squat structure that resembled a giant snuffbox. But Wyvernc House had the advantage of quiet and order. It swallowed noise and drank light. Albemarle Street was overfull of both.

Michael's back began to knot as he marched up the steps to her front door. Caroline was a surprise, and surprises often made him tense.

Not because of her persistent beauty. No, it was her unshakable confidence. Her certainty that he wasn't mad—yet she offered to help him, as if she recalled their last, disastrous meeting with pity. As if determined to fix something that was broken.

Michael was used to being the one who fixed; he did *not* intend to be seen as broken. He had come today to prove her impression wrong.

But once admitted to the house, Michael found himself blinking amidst a blast of sparkle and color. There was too *much*. The walls were a vivid blue; the polished brass chandeliers, gilt picture frames, and glossy marble floors winked and shone in the slanted sunlight. From inside the drawing room, Michael could hear a dozen voices raised in babble and laughter.

Too much—much too much. Yet entirely normal for the *ton*. Michael gritted his teeth and hoped the expression resembled a smile, then trudged upstairs to the drawing room.

He eased open the door and saw at once that the room was crammed full of men. A riot of dark wool, glossy boots, nasally voices. And vases, too—bunches of flowers, riotous in their color, covered every surface that wasn't draped with male callers.

Too late, Michael realized he should have brought some sort of nosegay with him. But he couldn't back out and return with flowers; already everyone in the room had swiveled toward the doorway to regard the new arrival. Their expressions held all the suspicion of schoolboys scrutinizing a student who arrived in the middle of term.

Michael was fairly certain his would-be smile had turned into a grimace. "Good afternoon," he said.

At the center of the room sat Caroline, fair and tranquil amidst the sordid jostlings of her callers.

"Wyverne!" she called out. "How good of you to come. And I'm glad you remembered what I said about the flowers."

"Hmm," he replied noncommittally, having no idea to what she referred.

"You aren't getting tired of flowers, are you?" A young man turned dark, worried eyes to Caroline. "I didn't know."

"Not at all, Bart." Caroline spoon-fed the youthful swain a bright smile. "I adore daisies. So cheery, aren't they?"

She drew a fingertip over a thin, white petal; as the flower bounced back, pollen scattered across her lacquer-topped table. "His Grace has promised me a special bloom that grows only in Lancashire. He brought the seeds with him to London, and if they blossom, I shall have the only coquelicot carnation in the entire City."

She dimpled in her delight, and the so-called *Bart* who had looked pleased about his daisies now appeared crestfallen.

"Will you, now?" One of a pair of identically dressed dandies raised his brows and shot a cautious look at Michael. His thumb dandled a snuffbox, tracing its enameled top. "I should like to see it once it's in flower. I hope it will do you justice, Caro."

Since he had just been transformed into a botanist, Michael felt as though he ought to contribute something to the conversation. "It will not."

His voice rang like a slap through the room, and the dandy—his shirt points starched so high he could hardly turn his head—allowed an amused smile to creep over his features.

Michael lifted his chin, ignoring the pressure at his temples, and tried for one of those Galahad comments. "There is no bloom that could do justice to Lady Stratton."

Wait. That didn't help. He had just dismissed the elaborate offerings brought by all the callers, hadn't he? Indeed, the other men shifted in their chairs. If Michael were a ship captain, he would have a mutiny on his hands soon.

"Though these are very nice." He nodded at a random vase in a random part of the room.

Caroline looked as though she was trying not to smile. "I did allow you to call me Caro, if you'll recall. And thank you for the compliment, Wyverne. I've no doubt that anything you turn your hand to will come to fruition, or in this case, to blossom. Why," she addressed the other callers, "he's making the very moors bloom. Did you know that?"

The two dandies turned to Michael, blinking at him like cravat-choked bookends. "Yes, of course," faltered the one who had not yet spoken. "In Yorkshire, isn't it?"

"Lancashire," Michael corrected. Dimly, he wondered why Caroline knew so much about his determination to stretch rich fingertips of farmland onto the stark moors of his dukedom.

A fourth caller spoke up now, a man with a thin, dark face and plainly tailored clothing. "I've never heard of such a flower. Is it a new cross-breeding?" To Michael, his question seemed to hold more satirical disbelief than polite interest.

Michael nodded. "Indeed. It is a very recent creation." *Two minutes ago.*

"Do sit, please, Wyverne." Caroline indicated a chair several feet away from the other callers. "Draw that seat wherever you wish. There's tea if you'd care for some refreshment."

She reached for a silver bell, but Michael forestalled her with a shake of his head. He was willing to stand aside until these foolish callers melted away, taking their fuss and noise with them. Until then, there was no sense in the infliction of compulsory niceties.

He sat down in the inconspicuous chair, not far from the dark-faced man. "Wyverne," Michael said by way of introduction.

"So I gathered." Again, the man wore a damnable look of humor, as if everything was altogether too amusing for words. "It is an honor to meet you, Your Grace. I am Josiah Everett. Just plain mister."

Michael inclined his head. At this slight shift in posture, his chair creaked.

Hmm. A creak? He wasn't *that* heavy. He gave the thin, gilded arms a shake, and one of them pulled loose from the seat.

It might be as simple as a peg that had come unseated, or it might need a few nails. The drawing room was littered with chairs like this one; Caro would undoubtedly wish to have it repaired to preserve the set.

Michael slid from the seat, knelt on the floor, and laid the chair on its back facing him. Ah, there was the problem; the carefully fitted pegs holding the arm in place had pulled loose. No doubt the old wood had dried and shrunk.

"Another casualty of the endless winter," he

muttered. "Even the chairs feel the cold in their bones." More loudly, he said, "Everett, please get me a nail or two. Long enough to pass through this piece of wood. Do you see? And a small hammer."

When Everett didn't reply at once, Michael looked up at him, impatient. "Come now. It'll only take a moment to set this chair to rights."

Then he noticed that Everett's face had lost its look of humor; instead, he appeared bemused. And *then* Michael noticed that the room had gone quiet.

So quiet that he dimly heard Caro tell a servant, "Please fetch whatever His Grace requires." And then the whispering began, as nearly a dozen men felt the need to communicate their opinions at once.

Oh, damn. He shouldn't have tried to repair the chair, should he? At least, not with other callers here. Though it seemed senseless not to take care of a minor repair as soon as one saw the need.

He hoisted himself from the carpeted floor and stood behind the prone chair. Keeping his gaze lofty, high above the heads of the other callers, he ignored them, though their stares made his skin prickle, and their voices rang in his ears.

When a footman returned with a hammer and a handful of assorted nails, Michael explained the necessary repair, then permitted the man to exchange the rickety chair for a more solid one.

Did the footman know which was the right size of nail to use? Would he bother to fix the chair at all? Michael's fingers itched to take the hammer from him, to perform the repair himself. He'd know it was done right then, and he wouldn't have to think about it anymore.

But he wasn't in Lancashire, amidst his holdings; he was in London. And it was Caro's business whether her chairs were solid or falling to pieces.

A headache tapped at his temples, a warning pressure as of tiny nails being driven into wood. Michael sank into the new seat at Everett's side. "I beg your pardon."

"No need." Everett's look of humor had returned. "You've given them something to talk about besides their own clothing. And you've left your mark on this house in a way that none who brings a bunch of posies does."

"Ah, but I shall bring a coquelicot carnation too." Michael would have rolled his eyes if it would not have given away the deception. Between Caro's deception and his own blunder, he would have all London convinced of his eccentricity before the day was out.

Everett grinned, quite undeceived. "An offering that clearly holds great value to Caro."

Though their lowered voices could not possibly have reached Caroline, she turned her head in their direction and shot Everett a wink. A *wink*.

Michael might as well be a Bow Street runner, trying to sort out a tangle of motives from an uncooperative mob. He always felt thus in society. "Mr. Everett, I have no idea what our hostess values."

Certainly not a lofty title or the stretching lands of a dukedom. Perhaps nothing more nor less than the hearts of the male half of the *beau monde*. If so, no single man could possibly please her.

"If anyone could divine that, she would be snapped

up again in marriage." Everett gave an elaborate sigh. "Alas, a mere mister such as I has no chance at her hand. I must work for my bread and can spare only an hour here or there to visit this foreign world. It is as entertaining as an evening at the theater and far more economical." He turned his head, lifting his chin. "Shall I aspire to fashion? Do you think I could achieve collar points like our dear dress-alikes?"

"Perhaps if you used a wire framework." Michael's answering smile felt strained. "Though you are incorrect in your assumption about Lady Str—Caro. She doesn't care about rank."

"Only because she has a fair degree of it already," replied Everett. "It's easy to scorn that which one possesses. But it doesn't mean one doesn't wish to continue possessing it." He looked aslant at Michael. "For example. You wouldn't wish to join me among the ranks of the mere misters, would you? As a man of business to a baron who hardly admits I am his cousin?"

"Naturally not, though I do not mean to offend you. But I have never scorned my title. I am accustomed to a life in which people rely on me."

His headache tightened like a vise; only then did Michael realize it had relaxed for a few moments.

"If you were a mere mister," said Everett, "no one would rely on you, though. Except your landlady on rent day. And your tailor, such as he is." He pulled a face, tugging at his simple neckcloth.

"And your employer."

Everett shrugged. "I haven't yet managed to convince him of that fact."

"I cannot imagine living such a different sort of life," Michael replied.

"A pity," sighed Everett. "You won't trade positions with me, then? I rather fancy a duke's life."

"It's not all luxury." Michael regarded his own dark blue superfine coat dubiously. His name still carried enough weight with tradesmen that he had been able to kit himself out in style, though the fashionable garb seemed overly elaborate. He would much rather clad himself in something rough, warm, and comfortable for striding around his lands, inspecting the progress of improvements.

He realized Everett was scrutinizing him again. "What?"

"I've heard much about you. It's interesting to meet you, Your Grace."

"I can only imagine what you've heard. Rest assured, nothing but the most pressing of business would have brought me to London."

"And to Caro's drawing room?"

Michael hesitated. "Also business." Everett was prying, but Michael didn't mind his questions. The man managed curiosity without animosity, a welcome combination.

"I wish you good fortune," the dark young man said. "Though I think we all hope for a bit of good fortune when we come to Caro's drawing room. Her beauty brings all of society together."

Caro again. It still struck Michael as strange that she allowed this familiarity to so many—and that Everett spoke of her with admiration, yet not the smallest expectation. She made herself accessible yet unreachable, all at once.

Yes, she was a surprise.

"I don't care about her beauty." *Liar.* "That is, I am not in attendance because of her appearance."

Just then, the Earl of Stratton—that presumptuous fellow who had pestered Caroline the night before—bowed his way into the room, half hidden by a bundle of flowers as lush as flesh, their fragrance so heady Michael wondered if the earl had doused them with perfume.

If the man wanted for money, he could certainly have economized by not bringing such an extravagant bouquet.

Michael watched Caroline for her reaction. Did she still hold a grudge against the earl for harassing her at the Applewood ball?

"Stratton," she said. "Welcome. I'm as delighted as ever to see you."

"These are for you." Stratton tumbled his heavy burden into Caroline's lap. A spike of gladiolus slapped her cheek.

"How lovely." She craned her neck over the lapful of flowers. "Hambleton, if you would ring for a maid? I think these must go in one of the great urns in the corridor."

Obligingly, one of the bookend dandies jangled the silver bell, and Caroline handed the armful to a wide-eyed maid. Stratton frowned as his flowers were marched out of the room.

So she *did* hold the earl in disfavor. Michael felt as gratified as if he'd done something far more heroic for her than stand under a lantern and allow her to grab his arm. "The peace offering declined," he murmured.

"Indeed," Everett said, equally low. "The villain, such as he is, vanquished. Poor fellow."

Michael's mouth twitched. Everett was turning out to be amusing company, especially when he directed his observations away from Michael.

This desire to observe seemed to be what had split Everett from the remainder of the callers—whether by his doing or theirs, Michael knew not. But it made sense to Michael to do the same. He could search for clues about Caroline: why she had offered to help him; what she thought of him.

His eyes needed training in the subtle rules of society, just as they had once learned to interpret an engineer's mechanical drawings. Already, Michael had forgotten an essential component: a bouquet. And the fact that one ought not to flip the furniture upside down.

But people had fewer moving parts than the simplest of machines. It should be possible to understand them, inscrutable though they seemed now. Trevithick's steam engines had seemed mysterious too, until Michael familiarized himself with their inner workings.

"Gracious," said Caroline as Stratton began to nudge himself onto her settee. "Can it really be quarter of four?"

A dozen hands reached for fobs, drew out pocket watches. Unnecessary. A mantel clock squatted within sight.

"Yes, it can be," Michael said. "As of five minutes ago, it was forty past the hour."

Caroline shot him a look, though he thought she

smiled faintly. Then she began a flurry of graceful fidgeting, nudging dainty embroidered cushions, and smoothing her gown. "I am dreadfully sorry, you dear men, but I've an appointment I simply can't miss. I do hate to end our time together."

Her mouth was not a pout, but something much better. It showed not childish disappointment, but regret. And promise.

Michael had not known a mouth could say so much without uttering a word.

The other men obeyed the command to depart, bowing, babbling their promises of invitation, jostling one another as they tried for one last look at their queen.

Michael waited, and when the eddy of departing callers began to trickle away, he aimed a bow in Caroline's direction and trod toward the door. Wondering why he had come only to lie about a foolishly named flower, then make a fool of himself in turn. He understood no more about Caroline's offer than when he'd come.

Whap. Something heavy and soft struck him between the shoulder blades.

Michael turned. Caroline smiled at him and tossed a small embroidered cushion from hand to hand. Its twin lay on the floor at Michael's feet.

"So sorry, Wyverne," she said. "It must have slipped from my grasp. Do stay and I shall have a maid brush your coat."

To Michael's right, the last of the candied callers was thundering down the stairs to the ground floor.

He was left alone with Caro, then. "You did that on purpose."

"Of course I did. Don't tell me you've never wanted to hit a duke with a pillow."

He considered. The only other duke he had known well was his father. "Not with a pillow, no."

Caroline retrieved her embroidered missile from the floor, then pounded it into place among a litter of similar cushions on her long settee. "Did you enjoy mingling with society again, Wyverne? I am honored—or maybe you should be honored—to have you encounter the cream of London's bachelor society in my drawing room."

"They remind me of tame animals, actually. Puppies." Michael wanted to pace and shake out his feet. Instead, he lifted each booted heel and planted them firmly on the patterned carpet.

Rather than look insulted, Caroline grinned. "There is nothing at all wrong in playing with puppies." Michael snorted, and Caroline laughed. "You're not the first to call them puppies. The other was my cousin and companion, on whose judgment I always relied."

"Past tense?"

"Not exactly. I still love her dearly, but she married and ran off to a quiet little town outside London. It is the one decision she made that I could ever fault—not her marriage, which was wonderful, but her decision to leave the City." A rueful expression crossed her face. "Anyway, it's strange that you should use the same word for my callers. If I am not careful, I may find myself asking you for advice, as I did Frances."

Michael's mind tumbled with silks and slippers and lacy unmentionables. "It would hardly be appropriate for me to advise you as your lady's companion did."

"Honestly, Wyverne. I wouldn't ask you which bonnet went best with a certain frock, as I did my dear cousin. But if I wanted to know which shipping company was the most likely to guarantee me a return on my investment—"

"East India has locked up the trade in tea for the time being. The company is England's most certain investment right now, outside of the Funds." He blinked. "Oh. Is that what you meant? The manly sort of advice?"

"Well said. Yes. No one expects you to know how a woman lives in a man's world, Wyverne, only how a man lives. Knowledge such as yours could make you a leader in society if you wished."

"God forbid."

"It needn't go that far. But if you don't know the answer to a question, you can always act offended that the question was put to you in the first place. No one will think less of a duke for having a poker up his backside. In fact, it's almost expected."

Michael's head reared back. "I *beg* your pardon."

"Perfect." Caroline looked delighted. "That is exactly the tone of voice I meant. Now, if you could contrive to look down your nose slightly?"

Michael tilted his chin up thirty degrees. His eyes crossing over the bridge of his nose, he located Caroline's smiling face. It was hard not to smile back, to keep his voice chilly as he repeated, "I *beg* your pardon."

She shrugged. "Fair, fair. It'll take practice. It's only a shield, anyway. One of those things to say when you can't think of anything to say."

"Do you have such shields too?"

She considered. "*I'm as delighted as ever to see you*?"

The words she had used to greet Stratton. How had she greeted Michael himself? He couldn't remember right now. Nor was he sure why she had offered to help him, or kept him after her other callers departed—or when they might talk about his impending marriage.

So he barked, as he always did when his thoughts began to spiral fruitlessly. "What, pray tell, is a coquelicot carnation? Is it some joke upon me?"

"It is not a joke, but an excuse," Caroline said. "So that my callers would envy your foresight, rather than feeling superior to you for its lack."

"Do you require blooms as payment for your company? What is the significance of a gift if it is required?"

Caroline's eyes went glass-hard. "*I* require nothing, Wyverne. What flowers my callers choose to bring are just that: their choice. But there is an unspoken rule in society that a gentleman brings a gift when he calls on a lady. If you dislike the idea of flowers, sweetmeats are also acceptable." She paused, then softened. "Such gifts are for the sake of appearances, like changing one's clothing before dinner. In themselves, these acts may have little meaning, but they prove that one knows the rules of society."

Ah. Those unspoken rules. They had been beaten into him throughout his youth, but they wouldn't stay. His mind sieved them out like tiny herrings, holding fast to the meatier subjects of engineering, accounting, agriculture.

She did not deserve his harshness; she was only

following the rules. And he should too, until he had captured a wife. "I will bring a gift next time I call."

Caroline waved a careless hand. "There is no need, Wyverne. Simply tell everyone how well your coquelicot carnation is growing and postpone its delivery date, and I believe you will skate by on its uniqueness."

She meant to help him. *Had* helped him in a tiny way. His mouth opened and closed, not wanting to grant a *thank you* for something as small as falsifying a flower.

"Please call me Michael," was what came out instead.

She popped up from her recline. "May I? How extraordinary."

Michael splayed his fingers as he'd seen other gentlemen do and studied the buff on his fingernails. To the smallest detail, his valet had turned him out properly for a man of high society. Now his hands looked strangely decorative, as if they were no longer meant to be used.

"I would not have thought you would be surprised by this type of familiarity, since you grant it so often yourself." He tried to speak lightly. He was not successful.

"The world has trimmed us from very different cloth. I do not expect you to tailor your behavior to mine, Michael." A pause, as she tasted his name on her lips for the first time. He wondered if she recognized that such familiarity from him was a gift far more significant than a bouquet.

"We might not be so different, Caro," he replied. "We made a pact together, after all. We must want the same things."

"For you to find a rich wife? Truly, it has been my ambition in life this past decade." She toyed with a silken cushion tassel, her ripe mouth curved.

Michael frowned. "I didn't ask for your assistance. You offered it, which you needn't have."

"I did. I mustn't tease you, Michael. I know you don't like it." Caroline looked contrite.

"You may act in the manner of your choosing."

"Of course I may, you dratted duke. You needn't give me permission to speak my mind in my own home. I'm trying to be gracious, that's all."

He drew a chair near the settee and seated himself facing Caroline. "It is hardly gracious to call me a *dratted duke*, you know."

She grinned. "There's that ducal voice again. Well done. And you're right, I shouldn't have said that. In the privacy of my own home, I do tend to, ah, relax the proprieties."

Michael could not imagine why her cheeks flushed, but the effect was lovely against her golden hair and the grass-green of her gown. Heat shuddered through his body, and he folded his arms tightly against it.

"To return to the matter at hand," Caroline said, "propriety is exactly what we are concerned with. Namely, finding you a wife. A respectable one with pots of money. Need she be pretty as well?"

Michael only stared at fair hair, translucent skin, the curve of pink lips.

His mouth felt dry, his throat scratchy. A warning tap began in his head: *answer*. But he didn't know the answer. His hands fell to his sides, then found the frail arms of his chair and clasped at them as if they were oars on a lifeboat.

Caroline spoke on. "We can but try for it. I've thought of three possibilities. None of them titled, of course."

"Why *of course*?"

Caroline dropped the silk tassel she had been marring. "Because the *ton* thinks you mad. Despite the lure of your title, they'll be reluctant to ally their blue-blooded daughters to a line that might be tainted. You will do better seeking a wife in a family that wants to move up in the polite world. They're more willing to overlook eccentricity."

"Of course," Michael echoed.

So, it was just as Sanders had warned him. As his own father had predicted so long ago. Now he must find a wife who would marry him *despite*.

Caro tapped his arm. "Michael, I don't mean to offend you."

"You have not." He rubbed at the bridge of his nose. "I know that you are quite right."

"Money is what you need, not blue blood. If blood alone would answer your creditors' demands, you could tap yours and sell it by the tablespoon."

"That is gruesome."

"Merely practical," Caroline said. "I know you're here for the sake of your dukedom and your tenants. And I am guessing you would rather bleed yourself dry than fritter about London unnecessarily."

"Perhaps not *entirely* dry." He tried to smile. To his surprise, he was successful.

"I believe by the time your courtship is completed,

no one will think you anything but sane. More than sane, even. Brilliant. There's a fine line between genius and madness, you know, and the line can be easily bridged by coin."

The same notion had once occurred to him. "You think I can buy my sanity, then?"

"I have no doubt that you have always had it. The polite world has simply misinterpreted it. Having a full purse will encourage the *ton* to reevaluate you more generously. It made all the difference for me."

He huffed. "You were never scorned by society."

"As you have been away for eleven years, you cannot know what my life has been." She gave him a cool smile. "Now, are you ready to hear about the young women I have identified?"

Again, Michael's grip on the arms of his chair tightened. If Caroline's voice had taken on the slightest tinge of pity or relish as she referred to his speckled character, he would have left her house at once. But she simply shrugged it off, as though a reputation for madness mattered little more than a reputation for overspending one's quarterly allowance. She thought him sane; she offered her aid; she was confident of success.

She did not view him as someone damaged, after all.

The realization was freeing: he felt light and grounded at once, ready to do what was required of him not only as a duty, but with pleasure.

Though his duty and his pleasure had nothing to do with flaxen hair, with scandalous offers and floral figments. This was a matter of business.

The idea of trusting anyone, especially Caroline,

was… unprecedented. But Michael was not averse to the unprecedented. If he had been, he would not have dredged his money into canals and boiled it away with steam power. And she certainly knew the business of society much better than he. It was quite logical to consult an expert.

His hands relaxed. "Very well. I would be grateful for your help. When shall we start?"

Her cool smile turned warm. "As soon as possible, Michael. Tonight."

Five

MICHAEL SOON LEARNED THAT CAROLINE WAS AS good as her word. That evening, she spirited him off to a small dinner party at the home of her friends, the Earl and Countess of Tallant.

In Tallant House's gilt-papered drawing room, Caroline made the introductions. Their young hostess beamed at Michael. "I've been eager to make your acquaintance, Your Grace. Though we've never met, Caroline has mentioned you many times."

This was interesting information. "Has she? What has she said?"

Lady Tallant laughed. A woman of about Michael's and Caroline's age, she had warm auburn hair, a lovely face, and a mischievous smile. "I probably ought not to have said that. Now you'll be miffed with me—or with Caroline. Oh, do choose her, because no one is ever offended by her."

"I find that hard to believe." Michael shook his head. "No. Pardon. I mean, I find that easy to believe."

Lady Tallant beamed at him. "Truth *and* tact? We shall get along famously."

Caroline pulled a face. "Emily, hush. You will make His Grace uncomfortable."

"Not at all." Michael realized he sounded hideously uncomfortable.

"Oh dear." Lady Tallant looked penitent. "I assure you, Your Grace, I meant only to make *Caroline* uncomfortable. But she is the most hardheaded creature in the world. I simply cannot discomfit her."

"That is a marvelous gift." Michael could not imagine the blessed buoyancy of a life in which nothing discomfited him.

"Indeed it is," Caroline agreed. "I endeavor to provoke Emily into shocking impropriety for my own amusement, and she tries to do the same to me."

"I shall never triumph," sighed their hostess. "Tallant becomes so worried when I am—"

"Worrisome?" Caroline gave her friend a brilliant smile. "Speaking of impropriety, Michael, let us take on its opposite. There is someone you simply must meet."

Lady Tallant raised her brows. "*Michael*? Is this a courtesy title or a discourtesy?"

"It is a privilege with which His Grace has honored me, and I am grateful for it. There's no need to be such a harpy, Emily."

Their hostess laughed and waved them off as if *harpy* was the fondest of endearments—which, in Caroline's buttery voice, it might as well be. Lord and Lady Tallant seemed to be friends of such long standing that they permitted Caroline every trespass, whether a small one like teasing them or a larger social sin such as bringing an extra gentleman to an intimate dinner party with very little notice.

The other guests had clotted, small bunches of stares, blinks, whispers. Were they whispering about him? Or merely reluctant to have a stranger overhear their conversation?

Michael's throat felt parched.

Caroline spoke low in his ear. "Tonight you'll meet the first maiden who might suit you, a possible future Her Grace the Duchess of Wyverne. Do come and I'll introduce you." Instead of slipping her hand into the crook of his arm, she simply glided away. No touching.

Thoughtful of her.

So the mad duke's bride hunt began. He followed Caroline to a pair of women, both of whom greeted her as though they knew her well. One was as tall as Caro herself, with steely-colored curls and a gown that seemed to have been ornamented by a lunatic, all flounces and beads and lace and pearls and spangles.

Fortunately, his potential intended was the other lady.

Caroline presented lunatic-gown-woman as Mrs. Weatherby and the young woman at her side as Miss Weatherby; then she stepped on Michael's foot.

"I'm pleased to make your acquaintance, Miss Weatherby," Michael began dutifully. "Do you enjoy London?"

Miss Weatherby appeared to be about twenty years of age. A kitten of a maid, she was small and rounded, softly pretty, with a cloud of light brown hair and Wedgwood-blue eyes. Her little hands kneaded the golden handle of her reticule; she looked both delighted and frightened at once. "I do."

Even Michael, thick though he might be at reading social cues, could not miss the force with which her mother jabbed Miss Weatherby in the ribs.

She squeaked, then looked wide-eyed at her mother. Mrs. Weatherby cleared her throat, then flashed a dazzling smile in Michael's direction.

"I. Um." Miss Weatherby made another squeaking sound.

Meow, thought Michael. He wondered if he ought to offer her a bowl of milk or a herring.

No, that was unkind. She had already managed to speak four words to him, which was more than most women he'd encountered at Lady Applewood's recent ball.

He tried to look solicitous. Some sort of trick with raised eyebrows—that was what people usually did when they were interested.

"I, um, live here the year round," managed Miss Weatherby. "My father is a banker, so he always has business to attend to in London."

Weatherby. Like a gear, the name clicked in Michael's head.

Clever Caroline. He had not made the connection before, but Weatherby was one of the creditors who held Michael's estate in his golden grip. He would certainly relax it if Michael married his daughter.

What was the fair rate of exchange to transform a cit into a duchess? Was the price affected by the supposed madness of the duke?

He rather thought it was. Mrs. Weatherby was scrutinizing him, probably wondering if he was going to gibber and froth at the mouth. Though she prodded her daughter to speak more, he still had to impress the matron of the family. He must act rigidly, predictably, undeniably sane.

"How nice for you." He smiled. Both Weatherby women recoiled.

Ah. Perhaps he had displayed too many teeth. He closed his lips; Miss Weatherby still looked wary.

For the life of him, he could not think what to say to her next. He only knew that he must not offer her a herring. It would be a disaster.

"His Grace," chimed in Caroline, "has not been in London for quite some years. Miss Weatherby, perhaps you might tell him of some of your favorite shops and sites to visit."

"I would be pleased to hear it." Michael could not mistake a cue handed to him with such plainness.

"Oh, you must begin with Bond Street, then," began Miss Weatherby. Slowly at first, then with increasing breathlessness, she recited a list of milliners and modistes and mantua makers.

Surely the girl did not really think he cared who made her dresses, but just as his jaw tightened, he caught sight of Mrs. Weatherby's gimlet eye again.

He must smile. Not too many teeth. No teeth; yes. And nod every few sentences to show her how interested he was.

This choreography was sufficiently complex that he lost the thread of conversation. When the three women stared at him, he realized he was nodding into silence and had evidently missed some question.

The too-familiar headache gave a gleeful chuckle and made itself at home.

Michael squared his shoulders, then looked down his nose as he had at Caroline's house. Reminding Mrs. Weatherby that he was a duke, and rumors of madness or no, he had the right to cease attending to an inane conversation if he chose to. "I beg your pardon, Miss Weatherby. What were you saying?"

She flushed, cast her eyes down. "I asked if you intended to stay in London long, Your Grace."

"Yes." His voice sounded hoarse. He cleared his throat and tried again. "Yes, I imagine I'll be here for a while. Circumstances require my presence here for the time being."

"Do they, Your Grace? And what are those circumstances?" Mrs. Weatherby spoke in a voice of slate: hard and flat and carefully expensive. Michael felt each word like a blow against his skull, and again he lost the thread of conversation.

"His Grace is most dedicated to the management of his estates," Caroline replied. "As you are no doubt aware, Mrs. Weatherby, some matters of business can best be transacted in London, which is truly the financial heart of England."

She beamed at Mrs. Weatherby, and the older woman's mouth opened, closed, and then slitted open again to allow the words, "Of course, my lady," to spill forth.

Clever, clever Caroline. A subtle compliment at just the right time. Michael was having more difficulty than he had expected placing himself on the auction block, allowing himself to be judged and priced and judged again.

At least he did not have to do it alone.

Gratefully, his fingers found Caroline's where they wrapped around the handle of her fan, and he brushed them with his. Just a slight touch. A thanks.

She shivered, perhaps because of the wispiness of her red gown's bodice. Not warm enough for the cool evening. Summer had passed London by, just as it had Lancashire.

"How many estates have you, Wyverne?" Caroline asked idly, turning to him. "I know they occupy much of your time. Are there five?"

"Six properties." The floor seemed steadier beneath his feet at the very thought. "That is, five estates besides the house in Town. Though I spend the bulk of my time at the dukedom's seat in Lancashire."

"It is beautiful in the north of England," Caroline said. "Miss Weatherby, have you traveled much in that area?"

"I went to, um, Cumberland as a girl," replied the maiden. "Never Lancashire, though. What is it like?"

A question Michael could answer, at small or great length. His aching head was soothed; his tongue unlocked, free and glib, for the first time this evening. "It is like no other part of the world that I have seen. It is quiet and stark, and a man's living must be broken from the moorland. It's an honor to set one's will against the earth, then negotiate a peace with it."

As he spoke, Caroline excused herself and slipped from his side.

Well, Michael could not reasonably hope that she would stand six inches away from him all evening. So, clearly, he was being unreasonable in his disappointment.

For he realized: her work was done. She had built the foundation of this conversation, and now it remained only for Michael to complete the structure. She had created it in a form she knew he would like—reminding the Weatherby women of the grandeur of his title, settling on a topic of conversation he would enjoy.

And then she had gone to the side of a tall, fashionably dressed young man. Now she was laughing, putting a hand on his arm, and he was grinning back at her with a knowing smile—the smile of a man who enjoyed touching.

Michael could not help but remember how Caroline had rested her fingers on his arm, how the caress had tested him to distraction. Or today, how he had brushed her fingers with his, then pulled away. Such was the limit of his intimacy.

Life would be so much easier if he were someone else. Someone who always knew what to say. How to flirt and persuade people. Who didn't have a dukedom to take care of.

Easier, but to what end? He was Michael John Wythe Layward, Duke of Wyverne, Marquess of Vaughan, Earl of Beaumont, Baron Lumley, responsible for the well-being of thousands. With his weighty titles came responsibilities just as heavy.

So be it. There was only one thing to say.

"May I see you in to dinner, Miss Weatherby?"

By the time the men finished consuming their port and tobacco, Michael thought enough time must have passed for a journey to the moon by ox cart.

Two courses had been served—a rich array to Michael's eyes, since left to his own devices, he ignored mealtimes. When his stomach's rumblings grew too distracting, he simply grabbed for whatever food was available. But Lady Tallant set forth for her guests a soup, fish, and roasted beef, then removed them for creamed vegetables and fowls. Everything was perfectly cooked, beautifully seasoned, artfully presented—and this was but a small party of friends. The effort and expense involved in larger entertainments must be staggering.

Michael struggled through conversation with Miss Weatherby and her mother, returning to Lancashire whenever topics flagged. He could not tell whether they were truly interested or just being polite. It didn't matter; it was a comfort to talk of the land he loved so well, where he seemed to have left such a large part of himself.

When dessert was served, Lady Tallant apologized over the fare. "Our cook couldn't find any fruit today for love or money, and she assured me she tried both. At least the cold weather permits the transport of ices, or we should have to content ourselves with chewing on the candles."

Lady Tallant atoned for the lack of fruits by offering her guests an assortment of sweetened ices from the ever-fashionable Gunter's, located not far from Tallant House in Berkeley Square. Her husband at once took a large serving and spooned the frozen confection into his mouth with the glee of a child.

Michael accepted a delicate pink ice, which he realized to his dismay was flavored with rosewater.

He consumed it in small bites, nodding in response to whatever Miss Weatherby happened to exclaim over in her kittenish voice. And thinking.

So, there was no fruit for a countess in London. A subtle reminder of the famine wracking so much of Europe in this cold year. England had been more lightly gripped by hunger, but it was a small solace—and a small agony—to know that even the richest nobles in the nation's greatest city felt the chill of unnatural winter too.

The meal at last completed, Michael endured another round of distracted nodding as the men chatted over port until Lord Tallant deemed it appropriate to rejoin the ladies. Michael followed the other men into the drawing room, wondering if he could pen a letter to his steward. Surely Tallant had a writing desk somewhere. Michael hadn't written to Sanders for an entire day, and he kept thinking of new things he wanted to tell the man. Sanders might not remember which tenants' roofs needed repair, and he would have no idea from where to order materials.

Michael's fault, perhaps. Over the years, he had tugged charge after charge from his steward's control. But it was necessary to make sure everything went perfectly, as he sought to undo the damage his father had wrought. Michael trusted no one as much as he trusted himself.

"Your Grace? Would you care to make up a hand of whist?" Lady Tallant asked. "Do say yes, or I shall have to partner my husband, and he has the most abominable memory. I shall be impoverished if I am forced to rely on him."

Lord Tallant's mild countenance looked wounded. "Em, I always replace the pin money you lose."

"True, and that's very dear of you, Jemmy. Though as there are only four suits, one would think you could recall which was trump."

"We could try writing it down," the earl suggested. "I'm sure I could remember it if I could only look at a note."

Michael seized the opening. "Do you have paper and pen here? Allow me, Tallant."

"But, Your Grace, surely you would prefer a game?"

"Call me Wyverne, please," Michael said. "There is no need for greater ceremony. And I would be delighted to encourage harmony between husband and wife. You might write down the suit; then there's a letter I'd like to dash off."

That sounded almost carefree. In truth, he *felt* almost carefree. The prospect of disgorging a list of responsibilities onto paper was calming him. His fingers twitched not from tension but from eagerness to hold a pen.

After giving Lady Tallant pen and paper, which she used to inscribe the word *hearts* and slide it in front of her husband's fistful of cards, Michael retrieved the writing implements and returned to a desk at one side of the capacious drawing room.

At once, his tangled thoughts began to flow as smoothly as ink from his pen.

First, there were the tenants' roofs to mind; then he wanted a report on the weather: temperature, snowfall, rainfall, everything. And on the state of the harvest, such as it was. Ordinarily the flax would be stretching tall in the fields now; this year, the plants were stunted by frost and starved for sun. With few crops to harvest and sell, Michael would have to buy food to help his tenants through the lean months. Unless, miraculously, the winter relaxed its grip.

Michael was past hoping for a miracle, which meant he had yet another reason to strike up a flirtation with Miss Weatherby.

He bent over his paper, shutting out that thought, the other guests, the room, London. He thought only of what needed to be done in his absence from Lancashire, scribbling lists and questions and reminders. Since Michael had come to London, he had heard from Sanders distressingly seldom. Only often enough to be told that, since Michael had come to London, Sanders was no longer dogged by the dukedom's creditors.

If Michael had lost their faith through his supposed madness, he was regaining it now by joining in the season. Incontrovertible evidence in favor of his sanity.

He signed his name with more than usual force.

The letter done, his awareness expanded again—out from the paper before him, back to the drawing room of Tallant House, lamplit against the night, its gilt wallpaper burnished and quietly rich. The soft carpet and furnishings blunted the laughter of the card players.

And then there was Caroline, who stood near a wide fireplace with a painted glass screen. She was talking to that tall young man again. A Baron Hart, if Michael remembered correctly. Hart had fashionably tousled dark hair and a languid, confident bearing. He looked at ease. He looked like he belonged with Caroline.

And apparently Michael belonged by himself. Letter complete, there was nothing for him to do but meander around the edges of the drawing room.

He ought to make his way toward Miss Weatherby to advance his suit. Though how much more the young lady ought to be expected to hear about Lancashire, he couldn't guess.

For the moment, she was still playing cards. Her soft features looked gentle and pliant in the forgiving lamplight. Once she chose her next card, her eyes found Michael, and her lips trembled before her gaze returned to her cards again.

Was that a look of excitement or of apprehension? Was the offer of a dukedom not enough when it came tied to a duke's hand in marriage? To *his* hand?

His head pounded in the rhythm of these words. His dinner became uneasy in his stomach. The chicken fricassee pecked and fluttered at his insides; the beef pounded at him with heavy hooves. He swallowed hard.

He needed a trick to distract himself. He could master his body by waking his mind. Pulling in deep breaths through his nose, he looked around the room. The usual litter of amusements: books, newspapers, periodicals, a pianoforte.

And on it, a lamp.

A *Carçel* lamp.

He squinted at it to make sure he was not mistaken. Yes, so it was: the glass globe sat atop a sturdy bronze base, its reservoir of fuel tucked away, hidden.

His dinner became food again, and his head ceased its pounding meter. A Carcel lamp. Marvelous.

He had wanted one for years, but they were hard to come by. Lancashire shops refused to carry them because they were so delicate and complex, and every lamp Michael had ordered from London had arrived broken. They had an ingenious clockwork mechanism in the base, a pump that forced oil up into the wick. A great improvement over the old Argands that still cast their shadow-marred, top-heavy lights in every room of Callows, his Lancashire seat.

He could have fixed the shipments of Carcels, of course, if he had ever examined an unbroken one and understood how their delicate inner workings fit together.

Hmm.

Like a moth, he was pulled to the light of the lamp. He removed its globe-shaped shade, forgetting everything except the hot little flame at his fingertips.

Six

"What is Wyverne *doing* here, Caro?"

A fashionable dandy Hart might be, but Caroline had always known his tousled hair covered a head with no lack of sense. In this way, he resembled Michael more than any other man-about-town Caroline had met.

Her eyes turned to Michael himself, who sat at a writing desk. As she watched, he tapped the feathered barb of a pen against his paper, then began scribbling again at a furious rate. Likely that flecks of ink were spattering his cravat and the lovely malachite-green silk of his waistcoat. Likelier still he would neither notice nor care.

She looked back to Hart. He deserved better than this constant comparison with another.

"He is here at my request," she replied at last. "I am helping him."

"To what end?"

"To the end that preoccupies everyone in society: money. I am helping him find a rich wife." A small incline of her head toward Miss Weatherby. "What do you think of my choice?"

Hart shook his head. "Considering she's chosen to partner her mother at cards rather than approach Mad Michael, I'd say she's not amenable."

Mad Michael. Caroline had forgotten this old nickname for the Duke of Wyverne. If the *ton* still bandied it about, his rehabilitation might be more difficult than she had expected.

She adopted a careless tone. "I think it's gone rather well so far. I do not expect him to seek a special license right away or to drop to one knee and profess his love tonight. But see how she looks to him every time her attention is freed from her cards? She is intrigued."

"Either that or she's wondering what kind of madman comes to a dinner party only to catch up on his correspondence."

"A *busy* man. He oversees a dukedom even while he's in London."

Hart raised a curious brow. "I have a country estate, and you don't see me dragging my tedious affairs around with me. I know how to amuse myself, and others."

Unmistakable hint. Caroline ignored it. "Maybe so, Hart, but you've lived differently from Wyverne. He prefers to grip his holdings tightly."

"Yet they are now in danger of slipping from his grasp."

Caroline nibbled at her lip, a pensive gesture that drew attention to its fullness. "Yes, true. I cannot fathom how it's happened."

This was no exaggeration. How was it that Michael faced ruin when he kept a vigilant watch on his estates? When his care for them occupied his every waking moment and probably robbed him of sleep? How, too, could men such as Hart stay solvent when they gave more attention to the tailoring of their coats in a week than to the management of their holdings in a year?

Perhaps nothing but the everlasting winter had changed Michael's plans. Or perhaps it was something deeper within Michael—that unique quality the world stamped and sealed *mad*.

Where he was concerned, she kept running into that wall of incomprehension. She would not break through it with Hart, so she turned resolutely away to a subject she knew quite well.

"What do you think of my gown, Hart? The modiste told me this shade was all the rage."

"Coquelicot, is it not?" Hart smiled. "Isn't that the color on everyone's lips today?"

"Ah, so you heard about my promised carnation. I hope it will have a pleasant scent. I find the natural perfume of a flower intoxicating."

She felt weary—or worse, wearisome—as she said this. Flirtatious words fell heavily as stones from her tongue tonight, though Hart looked gratified enough.

"If it is worthy of you, then it will be intoxicating indeed." He lowered his voice. "May I call on you tonight?"

She mulled over the request. The idea of using Hart for her own pleasure did not appeal to her; it had not for some weeks. "Not tonight. I have too many things to plan."

This mitigated his disappointment by a fraction. "Do you? Are you preparing for a party?"

"Not at present. I am scheming strategies to advance the suit of my ward."

"Your ward?" His brows knit until Caroline nodded at Michael, who was still scribbling away at his letter. "Oh. Wyverne." Hart gave her an odd look. "He's a duke, Caro, and quite mad. He doesn't need your help, and he won't notice or care if he doesn't get it."

He grinned as though this was all rather funny, but Caroline went cold all over. *He doesn't need your help.*

Hart thought so. Maybe everyone thought so. It was what she feared most: that she was useless.

Oh, men wanted her money. They coveted her body. Women envied her prestige. But Caroline herself, the woman beneath the lacquered surface? No one needed her at all.

And if Hart was right, Michael had as little concern for her as he would a splotch of ink on his waistcoat. Just as he had eleven years before.

He was certainly heedless of her efforts on his behalf. Still he worked on his letter, ignoring Miss Weatherby, slicing away at his chance of success with every stroke of his pen.

"He is not mad, Hart," Caroline said with determined calm. "Only unique. And someone has to help him."

"If you insist." Hart still looked skeptical. "But why need that someone be you, Caro? No one expects that of you."

"Maybe that's why I want to be the one," she murmured. She smoothed the coquelicot taffeta of her dress.

Coquelicot. Not merely red; never such an everyday color as that. She had trained herself to think in intricacies of form and dress, and she could not stop now. It was foolish to wish to be more than lovely, wealthy Lady Stratton—especially when she had once been so much less.

She didn't realize Hart had heard her until he repeated her words. "You want to be the one."

"Never mind, Hart." She tilted her chin down so the lamplight would shadow her cheekbones, make her eyes deep and mysterious. Hart usually found the effect distracting in quite a nice way.

Not this time. "No, no. You merely surprised me, Caro. I didn't expect… well. I understand. I hope to see you again soon, one way or another."

With a bow, he left her. He walked over to the velvet-covered card table and whispered in Lady Tallant's ear. Something quite roguish, apparently, for Emily laughed and waved a slip of paper at Hart.

"Just because it's your name doesn't mean it's your property. All hearts are not your possession. This paper is a reminder for Jemmy."

"Dash it," said the earl, making a grab for the paper. "Leave it on the table, Hart. Em and I are up by seven pounds."

Caroline smiled. The earl's abysmal memory for card play was surpassed only by his unflagging good humor.

On another evening, she would have joined the small group at the card table, perhaps finding someone to flirt with, soaking up compliments until she stopped feeling quite so empty.

That last thing Hart had said—that *I didn't*

expect—nagged at her. What did he mean? Had she grown so predictable, living in the tight little box of her Albemarle Street house, seeing the same people all the time? Spending her days with fashion and flowers and laughter?

When one had grown up as poor as she, it was difficult to get enough of such luxury. But maybe her decorative tendencies had become a golden chain, holding her back from accomplishing… well, more. Somehow.

She blinked. The light had gone dimmer, and Michael was no longer sitting at the writing desk.

He was standing at the pianoforte, holding a—what was that? It looked like a small metal gear.

Then she realized: the lovely cast-bronze lamp that had stood on the pianoforte was now lying across its lid. In pieces. And Michael was poking through them with the furtive eagerness of an anatomist, afraid his precious stolen corpse would be taken away at any second.

Damnation. When she had called him a *dratted duke* earlier, that was a much milder epithet than he deserved.

She marched over to him and, without preamble, hissed, "This is no way to convince Miss Weatherby of your sanity."

At the sound of her voice, he flinched, startled. The gear slipped from his fingers and pinged off of the etched glass globe.

Caroline affixed a pleasant smile over her face, then ventured a look at the card table. Indeed, Miss Weatherby's pale face was turned in their direction.

Caroline hoped the young woman continued to

be intrigued rather than dismayed, though she could imagine no one but Michael being intrigued by the innards of a lamp.

"What are you doing?" she whispered, keeping her smile carefully hung in place.

To her surprise, he smiled back.

The change in his face was startling. The faint, careworn lines at his eyes became crinkles of joy, and his sharp cheekbones softened with the press of his mouth. His teeth were even, his mouth a delight. This was a revel of happiness, as it could only be felt by a man for whom it was rare.

And such happiness was over nothing but a damned lamp. He had never chosen to bestow that expression of bliss on Caroline for her own sake.

"It's a Carcel lamp," he said. "Isn't it marvelous?"

Her voice was harsher than it might have been had he looked less transfigured. "It might have been once. Now it's nothing but a pile of rubbish."

"I wanted to see how it worked," he said, as if this were an obvious sentiment. "Look at this gear, right here. It drives the most ingenious clockwork pump. Do you know how a Carcel lamp works?"

"Of course I do," Caroline lied. "Keep your voice down. Miss Weatherby is watching."

Michael seemed not to hear her. "I haven't been able to get one of these in Lancashire, and I've always wondered how the pump operates. See how it drives the oil upward? That way, you needn't have a heavy oil reservoir above the light itself." He smiled again. "Thank you for bringing me tonight. This is a genuine pleasure."

Caroline choked. Michael ignored every fatted calf the *ton* could offer and instead glutted himself on lamp oil.

She really shouldn't be surprised. "I'm delighted to have fulfilled the first day of our contract to your satisfaction. But you must put the lamp back together and quickly. Can you?"

Michael shook his head. "I'm not done studying it yet."

"Michael, you are in London. You can buy your own Carcel lamp and spend the whole night taking it apart. But you must put this one back together. *Now.*"

He stared at her, seeming taken aback. She pressed her lips together, counted to five, then tried again. "Did you not promise to rely on my judgment?"

A long pause, as his evergreen eyes searched her face. Then he nodded and began sifting through the litter of glass and metal.

"I'm going to earn every bit of our eventual triumph," she murmured, handing him a gear that went rolling toward the edge of the pianoforte.

"Our triumph?" He squinted at her.

"Finding you a rich wife. You won't make it easy if you insist on conducting mechanical experiments in the middle of a dinner party."

His eyebrows knit. "I did not intend to tax you with a great burden. If you recall, you made the offer of assistance unprompted by me. And you may decline to continue it at any time."

"You *have* to stop saying that every time I tell you something you don't like." She laid a hand on his arm, remembering his aversion to touch only when he froze, tensed. She lifted her hand at once. "Michael, such aid is more than I've ever offered anyone else. You might not see it as an honor right now, but I'm asking you to trust me. You will get what you want if you do."

He studied his sleeve as if her fingers had left scorch marks on the fabric. Then he looked at her again with that unnervingly focused attention. "Do you truly know what I want?"

His voice vibrated through her, soft and deep, and her throat went tight with a longing to swallow the sound and hold it inside of her. She didn't know how to answer, for she could not again offer perfect frankness of her own: *I hope so. Oh, how I wish.*

Her scheme was failing. Rather than learning his secrets from a safe distance—placing another woman between them as a shield—she was only tying herself to Michael more intimately. And he did not even know it.

Then a massy figure bustled up next to her, calling, "La! Whatever are you doing, Your Grace?"

Mrs. Weatherby had abandoned the card table, and her pale daughter had flitted after her. The banker's wife sounded like a displeased governess, and Michael lifted his chin—probably ready to say *I beg your pardon* in a devastatingly cool tone.

Caroline hurried to intervene. "His Grace was simply showing me the workings of the Carcel lamp. Isn't it fascinating? It's clockwork, you know." She spoke blandly, as though she hadn't only learned this five minutes before and against her will.

"Er… yes, my lady." Mrs. Weatherby stumbled over

the words. "Yes, I believe my husband keeps one in his study. They *are* rather fascinating."

Miss Weatherby did not smile. She only looked gravely up, up, at Michael's tall frame—as though he had disassembled a dream of hers along with the lamp's inner workings.

And maybe he had. A banker's daughter might aspire to a noble husband, but not to an indifferent noble with eccentric interests. Miss Weatherby held one of the richest dowries of the season. No doubt a marquess would do as well as a duke for her if it meant she'd have a fashionable, predictable husband.

She was a pleasant girl, but Caroline now realized: she was far too mild for a man such as Michael.

This did not feel like the failure it ought to have.

For the next few minutes, Mrs. Weatherby chatted about the appointment of her husband's study. Caroline, ornamental as any gewgaw, could discuss fabrics and furnishings as long as needed. Long enough for the formidable duenna to forgive any social trespasses.

Not long enough, though, for the daughter to shake off her disappointment. And not long enough for Michael to understand what had gone wrong in the first place.

Caroline finally managed to coax the Weatherby women back to the card table. Hart had slipped into a seat in their absence; as he stood, he caught Caroline's eye. If expressions could be written in words, this was as bold an *I told you so* as she'd ever seen.

She hoped he could read her own expression: *oh, shut up*.

"Everything all right, Caro?" Emily lifted her eyebrows.

Caroline had too much pride to entrust her old friend with complete honesty in this case. "Of course, darling. His Grace has been edifying me, that is all."

Emily's mouth crimped. "Do let me know if he has any luck. I've never held out the slightest hope for your edification, myself."

"I hold out as much for mine as I do for yours," Caroline said sweetly, patting Emily on the shoulder. "Brutus, darling."

"If I'm to be called a traitor, I prefer Benedict Arnold." Emily picked her cards back up and rearranged a few. "A much fresher reference."

"Bond Street," said her husband, his brow furrowed as he searched his own cards. "Em, what was trump again?"

Hart laughed; Emily sighed. Caroline said, "What about Bond Street?"

Jem looked up from his cards. "That's where we got the lamp. Can't think of the shop name, but Sowerberry can help you with that. Our butler, you know. Wyverne seems to like the lamp. He should get one."

He looked down at his cards again. "Can't think how I've got so many cards left. Are you sure you've dealt correctly, Hart?"

Caroline slipped away, back to Michael, who was still fitting gears together.

She had called him her ward. A joke, yet she did feel responsible for him. She'd brought him tonight. She had asked him to trust her, to place his future in her hands. It was a great deal to ask of any man, much less a duke. Much less of Michael.

As he struggled to fit two gears together, his hand bumped the lamp's glass shade. It smashed on the carpeted floor much more loudly than Caroline would have expected.

"Damn," said Michael. In unison, Mrs. Weatherby and her daughter gasped.

Damn, indeed, thought Caroline. With that single unguarded syllable, he had ensured that Miss Weatherby would never consider his suit.

That stupid lamp. Caroline would have hidden it as soon as dinner was over had she known what it would cost: not only a glass shade, but a wealthy bride. A maiden who could afford anything in the world except the unexpected.

Caroline rolled her annoyance into a tiny ball. "Michael, please call on me tomorrow morning. I have much business to discuss with you."

He bent to pick up the shards of a formerly beautiful frosted glass sphere. "Business? How so?"

"For business you have come to London, and for very particular business, we have made a pact. I *am* capable of deeper thought than flowers and flirtation, you know."

"I've never doubted that." He stood, setting the pieces of glass gently atop the pianoforte. "Will your other suitors be there tomorrow morning?"

She noticed the word *other* and tucked it away for closer examination later. "If you call early enough, we will be alone."

He nodded, then looked over the pieces of the

lamp, still spread out before him. "I know I can figure this out," he muttered. "It will just take more time than I thought."

I feel the same way, Caroline thought.

But all she said was, "Tomorrow, then."

Seven

Despite the ridiculous buff on his fingernails, Michael was not a vain man.

Oh, he knew he had a knack for some things, such as totting up columns of figures or finding the problem with a rickety chair.

He also knew he was quite bad at some things.

Such as, apparently, charming the daughter of one of his creditors. Or putting a Carcel lamp back together upon a moment's notice.

So when he called at Caroline's house the next morning—quite early, as she had suggested—he expected that she would shout at him a bit. He had blundered. He had let himself get distracted at exactly the wrong time. All in all, yesterday hadn't contained his finest efforts at reputation redemption. Or bride capturing.

Really, he deserved to be shouted at.

But she greeted him with a smile when he entered the sunny-walled morning room. As she stood, the shiny green beads on her gown clicked faintly.

"Michael, do you prefer coffee or tea? Or chocolate? I think the kitchen has some chocolate too."

He looked at her warily. "Nothing. I don't need anything."

With a nod, she ordered tea and biscuits from a servant. Turning back to Michael as the door closed them in, she said, "It's not for you; it's for me. I've a feeling I'm going to need all my energy this morning."

He looked at her closely; never a hardship. Today her blue-green eyes appeared shadowed. "Are you tired?"

"I'm all right. But if today goes as yesterday did, I will soon become very tired indeed."

Ah. There it was. "Go ahead. Shout at me. I don't mind."

She motioned him to a chair. "Sit, sit. I had it checked for soundness." Did she wink at him? Seating herself in a matching chair, she added, "Now, what would be the purpose of shouting at you if you don't mind it? It would be a waste of air and would probably unnerve the servants."

"Then you aren't annoyed with me?"

"I didn't say that. Respectable and wealthy heiresses are hardly as thick on the ground as horse droppings. If you wish to catch one of them for yourself—an heiress, I mean—then I'll thank you to behave yourself in a reasonable manner."

He blinked. "Let me understand you clearly. Are you referring to Miss Weatherby as a horse dropping?"

Caroline folded her arms. "No, of course not. It was merely a figure of speech. Miss Weatherby is a lovely girl. If anyone is to be tagged with the epithet of *horse dropping*, it shall not be her."

Just then, a servant entered the room with a tray of

biscuits, a covered teapot, and a few fragile little cups. Michael was forced to bite his tongue until they were left alone again.

As soon as the door glided closed again, he spoke up. "I am not so unbearably thick-witted as you seem to think me, Caro. I understand your meaning perfectly well. But I cannot imagine what I've done to be called unreasonable."

"Are you certain? You thought there was reason enough for me to shout at you." She poured out a cup of tea for herself, then inhaled its fragrance. "If you've forgotten what happened yesterday—"

"I have *not*," he ground out, "forgotten. I broke a Carcel lamp, which was an accident."

She raised her eyes to the ceiling. "I suppose that's not false. But it would not have broken if you'd never taken it apart during a dinner party. Could I recollect a thousand more *faux pas* you had committed last night, that single one would stand as reason enough for my displeasure."

Michael held himself rigid in his chair. "Dinner was over. And there is nothing unreasonable about finding something sensible to do, given that I had chosen not to play cards."

"Indeed there is not, though we disagree on what *sensible* means. *Sensible* means that you play the pianoforte. It does not mean that you dissect the lighting atop it."

"I don't play music."

"Then *talk* to someone, Michael. Make a new acquaintance. Use that title of yours for your own benefit. Or if you can't bear to do that, simply stare out the window as though every pastime is tooth-grindingly dull and far beneath your notice. But for God's sake, do not take apart your host's lamp."

Michael crossed his arms, holding himself steady. Any second now, a headache would erupt, burying his control under a lava flow of pain.

"I realize," Caroline continued, "that my advice to you not to dismantle lamps will not apply to many situations. But we will take it as a starting point: the host controls the lamps. Bear that in mind. If you ever hold a house party at Callows, you may lead your guests in a cheerful disassembly of every lamp in the house." Her eyes widened. "I say, that's a good idea."

Her tone made Michael suspicious. "Taking apart my lamps?"

A ghost of a smile bent Caroline's mouth. "Hardly. I mean, convening a house party in Lancashire after the season. If we haven't already got you betrothed by then, that is. I'm sure you'd be irresistible in your own environment."

Ah, here came the headache, knocking at his temples. It was late to arrive; he had expected it minutes ago.

"My steward informed me that the polite world thinks me..." Michael choked on the word *mad*, then cast about for a substitute. "Ungracious."

"I agree with him completely, and after last night, I think Miss Weatherby does too. It is indeed ungracious to ignore a gently bred young lady, then dismantle a lamp in a fit of childish boredom. And then break its fine glass globe and allow a curse to slip out in that same young lady's hearing."

"I was not bored at the time I took apart the lamp."

She shook her head, then made a complicated ordeal out of sipping her tea, adding a bit more milk and sugar, then drinking again.

He wished he could interpret her face. He understood the elevation of land, but how to read the elevation of an eyebrow? He knew how to grade for the best growth of different crops, but what did the different grades of a smile mean? Why did a cheek bloom rosy?

He could not ask her. But he had to trust her to some degree. She had offered him help.

Long ago, she had offered him much more than that.

Warmth shot through his body at the memory. The very thought of it ached; it was so sweet and so terrible.

"I wasn't bored," he repeated. "I was—well, tense. You weren't there. You were talking to that other fellow."

Clunk. She set down her teacup so hard that tea sloshed into the saucer. Her hands pressed to her mouth. With pity?

"And," he added more loudly, "I've always wanted to know how those lamps work."

"Yes." It sounded as if she were answering a question.

All those years ago, passion had bloomed as swiftly as it had been killed. Michael had thought he'd go mad from the conquest—*her* conquest—and the loss. But still, against all logic, he wanted to touch her cheek, to see if it was really as pliant as the skin of a peach. He wanted to rub a thumb over the arch of her brow and slide his hand down her neck, her shoulder, the smooth length of her arm. If he could wrap his hands around her form, maybe he could wrap his mind around this pull, this want, and master it.

But he must not touch her. The idea was ridiculous. Completely out of the question.

He laced his fingers together so they wouldn't become disobedient.

"You've gone away again," Caroline said.

Michael looked up from his carefully arranged hands. "Pardon?"

"You." She swiped a hand through the air. "You're sitting here, but you're not really listening to me. You're thinking of something else. Worrying about your dukedom, aren't you?"

"Of course," Michael blurted. Better she think he was preoccupied with Wyverne than by the curves of her face and body.

"Tell me, Michael. Is your steward competent?"

Michael watched her lips form the words, the tip of her tongue peeking forth on the liquid consonants. How did they taste to her? Was speech sweeter in the mouth when one always had honeyed words?

He had to repeat her words in his mind before he could divine their meaning. "Competent?"

"Yes, competent. I assume he is, or you would surely have dismissed him by now."

"True. Yes, he is."

"Then you have nothing to worry about. As long as you have funds to pay him—you *do* pay him, do you not?"

"For now," Michael muttered.

"Then you can trust him to serve you, and you need not worry about things you are unable to influence, fix, or oversee." She smiled, as if she thought this was reassurance.

But it was not. It turned lust to anxiety, reminding Michael that he was far away from Wyverne and that everything lay in Sanders's hands now. All he could do was write letters: letters that took too long to arrive and were not answered nearly often enough.

Hectic darkness flickered before his eyes, and he tried to pull in a deep breath without Caroline noticing.

She did notice, though. "Good heavens, what is the matter?"

"Just… tired," Michael managed.

"If you are merely tired, then I am the Prince Regent's favorite horse. Are you ill?"

"Of course not," Michael rasped, remembering to tilt his chin up and stare along the length of his nose.

"Then it must be that you didn't like what I said," Caroline murmured. "About not being able to oversee every—well, I'd best not repeat it. Michael, I know the doing isn't as easy as the telling, but you must trust your steward. Has he been with your family long?"

"Yes. But I've been…"

He trailed off. He could not admit to her the neglect his father had bequeathed him, having gambled away the livelihood of Wyverne's tenants and mortgaged their future. He could not, in this bright, brocaded morning room, talk about slogging through debt, dredging his land, excavating canals. Anything, anything to squeeze a bit more life from the chilly, rocky land.

He had given his land his whole life, and it was still not enough. Even now, his mind ticked with tasks like an over-wound pocket watch. *Should. Must. Need to. Ought.*

Caroline's voice seemed to come from far away. "In your absence, will your steward be able to cope with whatever arises?"

How could he know? Nature was in charge, as always, and she would not be gainsaid. What did it matter whether he built the most advanced irrigation system in the world if the earth denied him a growing season? "No one can possibly know the answer to that question," he ground out. "Why have you requested that I come this morning? Is it to harangue me about things you know nothing about?"

Too harsh by far. He knew she meant well. But where another woman might have crumpled, she only raised her eyebrows.

"No, it's so that you'll tell me more. Do understand, Michael, my intention is not to make you uncomfortable." She flashed a grin at him. "That is only an unexpected benefit."

Her grin died, and she added, "Only teasing, of course. So touchy, aren't you? What I mean is that you must trust me, and you must trust your steward, and that will only come through offering each other honesty."

"I do not care to trust anyone but myself."

"Truly?"

"Yes."

Caroline looked the way Michael had felt when he first saw a Cornish steam engine: fascinated yet a bit appalled by its strangeness. "If so, I don't wonder you are in financial trouble. Why should bankers trust you if you don't trust them?"

"If others choose not to trust me, that is their right, and indeed they are exercising it this year. But I know that I can be trusted. For my part, I lend only to people who rely on me, such as my tenants."

"Because they are your responsibility, and therefore in a way the money is still under your control. You really *don't* think you trust anyone, do you?" She paused, teeth pulling at the fullness of her lower lip. "Yet I wonder if it has occurred to you that you are trusting me now. And your steward too."

"I—" He slammed his mouth shut before he could say something ungracious again. She was right, and he disliked that she knew that. He could not be in two places at once, or live well in two worlds.

So yes, he had to trust her for now. He had called on her this morning, after all. And he had accepted her help because he could not quite manage to deny himself every part of her.

Caroline poured out another cup of tea. "I don't mean to wake your anxiety again."

"I am *not* anxious."

She shot him a Look.

"I'm not. I simply get headaches sometimes." Damn it. He hadn't intended to admit that.

She handed the cup to him. "Drink that. Then tell me about the headaches."

"There's nothing to tell. Everyone gets headaches sometimes." He felt oafish, blunt fingers cradling an eggshell-thin china cup. Since she was still watching him, he sipped at the tea.

And sipped again. And again. Before he realized it, he was looking at the dregs in his cup.

"The warmth is pleasant," he said to excuse himself. "Thank you."

With a knowing smile, she refilled his cup and handed him a plate of biscuits. “Some people get headaches when they forget to eat and drink.”

“Ridiculous. That’s not why I get headaches.” In less than a minute, his cup and plate were somehow empty.

Again, Caroline replenished both. “So you’re neither anxious nor hungry. Yet these headaches distract you? Might you be ill?”

“I’m not ill either. I simply prefer to retain control of my surroundings, because if I do not, I get a headache.”

She blinked at him.

“I assure you, it is *not* due to anxiety.”

She raised one eyebrow.

“It’s *not*. And I do not have a problem.”

“But you do,” she said. “You need money.”

“Oh.” With a clatter, he set his cup and plate down. “Yes. True. I do have that problem.”

“You probably won’t find your future bride until you stop thinking of this time in London as a brief chore to be escaped as soon as possible. A duke can never be completely forgotten by society; at most, he can be contorted in the minds of others.”

“I know that well enough,” Michael said grimly. “People love to whisper about me.”

Caroline clapped her hands. “Very good, Michael. Far more ducal than even I expected.”

“How do you mean?”

She smiled. “You think everyone is talking about you all the time?”

He realized how it sounded. “Not talking. Whispering. It’s different.”

“Fine, then. Whispering. By which *I* merely mean

talking very quietly, but I assume *you* mean something more sordid."

Michael crossed his arms. "Perhaps."

"Even if they whisper about you, what does it matter? You outrank them all. You can tell anyone to go to hell anytime."

"That would certainly scotch the rumors of my..." He paused, not liking to say *madness*.

"Actually," Caroline interrupted his unfinished sentence, "it might. It would be more in keeping with the behavior expected of a duke than would, say, taking apart a lamp."

"Not the lamp again, please," groaned Michael. "As I can't undo my dissection, as you called it, I beg you to drop the subject. I promise you that I will never take apart a lamp again, unless it is my possession and in my home."

"All right, no more lamps," she agreed. "Then let us return to the whispering. You think everyone is talking—pardon me, whispering—about you."

"Yes."

"Let me ask you this, Michael. If they are whispering about you—which you don't know for certain, not being a Gypsy prognosticator—could it be for a pleasant reason?"

"I doubt it. Why would they whisper if so?"

"Because a lady cannot say aloud, 'look at the delectable arse on Wyverne.' But she can whisper it in her friend's ear. And then they will both look at you. They might even laugh. And it won't be because they think something is wrong. It will be because they are appreciating your delectable arse."

Michael had to smile. "Women don't talk like that."

"But I just did, did I not? I assure you, women do talk like that. And about you. Surely you've encountered flirtation before."

He had, yes, the last time he'd been in London. He'd been only twenty-one, determined to escape the eccentric reputation that had dogged his youth. Determined, too, to show the world he had nothing in common with his debauched father.

Then he met Caroline, and he had positively boiled with thwarted lust. Fortunately, Lancashire and eleven years' more maturity had chilled those urges out of him. He had honed his body into a vehicle for completing the tasks of his dukedom. There was no sense in feeling lust, since he had no intention of acting on it.

Perhaps this was why he disliked being touched. He did not want anyone to wake his sleeping desire.

Yet it awoke as he stared at Caroline, spellbound by her calm understanding. It was as seductive as a proposition, this slow exchange of confidences.

He was separated from her by no more than a few feet, but Michael felt it as a chasm between himself and unknown territory. Like the legend on an old map: *Here there be dragons*. Yes, there she sat, and his whole being heated at the thought of drawing closer.

Out of habit, he denied himself. He leaned back in his chair and steepled his fingers. "Thank you for your kind words."

Caroline pursed her lips. "Certainly. Any time you wish for a compliment on your arse, I will be happy to oblige you."

This was sufficiently ridiculous to break the steely tension, giving both of them permission to laugh.

But Michael's thoughts were left behind, perilously close to those dragon waters, licking heat over his skin. He was simmering and feared he might boil away, yet he craved the sensation.

There must be something of the beast within him as well.

This new type of madness was unlike the eccentricities of which the world suspected him. It was nothing more or less than a letting go, an unlocking of himself. And it was the sweetest terror he had ever known.

Eight

"NOW THAT WE HAVE DISPENSED WITH THE SUBJECT of your arse, let us discuss your courtship." Caroline sat up straighter in her chair, making her voice resolutely crisp. "I think we must assume that Miss Weatherby will not be amenable to further attentions from you."

Much better, putting another woman in the room with them.

Caroline had suspected her plan wouldn't go smoothly. If Michael hadn't strewn a lamp across the drawing room of Tallant House, he would no doubt have done something else to complicate his reentry into society. She had counted on unexpected behavior.

But she had not prepared for untidy emotion—not his and especially not hers.

Caroline had planned to master her foolish fascination, binding it up tight with her common sense, her money, and her wiles. But it was stronger than she had known. Every time Michael's forest-dark eyes met hers, the old desire struggled and woke.

She clamped down on it ruthlessly. "Miss Weatherby

may put a flea in her father's ear about you, and that will not do your financial situation any good."

"Agreed."

"Are you ready to consider another possibility, then? The second lady I have in mind is Augusta Meredith, an orphan and an heiress, already of age. There will be no intrusive parents when we make her acquaintance. At a ball, I think. You can ask her to dance."

As she nattered on, buttering over her rebellious feelings with everyday words, she marked a change in him. His shoulders grew stiff, and the corners of his mouth pulled tight. He looked like a man turned to stone. What was the word for that? Oh, yes. *Petrified*.

She broke off in the middle of a sentence about Miss Meredith. "What on earth is the matter, Michael?"

"I don't care for your society type of ball."

She should have realized that a man ill at ease with touch would not care for the press of crowds or the din of voices. "Ah. That's why you were out on the terrace at Applewood House. You were escaping."

He pressed at his temple with the heel of one hand. "I was enjoying the weather."

"Rubbish," said Caroline. "No one's enjoying the weather this year, especially not you. Very well, let me consider this. Because you will have to take part in society if you are ever to be accepted by it."

She fiddled with the bugled trim that adorned the skirt of her gown. Michael swallowed heavily, watching her fingers.

"All right," she decided. "We'll figure this out using one of your scientific methods, as we did with the whispering."

"You didn't figure out anything related to the whispering. You only said something coarse to amuse me."

Coarse? He had no idea. But she only smiled as though he'd caught her in a pleasant little trick. "If you were amused, then I am delighted. But let us call it a hypothesis too. That sounds like something you might enjoy. You *do* enjoy dealing in hypotheses, do you not?"

He inclined his head, giving her permission to continue.

"My hypothesis, Michael, is that when people whisper about you, it is because they are either admiring you or are intimidated by you. They hope, yet fear, that you will take notice of them. A word from you, a few minutes at your side, can give them a memory to feast upon for long days ahead."

Thus she revealed her long-ago self to him, cloaking it in wrong pronouns and false hypotheticals. Though her memories had held their sweetness only for a short time, they had long since grown stale. She was determined not to let them become bitter, though. She had gained too much to dwell on that old loss.

And it was sweet again to have him watch her so intently. "That is what you truly think?" His lips pressed together; his dark lashes shadowed his cheekbones with every blink.

She ached to take away the pressure and the shadows, to learn every angle of his body and mind. Like a Carcel lamp, he was constructed in a unique and intricate way that few people could understand.

Caroline was trying, though, and she was determined to succeed. She could never understand a lamp, as Michael did, or calculate the volume of earth to be removed to make an effective canal. But she had pierced her own heart long ago, and she knew how people worked.

She understood the need cloaked by Michael's deep eyes: he craved help, though he would never ask for it. He was a man, and a duke, and he was unimaginably proud—three reasons to keep that wall around himself.

She took metaphorical chisel in hand. "The next time we go to a ball together, Michael, task yourself with noticing the way people act. If their eyes crinkle at the corners, they are pleased. If they laugh, they are likely still more pleased. Only if they turn their bodies away from you need you suspect a snub."

"*We*, you said. You will accompany me, then? To the next ball I attend?"

Her stomach squirmed. "I can, since it is in pursuit of your goal. We shall call it the second event of our contract, and if all goes well with Miss Meredith, perhaps it will be the last we need."

She gave him precisely two seconds to digest this information: long enough for the words to soak in, but insufficient for a reply. "You now have a means of analyzing human behavior at a ball. We have already disposed of the question of whispering. You will add it to your quiver of testable hypotheses. Is there anything else?"

He shifted in his chair; through the thin knit of his trousers, she could see the long muscles flexing in his thighs. Half rising, he shot a look at her and lowered himself back into his chair.

"Stand if you must," Caroline said. "I can conduct a conversation just as well if you are on your feet as off them."

A sideways glance. "You will not think me impolite if I pace?"

"Pacing is one of the least impolite things you have done since we renewed our acquaintance," Caroline assured him. "Please proceed. My carpet is quite comfortable to the foot."

Michael's mouth twitched. He stood, walked to the window, then back to the door. Each time he crossed, he picked up speed. When he fell into a step as regular as the tick of a clock, he finally spoke.

"I dislike the conversation that must be made with people one does not know." His voice was clipped off with every step he took.

"How can that be? You carried on at great length with the Weatherby women."

His steady stride broke, and his gaze found hers. "You were with me."

Her mouth dropped open; she slammed it shut. He had admitted something astounding: that he had needed her.

How precious, to be needed for something beyond the selection of a fabric, a pleasant afternoon call, a luscious night. For something far more valuable than all her wealth. For herself.

You were with me, he said, and it mattered to him. Delight bloomed within her.

She covered it up. Let it rest, hidden, alongside her old desire for him. Instead, she returned to the scientific language he favored. "What I said to the

Weatherbys was commonplace enough, Michael. You could certainly duplicate the results."

"I doubt I will always find occasion to speak about Lancashire."

"Maybe not to begin with." She looked over her neglected teacup, her plate of untouched biscuits, and crumbled one as she thought. "One often starts a conversation by commenting on the weather or the dinner or some common point of experience. Once the first reserve has been breached, you may find additional points in common or make a remark that is sure to interest others. This makes others feel comfortable, which allows them to enjoy your company."

Until she spoke, she had not realized how many interactions each day could be reduced to such interchanges: the greasing of social wheels, the reassurance of everyday topics of conversation. So much that was almost scripted in its regularity. She could certainly teach this method to Michael.

And thank God, that meant she *was* needed, just for now. There was more pleasure in that than in receiving a roomful of suitors who sought only to get inside her purse or her skirts.

Michael was different from other men; she had always known that. Without even trying, he was twining himself through her mind. He would breach her heart too, if she let him.

But he had no use for a heart, so she would not allow him close to hers. No, she would permit every other liberty before she would permit that.

Michael had never thought of conversation in terms of discrete tests and tasks. The idea was intriguing.

"Simple as that, you say. One should talk of the weather and then identify something in common." He blew out a deep breath, then returned to his seat. "Let us test it out."

"What would you say, then, if I should ask you about the weather?"

Michael narrowed his eyes at Caroline. There was nothing in her question that could be tested. "I would ask you if you had looked outside lately. That is where the weather is always to be found."

She smothered a laugh. "It's not a literal question, and that is not a polite reply. But I'll ask it of you differently. What do you think of the weather?"

Better. There was room to supply information here. "I think it is unusually cold for this time of year, though less so than in Lancashire. Perhaps the fog helps hold heat in to the City." An idea ribboned through his mind. "Caro. Has anyone has ever recorded the relationship between the temperature and fog density? It bears further study, I am sure."

Caroline held up a hand. "Michael. Stop. I have no idea whether anyone has cataloged the… whatever you said. And neither will anyone else. If someone asks you what you think of the weather, they do not expect a detailed discussion of temperature. Simply say something like, 'Deuced cold, isn't it?' That's all."

"But that's a meaningless answer."

"It's not meant to provide information. It's meant to reassure the other person that you are of his class, of sound mind, and reasonably pleasant to be around.

From such reassurance comes social success. Now, try again." She lowered her voice to resemble a masculine rumble. "Rotten weather, what?"

Michael parroted, "Deuced cold, isn't it?" Even as Caroline smiled, he shook his head. "That might work as a semblance of a greeting, but I can't simply repeat that all day. And what if the weather should warm?"

"Then you say, 'Deuced warm, isn't it?' I should have thought that would be obvious." She gnawed on her lip; the gesture made him shiver. Deuced warm. "But you are right, it's only the first step. And it must feel natural, or you'll sound as though you're speaking a part on the stage—and badly. Can you give me a brief version of what you said before? About the cold or the fog?"

Michael stretched his mind back. "You ask me about the weather. Then I could say that it's cold, but less so than Lancashire."

"Perfect." Her sunbeam smile struck him in the solar plexus. "That sort of reply will do wonderfully. It is no social trespass to speak of what you like best, only to talk on for too long. Remember, we always want to make other people feel at ease."

"Ha." Michael could not remember feeling less at ease in recent memory. This physical turmoil was as distracting as his usual headache, though in a different way. It was not a wish for pain to end, but a yearning for something wakeful and exotic to begin.

Caroline talked on. "Do you take snuff? That's another topic you could introduce. Gentlemen can easily spend hours talking about their favorite sort and why it's the only one that's worthwhile."

Michael stared at her lips. He wanted to rub his thumb over that mobile mouth, to see if it felt different from his own. He needed to touch her, to feel the skin of another human being against his. He needed to…

He needed to answer the question. Snuff, wasn't it? "Ah—no. I never have taken snuff. What is the pleasure in forcing oneself to sneeze?" As if his body didn't grow agitated enough on its own without prompting from inhaled particles.

It was growing agitated now. Not from a headache, nor from the tension that often corded his arms. Instead, his fingers tingled, as though wanting again to cast everything away and forget himself.

"What is the pleasure in anything?" Caroline looked quite serious.

"What do you mean?"

Caroline spread her hands. "There's no pleasure in snuff. There's no pleasure in talking to the *ton* and forming everyday connections. You do not play cards or music. I have never known you to dance. In what, then, *do* you find pleasure?"

It was not a question he was accustomed to hearing, much less asking himself. Possibly because there were indeed few pleasures in his life. His mother had died in his infancy, and thereafter, his youth had been a bitter war of opposing temperaments until his father abandoned the battle for the grave. Even the satisfaction Michael once got from resurrecting Wyverne had slid away from him as his plans burgeoned, as details and money slipped from him and never came back within his grasp.

It was already more than he could keep within control, so there was no room for any other kind of pleasure.

Though he could almost forget that as Caroline watched him, her lips parted. She smelled faintly of jasmine, like spring brought to life in the middle of the City. He could spring to life too, if she would show him how. For what other reason would he be here with her today?

For Wyverne. Always, only, ever.

For Wyverne, now, he wrestled with himself until he choked off his want, managing an acceptable reply. "There is pleasure in taking apart the clockwork mechanism of a Carcel lamp."

Caroline lifted one eyebrow. "So you say." But the crimp of her mouth was, Michael thought, evidence of amusement rather than annoyance. "Let us try again, then, and we will seek a kernel of pleasure in the everyday. You have your introduction in a moderate discussion of the weather."

Michael sighed. "Yes. And no experiments."

"Quite right. What next should we vanquish, to increase your enjoyment of London life?"

The answer came to mind at once. "Dancing. I know it is an inextricable part of courtship, though it is really nothing but an excuse for touching a lot of attractive strangers."

"And unattractive ones too. Sadly." Caroline dusted biscuit crumbs from her fingertips. "I suspect you're not the only man in London who has qualms about dancing. It is one of the most complex of our rituals, you know. Every step heavy with meaning, every gesture holding import."

"That is not a helpful observation." Michael's right leg began to bounce, agitated. "I thought dancing was intended to be diverting, but where is the diversion if every dance holds more significance than the average speech before Parliament?"

"This." Before he understood her meaning, she rose from her seat to flatten a palm on his chest. His heart thumped for her notice, but then her head bent close to his, and he felt the warmth of her breath on his ear. "This, Michael."

His scalp prickled; he had no idea whether his heart continued to beat. He only felt, wanted, craved as she took his hands, pulled him to his feet, then slid his hands around the curve of her waist.

His fingers flexed. "The sphere is no longer my favorite shape."

Stupid brain.

"You have a favorite shape?" She paused. "Never mind. Of course you do. Might I hope your favorite number is three? We're going to waltz."

"What? Here?"

"Here. Now. One, two, three," she murmured. Then she tugged at his shoulders, humming tunelessly.

His feet followed as they were bid, at first stumbling until he seized upon the pattern of the steps. Ticking off circle after circle, transporting him ever onward, to a place that was entirely distant from a morning room on a noisy street in London. They turned, silent and slow, deliberate as arithmetic, and there was nothing but the sum of their parts. Body and soul and the sweet feeling of Caroline in his arms.

They fit together, hands and bodies, in every way.

Two gears from the same wondrous machine, made to work together.

The tuneless scratch of her hum died away, leaving them alone in a roaring silence.

He had forgotten his body for a few minutes—a blessed gift. Now that it pressed upon his notice again, it was not as usual. Every fiber of his form felt taut, but the feeling was pure and bright, like feeling the sun on his skin for the first time after a long winter.

At long last, he thought as he bent his head.

She slid her hands to his face, then turned her head to breathe his name in his ear. "Michael. *This*. Let me show you the pleasure in it."

He had never known an ear was useful for anything but hearing. Yet as she breathed in it—as he could almost feel her lips upon its sensitive folds—pleasure arrowed through his body, sudden and startling.

Surely she could feel his arousal through their clothing. Would she pull away? But no, she caught his shoulders again and pulled him closer.

His hands framed her face, then tangled in her coiled hair. Delicately, he brushed her lips with his. So soft. So heated. She gave a little sigh and slid her arms down to encircle him.

Why—she was *embracing* him.

He had not been embraced since the last time he surrendered himself to her touch.

Of reflex, he waited for the gut punch of chilly tension, the intrusive pounding of his headache. But she tugged his head downward, and her hot tongue found the rim of his ear, and his every rivet simply popped. He was steam, mindless and formless and boiling, and dimly he heard himself moan as she gently nipped his earlobe.

He caught her mouth again, smothering it with his own, wanting to consume their every sound of need. This was a power both unprecedented and exhilarating: to please a woman with his body. He had never done such a thing before, never been so close or so passionate.

But his own flesh understood things darker and deeper and hotter than anything Michael had ever studied in a book. He knew just how to press back when Caroline rubbed against him. He knew how to match her mouth with his, how to invite the delicious torment of her tongue. The taste of her was indefinable, like heat itself, and he sipped at it to understand it more fully. There was no understanding it, though, none at all. It was wildness for its own sake, and it was marvelous.

His hands had their own will, stroking her back and pulling her more firmly against his body. He wanted her inside him; he wanted to be inside her. The touch of her was magical, more intoxicating than brandy could possibly be.

No wonder he had resisted such closeness. It was unmaking him. He was drunk on it, and the realization made him shudder with thrilling force. This, *this* was why people danced and loved, and why they offered one another night after night of pleasure.

But pleasure would not save Wyverne.

The thought was as heavy and painful as hitting his thumb with a hammer.

There was no reason to dance with Caroline, or

to kiss her. The solution to his problems was the prosaic circle of a guinea, not the sinuous curve of the woman in his arms.

He let his arms sink to his sides. They felt as weighty as if all the burdens of the world had been placed on them.

Which was a ludicrous overstatement. It wasn't the world. It was merely eighty thousand acres of it, scattered far away and sere, needing him more than he could ever need anything or anyone.

"I..." He began, but had nothing to say next.

That single syllable was enough, though. He could almost hear the fragile intimacy shatter as Caroline stepped away from him.

"I can do without pleasure," he made himself say. "It is not a requirement. Only money is a requirement."

"I am sorry to hear you say that." She was still too close to him, close enough to touch, yet she did not touch him again. "For I think an appreciation of pleasure would help you greatly in your cause. Without feeling it, you can never give it."

"I said I felt pleasure in taking apart the lamp."

She gave a dismissive wave. "Purely intellectual. That type of pleasure is cold and solitary. Instead, I'm talking of the pleasure of the flesh and of the soul."

Michael felt himself on unsteady ground. "This cannot be relevant to my search for a wife."

"It is relevant to everything," Caroline insisted. Now it was her turn to pace the room. With her hands tucked behind her back, the beaded bodice of her gown pulled tight over her rounded breasts. Michael knotted his fingers again, reminding them that they were not to touch. "Surely you want your wife to admire you, and one day even love you."

His mouth had gone dry. "That would be ideal, though it is not necessary."

She pivoted, faced him. "No? It should be. How much better would your inevitable marriage be if your wife smiled when she saw you each morning? If she caressed you because she loved the feel of your skin and knew that you loved her touch? How much better if you had someone to talk to who accepted everything odd that you said, because she admired the workings of your mind and trusted your judgment?"

He stared at her. The idea of such a wife, such a life, was like riding the *Catch Me Who Can* locomotive across the Channel from Dover to Calais. In a word: impossible.

"No one has such a marriage," he said. This was not, he knew, a statement of fact. It was a theory that could be disproven by a single counterexample.

"You're wrong," Caroline replied, "though that doesn't matter. What matters is whether you want that for yourself, or whether you only want to discharge your debts and carry on as you have for the last eleven years."

"Business before pleasure," he murmured. There was always business. There was never any time for pleasure.

That was Michael's choice. If he had wished, he could have hired himself an army of servants, left his estates in their charge, and gallivanted around London, whoring, drinking, gambling. Living as his father's son, allowing his land to dwindle irretrievably into poverty.

But he would not; he was not built to slough

his responsibilities onto others. Such pastimes were meaningless and therefore worthless. Instead, Michael chose their opposite: the business of his dukedom. He devoted his considerable intellect and energy toward improving finances and land matters, and each year—until this one—had seen progress.

Wyverne was his responsibility. And discharging his responsibilities fully and well held pleasures of its own.

"Business before pleasure," he repeated, catching Caroline's eye. "That is the way it must be. Finding a wealthy wife is my business. If pleasure comes later, so be it."

She watched him for a long, unblinking moment. Michael felt as though she saw through his veneer of determination to the desperate longing within.

"So be it," she echoed. "Then we shall seek out Miss Meredith."

After spearing him with such a look, he wished she had not accepted his answer without demur.

But why should she not? Theirs was only a tie of business, after all. No matter how pleasurable it might seem for a moment frail as crystal.

Nine

"Deuced cold, isn't it, Your Grace?"

Lord Kettleburn clapped Michael on the shoulder and grinned at him. With a fluffy crown of white hair and a fleshy nose webbed with burst capillaries, the elderly baron was as inelegant as he was jovial.

"Deuced cold," Michael agreed. At his side, Caroline coughed so much that he suspected her of covering a laugh.

The Kettleburns made an unlikely pair: he, a rough-spoken *pukka sahib* who had made a fortune in shipping; she, a viscount's daughter several decades his junior, whom he had purchased shortly after receiving his barony for economic services to the Crown.

In other words, Kettleburn had started with money and used it to gild his way to a position in society. Precisely the reverse of what Michael intended to do.

He only hoped his union proved more harmonious than the Kettleburns'. The baron's money might have bought lobster patties and a large orchestra, but as far as Michael could tell, no one particularly wanted to talk with him.

Except Caroline, who was clasping the old rogue's hand. "I adore your new chandeliers, Lord Kettleburn. Such beautiful crystal. Are they Venetian prisms?"

The baron cleared his throat. "Can't say, honestly. M'wife's picked out all the fripperies and furnishings. She does the choosing, and I do the paying. Suits us both, what?"

The young baroness smiled tightly. Several inches taller than her husband, she reminded Michael of an icicle: thin and brittle in a frost-silver gown, with pale hair pulled back tightly from austere features.

By contrast, Caroline was all warmth. Her gown was dark red, so velvety looking that it seemed to invite touch. In the candlelight, her upswept hair appeared as golden as a sodium flame—though somehow he had thought it prudent not to blurt out this comparison.

"I admire your selections, Lady Kettleburn." Caroline turned her smile to the young baroness. "And I congratulate you on your fortunate household arrangements. Not many women of my acquaintance enjoy such husbandly trust and indulgence."

The young woman relaxed visibly, and Caroline turned to their host again. "My lord, the punch is your own concoction, is it not? I've heard it's the perfect complement to an evening of dancing and merriment. Wyverne, you must try it."

The baron blinked hazily. "Er… yes. I'd be honored, Your Grace. May I show you to the refreshments?"

"No need, my lord." Caroline waved him off. "Your other guests would miss the pleasure of your greeting. I'll steer Wyverne in the right direction."

With a flurry of nods and smiles all around, they

moved into the arcade of rooms their hosts had opened up for dancing.

"Truly, I have no idea in which direction you are steering me," Michael muttered. Like his own London residence, Kettleburn House was a stretching home in an elegant but not modish part of London. But as quiet and dim as Wyverne House was, this one was tumultuous, full of winking candles and babbling voices, the heavy scent of meats cooked in butter and lard, the bleat of oboes and thrum of strings. Already his head pounded in time with the country dancing; already he was tense from holding himself out of Caroline's reach, from reminding himself not to reach for her.

Tonight, he had another chance to show the world who the Duke of Wyverne was. And by God, he'd better not cock it up again.

Caroline nodded at a gaggle of richly dressed women then waggled her fan at another group. "I am steering you into society," she said. "Is it not obvious? Lord Kettleburn is now convinced that you are keen to try his punch, than which he can imagine no greater honor. And his lady wife is of better cheer knowing that her domestic arrangements are admired rather than scorned."

She turned to Michael, lovely as a wicked angel. "This is how we shall proceed. All you have to do is say 'Deuced cold' when the moment is right and think of something kind to say whenever you can. Just as we practiced last Saturday."

"Why need we waste such efforts on people such as the Kettleburns?" Michael asked. "They have money but no influence, no daughter for me to pursue. Surely our time would be better spent courting the favor of someone else." Unkind, perhaps, but his reserves were finite. He already felt like a spring over-tightened, tense beyond bearing.

"Spoken with a duke's hauteur. Why waste your favor on your inferiors?"

"That's not what I meant." The rhythmic headache added a brutal glissando. "I speak of time being limited, not favor. I am only conscious of the need for haste."

"Ah. So you wish to focus your attention on the best people."

"I—"

"Aristocrats, you mean. Dukes such as yourself."

He wondered whether she was being deliberately obtuse. "If they have money and unmarried daughters."

Caroline snapped her fan closed. "Someone such as the fifth Duke of Devonshire, you mean? He was blessed with both daughters and deep pockets. A prince among men, to be sure. He made his wife's life a hell by taking up with her closest friend under his own roof, yet when the duchess strayed, he had her exiled to France."

"I don't mean—" Michael tried to break in, but Caroline continued ruthlessly.

"Or do you mean to confine your definition of the best to royalty? Perhaps our Prince Regent, who has a wife yet not a wife in the abandoned Mrs. Fitzherbert? Or whose cousin bore him such a disgust that, once they were married, she left him after the wedding night?"

"*No.*" Michael pressed a hand to his temple, but he could not silence her voice.

"Or best of all, the king, who speaks in tongues and froths at the mouth?"

"Quiet, woman!" Michael barked.

Caroline went still. "You refer to me as *woman*?"

Michael let his hand fall. "It's biologically accurate. And I also said 'quiet.' You have willfully misunderstood me. You are attributing great snobbery to me when I only stated my desire to focus my limited attention on finding a wife. I cannot become friends with everyone in London. I do not possess your skill."

Caroline blinked several times. Then she flicked her fan open again and continued walking as though there had been no outburst. "I am friends with only some of them. But I am courteous to all. The nobility, as you know, deserves respect by virtue of their blue blood. The happiest accident of birth."

"Yes." Michael hesitated. "Well, that is the way of the world."

"It is, and I neither disagree with it nor dispute it," Caroline said. "The world must have its ways. But I save my highest regard for those who make the best of the gifts they have been given, whether that is a title or a fat purse or—"

"A beautiful face?" Michael gazed down at hers.

"Yes, that is a woman's greatest currency. If she gambles well, she can parlay it into a title and a fortune." Her smile looked fragile.

Deuced cold.

Then it melted away. "Do not think I criticize you, Michael. To the contrary, I admire the way you care for your dukedom. I know that's why you now seek a wealthy wife, no matter how distasteful you find the task."

"I don't—"

"But you never know who might help you or Wyverne. My opinions need not be yours, naturally, and maybe you won't care for some of the people to whom I introduce you. But I aim to help you. And therefore, I ask you not to dismiss anyone out of hand."

"Of course I won't," Michael said, insulted. "I am no schoolboy who needs a drilling in manners."

"Is that courteous, then?" Caroline leveled a finger at him. Michael realized he was looming over her with arms crossed, shoulders square, and chin high, as if he could use his size to intimidate her into silence.

Not that it would work. He could never silence this woman; not even if he were the size of an elephant. And to be fair, he shouldn't. She had said nothing so radical, only urged him to mind his manners, so to speak, for one never knew who might do him good.

For all that it appeared selfless and sentimental, such courtesy was quite logical. Still, he felt the tension of an unfulfilled goal, of too little time and too much uncertainty.

Maybe she saw this, because she relented. "It can never be bad to spend a minute setting someone at ease, Michael. To put it in the economic terms you favor: for a small investment of time, you will yield a great return of esteem. Observe."

She turned to a plump woman brushing past them. "What a fetching gown, Lady Halliwell. I've never seen anyone look so well in peach as you do."

The woman halted. "Darling Caro! You're a vision, as always." She looked curiously at Michael. "A new escort for you tonight?"

"His Grace, the Duke of Wyverne. I am but a chance companion this evening. He's honoring us this season due to…" She winked. "His desire to embark upon a certain state."

Michael straightened his shoulders and tried to look eager and soppy.

He must have done well enough, for the round Lady Halliwell beamed at him. "*Are* you? How delightful. I had rather heard… well, never mind. If you're looking for a… well, then obviously you are… That is… how lovely! I wish you good fortune. Ah… do you intend to dance tonight, Your Grace?"

"I…" Michael trailed off. His dance with Caroline had prepared him for nothing; it had only taught him the meager limits of his own control. Would it be the same if he danced with someone else? Would he make a spectacle of himself in Kettleburn House, smothering every young lady with kisses if she dared draw near him?

But no… she kissed me first, he realized. Caroline had begun it all.

This realization was hardly conducive to his self-possession.

"Yes, His Grace is eager to dance tonight," Caroline trilled, causing her peach-clad acquaintance to pat plump hands together in ecstasy. "But we've promised our host to sip some of his excellent punch first. Did you know he concocts it himself?"

"Does he?" Lady Halliwell looked interested. "I heard some young bucks talking of it earlier. Scandalously strong, is it not?"

"I hope so." Caroline grinned.

Lady Halliwell laughed and turned to resume her path through the crowded room. "An honor to meet you, Your Grace. I shall see if I can send some lovely young ladies your way, shall I?" Her round face dimpled, and Michael found himself returning what was really a rather pleasant smile.

"The lovelier, the better," Caroline said, and both women laughed again before Lady Halliwell moved on with a parting wave of her fan.

"Do you see what I mean?" Caroline said quietly as she and Michael pressed in what must be the direction of the much-discussed punch. "With the right word in her ear, Lady Halliwell was perfectly willing to be charmed by you. Now she will tell everyone what a delightful man you are. *And* she'll help circulate the news that you're looking for a wife, which could help your cause with creditors as well as wealthy young ladies."

This sounded less appealing to Michael than it ought. "I said nothing more to that woman than a single syllable. How could she find me charming under such circumstances?"

Caroline tapped her chin with her folded fan. "I believe it's something like agriculture."

"I beg your pardon."

Caroline chuckled. "Your ducal phrase, always upon the tip of your tongue. What I mean is, it's much easier for a seed to grow when the soil is prepared carefully. Correct? So it is with people too. If you prepare them for what they ought to see and feel, they are more apt to see and feel it. I acted as if I found you charming, and so Lady Halliwell was charmed."

"You only acted?" Michael knew the question was irrelevant. Whether or not Caroline found him charming had nothing to do with his purpose in London.

Except... when they had waltzed, he'd felt himself come alive. He had craved her touch, yearned for that closeness. His body had become an essential part of his being, rather than a dull weight on his mind.

In a way, she had made him feel whole. And that meant he hadn't been whole before, which was as terrifying as the feeling of wholeness was exhilarating. But it *was* exhilarating. And he could not bear to think it was all an act when for him it was so painfully real.

"I act every day, Michael," she said. "All day, every day. But that does not mean what I say and do is a lie. I may sweeten my true feelings with kind words, but I will not play myself false."

Her eyes went hard; her face, stern. Michael knew sternness well, because it sat so often on his own features. Sternness was effective at covering other feelings. Fear. Worry. Longing.

This type of acting, Michael did not mind. Some emotions were too private to share.

"I can accept that," he replied. "But I do not wish you to sweeten anything you say to me. You cannot offend me as long as you are honest."

"I wonder." She swooped behind him and nudged the tails of his coat. Straightening, she said, "Michael, you have a remarkably fine arse."

It was not dignified for a grown man to redden. Of course, it was also not dignified for a gently bred woman to compliment a man on his... posterior.

So Michael and Caroline both cast off dignity. He glared down at her with a flaming face, and she gloated. "Are you shocked, Your Grace? And I thought you could not be offended by the truth."

"By the truth I cannot, but by mockery I can. I have asked you for the favor of your honesty, and instead you seek to discomfit me."

"I have given you a greater favor than you know." With a sharp flick of the wrist, she snapped her fan open again. The painted semicircle was deliberately provocative, showing a nude Venus reclining on a tussle of draperies. It covered Caroline's mouth and nose, made a shaded mystery of her eyes. When fronted by Venus, none could fail to make the association: Caro sought desire as her due.

Oh, she had it, little though it meant to her. Like a bouquet, presented and received out of obligation.

"We ought to make our way to the punch bowl," Michael said.

"I could use some strong spirits myself." Caroline lowered her fan to the level of her bosom. "Come. I believe we'll find Lord Kettleburn's concoction at the center of that group of raucous young men."

Kettleburn had left the side of his lady wife and was now elbowing his way through the mass of imbibing men. The baron was red-faced and jovial, though the other men ignored him as they would a servant. As the crowd peeled back, a table of refreshments and an empty crystal punch bowl were revealed.

Kettleburn waved for lemons and sugar and several bottles Michael could not identify at a distance of several yards. The baron laid out all the ingredients on the snowy linen tablecloth, then mixed and mingled the complex beverage with swift, precise movements.

It was a pleasure to watch anyone so sure of his work. Kettleburn's quiet bustle drew even the interest of his inebriated young guests.

"Well done, Kettleburn. Well done," Caroline murmured behind her fan. "He forces them to recall whose hospitality they have accepted. After all this fuss, I can only assume the punch is something very special." She looked up at Michael. "Do you see the power of such conviction? He has convinced me of his skill, just as he has everyone surrounding him. He believes that his recipe is astounding, and without taking a taste, we are ready to believe it too. It is always thus with a reputation."

"And what is your reputation, Caro?" He could not resist the question. He had no idea of the answer.

Those blue-green eyes narrowed. "Mine is what I've made it over the course of a lifetime. But we're here on account of your reputation, not mine." Her mouth stretched into a tight little curve. "You've made your bed, and now you find it too austere to lie in. So we'll stuff it with bills and frame it with coin, and once the work is done, you shall sleep soundly for the remainder of your days."

Stung, he said, "I suppose I asked for honesty. You think me a wastrel, then?"

"No. Not that." She sighed. "No, I spoke too harshly. Please, forgive me. I don't think you a wastrel. But I've never really known what to think of you."

"You think of me?" This was the wrong question

to ask. He cleared his throat. "That is—you ought to think of me as—as a good duke. I wish you would."

"I do that." Venus covered her face, then was folded up. "I most definitely do that."

Was she happy with him, or was she not? He could not file this conversation into either category, so he could not, as yet, understand it.

Not that he needed to. But he was finding that he *wanted* to very much.

Before him, men were dipping out Lord Kettleburn's punch for themselves and a few bold ladies. Now that the baron's magnificent display was completed, he was shunted aside again. Lady Kettleburn sliced through the crowds in her home with chilly splendor, Caro's warming influence apparently quite dissipated.

So it was: people always returned to the behavior they knew best, and no one could change them beyond a single moment.

If the *ton* thought Michael mad, then he could not change anyone's mind. Not even if he stayed for a whole season of balls, dressed his finest, and danced every dance Almack's could offer.

Which meant he would have to find someone who would marry him despite his reputation. *Despite*: it came back to that word again.

Michael wanted not to care. But the truth was, he cared very much. That was part of the reason he'd stayed away from London so long. Why choose to spend time with those who spoke ill of him? The only possible end was that he would grow to think ill of them and of himself. Neither outcome was desirable.

And neither was the idea of a trade such as Lord

and Lady Kettleburn had made: a fortune for a title. A sacrifice on both sides seemed inevitably to lead to a sacrifice of all tender affections. He might have accepted that once, but Caroline had made him think. Think, of the joy of having a wife who esteemed him. Even loved him.

Think, of pleasure.

He drew her hand within the crook of his arm, hoping she would let him pull her close.

But she only smiled up at him as though he had obeyed an order. "Why," she said, "I believe I see Miss Meredith. Shall we get on with the business of introductions?"

Ten

For two reasons, Caroline thought Augusta Meredith an excellent candidate for Michael's hand. First, Miss Meredith had money enough to turn every sow's ear in London into a silk purse. And second, she was an orphan.

After Michael's calamitous encounter with the Carcel lamp, and the Carcel lamp's calamitous encounter with the drawing room floor, Caroline thought it prudent to eliminate disapproving mothers from the courtship situation.

Yes, she might have found the future Duchess of Wyverne this time. Miss Meredith was twenty-four years old, in control of her own funds, and quite bold enough to overcome Michael's formidable reserve.

And she was beautiful. That wouldn't hurt matters.

So Caroline had thought in the haven of her own carriage. Pleased with herself. Quite the matchmaker. Smug, really, that at last, she would prove there was no one she couldn't handle—not even Michael.

Now, standing next to Augusta Meredith—all dark-red hair, wide smile, white teeth, pleasant laugh—Caroline was almost struck dumb by the difference between twenty-four and her own thirty years. Between her own gown, cut to skate over her imperfect figure, and Miss Meredith's tight-bodiced garment, which left no question that her young form was flawless.

No doubt Michael noticed. No doubt he was noticing every inch of Miss Meredith's generous bosom, barely covered by copper moiré.

"I'm honored to make your acquaintance, Your Grace," Miss Meredith purred into Michael's ear. "I've heard the most fascinating things about you."

Michael stiffened.

"All good, no doubt." Caroline's smile showed a confidence she did not feel.

"Oh, yes." The younger woman tossed a roguish look at Caroline. "Isn't he the talk of the *ton*, Caro? Why, Your Grace, I heard you took apart every stick of furniture in the Tallant House drawing room." She trailed a gloved hand up Michael's arm. "I can tell you have the strength for it."

Michael stared at the hand on his arm.

He had said he suffered from headaches, and Caroline could see one taking hold. He squinted, and his firm mouth—*oh, he had kissed her with that mouth*—went tight.

Yet he allowed Miss Meredith to continue touching him: progress indeed. When Caroline had first flirted with him—no, no more than *touched* him—he had twisted away and barked at her as a dog would. And in turn, she had chased after him, teasing and taunting so he would play fetch with her.

Miss Meredith didn't have to chase. She was, herself, fetching.

That lady gave Michael's biceps a squeeze. "You must call me Augusta, Your Grace."

"I need do nothing of the sort."

Headache or no, that was no answer to a lady. Caroline kicked him in the heel. Not very hard, of course. Not nearly as hard as he deserved.

"But I will do so all the same," he added. "Thank you. And you must call me… ah, Wyverne."

Caroline kicked him again. Without another word, he took a step back, which removed him from grabbing range of one woman and kicking range of the other.

Well. No one had ever accused Michael of being stupid.

"Do tell me, Wyverne," Augusta asked, "what do you think of the orchestra? Do you intend to dance this evening?" Closing the distance between them, she again caught his arm and began to walk her satin-gloved fingers up and down his biceps. "Or if you are weary of that pursuit, I'm sure we could think of another. Something… equally pleasant?"

Michael stared at her hand. *Glared*, more like. His head must be clanging with dismay.

Despite herself, Caroline smiled. She couldn't blame Miss Meredith for her instant attraction to the duke. In the polished ballroom of Kettleburn House, he stood out as a little taller, a little broader, a little leaner than others. Though his dignity proclaimed him a nobleman, his physique showed him to be a man who understood work and labor. The contrast was irresistible.

And his gravitas—ah, that was the best part for Caroline. That serious face, that stern manner. The best thing about a man who worked so hard was teaching him to play.

Since he didn't have a playful answer at the ready—when did he ever?—Caroline chimed in. "Do you have a suggestion, Augusta? I know well, you're always full of clever ideas. And His Grace is still fairly new to London. As you can see, he needs some amusement."

She permitted herself a cavalier wave at Michael's granite expression, which cracked with grudging humor.

"Let me think about that." Augusta considered. "Vauxhall Gardens might be pleasant, with all its secret paths. But for tonight..." The younger woman crossed her arms under her bosom as she mused, pushing up her impressive breasts until they came perilously close to escaping her bodice. Naturally, Michael's eyes flicked down to them.

His face flushed beneath its tan.

Caroline guessed he had little experience with women. As reticent, yet aroused as he had been during their dance, it could be no commonplace event for him to be alone with a woman. For a man so hungry for control, passion would be a devastating loss. Even so, Caroline wanted to wake it, to take that control for herself.

But he was not hers to wake or control. He was in Augusta Meredith's hands now, and soon Augusta might be in *his* hands.

Oh, damn. Caroline couldn't deny it anymore: she was jealous.

Well, there was nothing to do but squelch the

feeling. Michael had been quite frank about wanting Caroline's help, but no more than that. And there was no sense in ruining his chances with another woman. Gossip and envy had been Caroline's enemy eleven years ago. She would not befriend them now.

Instead, she took care to adopt their opposite: graciousness. The young lady wanted a moonlit garden walk with secret paths? Very well.

"My dear Augusta," she broke the younger woman's reverie. "His Grace has never been to Kettleburn House before. Would you show him the famous rose garden?"

Augusta looked pleased, and Caroline had all the gratification of having done a small kindness against her own will. "That's a wonderful idea, Caro. What do you say to it, Wyverne? Shall we take a turn through the garden?"

"It would be my pleasure." His voice sounded stiff, as though he had no idea to what he had agreed, no idea what pleasure was.

Caroline affixed her brightest smile and waggled her fan at the pair. "Have a delightful time. Do let me know, Wyverne, if you come across a coquelicot carnation in the course of your botanical fumblings."

"Ha," he said, and with one more hint of a smile, they had disappeared into the crowd.

So. Her work was done, and she was no longer needed. If she had chosen well, she wouldn't need to consult with the third marriage prospect she'd identified. Perhaps even now, the future Duchess of Wyverne was strolling with her duke through the tangled roses behind Kettleburn House.

If so, they deserved each other, and that she did mean in all kindness. There was no joy in wishing people unhappiness.

She only wished she could find a little happiness for herself.

With seeming carelessness, she scanned the crowd for familiar faces, nodding whenever she locked eyes with a friend, acknowledging greetings with the perfect incline of her head, a graceful curve of lips. But no one sprang to her side to draw her into a deep conversation. No one called to her with any comment beyond a compliment on her appearance. She was surfeited with quantity yet wishing for a little more quality.

Damn Michael. He had spoiled a perfectly lovely party. He'd jolted her awry with his response to Miss Meredith, and she couldn't regain her footing.

So it had always been with him.

A voice in her ear recalled her to her surroundings. "Caro. You look ravishing tonight."

Reflexively, she turned in its direction. "Oh. Stratton." Her smile vanished.

Her late husband's great-nephew and heir looked as fashionable as always. The high points of his cravat did little to hide the weakness of his chin, though, and the scented pomade in his light brown hair only accentuated his receding hairline.

She tolerated a kiss on the hand, but it was impossible not to compare him to the man who had just left her behind. "What do you want from me, Stratton?"

The earl offered her an oily smile. "Only a dance, dear Caro. Only a dance for now." He gestured toward the couples assembling for a country set. "Shall we join them?"

Inside, Caroline sighed. But there was little he could do to harass her in a crowded room. "Very well. But no proposals tonight, do you understand me? I simply cannot abide another."

He pressed a manicured hand to his heart. "How you wound me."

"I only wish I did," she muttered. She would not soon forget how he had tried to manhandle her at the Applewood House ball. Such had ever been her fate when she floated out onto that terrace—though this time, Michael had been her savior rather than her ruin.

Perhaps Stratton had heard her, for his eyes narrowed. "Wish what you will. Do you intend to dance with me, or shall you make a spectacle in the ballroom?"

No. Not that. Dutifully, she laid her fingers on his arm and fell into step. "Very well, Stratton. Only stay in the middle of the crowd, and we'll have a fair enough time. Shall we stand at the bottom of the set?"

"Let's go to the top, so everyone can see us." He beamed at her, proud as if he was already pulling gold from her pockets.

This was the way of her life, her world: through her money and manners, she left people happy. But did anyone think of her when she wasn't around? Would anyone care for her if she had no fortune or a plain face?

She had no means of testing this hypothesis, but she suspected the answer was no.

She might as well dance with Stratton, after all. What else was left to her this evening?

"This is the most notorious garden in London, Your Grace," Miss Meredith whispered to Michael. Her hand was tucked into the crook of his arm, and as they walked, she kept brushing his arm with her undeniably splendid bosom.

Michael didn't mention it, of course. She would be embarrassed if she knew how she was displaying herself.

The Kettleburn House garden was not large by the standards of London's mansions, but it was intricately laid out. Already Miss Meredith had led him through a maze of pitted gravel paths, past sedgy undergrowth and tangled, spindly rosebushes. An occasional torch split the night; an occasional giggle too. They were not alone in taking a moonlit stroll, then.

"What gives this place its notoriety?" Michael said.

"Ah." Miss Meredith raised herself on her toes to murmur in his ear. "It was born in scandal."

The full weight of her breasts plumped onto his forearm as she dropped back onto her heels. Despite his best intentions, he twitched at the contact. Caroline had prepared him to discuss the weather, not to be bombarded by breasts. He could not fathom the proper response.

So he pretended that all was normal. "A scandal? How so?"

"It used to be quite a showplace, as Lord Kettleburn had hired the best gardener in all England. But some say the gardener spent as much time cultivating her ladyship as he did his flowers, and so he was let go. No one else has been able to do a thing with the garden since."

Michael frowned. This reminded him too much of the long-stirring rumors about himself, so often seasoned with salacious undertones. Lust or madness, the subjects were irresistible to the *beau monde*'s gossips.

"The place looks well enough," he contradicted. "Though the cold weather cannot be helping the roses to bloom." His own lands looked far worse, the dead vegetation rotted in boggy lowlands and stick-dry on the windswept higher ground.

"But the scandal of it!" Miss Meredith sounded agitated. "The clandestine affair!"

"It need not concern you," Michael said. "No guilt can come by association with a location, only with a person."

Miss Meredith stood still for an instant, then dropped her fan from her free hand. "La! How clumsy of me."

She bent over and began to pat the ground. "Oh, mercy, where can it have got to?"

Good God. Her round derriere was waggling in the air, and her generous bosom seemed about to spill from her bodice as she leaned over.

The curvaceous Miss Meredith was pretty, but Michael was embarrassed on her behalf: she seemed unaware of the prurient way she displayed her body. Had she enough dignity to serve as his duchess?

The headache decided to join them for this rose-garden interlude, but Michael willed it away. If Miss Meredith wished, she could roll all over the ground. She had money enough for them both, and so they might deal well together.

He tried a courtly maneuver. "Miss Meredith, do allow me."

He shut his eyes to accustom them to complete darkness, then crouched and opened them. Right away, he saw the dim outline of the ivory fan on the gravel path, snatched it up, and slapped it into Miss Meredith's palm as he stood.

"Oh. Ah. Thank you, Your Grace." She looked at the fan for a long moment, then smiled up at him. It was a rather impish expression that reminded him of Caroline.

The young lady dusted off her gloves and slid her hand into the crook of Michael's arm again, leading him further into the winding garden. Her grasp was tighter than ever, her fingers tight as unsheathed claws. If young Miss Weatherby had been a kitten, Augusta Meredith was a tigress. She seemed not to know her own strength.

After a few minutes of wordless crunching down the gravel paths, she spoke. "What brought you to London after so long away, Your Grace? I've lived here all my life, but I haven't heard of you being here since… oh, I must have been a child at the time."

A child? Michael felt suddenly out of step as they walked on. Had he been away from London for a half a generation, then?

Yes, so he had: eleven years. And if he had no one's welfare to consider but his own, his absence would have continued indefinitely.

He looked back to the house again, almost wishing to return to its churning, glittering, crowded rooms. Though he and Miss Meredith were alone, he felt somehow more exposed than he had in the ballroom. "I returned to London because I thought it time to find a bride."

"Ah." Miss Meredith's hand relaxed its grip by approximately twenty-five percent. When she spoke again, her soft coo had been replaced by clear, clipped tones. "I'm sorry, Your Grace. I didn't know. It seems I've led you down the garden path."

He looked at the scrambled plants behind them, the shuffled pebbles of the path, the guttering torches that left them only half-enlightened. "Yes, of course you have. That was the purpose of our walk, after all."

"No, I mean..." Miss Meredith tugged her hand from his arm and wrapped it, like its twin, around the sticks of her fan. "I had a different purpose in inviting you outside."

Bewildered, Michael asked, "How so?"

Miss Meredith shuffled her feet. She studied her fan and shrugged.

She was reluctant to admit the truth, then? He ran through possible reasons. "Did you intend that I should compromise you? There is no need for such machinations. I am quite ready to propose at any time."

Miss Meredith laughed shakily. With her back to a torch, her face was thrown into unreadable shadow. "They warned me you were mad."

Michael ears rang as though she'd slapped him. "I *beg* your pardon."

"I intended quite the opposite of a proposal, Your Grace. I thought you might... oblige me."

"Oblige you in what manner? I have no money to—oh. *Oh.*"

"Yes. Exactly. Oh."

"I— That is— You can't possibly mean—" Every sentence Michael tried was impossible. He shook his head, hoping the world would rattle back into place.

"Unmarried women don't enjoy the pleasures men do," she said. "But I want to. That is all."

"You could marry." Michael squinted at her silhouette. "You could enjoy fleshly pleasures in a respectable way."

"If I married, I would lose control of my money." She shook her head. "I can't have that. I simply want to be… obliged."

"And why did you choose me for this singular honor?" He could not keep the ice from his voice. He had never *obliged* anyone in his life, and he was damn well not going to begin with a gaudy stranger in the outdoors.

"Because you are an eccentric, Your Grace. It is well known that you care little for the rules of society. If anyone is willing to cast off propriety, it is surely someone like you. And you are quite a fine figure of a man, you know."

"I am most gratified to hear it," Michael replied stiffly.

She seemed at last to comprehend his displeasure, for she fell silent. Her arms folded in front of her body, then dropped to her side, then refolded.

If she felt anything like he did, she had no idea what to say or do now. Surely they had plumbed the very depths of embarrassment. Nothing Caroline had taught him had prepared him for a situation such as this: a woman rejecting his respectable proposal and making him an indecent one.

He didn't know whether he wanted to laugh until the buttons popped off his waistcoat, or to sit and let his headache take full possession of his senses.

So he did neither. Instead, he said the only thing he knew was always appropriate. "Deuced cold, isn't it?"

"It is," Miss Meredith said with admirable calm, stepping out of the torch's shadow. "Shall we return to the house? I don't suppose there's any purpose to our remaining out here any longer."

Michael held out his arm to her. After a long pause, she took it. They retraced their steps in silence—on her side, maybe chastened or embarrassed. Michael could destroy her reputation if he wished to.

Of course he would not. A reputation was a fragile thing; he would never damage a lady's simply because she had the verve to admit what she wanted.

In fact, he had a marvelous idea. One that might help this lascivious maiden and achieve a small victory of his own at the same time.

"Miss Meredith," he broke the taut silence. "Have you ever made the acquaintance of Lord Hart?"

"N-no," the young woman faltered.

"I have been thinking of your stated aim, and I believe he'll answer your purposes admirably. Shall we see if he is in attendance tonight?"

She halted. "Is this a jest?"

"Not at all. You have done me the honor of entrusting me with your confidence. I would like to assist you, though I cannot do so—ah, directly."

Help. Simply help. This was how Caroline had repaid his own clumsy proposal. He could do the same for her friend.

And perhaps distract Caroline's preferred admirer from her side too.

Miss Meredith turned toward Kettleburn House, then nodded. "Very well. Thank you. I should be glad to make his acquaintance. But you need not concern yourself in the matter; I'll ask our hostess to perform the introduction."

They resumed walking. For the first time this evening, the drumbeat in his head relaxed. Michael was not what Miss Meredith wanted, but he had made amends for that. And so her hand on his arm was simply a matter of courtesy; there was no further expectation that he would flirt and no chance that she might accept his hand.

And that was all right. She was not who he wanted either. Though it was not her place to make amends for that.

No, that was Caroline's fault, and Caroline would answer for it.

By unspoken agreement, they strode quickly back to the beaming house. Before they climbed the steps up to the stone terrace, Miss Meredith stopped Michael again. Light from the ballroom filtered down the steps, gilding her bright hair and pale skin.

She was a vision; she just wasn't *his* vision.

"You're quite kind, Your Grace."

"I am most gratified to hear it." This time, he could speak the words with a smile.

"I hope you find the lady you're looking for."

"I hope you achieve your goal as well." He bowed over her hand, then led her up to the terrace. With a curtsy of farewell, she returned to the house.

Enjoying the slight breeze, Michael leaned against the balustrade and soaked in the quiet. The sense that he had done right by Miss Meredith was a small triumph.

The sense that Caroline had not done right by him? That was thornier.

He often felt as though society spoke a foreign language. In recent days, Caroline had served as his translator, putting the proper words in his mouth when he had none of his own. All in pursuit of a goal: a wealthy wife.

So why had she chosen to introduce him to Miss Meredith? Surely she had known about the young woman's proclivities. She certainly knew of his own preferences, his reluctance to be touched or to trust anyone. Yet he had touched Caroline, kissed her, trusted her.

Splat.

A fat, cold raindrop slapped him on the cheek. He wiped it off, but another spattered his still-raised hand at once. With a suddenness familiar to all Englanders, rain began to pitter over the terrace, darkening the buff-colored stone in blotchy circles.

It was refreshingly cold, damping the air's acrid heaviness. But much as Michael wanted to stay and let it wash away his thoughts and clean his skin, he could not. He wore linen and wool and fine knit, and his elegant clothing would be ruined by the rain.

How he had changed since he had come to London not quite three weeks ago. He was protective of his clothing. He was conscious enough of propriety to turn down an *affaire*. Maybe he really was mad.

He actually managed a smile at the idea.

He strode to the French doors and shoved them open. At once, the chilly drizzle was exchanged for the humid, close air of the Kettleburns' ballroom.

No matter. He would clear the air soon enough.

Eleven

MICHAEL FOUND CAROLINE SIPPING AT A CUP OF punch, listening to an overweight gentleman of indeterminate years and liquor-red face holding forth about horses.

"Y'see"—the man squelched a hiccup—"a chestnut has no get-up-an'-go. Everyone knows that. If it's a fine trotter y'want, choose a bay every time."

"How fascinating. I had no inkling," Caroline said over the edge of her cup. "I know it's important to have a matched pair, but that's the limit of my insight."

"A matched pair of *bays*." The man hitched at his waistband and braces. "You'll never go wrong with a bay. Deep through the chest, they are." He leered at Caroline's bosom as he spoke the final word.

Michael had enough of this nonsense. "Pardon me, I need to borrow Lady Stratton. There is something particular I need to discuss with her."

"Eh?" The man looked around blearily. "Caro?"

"His Grace, the Duke of Wyverne," Caroline introduced hurriedly, as Michael began to tug at her arm. She bobbed a farewell, handing off her cup to the man. "Do excuse me. I always enjoy our chats, Lord Caulfield."

"About utter rubbish," Michael muttered, as he dragged Caroline after him through a crowd of people.

He was tugging at her with more force than he'd realized. Before he could halt, he blundered into the space cleared for dancing. A reel was going on, with small groups of people stepping and interlacing and twirling as the orchestra sawed away.

Michael froze.

He might as well have stepped onto an opera house stage in the middle of an aria. Dancers shuffled around him, glaring at his disruption. His heart thudded, readying him for escape—but no, he couldn't turn tail. He flailed for the memory of his waltz with Caroline, for the thrill of it, but it was stomped away by the shifting patterns of booted and slippered feet.

His vision dimmed; his head felt light. *Too much.*

Someone seized his hands, tugged. He was pulled forward; then someone pushed at his stiffened forearms until he stumbled backward.

"That's it," murmured a familiar voice. "Now hey to the left and thread through the next couple."

Michael blinked, shook his head. The haze in his eyes and ears resolved into the brass-bright ballroom of Kettleburn House. Caroline had tugged him into the bottom of a reel and was beaming as though this fumbling dance delighted her. She nodded and laughed greetings at the other dancers, even as her hands kept a steady, guiding pressure on Michael—one hand, then two, then just a touch as the dance forced them apart.

Years ago, Michael had learned these steps. He

would not have expected his feet to remember them after all this time. Perhaps they did so only because his mind was distracted by the unlikeliness of the situation. He had been preparing a splendid rant for Caroline, and instead she had rescued him from yet another social trespass.

She was always right, damn her. When he'd thrown a few manners at Miss Meredith, the young woman had rolled over like a puppy—more swiftly, by far, than he had expected. Now that he was stomping through a dance, the glares had turned to curious stares. Even smiles. When Caroline smiled, the world smiled back.

Prepare them for what they ought to see and feel. Just as she had said. She was mistress of society, wholly and completely. So what need had she of Michael? Was he an experiment? A test of her skill?

Why are you helping me? The question battered at his teeth and lips, but there were too many people around for him to ask her, the dance too shifting and swift to permit speech. And he did not want to know the answer—not to this question, not to a multitude of others. *Why did you kiss me? What do you want?*

The reel scraped to an end with a spirited flourish from a trio of violins, and Caroline tugged Michael into a bow.

"Creditable," she said as they straightened up. "I had no idea you meant to dance tonight. Lady Halliwell will delight in telling the polite world that she heard of your intention first."

"I had no intention, as you know quite well," he ground out. "Come with me. I was seeking a secluded area. I need to speak to you."

"In seclusion? How intriguing." Again, they made their way through the crowd. This time Michael kept his wits about him, not wanting to blunder into another pocket of dancing or a card game or—God forbid—an assignation.

He drew Caroline on until they reached what was usually the Kettleburn's dining room. It made up the end of the long suite of rooms the baron had opened up for dancing, but as it held neither food nor musicians nor punch, the dark-paneled room was nearly deserted.

Michael found a spindly chair, set it next to a large potted fern, and pressed Caroline onto the seat.

"Are you quite well?" As usual, she sounded completely self-possessed.

He could not nonplus her by any means he knew, but it was all too easy for her to discomfit him. All she need do was stand close enough for him to breathe in her flower-scent; all she need do was touch his hand.

Or, of course, send him out for a garden walk with a woman who wanted a tumble more than a proposal.

"No. I mean—yes. And I do apologize for pulling you away from your conversation with… Lord Drunken Horse."

"Such delightful manners, Michael." Caroline raised a brow. "Well, it's quite all right. In case you hadn't noticed, you managed a dance with me and a fair bit of touching too, all without becoming agitated."

"I was already *agitated* when I reentered the house. And I became more so when I found you listening to a bundle of nonsense about chestnuts and bays, as if you hadn't a care in the world."

On the wall, above Caroline's head, hung a life-sized portrait of a hook-nosed gentleman in a powdered wig and the ruffled fashions of an earlier century. He seemed to look down his large proboscis at the two intruders. *Yes, try to explain yourselves.*

"Quite correct. I hadn't a care." She laced her fingers together and stretched out her legs. "That is, not beyond helping Lord Caulfield have an excellent time. I owed him that much out of gratitude."

"How so?" Michael wished the hook-nosed gentleman in the painting would glare at Caroline instead of at him.

"Because of Lord Stratton, as usual. My most devoted and contemptible suitor. He argued me into a dance after you went for your romantic stroll, but Caulfield retrieved me soon enough."

"I hardly think you were better off."

"I considered myself so. Lord Caulfield contents himself with talking and is pleased with very little by way of reply. Stratton is neither of those things, and so I'd rather talk to Lord Caulfield about rubbish than Stratton about the most fascinating thing in the world."

"And what is that?"

She searched his face, then laughed. "Oh, a new gown, of course. What else?"

"You're teasing me."

"No, I'm teasing myself. Anyway, I'd rather speak with you than either Caulfield or Stratton, as long as it has nothing to do with Carcel—"

"Don't say it," Michael threatened.

"—lamps. Ah, too late."

Michael frowned. "Surely you have friends whose company you genuinely enjoy. Or is Lord Caulfield's conversation more of your nonsense about being kind to everyone?"

Caroline straightened up. "Lord Caulfield was the finest horseman in London in his youth. He only turned to the bottle after an unruly colt kicked him in the ankle and shattered it. It would behoove you to remember that just because someone may *appear* ridiculous does not mean he truly *is*. After all, Michael, how do you suppose the Weatherby women view you?"

Michael was beginning to dislike Caroline's insights intensely.

He rolled his head on his tense neck, not caring that he was spoiling the starched folds of his cravat. Then shaking out his arms, he imagined tossing away the distasteful bits of the evening. But no, they still clung to him.

Caroline bit her lip. "Well, we've already ransacked this subject quite thoroughly. No need to go over it again. Do tell me, though, Michael. What in heaven's name has made you so frantic that you don't even notice when you're bumbling into the midst of a scotch reel? And what has you so determined to start an argument with me?"

Michael's face heated. He longed to tell her *I am not*, but contradiction would only support her impertinent accusation.

He glanced around to make sure no one was within earshot. Seeing no one, he dropped into a chair next to Caroline. The potted palm stretched its spindly fronds over his head, giving him an adequate assurance of privacy. No one could hear them except the bewigged, hook-nosed portrait, and as he was nothing but oil on canvas, he would keep their secrets.

"Miss Meredith," Michael hissed.

Caroline squinted at him. "I don't understand. Has she captured your interest?"

"She tried to capture a great deal more than that. She's looking for a… a male barque of frailty."

He looked away, jaw set, but Caroline was silent for so long that he turned back to her. She had a hand pressed against her mouth, and her eyes were swimming.

"What?" he demanded.

She flapped her free hand at him, then drew a deep, shuddering breath behind her palm.

A giggle slipped out.

Michael folded his arms. "You are amused. I should have known it was all a joke to you."

"No, no," she protested in a shaky voice. "That's not it at all. I swear to you, I never thought she'd try anything."

"You *knew* she was like this?" His sense of injury increased—and, were he fully honest, disappointment. Society life held pitfalls enough for Michael without Caroline tripping him up too. She, of all people, had vowed to lead him aright.

Caroline swallowed one last laugh and, with a clear effort, drew in a deep breath and composed herself. "I never"—she choked—"never suspected she would be anything but quite proper with you, Michael. She got in a bit of trouble last season by acting shockingly fast while she was still in mourning for her parents."

"I'm not shocked, actually."

"Yes, well, she's out of mourning now, but her reputation has persisted. She might never make a respectable match. Yet she wants nothing more than the pleasures in which her male counterparts regularly indulge."

"So you thought you'd foist this pariah off on me." Michael wished he could fold his arms tight enough to slow his hammering heart; to wall out the sense of betrayal.

"She's not a pariah," Caroline said. "She's a lovely woman with more money than sense who flits at the edge of respectability. As you occupy the same space, and as you have more sense than money, I thought you might deal well together."

"She's not interested in marriage." Michael paused. "But I do believe she's interested in Lord Hart." His face heated, belying his casual tone.

"Hart?" Caroline's brow furrowed. "I didn't know they were acquainted. I've never heard him speak of her."

"Do you know him so well, then, that you are familiar with his every friend?"

Caroline's chin drew back. "I do know him well, yes. And now that you mention the possibility, he might suit Miss Meredith admirably."

Michael was not sure whether this admission ought to deflate him or encourage him. She certainly seemed willing to hand off her paramour to another woman. Not that it mattered. Michael had as little claim on Caroline as she had on him.

She looked thoughtful. "I haven't seen Hart here tonight, but if he does stop by, Miss Meredith will find him soon enough. She's a very determined creature."

"Determined," Michael said vaguely. His skin was tingling, sensitive under his clothes, as thoughts of *flirtation-lover-marriage-paramour* flicked through his mind.

He was jealous; jealous of everyone else Caroline had chosen. He wanted her damnably, and he never wanted anything damnably. And this desire was more illogical than most. He had already offered her marriage; she had already turned him down.

Caroline started laughing again. "So she tried to seduce you in the garden? Well, I can't blame her for that."

"I *beg* your pardon."

"I tried to do the same once upon a time, didn't I?"

This was the first time she had referred openly to that night. Eleven years ago, a passion that had shaken him, unmade him. He had fled the force of it, the evidence of his own madness, and transformed himself instead into Wyverne.

It was far from the first time Michael had thought of it, though. But he'd thought of it clandestinely, as an offer forbidden him by his strictest disciplinarian: himself.

Now Caroline brought it into the open with a curving bow of a smile that shot an arrow into Michael's inflated resolve. When she flexed her shoulders, the swell of her bosom pressed enticingly against the red fabric of her gown. *Scarlet.*

"You are nothing like Miss Meredith." Force made his voice unsteady.

"I know it," Caroline sighed. "She's like a flame, isn't she? So bright and lovely and warm."

"*In heat,* I should rather say."

She gave him a wicked smile.

"That is not the point. You are perfectly respectable." His voice echoed oddly in his ears, the air growing hot and hazy around him. "I've never doubted it."

"I'm no better than I should be, though I'm much better than you can imagine."

"I'm sure I can imagine."

Oh, how he could imagine. He alone, out of all the men at this ball, could imagine with the fire and fervor of lust unrestrained by experience.

Since coming to London, his imaginings crept into every unused corner of his thoughts, kept him awake at night. He was unsatisfied, hungry, and no food would sate him. No body, no woman, but *her.* The clean sculpture of her face, her lush form—they were so lovely that he almost forgot to breathe.

"You don't have to imagine, you know." How demure she sounded.

"I know." His voice was no more than a croak.

"You know."

"Yes," Michael said, aware that he was agreeing to much more than a simple statement.

She watched him. Maybe waiting for him to draw back, as he always forced himself to. But he couldn't budge this time. A singular need had crept over him, putting in roots like ivy climbing stone. His careful control was cracked into pieces by something vibrantly alive.

It could not go on, this slow grinding away of his

regimented self. He would agree to anything, anything at all, only to be with her. To find himself at last, or to throw himself into a crucible of madness and be melted away.

"I know," he said again.

Caroline nodded. "Then see me home."

Twelve

THE LAST TIME MICHAEL HAD SEEN CAROLINE'S HOUSE, it seemed like a tooth in a chattering mouth. This time, the house stretched tall and quiet, and moonlight plated all of Albemarle Street a soft silver.

This was London at its finest: at night, when the crowds vanished and the world was hushed and muted. It was easy to see the City's beauty now, without the clamor of distractions to every sense. It was easier, too, to feel sensual joy when one's senses were not overwhelmed.

For now, there was no color in the world but what the moon granted. He rode in Caroline's carriage in darkness and silence, with no lamps and no words. Only an awareness as heavy as touch, that the wait would be over soon.

There was no harm in waiting a little longer to make sure everything was right.

"Home at last." Caroline's words snipped open their cocoon. With a bounce of carriage springs, a footman dismounted from his perch and lowered the steps of the vehicle.

"How lonely a silent house always seems," Caroline murmured.

Michael stepped out and handed her down, the brush of her fingers distracting him from the thought that he held precisely the opposite opinion. Or the fact that *lonely* was the last word on his mind as he escorted her inside.

They climbed a proper flight of stairs to the equally proper environment of Caroline's drawing room. It held no suitors this time, only the flowers they'd left behind as tribute to their favorite. Michael had never given a gift to Caroline.

Yet.

Now that they were alone in her house, he felt a fizzing anticipation, the sprightly cousin of the anxiety he denied. Like anxiety, it made his fingers tingle, forced his breath to labor.

But ah, this time there was pleasure in it. There was pleasure in watching Caroline sway about the room, straightening things that didn't need to be straightened, trimming a lamp wick that didn't need trimming. Old habits came forth in times of nervousness, and Michael remembered that she had not always been a countess. She had been raised in a parsonage, and cosseted though she might be now, she was efficient and graceful in her bustle.

And she was nervous. As nervous, maybe, as he. Pride pooled, low in his belly, that he had discovered something about Caroline that he had not known before.

"Thank you," he said.

She stopped fussing about, turning to look at

him. "Gratitude from a duke? To what do I owe this honor?"

"Caro." He shook his head. "Don't."

"No teasing. I forgot." Her laugh sounded jittery.

Michael drew a deep breath. "Thank you for…" He trailed off, not sure how to confine what he wanted to say in the small packages of words. It sounded so grandiose any way he framed it: *For showing me that my limits are not what I thought. For helping me when I didn't know I needed it.*

For being a fantasy, come to life: a friend, in the body of a goddess.

"Thank you for welcoming me," he finally said, and it was close enough.

Her mouth made a shape that he supposed was a smile, though it curved down like a rainbow. "You are very welcome."

She sat on her long sofa and patted the upholstery next to her. "Come, sit with me."

Michael sat.

He could sense her body next to him, too close and too far for comfort. His back was stick-straight, his legs tense, his hands flat on his thighs. Out of the corner of his eye, he looked at her, wondering what to do next. Should he touch her? Would she touch him?

She sank against the back of the sofa. Then, before Michael could unbend, she turned sideways and kicked her feet up into his lap.

Michael froze. His mouth opened, then closed again. A wooden dummy without a puppeteer. Caroline sighed and shut her eyes.

When she didn't move again, Michael allowed

himself to lean back a bit. He stared at the feet in his lap.

He had never seen a woman's feet so closely before. Had never thought much about them, truth be told. Feet were useful, quite literally pedestrian. They were hardly erotic or intimate.

Yet there was something very intimate indeed in the way Caroline had stretched out next to him, laid her body across his lap. As if they belonged, intertwined.

As if they were lovers.

Cautiously, he slid his hands from his thighs, where she'd pinned them beneath her ankles. He held them up to the level of his shoulders, half curled, unsure where to place them. He could not, *not*, stroke her legs through her gown, her stockings. He could not slide her slippers from her feet and stroke their arches to see if she would squirm or laugh.

He could not, because it was new. And unless he knew he was going to do something perfectly, he would rather not try it. Not in front of someone he wanted so much to please, in a moment when so much seemed at stake.

Caroline rescued him, curving forward to capture one of his hands in her own. Grateful, his other one flew to cover hers.

They sat like that for a minute or two, while Michael simply held her hands. Through their gloves, he pressed the graceful taper of her fingers, the rounded crescents of her nails. Hands were so much more than tools, than instruments for pouring out tea or scrawling a letter. Hands were… comforting.

Not an exhausted comfort of the type he felt when

he slid into bed after a long day's work. This comfort was a balm that strengthened him. She chose to be with him; she held his hand. There was nothing small about this small gesture, because it was not *despite*. And maybe because of that, he didn't want to pull away. He only wanted to feel her fingers in his and see what came next, and next.

"You are always welcome, Michael," she repeated, "especially if you are content to sit with me in this way. It is very tiring to constantly convince the polite world that I am delightful and that I find them so too."

Michael's hands jerked, surprised. "You do not?"

"I do, usually. I enjoy this life. It's the same every year but different too, as faces and politics change. But living in society is also a performance. I must be my brightest, my most vivid, my most pleasant." She wiggled her feet. "Sometimes it is a relief to take off the costume and simply lie down and admit that my feet hurt."

She grinned: a girlish expression, paired with woman's words, a woman's body, lying lush and low before him. Honest and tired from carrying the weight of expectations.

Would she take off the costume too? He tried to swallow, but his throat was dry.

"You don't have to act a part with me," he managed. "But I do not think you could ever stop being delightful."

Her fingers tightened in his. Then she struggled against a cushion and slid herself to a sitting position. Her feet scooted across Michael's lap, teasing his groin before she folded her legs next to her.

"Why, Michael, that was quite charming of you. Thank you." She did not smile. If anything, she looked puzzled.

Michael was puzzled too. For the first time in his life, he had managed to be charming. He was not sure how he had done it.

"I do enjoy your company, you know," she added.

"And I yours." Was this a flirtation or nothing more than a handshake of friendship? Had he misinterpreted every cue? He had thought they were moving to passion, frantic and hot, but this was slow and rather sweet.

Rather… yes, rather comfortable.

He sighed, letting the bloom-scented air of the room fill his lungs, pervade his body. Seldom did he feel comfortable. There was always something to do, some guard to maintain. But tonight, there was neither. There was nothing he need do but sit and hold Caroline's hand in his own.

Then she lunged for him, catching his shoulders in her hands, and was on his lap with her lips pressed to his before he could finish his deep exhale.

Just as suddenly, she pulled away and slipped back to his side, demure again. Or as demure as a woman could appear with lips flushed and bodice slightly askew.

Michael moistened his lips. "What…?"

"It was time," she said. As if in response, a clock on her mantel bonged out the hour. Midnight. If Michael were at all superstitious, he would call it the witching hour.

But he was not. Midnight was only the start of a new day.

He swung her weight from his legs, then stood. With as courtly a bow as any prince could have made his queen, he held out his arm, and she took it, rising to her feet. She stood facing him, waiting for him to make the next move.

He wanted to. But he did not want to move wrongly. He tried something that had worked before: a kiss, a slow brush of lips on lips. His free hand was clenched at his side, an anchor of sanity, reminding him with the cut of fingernails into his palm: *keep your wits about you.*

Caro pulled back. "I am not a Carcel lamp, Michael."

He stared. "What are you—what?"

"You're analyzing me, are you not? You're holding back."

He dropped his other hand to his side. "You didn't enjoy my kiss."

This was a raw realization. Illogical, since it was only an evaluation of behavior. It should be no more painful to hear than if she informed him she disapproved of the incline he'd chosen for his canal walls in Lancashire.

He could not be offended by the truth—but he *could* be wounded. Especially when he put something of himself forward, something he thought represented the best of him.

Caroline shook her head. "It was pleasant enough. But I didn't invite you here to be pleasant. I invited you here so that you might share yourself with me and so that I might share myself with you."

Michael's fists clenched tighter.

"If you want to give me pleasant kisses," Caroline

continued, "I will take them, and gladly. But you've given me more than that before, and I want to see that part of you again. If you'll let me."

She stood before him, straight and watchful. Not touching him, not clasping her hands. Only waiting for him to react or reply.

He felt himself at a crossroads: continue on his cautious road or take a sharp turn. Be daring with his body, as he had with his money.

He had always meant the best for those who depended on him; he had tried to do well by them. But he had not done well by himself. He was tired and pinched, and the solitary road was narrow and cheerless.

He did not know what the other path held, but he wanted to try it.

He took a step toward Caroline, his feet noiseless on the fine carpet that stretched across her floor.

She smiled at him as he stepped closer, and he forgot that he possessed feet. He forgot everything except Caroline, face to face with him. Her eyes were the color of a tropical sea. She was an escape, a haven, warm and bright. With her, he could shed the cold of this unnatural summer, shed the wintry isolation in his heart.

He took her face in his hands, and she blessed him with a smile. "What a relief."

His mouth covered further words; he stilled her tongue by brushing it with his own.

He was blasted by a lust all out of proportion to the chasteness of her embrace.

This was the Venturi effect in life: the speed and pressure of rushing heat. As his awareness contracted, he felt he would burst with the unfamiliar, perfect dissolution of Caroline's mouth on his, her tongue tasting his, soft and hot and fiendishly wet. She seemed to be licking his whole body with that tongue; his muscles knotted and bunched, and his cock pressed against his trousers, wanting release.

There was no release, not from this anguished ecstasy. Michael would not have it so. She wanted him, and he would have every bit of her. He would understand a woman's body; he would bring her so much pleasure that she would never be able to give him up.

Dimly, he realized the illogic of his thoughts. The unlikelihood of bringing Caroline to ecstasy when she'd had many lovers and he'd had none. What did he know about giving a woman pleasure or gaining her heart? He had never experienced either.

Silence, he told those doubting thoughts. He had always been a fast learner.

Against her neck, he tested the pressure of each kiss, noting the reactions it evoked. Light, and she shivered under the brush of his lips. If he touched her skin with his tongue, she laughed, a low, smoky groan. And if he sucked at the fragile skin… good God, she fell apart, sagging against him, her eyes falling closed as if drugged by the sensations of her own body.

Each moan, each caress, was a triumph. He had waited a lifetime for a woman who would touch him not *despite* but *because*. A woman who cared nothing for his title, yet wanted him all the same. A woman who knew his fears and faults.

Who thought he had a remarkably fine arse.

The thought made him laugh. Caroline's eyes fluttered open. "Something funny, Wyverne?"

"Michael," he reminded her in a gruff tone. Sliding his hands around her, he cupped her own pliant rear and pulled her close. Chest to chest, heat to heat, they fit together. He had never felt anything so wonderful as Caro in his arms, filling his sight, her cheeks flushed and her lips red from the abrasion of his kiss, intoxicating him with her faint floral perfume and a muskier smell that must be desire.

She pulled back just enough to slip free the buttons of his waistcoat, then slide her hands beneath his shirt. His coat bound him tightly as she explored his chest with eager fingers, and Michael was glad for the lean muscle he'd earned through years of riding, walking, surveying, digging. Through much work, he had built this body, and she liked it. Her gloved fingers brushed across his chest, and his knees buckled before he locked them, his breathing shallow and quick.

Thank God, it had all been worth it. Eleven years as the duke of huge, troubled holdings, and it was all reduced to these minutes, or hours, in her arms.

The linen of his shirt was a delicious agony, teasing nipples he had never known could grow so sensitive. His body was painfully alive and aroused, and he no longer knew anything except the feathery pressure of Caroline's fingers on his skin.

"Come to my bedchamber." Her voice vibrated against his chest, a kiss in itself. "If you want to, that is."

"God, yes," Michael said.

She pushed back, cradled his face with one hand, and smiled. "You know this will change everything."

Out of habit, Michael stopped, considered. What would that mean if everything changed?

He was a duke with a dying dukedom. He was a man who had always denied himself a woman's most intimate touch. He had too much control, too many worries, too few friends.

Since coming to London, he had already become a man with whom women flirted, a man who could hold a woman's hand, kiss her skin, bring her pleasure and gain pleasure in return. A man who accepted the help of others and was neither shamed nor lessened.

All things considered, it was time for change. Past time.

"I hope it will," he said, then followed her upstairs.

Thirteen

He had never seen a woman's bedchamber before.

The sight was strikingly exotic, like the Taj Mahal—yet like that structure born of love, it was instantly familiar. Caroline's most intimate room held a mahogany wardrobe, a chest of drawers, a dressing table with a shield-shaped tilt mirror, a small tamboured desk on castored legs, and a bed. Save the dressing table, the same essential furnishings were in Michael's own chamber.

But there was something unmistakably feminine about this space, besides the heavy weight of green damask bed coverings. Maybe it was the frippery of bottles and jars scattered across every flat surface. The discarded fan that had been cast onto a chair. The faint floral scent that perfumed the air.

Take it in, he told himself. *You might never be here again.*

Michael felt a clutch of the familiar distress pumping his heart. This night was irrevocable.

She must have felt him grow rigid, or sensed it. "What is the matter, Michael?"

He only shook his head. His tongue was locked; his head, light. "I..." His voice trailed off.

He cursed his own hesitation. This might be new to him, but he was a grown man, for God's sake. A *duke*. He had handled any number of unpleasant tasks that would have overwhelmed his peers. Surely he could manage this exceedingly pleasant one: to divest himself of his virginity with a beautiful woman.

"I have never done this before." His voice was not as loud as he would have wished, but it was clear enough.

Caroline unbuttoned the pearl closures at the wrist of her right glove, then tugged at it, finger by finger, until it slid over her elbow, down her arm and hand. A long glide of creamy flesh shone silvery pale in the moonlight that filtered through the draperies.

"You've never come to a lady's room?" She began on her left glove, and Michael's throat clutched tight at the unbearable, unbelievable pleasure of Caroline, revealing her skin to him alone.

But she had revealed it to others too. He knew this. He could never matter as much to her as she could to him, for he was virgin territory. He would fall under her dominion as soon as she brought her body onto his.

"I've never come to a lady at all." He straightened his shoulders.

Caroline stared at him, her left glove only half shed. "You've never... ah. I see."

After an agonizing pause, she shook her glove to the floor. It lay coiled, like a discarded French letter. "I am very honored, Michael. Very, very honored.

And I shall do my best to ensure that you are glad you placed your trust in me."

Trust. Yes, he was trusting her with a great deal—he, who for so long had trusted no one but himself. She'd been insinuating her way through his guard since he came to London. How glad he was, finally, to have a companion in the solitude of his keep.

Then she grabbed the hem of his shirt and slid her bare hands beneath it. Under her touch, he shuddered, all tremulous sensation. Her hands were cool and gentle as they stroked over his chest, his abdomen. For an instant, they slid to grasp him below, and he could only shut his eyes and pray that she would continue.

But her hands lifted, left him, and Michael opened his eyes, half expecting she would laugh and order him out of her bedchamber—half expecting… he did not know what.

The unexpected.

Even so, she surprised him. She pecked his cheek, chastely as the clergyman's daughter she had once been. Then she turned her back to him and kicked off her slippers before the fire as though ready to turn in for the night.

She turned her head, peered over her shoulder. In the warm light of the coals, she appeared as the devil's most beautiful temptress. "Will you help me remove my gown?"

"Of course." He cast an eye down the garment's heavy red length. It was fastened up the back, but did it pull over the head or slide down? "Only you must tell me how to operate it."

She laughed. "One operates a lady's garments in

this way." And she instructed him in solving the puzzle of buttons and laces, plucking pins from her heavy weight of hair, sliding an expensive gown from a woman's form without damaging its fabric.

And then she stood before him… actually, still quite clothed.

There was something exciting to the point of breathlessness about helping a woman take off her clothing, but Michael had not known there would still be so much of it once the gown was removed. If he had, he would have calmed his nerveless fingers until Caroline was divested of another layer; he would have postponed his dry mouth until they had removed the corset, perhaps, or the… were those petticoats? A chemise? He didn't know what they were all called. There was so much fabric still swaddling her body, and he could not take any more of this tension. If it did not snap, he must either slide into her at once or spill in his trousers.

Both were unthinkable. So Michael snapped the tension instead and distanced himself.

He had often done this during unpleasant tasks; he had never before done so during a pleasurable one. The concept was the same, though. When the body became too oppressive on the mind, the mind silenced it. He often did sums in his head; compiled a list of native plants; considered improvements, cottage by tenant's cottage. He kept his mind busy and so silenced his body—whether mucking through knee-deep mud or making a muck of Caroline's corset strings.

He calmed his breathing with slow, practiced inhales. With every breath, the warm smell of skin and the fading sweetness of flowers filled his senses, but the discipline of rationing the very air in his lungs also calmed him.

There. He could study her again without becoming overwhelmed by his baser urges. He could examine every swell of her body as dispassionately as he would a… a… a bridge. Yes. Excellent notion.

The catenary curve of her neck was beautifully constructed, graceful and sloping under the weight of her fine-boned head and long tumble of hair. The trusswork of her corset was an intricate architecture of laces and nodes preventing her from torqueing. His fingers traced the stiffened fabric, marveling that it should shape a body yet cover it so unfeelingly. The laces were tight and scratchy beneath his fingers, rough as cast iron, and as difficult to untie.

"Haven't you a maid for this?" Michael asked, growing impatient with his own ineffective fumblings.

Caroline coughed. "Well, yes. But do you really want me to summon her right now?"

Michael had a vision of a young woman in a mobcap picking apart the knotted laces of Caroline's corset, then curtsying politely to him as he covered the bulge of his rampant cock with a bolster from the bed.

"Best not." He studied the corset again. "Are the laces valuable?"

"You're welcome to cut them, if that's what you're asking."

"Do you have a knife?"

"I hardly keep weapons in my bedchamber. But I'm sure I can find something that will answer the purpose."

She stepped out of his reach and slid back the

tamboured lid of her desk, then sifted through a litter of writing paraphernalia. After studying then rejecting a letter opener, she laid hands on a penknife.

"What do you think of that?" She pressed the small tool into Michael's hand. "I do have a knife in my room, after all. I feel strangely powerful all of a sudden."

"There's nothing sudden about it," Michael murmured as she pivoted, presenting him with her back again. She held up the fair weight of her hair, and with a few snaps of the small knife, Michael cut the knots he'd clumsily created.

Caroline drew a deep breath, her shoulders flexing as she wriggled the corset to the floor. She turned again to face Michael, her waist sliding smoothly in his hands. Her skin yielded under the thin layer of her shift.

To hell with dignity. He groaned. She smiled.

Then she touched his cheeks, trailing her fingertips over the ridges of his cheekbones—hesitantly, as though she were as virgin as he, and with a tenderness that surprised him. She was entangling him, enfolding him. It was impossible to keep any distance from her when she would keep none from him. When she offered him herself with such sweetness, and he wanted so badly to accept everything.

Quickly now, Caroline guided his hands in removing the rest of her clothing, and then she began on his. Before he could begin to feast his eyes on her body, he was jolted and pulled as she tugged off his cravat, shook him out of his coat, tugged free his boots. She was swift to undress him; whether his clothes were simpler, or she more practiced, he didn't want to know.

When he was naked, as she was, he felt cold. His shoulder blades jumped under his skin, wanting to pull his arms before him in a protective shield.

That would be undignified. So he tried to sidle sideways to the end of her bed, thinking to work his way around to the far side.

"It's as fine as I suspected."

He looked at Caroline, keeping his eyes rigidly focused on her face—as rigidly as another part of him was focused on other needs.

"Your arse." She grinned. "It's a work of art, Michael."

"You are achieving a comical level of hyperbole," he said, feeling pleased if not less self-conscious. He had honed his body, though unintentionally, and he could only be glad again that its form delighted her.

"A little laughter in the bedroom is never amiss." She folded back the heavy counterpane and crisp sheets of her bed. "Nor is hyperbole. But I'm giving you honesty in return for a peek at that lovely—"

"Don't say it again." His poor, beleaguered buttocks had never received so much attention before.

Caroline laughed and clambered onto the bed, pulling a sheet over her body and lying back.

The linen covered her demurely but outlined her immodestly. It draped over her curves, its indentations and swells like snow over hills. Fresh and ready for exploration.

"Would you care to join me?" She stretched, squeezing her eyes closed. Her breasts bobbed, high, tight nipples making tiny peaks under the sheet.

"I would indeed." In a matter of seconds, he was in the bed, under the sheet at her side.

"May I touch you?" Caroline had opened her eyes and was watching him now, intent.

The offer was more tempting than any other one life had brought his way. But in this, he wanted to take the lead. He would learn her body, learn the essentials of pleasure.

He shook his head. "Let me touch you first."

"All right." She looked soft and wistful. Or it might have been the warmth of the fire, the coolness of the moon, casting contradictions over her skin. It was so difficult to tell, especially now, when Michael's every sense was surfeited.

He drew back the sheet and began slowly, stroking her bared belly. He had never felt anything so soft and vulnerable as the skin of her abdomen, shivering under his palm. His hand looked sturdy and dark atop her unsunned fairness; her navel was a perfect little bowl just the size of a fingertip. He touched it, finding the firm center, and Caroline breathed a little harder.

He met her eyes, and she jerked her chin in an unsteady nod. "Yes."

Words enough, encouragement enough. He leaned to lick at her navel with his tongue, pressing its tip deep into her belly. Shocking, to take such a liberty with a forbidden part of another person's body—but in this room, nothing was forbidden.

He slid his hands over the span of her ribs, nuzzling her belly, her breastbone, and she shifted her shoulders as though settling into his touch more deeply. He marveled at the shape of her form, so strong yet so much more delicate than his own. His hands roamed ever upward, seeking the sleek curves of her breasts, then capturing them under a cage of his fingers.

The perfect size, the perfect shape. He could not remember ever seeing anything so lovely. The skin was softer than the fine fabric of her gown, the nipple red as a currant. His mouth belonged on it; he was sure of that. He fitted his lips about its roundness, then touched its tip with the point of his tongue.

She made a low hum deep in her throat. It sounded like pleasure.

Her skin was warm, tasting faintly of salt, and scored with pink striations where her corset had bound her tightly. He rubbed at one of these indentations, soothing the marked skin, then licked at it, as if he could draw the evidence of her daily discomfort from her body. She stiffened, arching her back under the pressure of his mouth, serving her breasts up to his eyes in a feast for the senses.

Her nipples were hard, as hard as he was below. Her breasts were soft and yielding, her voice throaty and sweet, and the contrasts nearly scrambled his senses. Her body was so different from his and so lovely in its differences. Where he was prosaic, all long sinew and bone, she was a sonnet of softness over strength. His every depth was exposed in the rangy structure of his body; hers was cloaked in a gentle façade. They might both be strong, but his limits were obvious to anyone, while hers were uncharted.

But she had sworn she did not lie to him, had she not? Nor did her body. She could not falsify her gasps, for her creamy skin blushed all the way down to the nipples that drew him again and again. She writhed under his persistent, curious mouth.

He was rather proud of this realization. There was something elemental and masculine in the idea of giving pleasure to a woman. If only he had known how pleasurable it was for himself, he might have overcome his reservations sooner.

No. No, he wouldn't have. Couldn't have. The idea of being so bare with another person—so literally naked—was unthinkable. Only to Caroline could he entrust his very self.

He shut his eyes against the realization, letting it pervade his body. This was the deepest sort of trust. Yes. As he had trusted her with his secrets, his weaknesses, they had seemed to recede. The burden was split among two and lightened, rather than borne always alone. Now they were bound together.

He opened his eyes to see her regarding him gravely. "Are you all right?"

"Very much so." A smile spread across his face. "I was simply savoring you."

"Is that so?" Her eyebrows lifted. "Well, I shan't stop you from such a noble purpose. Please, savor me some more."

Always used to giving the orders, he found that in this moment, he was quite happy to obey instead.

His mouth played with the curve of her breast, the intriguing darkness and tightness of her nipple. If he used his lips on her, she gasped, and a slight scrape of teeth changed the gasp to a moan. It was remarkable, how he could enslave her with ministrations to such a small part of her body. He nestled his body against hers, raised himself on one elbow, and unleashed himself upon her breasts, playing and licking and nipping and stroking until her eyes closed, her feet twitched.

She was trembling now, and he thought he would never get tired of touching her breasts. But her knees loosened and parted, and he recalled, there was much territory yet unexplored.

He raised himself up to a seated position and let his hands roam over her body, rubbing her to moaning life, caressing her face, the spring of her ribs, the pool of her navel… the mystery of her most private of parts.

She was slippery against his fingers. The wetness shook his control. He wanted to stroke it, sleek against his hand. He fingered the slick folds, explored the stiff apex, slid a finger through her fine hairs and down over the welcome of her passage. He was gentle and slow, wondering at her loveliness, her furled sexuality. In this, as in so much else, she was subtle where he was gauche. His desire jutted out before him, obvious and brash. Hers was hidden; it required searching, waking.

But waking it he was. As he stroked her thighs, let his fingers dance through her wetness, she began to clench her muscles and breathe more deeply, more quickly. She was even more slippery now; his fingers glistened. Caroline watched, eyes avid under half-closed lids, as he brought a fingertip to his mouth and touched it with his tongue. She was tart yet musky, like nothing else in the world.

"Enough," she said in an unsteady voice. "Enough, now. I shall have my turn."

"Um," said Michael, as she pressed him flat onto his back. She knelt next to him, then raised her arms to coil her hair into a long, gentle twist. Her rounded breasts bobbed, and one of his hands reached reflexively for a touch.

"Yes," she said again, cradling his hand, sliding it over her hardened nipple, the soft curve of her breast. Then she slung her twisted hair over one shoulder, and it fell in a flaxen rope to tickle his abdomen, his cock. Her hands glided over him in languorous strokes.

He tried to say "um" again, as she trailed her fingers over his body, but all he could do was gasp. And then she stroked him and bent her mouth to him, and he couldn't even gasp anymore. As she stroked him hard and long again with her fingers and tongue, he forgot everything he knew, everything he prided himself on. There was no logic or learning or Lancashire now—only Caroline and her clever fingers and her mouth.

Her mouth was shockingly wet and so hot that he almost lost his grip and plummeted. His hips jerked, his hands fisted on the sheet. His sac tightened, and his eyes flew open. *No no no no not yet.*

He clenched every muscle in his body, holding back his release with an effort of will, then clambered away from her, his body swifter than his dazzled thoughts.

Caroline uncurled and stretched out on the bed. "Too much, was it?"

"What did you do to me?"

"It's only a little fornication." Caroline laughed. "I can see that you liked it."

Only a little fornication, she said. Taking away the import of the moment. He wondered if that was a good thing.

Michael suddenly felt the cold on his bare skin, and

he trembled, his staff sinking a fraction. "I almost… it would not be seemly to…"

She raised her eyebrows, touched her tongue to her lips, and he could have groaned at the sight. Why did he always have to think so damn much? Why couldn't he have let her draw him to release?

Because he didn't want to use her in that way. He wanted his first orgasm with a woman, his first intercourse, to be a true joining, not a service.

Though God, what a service it was.

She shrugged. "I liked it. But if you think it wouldn't be seemly, then we'll do something else." She moistened her lips again, and looked at him with an imp's eyes, a siren's smile. "Maybe we can try it again sometime."

Michael shivered.

Caroline slid a hand back and forth over the bed sheets. "Come back to bed. Come back to me."

He could not resist such a plea. He could not imagine anyone who could. As if transfixed, he climbed back onto the bed and covered her waiting body with his own.

He'd never been in this position before—literally. But his body had hidden, instinctual knowledge. It knew how to support him, how to fit him into the cradle of her thighs. His cock lay hot and hard against her, the tip wet and slippery from his fluids and hers.

He locked eyes with Caroline, and she nodded. And with a quick thrust, he sheathed himself.

Simple as that, he wasn't a virgin anymore.

That was the last coherent thought he had, because the tight wetness of her, clenching him, was… it was unimaginable. *Oh, God.* There was nothing for the moment but blasphemy or a cry to heaven. The feel of her around him and under him was fire, oil, water. Impossible and combustible. Sleek and liquid and hot and deep. This unmade him, this joining. It would rip him apart.

He could not leave her; he could not keep still. He lowered his full length upon her, bracing himself on his elbows, and he pressed his hips into her deeper, more fully.

They both moaned at once.

He knew what to do next; even if his body had not known it instinctively, he'd picked up enough bawdy talk to know about the thrusting that brought on the crisis. But he *did* know. It felt right, to draw back, to let the work-hardened muscles of his arms and thighs bear his weight, allow him to pull back, then glide home, welcomed and eased by her wetness. Then again, again, until the world was only his body and hers.

He could never have imagined the tightness, the glide, the perfect slick friction. He could never have understood the fit of body in body, the rightness of it all. Never, without her. He could never have come to this.

Never, never, never. Never, without her, his body pounded. It was like the rhythm of his headache, but it echoed with a joy that resounded through his skin and muscle, bone and blood. It washed away tension and hurt, filling him with a roiling pleasure that bore him higher, tighter, faster, onward, more frantically, until he flung himself from the edge of the cliff with a cry.

He landed in a heap, so stunned by the force of his sudden ecstasy that he was unable even to breathe.

What an extraordinary feeling: to be exhausted yet tingling with life.

Sense returned in slow flickers. His heart pounding with the force of sweet exertion. The hush of Caroline's swift breathing in his ear; the softness of her breasts beneath the wall of his chest. Still joined, still one, he felt as if his heartbeat were hers, as if every breath she took gave him the air of life.

He breathed in deeply at the curve of her neck. Delicate and floral; earthy as passion. "You are perfect." He could hardly speak the words; he didn't want to stop inhaling her scent. "Is it always like that?"

She laughed, trailing her fingertips over his back. "If one is fortunate."

"I consider myself very fortunate." He raised himself onto his forearms, cradling her. Resting his forehead upon hers, he pressed light kisses over her face—the bridge of her nose, the curve of her brow, the angle of her cheek. So many lovely shapes, yet they could not compare to her heart and mind. To the wonder of the passion that had unfurled between them.

He had never expected such a thing: to let himself be mastered by desire yet to remain master of himself. "Very, very fortunate," he repeated. Another kiss, this one lingering on her lips.

Her nails bit lightly into his skin, firing his nerves again. More deeply, he sank into the kiss, brushing her hot tongue with his—until with gentle hands, she caught his shoulders and pressed him upward, away. As the kiss broke, he realized he had been crushing her with his weight. Withdrawing from her heat, he freed himself from their tangle of limbs.

She raised herself up on one elbow and looked down at him. "Do you really think so? That you're fortunate to be here with me?"

Still trying to master his breath, Michael nodded. "Yes, of course I do. I don't underestimate the gift you've given me."

Her lovely face crumpled for a fraction of a second. "Nor I you." In a bright voice, she added, "How do you like sex, then? Rather amusing, is it not?"

"Unh." Michael had no word for the feeling, so he settled for a meaningless syllable.

Caroline laughed again. "I couldn't say it better myself. The best lovers always reduce one to a state of complete incoherence."

"Well, you're the best lover I've ever had," Michael said truthfully.

Caroline smiled and walked her fingers across the width of his chest. "Mmm."

A noncommittal murmur or a sound of pleasure? Either way, she did not return the compliment. But this was to be expected. He had not wielded a hammer or an awl perfectly the first time he'd used them. It did not make sense that the tools of his body would be any different.

Still, though. "Let me try again. I can do better."

"So soon?"

"At once." He raised himself on his own elbow and pressed her back to the bed. Now that the urgency of his own arousal and climax were past, he felt clear-headed, replete, and calm, as though his world had finally marched into order.

Here was Caroline, a banquet for the senses, all pale

skin and long limbs and rounded curves, so lovely that he could scarcely believe he was permitted to touch her. In the low wink of the coal fire, her face looked flushed. She was beautiful as a goddess, yet touchably warm. As he trailed his hands over her form, she covered his fingers with her own and smiled. "I am fortunate too, Michael."

This was his chance: now, while all seemed right with their world. In everything he had done in London, he saw Caroline's hand. Why, then, should he seek the hand of another?

She always knew the right thing to say and do. She could be everything he needed. She could save Wyverne, remake it, just as she was remaking him.

"Caro. Will you marry me?"

Fourteen

Another proposal. Damnation.

Caroline squeezed her eyes shut—a vain attempt to shut out the world.

Oh, she could close her eyes to the familiar heavy folds of green fabric that hung over the head of her bed. And most of all, the face above her.

But she couldn't stop her ears. And now Michael offered what he no doubt thought was a convincing argument for her agreement. "Caro, please accept. You are everything you have been pushing me toward in a wife. Wealthy and respectably bred, but not of noble birth. And you're unencumbered in every way. It makes sense. Don't you see?"

No. She did not see that or anything else: she kept her eyes shut. But in her head, she screamed, *Why?*

She did not want an explanation of his reasons for proposing. She wanted to know why he had broken the spell.

She opened her eyes, saw him staring down at her. He looked patient but sure, as though waiting for his ship to come in so he could see to the unloading of its cargo. He did not look as if he'd just had a transcendent sexual experience.

Caroline sat up. "You support your proposal with many arguments."

"You agree, then."

"No. I can't. Everything you say—Michael, it doesn't have anything to do with *me*."

"Nonsense. It has everything to do with you. I just described all the reasons I wish for you to be my duchess."

"Those reasons could apply to many women. Why me in particular?"

His brows yanked together, as though her question made no sense to him. "Well, I feel comfortable with you. And I like you the most. Obviously."

She ignored this reference to their spent passion. "My fortune has nothing to do with your proposal, then?"

He paused before answering. Wise of him. "It is far from my only motivation. But you know quite well I could not offer marriage to someone without money."

Unwise of him.

And unwise of her too. "I do know that quite well," she murmured.

It had been nothing but a fantasy to think that he wanted her for her own sake. In reality, nothing had changed since the ball at Applewood House a week ago, or eleven years ago. So important were his goals that he could not abandon them for an instant. Not even in the bedchamber.

And so his proposal had turned their intimacy into a transaction.

"So, you propose because I suit your requirements, then. Oh—and I am 'comfortable' too? How convenient."

"'Convenient' isn't the right word, exactly."

Caroline felt all the cold of her nudity now. She clutched for the rumpled bed sheet and tugged it free, pulling it over and around her body like a Grecian robe. She swung her legs over the edge of the bed and stood up unsteadily, still boneless from their lovemaking.

Never mind that. It was over. Done. She held the sheet to her breastbone, shielding her body from his scrutiny.

Even now, she was aware of the effect in the back of her mind—how the sheet would outline her body with tantalizing elegance. But Michael was not tantalized. He seemed to take this as a cue to wrap himself in bedcovers too, and he wadded the heavy, green damask coverlet into a fabric washtub around his waist.

Efficient yet graceless. If that didn't typify him, nothing did.

"How inconvenient, then, that I must refuse again."

His brows were still a dark vee. "I do not see why."

"I wanted you tonight," she admitted. "I've wanted you for a long time. But I can't be the wife you need."

"Of course you can." He looked puzzled, as though she'd misunderstood a simple command. *Pass the salt. Be my wife.* "I just told you that you could. Besides this, you ought to marry me now that we've—well."

"What, you think you've ruined me?" She dug her fingernails into her sheet as passionately as she'd clutched for his body a few minutes before.

"'Ruined' isn't the right word, exactly." Those damnable eyes of his. They were so sharp but missed so much.

"Perhaps eventually I shall hit upon the right word for something. Until then, I thank you for your concern for my reputation. Or honor. Or whatever the right word might be. But as you're not the first man who has come to my bed since my widowhood, the responsibility for my ruination is not yours."

He looked as stunned as if she had clouted him. His lips parted, then closed again.

Damnable lips. Damnable eyes. Damnable chin and nose. He was too handsome to be so callous. It was impossible to keep up an icy guard when the sight of his face, so austere and yet so vulnerable, always melted her.

She hadn't cried since the death of her elderly husband, a kind man who had doted on her and bequeathed her the cachet and money to remake her life. She could cry now, though, for the death of another fancy as improbable as the clergyman's daughter marrying an earl. She might admire Michael for his honor, his dedication to duty, but he could offer her no more than this—not with his clockwork heart.

To help him save his dukedom, he needed a woman much like himself, a business partner who signed her name to a marriage license as she would any other contract, and who would be content never to be loved. Caroline could not be that person. Her heart was not clockwork, but human enough for two; twice tried and deeply bruised. She could only be ashamed that she had given herself away so cheaply, when she'd meant never again to give away anything at all.

Carefully, she measured her words. "I'm sorry, Michael. But I cannot marry you. You mean no more to me now than you did the first time we met, eleven years ago."

This was true, though he couldn't know what she admitted. The first time she'd seen him, she had tumbled for him with all the fascination of the young faced with the unfamiliar. Not even she knew how much of a soaring leap her feelings would require to exceed her early passion.

Just as he was fascinated by a damned Carcel lamp, so had she always been enthralled by him. She wanted to take him apart and master him, to ensure that she still understood the world.

Yet when Michael had taken apart a lamp, he had broken it. And in grasping for Michael's core, she had broken something too. She was not sure whether it was something in him or in her, or whether she had shattered something built between them.

Michael watched her with surprising dignity for a man sitting on a bed, wrapped in a wagon wheel of damask. "It meant nothing, then? Our trust?"

"I value your trust. But at the root, Michael, we do not want the same things." She attempted a smile. "Business before pleasure, isn't that your way? Yet it is not mine. I'm sorry, Michael, for both our sakes. I cannot marry you."

Michael's mouth opened as if to reply.

But no words came out; he only swallowed, his throat flexing visibly with the effort. Air fled his lungs in a rush, then did not return. His bare chest sunk, emptied, and he folded onto the bed.

Caroline blinked. "Michael?"

Was this a trick? He was not the type for tricks,

but she had never seen anyone behave in such a manner before.

"Michael, are you all right?"

Now curled on his side, his lower half still smothered in covers, Michael's chest snapped back to heaving life. He swallowed again, gasping, as though every hitching breath was a torment.

"Michael? Can you speak?" What could she do for this distress? She reached out a hand as if her touch could pluck away whatever was smothering him—but there was nothing there.

He swatted her hand away, arms shuddering. His breath came quick and shallow now, his eyes unfocused, darting around. An unhealthy dew of perspiration broke out on his forehead, in the hollow of his throat.

Caroline's own limbs took on the creeping numbness of fear. "What is the matter? Are you having an apoplexy? Let me call for a doctor."

He shook his head mutely. His whole body was shuddering now.

Caroline reached out again to touch him, pulled her hands back. He was flying apart, suddenly, and for no reason she could imagine.

"Is this the falling sickness?" She reached for a bolster. She had heard of this, though never seen it. She thought she was to keep him calm, make sure he didn't tumble off the bed and injure himself. How to calm him, though, she could not imagine. She feared even to touch him, lest she distress him further.

His face was ruddy and damp. "No," he managed through heaving breaths. "Water."

Caroline darted to the ewer and basin kept in her bedchamber. How much water did he need? She hefted the ewer and carried it back to the bed, thrust it at him, but his shaking hands only scrabbled at the porcelain surface. She tipped it toward his mouth, but he gagged and turned his head away. Water splashed on him, dampening his clammy face and the mattress beneath him.

"I'm fine," he said in a strangled voice. His face was the sickly yellow of half-churned milk.

To hear him speak was a relief, though he looked very ill. "Nonsense." Caroline tried to sound brisk and authoritative, as physicians always seemed to. She found such certainty comforting. "You need—"

She had no idea, no idea what he needed. She laid a hand on his chest and felt his heart thundering.

"I'm *fine.*" He pushed her hand away, heaving himself up onto an elbow. He pulled in a breath through his mouth, slow and deep. Then he pushed himself up to a sitting position and held his long body perfectly still, eyes closed. "I'm fine."

Caroline watched him, balanced on the balls of her feet, ready to dart off for anything she might need. The crisis, whatever it had been, seemed to be ebbing. But it had begun so suddenly, she could not be certain yet that it was over.

So still, he held himself. This coiled tension looked dangerous; it sent fear chasing down her spine. "There's nothing to be afraid of," she murmured stupidly. "It's all right. You're all right."

"So I said. I regret my—loss of control." He sounded raspy, and his eyes were still closed. "Will you give me a moment alone?"

Caroline studied him. His breathing sounded more normal; his face had lost its ashy tint. But he had not recovered his usual mien, the unconcern that came either from confidence or complete lack of awareness. No, his eyes were not closed gently but squinted tight. He did not want to look at her.

Half-moon indentations still marked his shoulders where her nails had gripped him, tugged him closer. His body had been used and loved as never before.

Yet now he wanted her gone. Was he ashamed of himself? Or of her?

Since they were both already alone, Caroline could do him the courtesy of leaving the room.

"Certainly," she said blandly. The long habit of politeness forbade her from lashing out at one already injured, though he was hurting her too.

She turned her back on him and dropped her bed sheet, then crossed over to her mahogany wardrobe and yanked it open. She found a red silk banyan within—a man's dressing gown. She had bought it for herself, preferring its luxurious weight to the filmy garments meant for women. There was something decadent and erotic, she had once thought, in wearing a man's garment that covered her so well, knowing she could shed it in an instant and be all woman.

Right now, she wanted to wrap herself in its warmth. And as she crossed to her door and let herself out into the corridor, she hoped Michael would open his eyes, see her leave, and wonder whose garment she wore. One last mystery, one last wound.

She already knew he would never come to her again.

She was more than a canal to be dredged, more than

one of his projects to tinker with. Yet he had treated her no differently. If she could not help him fulfill his next purpose—finding a wife—then he bade her leave him. He would abandon her as just another unsuccessful venture, ruined by the ungodly winter of 1816.

Her toes curled into the corridor's carpet. Savonnerie, Axminster, whatever it was—she had asked her cousin and companion, Frances Whittier, to choose it in accordance with the latest and most expensive fashion the year before. But Frances had married and left her behind, when Caroline had always thought to lead.

And now she was alone in the corridor outside her bedchamber, while a dream that had taunted her for more than a decade was destroyed by disappointing reality.

He used her, then sent her away. Michael was just like everyone else.

Except he wasn't, was he?

After fifteen minutes, Michael had emerged from her bedchamber, fully clothed but for his coat, which was slung over one arm. He looked pale, but his jaw was set.

"You are all right?"

"Quite well. Thank you, Lady Stratton."

Caroline winced at the distance but managed a cool reply. "I am glad of it, Your Grace. Do you—wish for tea?"

She felt as fluttery as a bride, and as nervous. Courtesy was her only refuge when confronted with this wall of stern, cold duke.

"No, I require nothing. Thank you. Will you ring for my carriage?"

The heavy silk of her robe weighed heavily on sensitive breasts. What if she opened her robe? Would the warm light come back into his eyes as he gazed on her? He had called her perfect. He had called himself fortunate. "What happened to you, Michael?"

He looked down his nose at her, the perfect angle she had taught him so recently. "A regrettable episode."

"Has it happened before?"

He looked away, and his taut posture sagged. "Once. Only once." His eyes caught hers for just a flicker; in the lamplit dim, his gaze was all shadow. "I must trouble you for the carriage. Please."

Her fingers reached for him; she clenched them into a fist, stuffing it into the deep pocket of her banyan. "Yes, if you wish, Mi—Your Grace."

She didn't dare ask any more questions. She didn't want to know the answers.

When the carriage rolled up before the door, she shook his hand good night. His fingers were cold; did he never wear gloves?

It was not up to her to ask or to care about such things.

She watched him stride down the steps; he did not look back. Dratted duke. He had given her his virginity, yet he took more than he gave. He took her ease, her sense of purpose, her desire for him; he caged them tightly and would permit her none. None, unless she would be his duchess.

In return, he *did* admit that he liked her better than a few others.

Her smile hurt.

Caroline stayed wrapped in her banyan for hours afterward, watching the silent street through her bedchamber window.

❧

The next day, she parsed the situation to exhaustion, and she thought she might have misjudged him. His sudden, wild attack of panic or whatever it had been—surely that could not be entirely motivated by the disappointment of a thwarted bargain. Surely he had felt some emotion beyond the fear of poverty.

Caroline was, as Michael would say, forming a hypothesis: that his iron will covered the same desires as other men. He was only better than most at hiding them, more determined than most to master and control them.

Yet the deeper she delved into Michael, and into herself, the farther she was from answering her questions. *Why? What did it all mean so long ago? And what does it mean now?*

She wanted to ask him. Needed to.

But try as she might, over the next week she could not talk to him or meet him or see him. Her notes went unanswered, and he seemed never to be at home to callers. She heard of him only by proxy. No one had seen him at any *ton* events, but everyone had a story to tell—and the more outrageous, the more they repeated it.

Mad Michael had set fire to a pile of invitations on the front steps of Wyverne House.

He had been heard shouting in his garden in the wee hours of the morning.

He had galloped down Rotten Row and nearly overturned the Duchess of Winterberry's landau.

He had ordered six dozen Carcel lamps from a shop on Bond Street.

Of all these rumors, Caroline credited only the last. But they caused her to wonder: was it worth it to try to rehabilitate *Mad Michael* by using her influence with her friends? The Weatherbys? Miss Meredith? Everything she'd done to reintroduce him to the polite world, he was throwing away with his impolite withdrawal from society. Only a madman would throw away something so hard earned as his reputation.

But anyone would throw away something he considered of no value, her devilish inner voice replied. *Perhaps he cares nothing for your efforts.*

Perhaps he did not. But he cared for his dukedom. And he hadn't yet left London.

For lack of a better idea, Caroline began to organize plans for the Lancashire house party she'd once mentioned as a certain means of finding him a wife. Now the house party that was to be his entrée back into the polite world would also be Caroline's way into his.

If she saw him in his own home, surely there she would come to understand him at last. She still had four events left on their fool's contract, with the excuse of finding him a bride. Four events to answer her questions with the excuse of business, no emotion involved.

She was determined that he would not leave her behind again, as he had so long ago, to stew in the humiliation of rejection. With a house party taking place in four weeks, he wouldn't be able to shake free of her. Not again. This time she was stronger. She would leave *him*, and on her own terms, when she wanted to.

Though as she laid her plans and sent her invitations, she wondered—was the right word *when*, or was it *if*?

Fifteen

For Michael, the fortnight following his encounter with Caroline was an agony of solitude. In the third week, he left London.

Out of sheer stubbornness, he waited until the beginning of August so that he would not be the first to depart the City. He would not have anyone say he turned tail and left before the end of the season, much good it had done him. He still had no wife and no money. In fact, he was even more impoverished than when he'd come to London, for he had given Caroline his secrets and his trust.

The journey back north, taken at the greatest speed Michael's aged carriage could manage, nonetheless left him too much time to think. At first he was able to smother his worries with work, scrawling notes with a pencil stub whenever the light permitted. But dusk came early. Rather than light the lamps and look ahead to Lancashire, Michael sat in the dark of the rattling carriage and thought of London—and Caroline.

He thought he had forgotten the feeling of sanity slipping from his grasp, of his world tipping and falling, knocking him flat and breathless. But as soon as the panic had struck, it was like meeting a lifelong enemy, ever-known, ever-despised. Eleven years was not too long between such episodes.

And somehow, they were always tied to Caroline.

He grimaced as he stared out the window of his carriage at a sliding, cold rain that obscured the fallow fields outside. A rain that pitted the roads on which he drove, turning country passes into slippery troughs of mud.

For the second time in his life, he left London behind, but this time he would not forget it. He had seen the kindnesses and comforts threaded through the shallow chaos of the *beau monde*, and he saw the value of moving easily within that world.

Now that he had slept with Caro, he understood the soaring joy of physical passion. But he also understood the pain of complete vulnerability. *Business before pleasure*, Caroline had said. That was his way, and he would not be permitted any other. The realization, the rejection, had shaken his body to its very marrow. The panic of this prison he had built for himself—it had threatened to unmake him, even as she watched.

Though he little resembled the caricatures of the scandal rags, they weren't entirely wrong. The everyday tasks that came easily to others—talking of the weather, dancing, laughing, flirting, lovemaking—were a struggle to him. Perhaps he really was mad, just as the *ton* said. Just as his own father had believed.

The carriage lurched heavily, knocking Michael's head against the window. He wished it could jolt free his unpleasant thoughts. They seemed to be wearing a groove in his brain as deep as the ruts in the road.

The relief of homecoming was delayed for endless dull days in a carriage, long nights in coaching houses. The land seemed wilder, rougher, bleaker than he remembered. After the macadamized streets of London, the sodden, mucky roads were bone-jarringly rough under his carriage's old, groaning springs. The public house rooms seemed colder than he recalled, the sheets threadbare. He noticed every instance of peeling paint, rotted wood; every slatternly servant who gave him food that was neither cooked nor served well.

As they traveled steadily north, the cold clutched more closely at everything, creeping through every gap in the carriage, stiffening blankets and joints, tiring the horses and drivers.

Had the world died yet a bit further while he was gone? Or was the change within himself?

He was annoyed with himself, to have developed a taste for the ease of London so quickly. Or was he seeing it all through Caroline's eyes now, imagining what she would think of Lancashire? Surely she would look with disappointment on the secret provinces of his life, his tattered dukedom.

Or maybe she had woken his flesh, and now it simply yearned for pleasure.

He could only hope that when he saw Callows, he would feel that sense of rightness again. For now, he had the uncomfortable feeling of having shirked his duty, of having let himself become distracted from his goal, ensnared by his own disobedient body. He had shared himself with a woman who would never do the same.

The human heart was far more confusing than any ledger. So he had long known. But he hadn't truly experienced the full, damning agony of that knowledge until now.

If he couldn't convince Caroline to marry him, after all that had passed between them, then why should *anyone* marry him? And how could he shackle himself to another when he had invested in her as surely as other men invested in the funds?

Now he was sure of nothing except that he wanted her again and that he could never trust himself with her.

Sanders's homely face was brown and creased as a walnut as he smiled a welcome to Michael.

"It's good to see you, Your Grace." The steward doffed his hat, working its brim in his thin fingers. The inevitable chilly drizzle plastered his gray-brown hair to his head and darkened the drab tweed of his coat.

"You needn't have come outside to greet me," Michael said gruffly, marching up the front steps of Callows.

But he was pleased all the same. He cut his eyes sideways at Sanders, and the older man smiled, his gold teeth glinting bright in the watery remnants of daylight.

Sanders was the same as always: nondescript, pleasant. For the first time since Michael's disastrous second proposal to Caroline, he felt a slow bleed of comfort through his chilled body.

Callows was the same, too. All solid dun-colored gritstone, its Elizabethan façade had scarcely changed since the stately home had been built. Solid and blocky except for its three watchful towers, their sharp-angled crenellations softened by centuries of wind and rain. The inner court was cobbled with many of the same stones that had helped along the wheels of carriages under the rules of Elizabeth, James, and the assorted Georges who had followed.

Michael and Sanders stepped inside, and Michael handed off his sodden greatcoat and hat to a waiting servant. The great door closed behind them with the familiar scrape and thump of determined wood against a resistant stone frame.

Here was Callows, reassuringly familiar, simple and sturdy, and beautiful in its usefulness. The rich, dark wood of the staircase, with its thick, turned balusters and smooth-worn treads. The wide, stained-glass window at the turn of the staircase. The peat fire that roared at one end of the great hall, frustrated by its inability to banish the chill. Above the fireplace—big enough to hold a dozen men—hung the Wyverne coat of arms. The history of his family, larger than life.

It had looked exactly the same when Michael returned from London eleven years earlier, not knowing he was soon to become Wyverne. Surely it would be the same after someone else was Wyverne in his place. He simply had to find a way to safeguard it.

A new way, that is. His grandiose plans for improvement had, to date, possessed the opposite effect.

At Michael's side, Sanders dripped quietly on the marble tiles and took on the mouthful-of-glass-beads expression he always adopted when he would prefer to avoid a subject. After champing his gold teeth together, he ventured, "Will the new duchess be joining us soon, Your Grace?"

Michael rubbed the bridge of his nose. "There is no such lady, Sanders."

The steward was silent for so long that Michael turned his attention back to the man's weather-beaten face. It held an expression he had never seen before.

"Sanders, you look ghastly. What is it?"

"I… I am sorry, Your Grace. I should not…"

"Should not look ghastly?"

Sanders managed a tiny smile. "I should not have suggested the journey to London. I see now that it was a hardship for you, and I am sure the fruitlessness is discouraging."

Michael looked up at the coat of arms and felt the weight of his title settle into position on his shoulders. It was his responsibility to care for everyone in his dukedom—even for his steward, who had served the family for decades, whose responsibilities had begun long before Michael ever became duke. It was understandable that Sanders felt responsible for Michael too. But it was not fitting; it was not fair to the older man.

"As a matter of fact," Michael said in a voice of determined cheer, "it was *not* fruitless. I have in one of my trunks two dozen of the finest Carcel lamps London had to offer. I have also refreshed my wardrobe. And I have consented to a small house party, to commence here in one week's time. I may yet find a duchess among its number."

He might. He had no idea. When Caroline had

sent her house-party plans to him by messenger, the sight of her rounded scrawl had made his head pound, made him ache with desperate want. In the end, he had simply inscribed *Do as you see fit.* That had put an end to her notes.

He was glad of that. Probably.

Sanders was still goggling at the revelation that they were to host guests, so Michael added, "I thank you for your concern, Sanders. But you must know it was entirely my choice to travel to London. And it is entirely my doing that I have somehow returned without a bride. On me lie Wyverne's problems, along with the responsibility for their remedies."

Now that he was back in the solitude of Callows, he felt all the farther from a solution. A small compartment of his mind wondered if Caroline would still aid him if and when she arrived for the house party. She had promised him her company at six events, after all, and only two had taken place.

Three, if one counted that glassed-in morning during which she taught him to dance.

Four, if one counted their outburst of passion.

He must not think of such numbers. He locked the treacherous memories away.

"Yes, Your Grace." Sanders lowered his eyes. "One week's time."

Michael surveyed the stretching hall, the staunch steward, his own drizzle-dampened garments.

He had never brought London into this world. The idea of doing so sapped some of the home's familiarity, like a favorite coat gone shapeless in the rain.

On that subject: "I must change my clothing,

Sanders," Michael said. "You should too, since you caught as much rain as I did. Once you're dry, if you'll see to the unpacking of the Carcel lamps, we shall meet in my study so you can inform me of all that went on here during my absence."

"Yes, Your Grace." Michael was not sure whether he imagined it, but at this barrage of orders, Sanders seemed relieved.

It was good for everyone that he was home again—himself, most of all.

❧

"You've done well, Sanders." Michael offered his servant what he hoped was a bracing smile.

The steward straightened with some effort, blinking groggily across the battered leather top of the walnut desk in Michael's study. Scarred and stained by decades of carelessness with penknives and ink, the desk was covered with ledgers of the household accounts, the tenants' affairs, observations on the weather, and any other scraps of information the steward had recorded during his employer's weeks in London.

Michael had been looking over these papers with Sanders for three hours, as soon as they could both dry themselves and fill and trim a Carcel lamp. Sanders had dutifully professed to be impressed by the superiority of the lamp's light.

For his part, Michael was impressed by the records kept by his staff in his absence. Here and there, they had departed slightly from his preferred methods of arranging figures, or they had made minor errors in subtraction on some account.

Subtraction, it always was. Never addition this year.

But these were minor considerations. It was pleasant to discover that few surprises had awaited his return.

Michael rolled his knotted shoulders and leaned back into his favorite chair, an ancient wood monstrosity with tatty velvet upholstery worn to the precise angles of his back and rear.

Arse, Caroline's voice said in his mind, and a spasm of heat gripped his body before he dismissed it with an effort of will.

She would not compliment his appearance now. All the garments he customarily wore in Lancashire were serviceable and shabby from long use: a plain cotton shirt with no neckcloth, a flannel waistcoat, worn breeches, leather boots rubbed raw by walks through heather and mud.

These clothes suited the cold weather and the work he liked to do. They suited *him*. But they would not suit his London guests. Soon enough, he would have to starch himself up again and go hunting for coin. He could not continue this subtraction indefinitely.

Sanders's jaw clamped shut on a yawn. "Thank you, Your Grace. Of course, the household accounts were kept by Candleforth and his wife." The butler and housekeeper. Relics of Michael's grandfather, they were as devoted to Wyverne as was Sanders.

The knot between Michael's shoulders loosened slightly. "I shall thank them for their excellent service as well."

Sanders bobbed his head. "About the money…"

Michael passed a quick hand over his eyes, willing them not to squint against a hard truth. He needed to see it, and clearly. "I'm about at the end of my rope, aren't I? Your letters to London did say that credit was extended for a short time, but…" He trailed off, not wanting to complete the sentence. *It's too much to hope that will continue after I withdrew into Wyverne House like the madman all London thinks I am.*

And who was to say they were wrong? He *had* gone mad after Caroline refused him. Mad enough to shake his body apart.

Sanders cleared his throat. "That's not precisely… that is, I can give you some assurance of a potential avenue for—"

Michael lifted his head and let his arms thump onto a ledger. "Sanders, please. Plain speech."

The steward sucked in a breath. "I was able to arrange funds to cover the servants' salaries and the interest on your debts, for now. But in approximately two more months…"

"I'll no longer be able to borrow, and I'll have to beg or steal. Or marry."

"Just so," agreed the steward with a gray ghost of a smile.

Michael interlaced his fingers with great care. "Best to know the truth. Let's have some coffee before we continue with the next ledger."

Again, that look of glass beads between the teeth—or somewhere rather more uncomfortable. Michael broke in before Sanders could begin another flurry of obfuscation. "Do tell. No coffee?"

The servant lowered his head in seeming shame. "I took it upon myself to economize in your absence, Your Grace, including such household luxuries as—"

"Never mind," Michael said. "That's all right, Sanders."

He wanted very badly to heave a sigh, gulp a hot cup of coffee, and banish the dry, grinding feeling at his temples. But he recalled that in London, Lady Tallant had not even been able to purchase the fruits she wanted, and she was a wealthy countess living in the foremost city on earth. Michael had neither money nor proximity on his side; winter had placed such everyday indulgences as coffee and hothouse fruits firmly out of his reach.

But he would have to reach them somehow. Absently, he squared papers and ledgers with the sides of his desk. "Sanders, we shall have to have coffee within the week for the house party. Beeswax candles too."

Nothing but the finest for his guests. It was a calculated risk, to gamble his remaining funds to try to win a wealthy bride. This must be the last in the long string of gambles that he had thought would help his dukedom. He had lost the others; he could not lose this one.

Confronted with a difficulty, his brain began to shuffle options. "We had better check the conservatory. It's too late to plant anything, but there might be some exotic foods in there to supplement what would otherwise be lacking." He started to stand, ready to stride off to inventory the great glass addition's holdings.

Sanders nodded. "Yes, Your Grace. I'll see to it."

Michael froze halfway out of his chair. He looked at Sanders. The older man was scribbling a note onto a piece of foolscap.

I'll see to it, Sanders had said.

It had not occurred to Michael to relax the grip in which he held Wyverne. Not once he returned and could get back to tramping through fields, climbing onto roofs, checking and rechecking to make sure everything was running as it should.

But it was not an unpleasant idea to let Sanders see to this small task. In truth, Michael was tired, and if no coffee was to be had, he was not sure how long he could stave off the weariness tugging at his eyelids.

He lowered himself into his chair again. This was a small matter in which to trust Sanders, after being required to trust him with such large matters over the past several weeks.

Sanders looked up from his notes. "Your Grace, how many guests are expected?"

"I estimate two dozen, though I didn't get a confirmed count from Lady Stratton before leaving London."

"Two dozen, give or take a few. Leave it to me, Your Grace. I shall work with Mrs. Candleforth to secure the food and household items necessary."

Leave it to me. That meant the same thing as *I'll see to it.*

If Sanders had been a woman, Michael might have suspected him of playing at seduction. There was nothing more desirable in the world, and nothing less certain, than the promise of a trust fulfilled.

But Sanders had proved himself worthy during Michael's absence, had he not? He had not done perfectly—but not even Michael had done perfectly. His penury was proof of that.

"Very well, Sanders. See to it." Both he and the

steward pretended that this exchange was everyday, rather than something more momentous. Almost as momentous as Michael going to London or dragging a passel of the *beau monde* back to Lancashire after him.

Michael leaned back in his chair and steepled his fingers, tapping them against his chin. "For my part, I must contrive a way to keep my illustrious guests so well entertained that they notice no deficiencies in the weather or the Town comforts to which they are accustomed."

The endless winter was, for once, not the most chilling thing on Michael's mind.

Sixteen

If Caroline considered the numbers, Michael's house party was not off to an auspicious beginning.

With seventeen other guests, she had spent the last four days jouncing north over rutted roads.

Two hours after their arrival, they had congregated in the Callows drawing room and prepared to head in to dinner.

But not one drop of brandy had been consumed, because no one knew where the host kept his liquor, and the host himself was nowhere in sight. And Caroline wanted a brandy like a pig wanted a truffle, because she didn't quite know what to make of her surroundings.

The drawing room was old-fashioned and cavernous, with dark red wallpaper, a scattering of heavy furniture, and a sour-smelling peat fire that promised, with its brightness, a warmth on which it entirely failed to deliver. The whole room looked well-tended, but also well-worn, as though no one much cared about making the place cheerful or fashionable.

Which was probably the truth of it.

At last, though, the numbers grew more promising, when five minutes after the gong, their host arrived. He made no excuses for his absence; he simply appeared, looking marvelous in dark blue coat and red—or was that coquelicot?—waistcoat.

Seventy-three inches of ducal grandeur, from his sleek dark hair to his hard mouth to his broad shoulders to his careful hands.

Before Caroline saw Michael, she had been ready to freeze him with icy dignity for neglecting his guests. For making her look foolish, dragging a dozen and a half fashionable Londoners northward to an empty drawing room.

But when she saw him for the first time in weeks, her ice melted. Her skin prickled, remembering—*this one*.

Based on her past experience with rejected lovers, Caroline knew Michael might have one of several reactions upon seeing her. He might act coldly to waken her shame; he might flirt with another woman to waken her jealousy. He might even attempt to flirt with *her*, to waken her lust. None of those would sway her.

As usual, though, none of her preparations did any good where Michael was concerned. Because he didn't act jealous or lovelorn.

He didn't even look at her.

And now that she saw him, stern and strong and distant, she could not imagine why she had thought *him* the one rejected. *She* was the one who had offered her body, who had surrendered pieces of her heart to his absent guardianship. *She* was the one who had sent notes and invitations, planning this house party to keep herself in his sights.

He had barely acknowledged her flurry of plans. Now that the names on her carefully considered lists were enfleshed before him, she wondered if he found her judgments fitting after all. She had selected the guests with great care. The men were either married and known to be pleasant company, or they were unmarried but judged not to pose competition to the duke.

Lord and Lady Tallant, of course; the earl's good cheer might put even Michael at ease, and Emily's friendship was essential. Josiah Everett was always amusing, and so Caroline had pried him temporarily free from his employer. Hambleton had been invited, for he was pleasant when separated from Crisp, the cousin whose lofty cravats he so unfortunately enjoyed emulating. The party was filled out by others from the fringes of the *ton* who had no objection to meeting a supposed madman of such elevated rank.

Including the third possibility Caroline had identified for Michael's hand, Eleanor Cartwright: lovely, wealthy, needle-sharp. She really might be perfect for him.

Michael's eyes roved over his gucsts, greeting them all with a slivered nod, sharing a word here and there. But for Caroline, he had nothing.

And Caroline added another possible reaction to her mental list: *he might ignore you—and waken everything*. Shame, jealousy, lust, all rolled into a spiked ball. She wished she could turn it into a mace and strike him with it.

Especially when, without meeting Caroline's eye or speaking a word to her, he interrupted her tumbling thoughts with a curt sweep of his arm.

Time to go in to dinner. So she smiled as though she were completely at ease, and she marched in at his side. Her fingers hovered over Michael's arm as they walked, wary of touching, of the effect it so often had on him—or might now have on her.

When she entered the Callows dining room, she forgot Michael for a few seconds; she simply dropped her hand to her side and stared. In the room's stretching height and width, it was as sturdy and graceful as a medieval cathedral: centuries old; stone-floored and timber-beamed. Completely unornamented by tapestry or carpet, painting or glass. Only a great iron hoop of a chandelier relieved the hard angles of rock and wood.

The chairs and endless table were huge and heavy and dark, Norman in style, and nicked until their finish was no longer glossy. Not fashionable, but made of the finest quality; well-maintained, but not precisely cared for.

Rather like their owner.

The rooms she'd seen so far made quite plain that Michael did, in fact, need a wealthy bride. His house had seen none of his fortune for too long. The realization made her stomach as heavy as though she'd dined early on a course of bricks—maybe because she didn't like to think of him rattling around alone in this Spartan house.

Or maybe because she didn't like to think of him taking a life's companion.

Well, it was his decision. As the nominal hostess of this party, she seated herself at the foot of the dining table and allowed Michael's servants to fuss unobtrusively with her chair, with serving dishes and glassware.

The service was good. The guests would approve.

But when the soup was served, Caroline's face fell. It was not the usual white soup she had expected; there were... *plants* in it. Strange little green coils such as she had never seen before.

Before she could consider this surprise further, at the head of the table, Michael raised a glass, and the guests fell silent.

"Thank you all for making the long journey north to my home," he began, his voice tight and chilly. He took a sip of wine, caught Caroline's eye for an instant before his wintergreen gaze flicked away.

It was the first time he had looked directly at her.

And then she understood: he had practiced a speech. He had withheld himself until the time came for a scripted greeting—with which he felt more comfortable than milling about in his drawing room asking everyone how their journey had gone.

Though that should have been easy enough. *Deuced cold, wasn't it?*

He continued, sounding less stilted now. "I have never before hosted a house party, so this will be a time of many new experiences for us. During your time here, I hope you will come to love Lancashire as I do."

The third and final candidate Caroline had identified for Michael's hand, Miss Eleanor Cartwright, sat halfway down the table on Michael's right side. Tall and fair-skinned, with dark hair and a high, intelligent brow, she was listening to His Grace's words with all the quiet attention of a student absorbing a lecture from a favorite professor.

"This soup," Michael said, "is the first introduction many of you will have to a Lancashire delicacy. Taste it, please."

Eighteen spoons, including Caroline's, lifted. Caroline caught one of the mysterious coiled plants in her spoon and took a hesitant taste.

Ah.

The soup was a revelation, creamy and buttery and savory. The mysterious plant was slightly crunchy, with a sweet-bitter taste that cut through the fat of the broth and enlivened it.

"This is a soup of bracken fronds," Michael explained. "I have heard them called fiddleheads. The cold weather has tinkered with our growing season here, as you can imagine, and bracken is almost the only plant growing well this year."

Out of a lowly bracken, such food could be made? Caroline studied the soup again. Marvelous.

Down the length of the table, spoon after spoon dipped down for more. Each bite added to the skein of flavors woven by simple ingredients combined well. Michael wasn't aping the sophistications of London; he was giving them something new, something uniquely of the land and of himself.

The evening was turning for the good, and Michael had not needed Caroline's aid at all.

Then, down the long length of the table, he winked at her.

It wasn't a subtle expression: he screwed up one side of his face until the eye closed. Then he grinned.

This was a reaction Caroline had never thought to prepare for: ease, humor. Her careful mask of courtesy shattered like spun candy. They were sweet, that wink and that grin, as if he shared a secret with her and they belonged together.

But they did not. Michael was so fond of the truth—so was he lying to himself, or was Caroline seeing only what she wanted to?

She couldn't tell.

So she winked back and drank her soup.

⁂

The rest of dinner didn't match the startling wonder of the bracken soup, but it was pleasant. Given enough wine, the guests were disposed to consider themselves well fed and were also prepared to be well entertained.

One awkward moment occurred when, as soon as the meal was completed, Michael requested that all his guests follow him into a drawing room they'd not yet seen. The male guests shared *we-knew-it* glances to be so denied their port and cigars by this madman, and even the women—who usually waited dully after dinner until the men rejoined them—were surprised to have the usual progression of the evening shaken up.

No more winks came from Michael; he was evidently impervious to the oddity of what he proposed. So Caroline smoothed over the situation, teasing the men about sharing their port with the ladies, speculating about the surprises Michael must have in store for them.

The room to which they were led was large and spare. At its center, atop a scarred marquetry table, squatted a black-painted metal device about the size of a lapdog. It looked like nothing so much as a tiny chimney atop a barrel.

As guests gathered around and blinked at this mysterious contraption, Hambleton gave voice to their puzzlement. "What is this, Wyverne? Some kind of tobacco pipe?"

Michael's mouth curved. "It's a magic lantern."

"I see," breathed Eleanor Cartwright. "Yes, this aperture permits the projection of an image. What is the light source? That's not the usual Argand lamp."

"Indeed not, Miss Cartwright," Michael confirmed. "I've modified this apparatus to use a Carcel lamp instead. I believe it will provide a brighter light, and consequently a—"

"A more vivid image." Eleanor nodded her determined chin, apparently having no qualms about interrupting a duke. "Without the shadow cast by the Argand style of lamp, all the illumination will be channeled through the glass slide. Excellent."

Michael blinked. "Thank you." More loudly, he added, "I hope you will all be pleased by this exhibition. Do be seated."

Caroline sank gingerly into a severe-looking chair next to the marquetry table; around the room, other guests found seats as well. There was no pattern to the furnishings in this room; velvet-covered chaises with carved Egyptian legs were intermingled with stiff, gilded Louis Quatorze chairs, sturdy Hepplewhite, and the human-sized mousetrap on which Caroline had, unfortunately, seated herself. Costly once, but now a complete jumble. Caroline's hands ached to tug and pull the room into order. She could make something of this place; she knew it. All the elements were here.

She slid her fingers under her thighs, reminding herself that she was not here to make any imprint on the place. She was here to cut ties. No more Michael. No more of this fascination. She would gain her greatest social success by marrying off the mad duke, and they would both have what they needed.

And they would be finished with one another.

That being the case, she should not have sat next to him. For instead of remaining indifferent, her eyes decided to follow his every movement. Watching as he retrieved a wooden box from a nearby table and slid open the top to reveal rows of glass squares and rectangles, separated by what appeared to be cloth wrappings. When Michael beckoned to a footman to snuff the lights, she couldn't help but gulp down the sight of those long, square-tipped fingers flexing, remembering how they had played over her body.

Fortunately, the lights went out—all but the one in the magic lantern—before she could betray herself with a blush.

For a few seconds, all the guests stared at the far wall of the room, on which shone a blob of light. Then, with the clean *snick* of glass against metal, a slide covered the light and an image shone forth on the wall.

It was Callows, sunlit and lovely, clean and golden, surrounded by a sweep of lawn so green the painter must surely have taken liberties with the choice of color.

Caroline had never seen a magic lantern show before; she had thought of them as nothing more than amusements for children. But no, this was a wonder.

"You may think yourselves in the north of England," Michael said, unseen in the dark room. "But those of us who make their lives here think it the center of the world."

He slotted in another slide in place of the image of Callows, this one of low, brown-gray mountains that stood out sharp against a sky the color of a bluebird's breast.

"This is the Forest of Bowland, which you'll see to the northeast of Callows if you approach during the daytime. I know," he said with a touch of humor, "there's scarcely a tree in sight, and so you'll find if you look outside. It's the ancient meaning of *forest* as a land that belonged to the Crown."

And now to me, were the unspoken words. Caroline wished he had spoken them aloud, reminding his guests that he was worthy of their respect.

Though he would be even if he didn't own a single acre.

"To the west of us is the Fylde," Michael continued, "which looks to the uninitiated like a stretching flatland."

"Damn right," muttered one of the men, a Mr. Watkins, whom Caroline had invited based on his thorough inability to appeal to young women. "This land's nothing to look at. Damned dull show. Wonder if he's got any bawdy slides in that box of his?"

Mr. Everett—Caroline recognized the wry, low voice of her impoverished friend—replied, "His land's a fair sight better to look at than mine, since I've none. Let's see what he has in store."

Michael, heedless of the slippage of his audience's attention, added, "This far north, we've a surfeit of space if nothing else. But the Fylde is bounded by a river that serves as our lifeline. I plan to expand a network of canals for irrigation and, one day, transport. We'll serve our cotton to the world, and our coal. We'll bring this plain to life. Perhaps we'll even make the mountains bloom."

His voice turned wistful, a wave of floating vision unmoored by reality. Caroline sank into the brightness of it, of the space on the wall that showed Lancashire not as it was nor even as the painter had seen it. She saw the unfocused flatness as Michael wanted it to be: a land of purpose, matching his own energy and drive. As he expected the best from himself, so he did from the land.

So he did from others. And surely he was disappointed by anything less than perfection.

The room was quiet around them, and Caroline could not tell if the silence was that of people spellbound or bored to distraction. She hoped for the former, for she felt the stirring of a strange magic within herself. Michael had told them how to feel, just as she'd told him at a ball in London only a few weeks before. With his words, he had woven and unrolled the tapestry of his life, his love for the land, his fascination with it—and his sorrow over its betrayal.

Could he possibly realize how much of himself he'd revealed to a roomful of near strangers?

Apparently not, for with a scrape and clink, Michael

drew out that slide and slotted in another. This rectangle of light displayed a scratchy pen-drawn image of a wheeled barrel, with a splash of red on a stretching smokestack. To Caroline, it looked not unlike the magic lantern apparatus itself. She turned to Michael for an explanation.

"This slide shows the *Catch Me Who Can* locomotive," Michael said. "A fascination of mine. I never saw it run in person, as I didn't journey to London during its exhibition in 1808. But I've corresponded with the engineer who designed it, and he sent a sketch that I've had transferred to glass."

"You've written to Trevithick?" Miss Cartwright's voice held all the awe that most young women expressed when discussing a court dress sewed by a fashionable modiste.

"Indeed," Michael said. "He's an eccentric fellow, I fear."

From somewhere in the darkness came a snort.

Michael shifted, and his face came into view close to Caroline's right side, up lit by the filtering lamp. His eyes fell into shadow, his cheekbones scooped hollow by the stark light.

"Thank you all for indulging me in this brief introduction to my world," he said. The glass slides clicked in their wrappings as he searched for another among their number. "Ah. I think you'll enjoy this one." He slotted a new slide into place.

They were faced with a velvet-blue night sky, spangled with stars and a benignly smiling moon.

As they watched, their eyes adjusting to this dimmer image, the moon and stars began to drift across the night sky, left, then right. Constellations floating in a way no astronomer would ever imagine. The guests gasped at the sight of galaxies dancing on a drawing room wall.

"How are you doing this?" Caroline whispered.

"This is a two-part slide." Michael sounded pleased by the murmurs of wonder. "The sky is on one, and the celestial bodies on another. They can move about in relation to one another."

"Ingenious," said the crisp tones of Miss Cartwright. "Have you any others of that sort?"

"Yes. But they might not be suited to..." Michael trailed off.

"Are they bawdy?" Watkins sounded hopeful.

"No, no," Michael hurried to explain. "They are phantasmagoria slides from France. They might be frightening to young ladies."

"Oh, nonsense." Emily, Lady Tallant, spoke out from across the drawing room. "Having been a young lady once myself, I can tell you that nothing frightened me so much as being left out of a rollicking good time. Do show us, Wyverne."

A chorus of agreement succeeded this, and Michael assented. The night sky disappeared, leaving behind a misty whitish rectangle.

Then a skull leered at them, sudden and huge and horrible. With a start, Caroline shrank back from its lurid gray-green bone, the grisly grin of its snaggled teeth. Bloodshot eyes rolled hideously in the misshapen sockets.

And Michael, bless him, was talking about it as though it was nothing more surprising than another landscape. "This is meant to be presented as part of a full show, complete with music and tactile effects."

"Tactile effects?" Caroline could not help but ask.

Michael reached out to draw a finger delicately up the back of her neck, and she shivered. "Never mind."

She thought she heard him chuckle.

From that point, the guests were enthralled. They gobbled up every sight Michael showed them—the bright and horrid wonders of his shifting slides; scenes of London parks; reproductions of famous paintings. Anything, it seemed, could be painted onto glass, and a magic lantern was indeed enchanting in its ability to transform a dark room into a feast for the eyes.

And Michael was quite as wondrous. Under the cover of darkness, he was bright, happy in their enjoyment, full of answers. His enthusiasm buoyed them all, convinced them that here was the most marvelous invention since... well, since the Carcel lamp.

For Caroline, though, the pleasure of the evening was not simply a reaction to the slides. She had never felt such sweet pain and aching want, and she could not put a name to it. She imagined it must be what a parent felt when a grown child married and moved away. As if one's abiding purpose had been fulfilled, and all that was left was—*well, what now*?

She forced out another peal of laughter as Michael changed the slides, showing them a rat scuttling in and out of the mouth of a snoring man. Clever, if rather repulsive.

Her laughter subsided when she saw, in the nimbus of the magic lantern's lamp, the confident way in which Miss Cartwright held out the next slide and

Michael took it from her. Such delight, such single-minded focus dwelled in his smile that surely Miss Cartwright would be pierced to the heart. Caroline was, and the arrow had not even been directed at her.

She felt a detached sort of marvel at the meeting of minds between Michael and Miss Cartwright. Her own frippery interests seemed slight and delicate in comparison. At last, Caroline had served him well—too well for her own good. She had served her purpose, and she'd returned to being ornamental.

The fortunate thing about being ornamental was that the surface always looked lovely, even when everything beneath was in complete confusion.

What she saw now was that he was quite capable on his own. Freed from the strictures of London, his alleged madness shone with brilliance. Eccentric brilliance, true, but wondrous in this dukedom that held scope for his dreams.

Folly winked at her from the lighted rectangle on the drawing room wall. He didn't need her after all. And sorry as she was for herself, yet a tiny part of her managed to be glad for him.

Hidden in the umbra of the magic lantern, Michael thanked the Lord for the cloak of darkness. He slid a finger under the edge of his starched cravat, which as usual felt as though it was choking him. He wondered if this was how stage players felt when they began a new show: the roiling anguish of uncertainty, the tingling excitement of anticipation.

Fortunately, Miss Cartwright was quite a helpful

young lady. She understood the mechanics of a magic lantern, and she handed him a new slide every time he grew distracted.

Much as he had dreaded the arrival of a houseful of Londoners, he had welcomed it too, as his only chance to pull Caroline back into his orbit. No need now to explain or apologize for what had happened the last time they'd met. They were on new ground now. Maybe they could begin afresh. At least he could prove to her that he was more than he'd seemed in London.

Even in the dark, he could find her; he knew the shape of her body as no other in the world. She laughed at the light on the wall, heedless of his need.

She usually saw people so clearly; had she seen, then, how he struggled through dinner? How everything he dared say had been rehearsed into woodenness? How often his eyes had turned to her, seeking a cue from the other end of the table?

What pleases people?

She always knew the answer. For him, most of all.

Seventeen

THE FOLLOWING MORNING, MICHAEL WAS AGAIN nowhere to be found. A quiet regiment of servants directed the ladies to appropriate indoor pursuits—reading, writing letters, plunking on decrepit musical instruments—while the male guests ventured out into the bracing wind in search of horses to ride or animals to shoot.

In the drawing room that had witnessed last night's phantasmagoria, Miss Cartwright tinkered with the magic lantern and examined Michael's collection of glass slides. Caroline tried to regard this as a marker of her own impeccable judgment, that Miss Cartwright was so drawn to an activity that pleased Michael.

Caroline sat a few feet away in a cane-backed fauteuil of rosewood; next to her, Emily, Lady Tallant, stretched out on a claw-footed chaise longue. Its striped silk upholstery looked dim and worn next to the vibrant yellow of Emily's gown, the startling jet of its trim.

"You look lovely this morning, Emily."

Emily shot her the kind of wry look that could only

be mastered by the oldest and truest of friends. With one single lift of an eyebrow, Emily communicated *I acknowledge the compliment, but I know there's something else on your mind that's completely unrelated to what you just said.*

All she said aloud was, "Thank you, Caro. You do too."

Caroline shook her head, smiling. *You're right, but I can't tell you anything in front of Miss Cartwright.*

She knew she was not looking her best. Her maid, Millie, had arranged Caroline's hair with unusual care, but there was no help for skin sallow from poor sleep and the jarring of a long carriage ride over a poor road. Given another day, though, she would shake it off. Surely.

Emily pushed herself up to a seated position. "Well, I've lazed about long enough. Shall we go poking around the rest of the house, Caro?"

"Certainly," Caroline agreed. "Miss Cartwright, would you care to join us?" As she'd expected, that young lady declined in favor of further examination of the optical toy.

Caroline and Emily ventured into the corridor and looked up and down its length. It was paneled in dark reeded oak, carpeted in a worn buff-and-green knotted rug that must have once been thick and costly as an ermine pelt. To Caroline, it looked warm and timeless, magnificent and neglected.

She had not been in a stately country house such as this since the death of her husband, the Earl of Stratton, who had whiled away his twilight years at his ancestral home in Somersetshire. Faillard Crest was a smaller, newer home than Callows, and far more fashionable;

Caroline had seen to that. But Callows had a grandeur that the Crest had lacked: it was steeped in history, built for the ages. Like Michael himself, it was heedless of expectations. It simply carried on as it wished, as it always had.

"Let's try this door." Caroline opened one at random. She found herself in a small, bright chamber wallpapered in a dizzying red-grounded Chinese print. Needlework furniture covers in the style of a few decades past proclaimed this a sitting room probably favored by the late duchess, Michael's mother.

Gingerly, Caroline lowered herself onto a spindly chair of worn gilt wood. Its embroidered squab cushion sighed a frail protest, then pressed as flat beneath her as though she outweighed an elephant.

"Well, that's lovely," she muttered, hopping to her feet again.

Emily laughed and found a chaise to stretch out on, its cover all swirling dark embroidery and fragile old lace. "*Lovely*'s not the word I had in mind for this room, Caro."

"It has potential."

"In the right hands, yes." Emily raised one of her annoyingly mobile dark brows. "Whose hands do you think those will be?"

"They'll never be any hands but those of a maid caretaking a museum if Wyverne doesn't deign to show himself at his own house party," Caroline said with asperity. "After all I've done to help him, the man can't even be found."

"Need he be available at every moment?"

"Not all, but at *some* moments." Caroline waved an

impatient hand. "I could slap him for his carelessness of manners, except that such an ill-bred gesture would undermine my point."

"His not making an appearance this morning, you mean?" At Caroline's nod, Emily shrugged. "I don't mind, and I doubt anyone else does, either. After all, it's a novelty to be hosted by Mad Michael, and we hardly expected cucumber sandwiches and lawn tennis. I thought the phantasmagoria was rather brilliant."

Caroline's chest hitched, and she began to pace around the room, fingers dancing over the backs of Norman-style chairs that looked old enough to have been carved by William the Conqueror himself. "Yes, it was an excellent evening's entertainment. But what has he done today? I can only presume he means to carry on as usual, even though he has a houseful of guests. He'll tramp about his lands and pore through account books with his steward."

Emily tapped her chin with a graceful forefinger. "Do you know, Caro, I think you sound a bit petulant."

"I do *not*." Caroline sank again into the chair that had protested her weight. She passed a hand over her face. "Oh, damnation, Emily. I do, don't I?"

"It's quite all right with me, though if you complain to His Grace, he'll have no idea what you're protesting."

"It's very clear what I'm protesting. I'm protesting his negligence of his guests."

"Guests that *you* invited, Caro. This house party was your doing."

Caroline was beginning to wonder why she had wanted to talk to Emily this morning. Her friend was completely lacking in the righteous indignation she ought to feel on Caroline's behalf. "It wasn't precisely my doing. That is, I arranged it, but it's to benefit him. To find him a wife."

"Miss Cartwright."

"That's who I intend for him, yes."

Emily blinked at Caroline. "And whom does he intend for himself?"

A pulse of futile, longing heat trembled up and down her body. "He'll follow my guidance. He's never thought about what he wants, Emily. He just bumbles around in a fog of responsibility, only coming up to grasp for money."

"Bumbling around in a fog? You make him sound as doddering as Lord Kettleburn. Why on earth should Miss Cartwright want such a man?"

Caroline's throat wanted to close, but she forced out the words. "Miss Cartwright is, I believe, much the same way. Perhaps not in the *utter lack of introspection*"—she pulled a deep breath in through her nose, willing herself calm—"but certainly in the logic and responsibility. I think she will be satisfied to exchange her money for his title."

"There is to be nothing more to their marriage, then?"

"Probably not," Caroline replied, her voice growing faint.

Emily picked at an ancient lace doily on the arm of her chaise. "If his marriage is to be nothing but a transaction, what need has he of your help? He could better make use of a solicitor than a matchmaker, it seems."

"I was more than a matchmaker," Caroline murmured.

Emily looked up sharply for an instant, then dropped her gaze back to the doily and studied it with feigned interest. "I see."

"I doubt it." Caroline sighed. "Emily, you remember what happened eleven years ago, and what a fool I made of myself over him. I fear I'm doing the same again."

"You were young, and he was handsome. There was nothing so foolish about desiring him. Or do you mean you've fallen in lo—"

"No. I couldn't allow it." Too fast she had blurted the words, and they sounded unconvincing even to her own ears. "Yet I meant well when I thought up this plan. This house party. I wanted to help him. And for myself—I wanted to be needed, even if for nothing but finding him a wife."

The countess teased free a strand of lace and met Caroline's eyes with the look only the truest of friends could master: sympathy without the slightest shred of pity. "That's cold comfort, to be wanted for the sake of another woman."

"Even cold comfort is better than no comfort at all."

Which was what she had now. Only a moment of lust had drawn him to her body, but now it had passed. Even if Caroline succeeded in matchmaking for Michael, she would end up alone.

This did not bear thinking of. She tried to lighten the conversation. "I can't complain that he's ever offered me a falsehood, nor expected them from me. He's always been quite plain about needing to marry for money."

"I must be overtired," Emily said, "because I'm not understanding why you don't simply marry him yourself. He's asked, hasn't he?"

"Oh, yes. He even deigned to tell me that I suited his requirements perfectly."

"Which were?"

"Being female. Having money. That's it, really. He did admit he liked me too, but that was an afterthought."

"What's wrong with that? An unencumbered fortune is hardly a detriment to your marriageability. He can't be expected to ignore it."

"But couldn't he pretend to be infatuated with me anyway?" Caroline knew she was sounding petulant again. She felt helpless, as if straining for a treasure held out of reach.

"No, I don't think he *can* pretend. Your puppy suitors are better fitted for that—though I am sure it is not all pretense, because you're quite ravishing, Caro."

"Oh, quite." Caroline folded her arms behind her head like a slumberous Venus, feeling neither ravishable nor ravishing this morning.

"Well, you are. Any man with eyes in his head would be drawn to your appearance, and his interest is sure to be kept there by your money. There's nothing wrong with that. Wyverne's simply the only one who went about it the other way around—sniffing from your inheritance to your… ah, other appealing qualities."

Caroline's arms dropped into her lap.

"Besides," Emily said, studying the worn lace beneath her fingertips with elaborate attention, "I don't for a moment think that all he wants from you is your money. And if you *do* think so, then there's not as much sense in your lovely head as I've credited you with."

Caroline stared. Could it be that simple? Her face and fortune were apparent to the world. But Michael did say he liked her. *Her.*

No, it all came back to money. Long ago, she hadn't had any, and now she did. Long ago, Michael had left her without a word; now he had proposed.

She had sold herself in marriage once. She would not do it again. She would never remarry without having all of her husband and giving all of herself—and she would not do the latter without the former.

"For heaven's sake, give me that doily." She snagged the tattered lace from her friend and began picking at it furiously. "Em, you can't persuade me he's looking for anything except a lifelong investor."

"Hmmm."

Caroline looked up, narrowing her eyes at her friend. The dark-patterned chaise framed a face of complete unconcern, as Emily studied the fit of her modish long sleeves.

"*Hmmm* is not an answer," Caroline said. "It is an exhalation. Even horses are capable of saying *hmmm*."

"A horse isn't capable of disagreeing with you, either. Since it seems an echo is all you want from this conversation, perhaps you ought to traipse out to the stables in search of a more sympathetic listener."

"I might if you don't cease your irritating observations. I've spent more time with Michael than you have, you know. Surely I can tell what he wants better than you can."

Emily reached for an embroidered cushion and stuffed it behind her shoulders, then settled back onto the chaise longue again, her glossy auburn hair a halo around a face of false innocence.

"What? Nothing to say?" Caroline's eyebrow shot up. Emily wasn't the only one who could speak a second language with her facial features.

"I'm not allowed to say *hmmm*, and I believe that's all I have to contribute at this point. You've decided he's mad, and that all he wants is your money, and so you aim to match him with someone who will be content to exchange a title for a fortune and who won't at all care how he behaves. Yes?"

"No."

Emily's expression shifted from wry to puzzled. "No?"

"I don't think he's mad. I've never thought that."

Emily sat up straight. "Hmmm. I mean—ah, yes, I see."

"Do you? How bright you are. We needn't continue picking me apart, then."

"Of course we need continue. So you don't think he's mad. Instead, you… oh, I can't recall what I said next. Was it the money? You do think he wants to marry only for money, and you think Miss Cartwright won't mind that."

"I suppose." She minded more than she should that Miss Cartwright could slot into Michael's life easily as a slide into a magic lantern. "If he *were* mad, it would have made my own humiliation so much less when I was a hopeful debutante and he left me alone at the center of gossip."

"Are you so sure he's not mad, then?"

"Yes." That answer, at least, came easily. "He doesn't care about the things other men care about, but that doesn't make him mad. He still perceives reality in an accurate way, as far as I can tell—if that is how one defines madness."

"I would define a madman as one who didn't tumble at your feet," Emily said loyally.

"He's done that, well enough." Annoyingly, her cheeks grew pink.

A grin spread across Emily's face. "Ah. So there *was* a tumble. I do wonder why you both persist in this cool distance of finances and contracts when it's perfectly apparent that you long to become entangled in a very different type of affair. Did you tumble for him as well as he did for you?"

"As well as he deserved," Caroline said crisply. She teased out a final knot of lace, then tossed the bedraggled doily to the floor. "Oh, Em. I don't know what he deserves, nor I."

"Then it's a good thing we're all together in this lovely home so you can find out," Emily said. "You've given yourself the task of finding him a wife, and I believe you shall. I've never known you to fail when determined. Not since…"

"Not since I went chasing after Michael the first time," Caroline finished. "I know, I know. Well, Miss Cartwright may do the trick. If all he wants is a ledger with a pretty face, she'll happily serve."

"If that's all he wants, he's a fool," said Emily in the same tone of certainty that she might use to pronounce a ribbon attractive or a joint of mutton undercooked.

"He's not the only one," Caroline said. "If he

wants too little, I want too much." She tried to smile. "You'd think that would make us the perfect pair, wouldn't you?"

"My dear Caro," said Emily, "I don't know what to think anymore."

"Nor I," murmured Caroline. No, not even about herself.

Eighteen

When she left Emily behind in the Chinese room, Caroline went hunting for Michael. As she had known she would.

She found him outside, as she'd also known she would.

He was barely visible from the front steps of Callows, his dark hair and clothing blending into the sere ground around his stately home. Only the vulnerable flash of pale skin between his hair and his jacket's collar showed that here stood a man, not a tree. A man with skin that must be chilled, for he wore no greatcoat or cravat.

The cold began to seep through the thin soles of Caroline's half-boots, so she started moving. She trod across the dry ground toward his heedless form, her resolve to give him a sharp correction already melting away. If, as Emily said, the guests had all enjoyed themselves last night, then surely Michael had earned himself a respite. He had never hosted a house party before; this must all be new to him and not precisely to his liking.

Yet he had done it anyway, so badly did he want

to find himself a bride. And thus far Miss Cartwright seemed quite, quite amenable.

Caroline walked faster, something cold and wild whipping up within her that had nothing to do with the wind plucking at her hair and pinching her cheeks.

She drew up a few yards away from Michael, wondering if he would turn to her. But he seemed not to have heard her approach; perhaps the sound of her footsteps had been covered by the loud whisper of the breeze.

Though dressed as simply as any laborer, he surveyed his land with an undeniable air of dominion. The chilly air had snapped his high cheekbones with color, and his breath was frost as he studied his land with the deliberate attention he had once given her body.

Caroline tried to swallow that thought, but that didn't help dismiss it. It only roiled more deeply inside her, remembering how she had once seen his quiet dignity transformed into passion. How much of herself she had given to him without his being aware of the gift.

How he had shaken apart then, and how he'd left her.

That was done. Left behind in London. Perhaps here, they could find a new equilibrium.

"Are you looking for my coquelicot carnation?" she said brightly.

At once, she knew she had said the wrong thing. This stark, stretching land was too large for petty emotion, too vast for her own small jealousies. She was glad when Michael did not reply and hoped he hadn't heard her.

She settled her boots onto the earth, liking the sound of dry grass crunching under her heels. She seldom walked over grass anymore. In London, there was little to be found, and such as survived the fog was manicured into a living carpet. But she remembered grass such as this from her girlhood in a country parsonage.

He turned to her at last. Blinked. "Caro? What are you doing out here?"

"Looking for you." *He called me Caro again.*

He only nodded. "It must be time I came back inside."

Before he could turn back to the house, Caroline caught his forearm. "Wait. Stay."

Stern brows knit over grass-green eyes. "Did you not come to fetch me back inside? I know I am neglecting my guests."

"I did come for that reason, yes. But your guests can look after themselves for a few more minutes." Now that she stood at his side, she wanted to join him in his peace. Here was no hoofbeat, no shout, no clamor. Only the wind through the dried heather, the faint gritty rattle of dust being reshaped, and reshaping, in the persistent push of a breeze.

And if she listened very closely, the quiet rhythm of Michael's breath.

As a younger woman, she had found country life too small to contain her. Only in London, bright and chaotic, had she drowned out the tumbling unrest of her soul. For the nine quiet years of her marriage to an earl old enough to be her grandfather, she had felt herself in rural exile, and she had waited. Wished. Hoped. She had never quite known for what; she had only known that she had never found it. Not even in London.

Except for a few fleeting minutes in the arms of a virgin duke.

And again, now, under the pewter bowl of the Lancashire sky. She had not known her hunger for more could be soothed. In London, all she could ever do was distract it, exchange one appetite for another. But here?

"This is different," she said, gesturing at the sweeping lands to the west.

"Yes."

"From—"

"Yes." He smiled. It wasn't an interruption, but an agreement. This stretching space wasn't different from any one particular thing. It was different from… everywhere.

She took a deep breath and understood what fresh air truly was. It seemed to scour her lungs clean of the smoke and smells of London, leaving a space within her that was somehow larger. "What do you do here as the Duke of Wyverne?"

"Whatever is needed."

"Without any restriction? You would… well, herd sheep?"

"If a shepherd is ill, yes. There is nothing shameful in doing what needs to be done. If the sheep need to be penned for the night and my hands would be of use, why should I keep them wasted and soft at a desk?"

Caroline could think of no reply except *Because that's not what other men would do*. He already knew that, surely. And that didn't matter to him. "Why, indeed?"

He cut a glance at her, as though checking whether she was teasing him.

"I'm not teasing you," she said.

He smiled. That smile—it changed him so. He looked younger, more playful. Utterly beautiful.

She made her voice brisk. "You see your body as a tool, then, making yourself as useful as possible, whether as a duke or a laborer."

"While I'm here. In London it was—"

"Yes." Now it was her turn to cut him off. She couldn't let him complete the sentence, not with her control so tenuous. The mere mention of London had freed treacherous memories of his big, roughened hands sliding over her bare skin. Her belly clenched, hot, at the thought.

She hadn't left all her appetites behind her, after all. But she would not indulge them again. She couldn't cheapen herself by taking the bits of him that he would allow her. If she couldn't have all of him, she'd best have none of him.

The wind blew harder, plucking coils of her hair from its pins. It rolled the locks into snakes and teased them high. Caroline brushed it back from her face, letting the breeze nip at her cheeks.

"You look as though you belong here," Michael said.

She laughed. "Windblown and covered in dust, you mean?"

"Not that."

Surprised, she met his gaze. That painfully sweet smile played on his lips again. She tried to think of something brilliant and witty to say, but his own words were so simple and true that she could only return them in kind. "You look as though you belong here too. I thought that as soon as I stepped outside and caught sight of you."

"I've never belonged anywhere else." He looked away to the rocky northern horizon.

I've never belonged anywhere. The words danced on the tip of Caroline's tongue, but she swallowed them down. They left a lump in her throat, made her eyes water. Or maybe that was just the wind.

Standing at his side, soaking in the space, she could almost forget that there was a giant stone edifice behind her, that she had filled it full of London dandies and ladies and schemes—anything to make herself indispensable, if only in some small way, if only for an instant. She could almost pretend she *did* belong here.

"It calms me, to stand here." Michael spoke low as he looked over the Fylde again. "I remember what I've done it all for."

"Your plans to find a wife?"

His mouth twisted. "Such as they are. It seems they were too grand even for a duke. Yet I meant well. There was so much to…" He trailed off, shook his head. "I always trusted the land, but it didn't return the favor this year."

"Deuced cold, isn't it?" Caroline wrapped her arms tightly around her body, wishing she had tugged on gloves and a pelisse before venturing outside.

He smiled at her small joke. But he still looked bleak, so she tried to offer friendly comfort. "The land needs you, Michael. This long winter has been terrible, but it won't last forever. With all your ideas—the canals you've had built—why, once spring comes, your land will obey your every whim."

"I hope. I suppose every relationship has its low times." He lifted his hand to shade his eyes against the sunlight, pale through thick gray clouds.

"Yes. They all do. But you are fortunate to have such a purpose, Michael. I could only wish to be needed as much as Wyverne needs you." Too raw an admission, but she couldn't call it back now. She tried to paper it over with smooth, flowery words. "I admire you for that, you know. For trying to make the most of your gifts."

"Do you? Then I wonder why you'll have no part of them."

His voice had gone cold as the wind; Caroline's lips felt numb as she answered. "What do you mean?"

Dropping his hand to his side, he fixed her with unsparing green eyes. "You want to be needed? Then be a duchess, Caroline. You'll have hundreds of people needing you every second of every day. Be a duchess, and take the responsibility for thousands of acres that won't grow. Find a way to squeeze guineas from ice and turn moorland into farms. Be a duchess, and you'll never again wonder what to do with your time; you'll only wish you had more."

Staring north to the low gritstone mountains, he added more quietly, "Be a duchess, Caroline, and you'll have the satisfaction of holding your fate in your own hands. You'll know that you can bring about your own success or your own downfall. For the sake of those who rely on you and the history that's entrusted to you, you'll do anything within your power to help them lead good lives. You'll try anything to atone for your failures."

He turned, piercing her with a needle-sharp gaze. "Be a duchess, and you'll never be free of the burden. And it will make you stronger than you ever imagined you could be."

He watched her, solemn as she had ever seen him, and Caroline could only stare and marvel. So this was what Wyverne meant to him; this was how Wyverne had shaped him.

She wanted to comfort him, to smooth the crease between his brows, kiss the anxious crinkles at the corners of his eyes. She wanted to rub her thumb down the faint lines that slashed from nose to the corners of his mouth, working them into the curve of a smile.

But it was not her place to reshape Michael. It was up to Wyverne to do that.

"Do you want me to be a duchess?" It was as close as she would come to begging. She had already humbled herself enough by following him across England.

His mouth tightened. "You are accustomed to doing what you like, are you not? You once told me so."

"Yes," she said cautiously. "But—"

"So you'd better decide. Do you want to do what you like, or do you want to be needed? I don't know of a life that offers both."

She took that in. Would a life in pursuit of her own desires make her fully ornamental? Completely expendable?

Had that already happened to her?

No, she rebelled at the idea. Surely *want* and *need*

were not always exclusive. Surely life could include both, even if neither of them had figured out how.

She lifted her chin. "Have you made your own decision, then?"

"About what?"

"About how you'll spend your life."

"There's nothing to decide. As I was born the heir to a dukedom, I've always known how I would spend my life."

"No, that's how you spend your *time*."

He narrowed his eyes. On another man, this might have seemed a glare, but Caroline could tell it for an expression of careful scrutiny. "I do not perceive the difference."

"My point exactly. You are a duke, first and foremost—but you've also become a duke solely."

All right, perhaps those narrowed eyes were a glare after all.

She continued, "You said that part of caring for a dukedom is being responsible for others, for their livelihood."

Michael dipped his head, a sliver of a nod.

"So your tenants cannot do without you. You are a very important fellow here in Lancashire."

"Are you trying to make me out to be some sort of arrogant overlord?"

"Quite the opposite." She took a breath, letting the cold air slice her words free. "If you're so important that your life is the center of others' livelihood, how do you preserve your strength? Have you considered what *you* need? Do you ever take a moment for rest or renewal or pleasure?"

Her voice tottered on this final word. He only

looked at her, his face still stern. His eyes seemed to have forgotten how to blink.

"Michael, I ask because increasing your own happiness might also make you better able to cope with the demands of your title. Does it please you to have people pressing at you all the time?"

"We're meant to be talking of your preferences, not mine. You're the one who said you wanted to do as you liked. I never made such a claim for myself."

"But you must consider it. How could you ask your future duchess to shackle herself to a life you don't enjoy yourself? Or *do* you enjoy it? Because there is little enough of pleasure in the picture you've painted for me."

He considered. "Life isn't only about pleasure or happiness, Caro. We have discussed this before."

"And come to no conclusion, if I recall correctly."

But they had, hadn't they? That conversation about pleasure seemed so long ago, but it was only a matter of weeks. Weeks only since the first tentative touches of their bodies, the first movement closer than friendship. The first time she had sought to pull him out of the rigid confines he'd constructed, to bring him closer to her.

It had worked, but only for a short while. Then he had closed himself away again.

He must have remembered this too, because his deep eyes studied her for a long moment before looking westward over the Fylde again. "There is pleasure of a sort in fulfilling a duty. I could not forgive myself if I shirked it."

"No, I know you could not. But now you seek help with these duties, a duchess to stand at your side."

He bristled. "I would not ask anyone to fix my errors, Caroline. I have always sought to resurrect the fortunes of Wyverne myself. I would not even seek a marriage for money if there was any means of extending my own credit further."

A sudden lift of the wintry breeze ruffled his dark hair, blew open the worn cotton of his shirt collar. He must be cold, but he seemed not to notice. Tall and strong and spare, he studied the sweep and flow of the quiet land. Its fallow moors, its rocky crags were his to protect.

But for all the uncaring land took from him, it could give him nothing back. Why could he not see this?

Caroline wanted to slide her arms in a living sash around his lean waist. To rest her face in the hollow between his shoulder blades until the tension that always tugged at them melted away. To press her warmth against his and whisper, *You are not alone.*

Stubborn man, though. Alone he had made himself, year upon year. His proposals had been nothing but matters of business; his heart remained shuttered away.

Even now, as his burdens grew, he trusted no one to help him carry them. Only when they grew unbearably heavy did he seek a marriage for money.

"Would you seek a marriage for any other reason?" she asked.

But the breeze flung her words away, and they never reached his ears. After another minute, she turned and walked back to the house.

Nineteen

When Caroline reentered the massive front hall of Callows, she momentarily forgot the manners instilled by a lifetime among the polite world.

This was, perhaps, understandable. Because the first person she saw upon reentering the great house, still stamping her chilly feet and rubbing together her chillier fingers, was her grand-nephew by marriage. Her late husband's heir. Her most persistent, least beloved suitor.

Lord Stratton.

Her head reared back. "What are *you* doing here?"

Considering she hadn't invited him, she could have said much worse to him than that. Stratton's defiant expression told her that no one else had invited him either.

Considering *that*, she *definitely* could have said much worse.

"Surely you didn't think you could escape me." He tried on a silky smile. "I'm so delighted to have caught up with you, Caro."

She shut her eyes for an instant, swallowed a shiver

of distaste. "This is very odd behavior, Stratton, showing up without any type of summons."

"We family members need not stand on ceremony with one another." He stepped forward, taking her hand. "What's yours is mine."

Family members. *Ha.* Like a bloodhound, he had the scent of her hundred thousand pounds in his nostrils, and he couldn't stay away from it. Money was life itself to Stratton.

Annoyed, she yanked her hands from his grasp. "That is not at all true. What's mine is mine, and I want nothing to do with what's yours." Since he was exactly her height, she stared him straight in the eye. "Might I add, Stratton, that unless you are secretly related to His Grace, the Duke of Wyverne, then you are not in a situation or a household in which family relationships apply. I am nothing more than His Grace's appointed messenger in the matter of arranging his house party."

"Nonsense. You sent the invitations."

Caroline wondered if this was the way Michael felt during social occasions: as though people were using the same words to speak two different languages. "And? Did I send one to you? I did not. There's no place for you here, Stratton."

Rather impressive that the smile remained affixed to his face. "I shall make a place."

The solid thump of boots across the marble floor distracted Caroline from what would undoubtedly be another futile attempt to hold Stratton at a distance.

Michael.

He smiled when he saw Caroline; then his head seesawed to take in the earl at her side. "Lord Stratton?"

They stood still as chess pieces on the black and white squares of the floor, all frozen in surprise. Caroline was the first to find her words again. "The earl has come to call, Michael. This must be quite a surprise to you, as it was to me."

Thus she hoped to communicate that: one, she hadn't invited Stratton; two, she did not consider it a pleasant surprise; and three, she did not do him the intimacy of calling him by his first name.

Unfortunately, Michael was oblivious to social niceties, while Stratton was determined not to comprehend Caroline's displeasure. So he only beamed at Caroline as though she'd thrown herself around his neck, while Michael narrowed his eyes in an expression of suspicion.

She would much have preferred the expressions reversed.

"Good to see you again, Wyverne," Stratton said. "Nice little home you have."

Michael stared at him, then turned his gaze to Caroline. "You did not invite him to attend?"

She shook her head.

He looked down his nose at Stratton. "Then you should not be here. Will you depart of your own volition, or must I have you removed by force?"

A puff of laughter escaped Caroline's lips. He sounded so *calm*.

Stratton began to perspire; she could see the dew break out at his temples. "Surely there's no reason for such talk between frien—"

"You decline to leave on your own? Very well." Michael marched toward Stratton. "I shall assist you to the door. Caro, never let it be said I have no manners."

"See here!" Stratton scuttled back a square. Distantly, a door opened and voices spilled forth.

Michael's jaw tightened. "See what? That you have displeased the lady, and therefore myself?" He rolled up the cuff of his right sleeve, an ominous gesture.

"Your Grace!" Caroline blurted. "He has indeed displeased me, but I should not like to alarm the other guests by drawing attention to his presence."

Both men froze. Caroline could hardly tell which was more surprised by her outburst.

"I—" She fumbled for words. Never before had someone risen so swiftly to her defense. Never before had she imagined Stratton would traverse the country uninvited.

With a shake of her head, she rattled her thoughts into order. "Here is my suggestion. The party intends to walk to Preston this afternoon—Stratton, that's a town about a mile and a half from here. You may join us at that time. I'm sure you can find adequate lodging there until you can arrange for your journey back to London."

The two noblemen continued to stare from their squares like frozen chess pieces.

"Is that acceptable, Your Grace?" she prodded.

Michael cast Stratton a freezing look, then returned his gaze to Caroline. "If it is acceptable to you?"

Warmth spread all the way into her cold fingers, making them tingle. "Yes. It will do."

"Then until the outing"—Michael nodded toward Stratton—"you are free to wait in the drawing room." He bowed to Caroline. "I shall have a footman escort him. You need not trouble yourself further."

"It's… fine." She still reeled a bit from the conversation. "Thank you, Your Grace. We'll be all right."

He hesitated, only withdrawing after she gave him an extra nod, a smile that felt tremulous. She watched him cross the floor in swift strides, then pound up the wide flight of stairs and disappear from sight.

Oddly, she felt a bit more at ease with Michael gone. Their conversation had ended in stalemate, neither offering terms the other could accept. If a third party were to broker their relationship, it would certainly not be Lord Stratton.

Damn her stupid relative by marriage. Damn his complete breach of manners.

Caroline turned back to face Stratton. "You heard your extremely temporary host. A footman will come to keep an eye on you. Until then, you might as well wait here."

Something sparked in Stratton's blue eyes, and he caught her arm as she tried to turn away. "Making awfully free with the duke's house, aren't you, Caro?"

She shook her arm from his grasp. "I am not required to justify my actions to you, Stratton. I am fulfilling the role with which His Grace has tasked me; that is, to serve as hostess of this party."

"So you do as Wyverne asks?" Stratton looked interested. "I wonder why. I wonder that he permits you such a free hand. Or is it you who has permitted liberties?"

A prickle of apprehension chased down Caroline's neck. "Indeed not. But I do as I like." So she had recently told Michael. The impulse sounded childish now—or foolhardy.

"You always have, haven't you?" A tight smile played on his lips; too close, he stood. "I remember what you were like before you married the last earl. You couldn't get—"

"*Enough*." Caroline fixed him with her chilliest look. "I take pleasure in helping friends."

"Yet you won't help me?" He blinked at her, all innocence, yet his hand brushed her breast. "I know you enjoy giving men this sort of help."

She would not step back; instead, she jabbed him in the chest with a forefinger. "If by *help* you mean *marry*, no, I won't. I shall not marry simply to convenience someone who seeks my purse. If you require any other sort of help, you may ask for it. Just as I may refuse to give it."

She turned toward the sweep of stairs Michael had just ascended. "Excuse me now, Stratton. I have guests to attend to. Stand here until someone comes to show you to the drawing room. I suppose you might have tea and a fire."

And with that, she left, floating up the stairs with a grace entirely at odds with the tumult inside.

How vulgar, how exhausting, to be subjected to men such as Stratton. She could understand why Michael kept himself away from the boil of society, where one never knew what might bob to the surface. One must be always vigilant, ready to skim off the undesirable scum.

She had been such an undesirable once, thanks to Michael. He had won her; she had lost him. And she had almost lost her good name too.

It had not quite come to that, thank the Lord;

specifically, the late Lord Stratton. He had been willing to marry her, dingy reputation and all.

Now it was up to Caroline to safeguard that reputation herself. It was, as she had once told Michael, what she had made it over long and deliberate years.

Caroline felt very tired standing alone. But if she wanted to do as she liked, she must draw back her shoulders and keep climbing the stairs.

I shall not marry simply to convenience someone who seeks my purse.

She could almost wish that Michael had overheard, or that she had thought to announce the same to her roomful of puppy-like suitors in London.

She was wanted by everyone, Emily had said? No, she was truly wanted by no one. Wealth made it impossible for her to tell the false from the true—to know who cared only for her fortune and who would be satisfied with the comparative poverty of her heart.

The Londoners seemed pleased by the prospect of a jaunt into the nearby village. Michael tried to communicate the small size of Preston compared to London, hoping to keep his guests from being disappointed, but he became mired in an explanation of the cloth-making achievements that had originated nearby. Too late, he saw that everyone had drifted away from him, then been herded out the front door by Caroline. Only Miss Cartwright remained at Michael's side.

"I apologize, Miss Cartwright." He followed Caroline with his gaze. "I was carried away by my own interest in the subject, though Preston's most notable achievements might not appeal to many others."

"Perhaps not," said the lady at his side, "though I myself share your interest in mechanical innovation, Your Grace. I was raised amidst coils of wire; I learned the workings of a spinning jenny at the age many children would instead learn to ride a horse."

Michael turned back to her, surprised, and her gray eyes met his. "Not the most fashionable upbringing, I know. But I am the daughter of a tradesman, not a gentleman."

He absorbed these glass-clear words. "I thank you for your honesty, Miss Cartwright. I welcome the chance to discuss mechanical innovation with you."

Color rose in her porcelain cheeks. "Thank you, Your Grace."

"Wyverne," he said, feeling as though he were extending a hand of friendship.

"Wyverne, then," she said with a nod of her pointed chin. "Ought we to join the others?"

Was her tone regretful? He couldn't tell. He didn't precisely feel regretful himself. When he took her arm, her gloved hand stirred him not at all.

This was good, though, a necessary step in assembling the machinery of a marriage of convenience. Best that his future wife's touch not unsettle him, surely.

Caroline had chosen well. Miss Cartwright seemed perfect for him: a fellow tinkerer, as logical as he might wish for a wife who was to improve his dukedom.

But would a life with a wife so chosen be like the chugging of pistons, inevitable and endlessly similar?

Who would make human a marriage between two such contraptions as he and Miss Cartwright?

It was in his nature to turn over unanswered questions, nag at uncertainties, sift through every contingency. But there were too many unanswered questions in his mind right now; he could never sift through them all. They were beginning to knock against the sides of his head, distracting him as he walked toward the rest of the party with Miss Cartwright. If he could only make a list, quantifying his confusion and thus controlling it.

But his guests were scattered over the lawn in front of his house, dressed in bright cottons and wools, chattery and spangled as a flock of starlings. And on his arm, requiring his solicitous attention, was the solution to his financial troubles.

"Please proceed down the road before you," Michael said to his guests. "You'll reach Preston in approximately one and one-half miles. The road should be in fair condition for a walk."

Uncertainty flickered over the faces of his guests, and Michael realized he had sounded too brusque. Of all the Londoners, only three did not show signs of confusion. Miss Cartwright, still at Michael's side, nodded her understanding. Lord Stratton beamed in a sickeningly triumphant manner.

Caroline, however, smiled at Michael as if he'd just said something delightful. Which was ridiculous, but it silenced his thumping headache anyway. The ache bled out of his head, swirling downward, twisting hungrily in his gut. He must have looked his hunger at her, because in the flicker before he looked away, her smile slipped and changed.

The headache returned with a dull thud. Michael twisted his arm within his coat sleeve, ensuring that Miss Cartwright's fingertips touched only the insensible bone of his forearm.

And they all began to march down the road to Preston.

For the second time that day, Lord Stratton intruded himself on Michael's notice. "Such a quaint part of England, isn't it?" The earl swung his amber-headed cane in conspicuous arcs. "This *is* England, isn't it?"

He swept a hand at the landscape, and Michael saw it through the eyes of a City dweller: deserted, quiet, rocky, barren.

How had he hoped to catch himself a wife here? What were the chances that any wealthy woman would love this place as he did?

"As you weren't married over a blacksmith's anvil during the course of your travels," Caroline said from a few feet away, "then you must be aware you haven't crossed into Scotland."

"I'm not interested in being married by a blacksmith." Stratton tried to draw Caroline's arm into his, and Michael felt a sudden urge to trip him with that glossy cane he kept dandling about.

"Drat. Pebble in my boot." Caroline crouched down and began fussing with the offending footwear. "Do go on without me, Stratton."

Stratton's brows knit, then he turned back to Michael. "Do the peasants hereabouts speak a local dialect? It might be amusing to observe them in their primitive circumstances."

Michael studied the shorter man's face. Was he mean-spirited or merely arrogant?

Neither was a commendation, and Michael was not pleased by the persistence of this uninvited guest. "They might recommend that you go to ecky, Stratton." An imp of delight danced down his spine.

"Would they? And where is Ecky? Some godforsaken place hereabouts?"

Michael wouldn't have thought he would enjoy insulting another man to his face quite so much; it seemed unworthy of him. But then, this was Stratton, and Stratton was unworthy of Caroline. "Not at all. It's a very popular place among the *beau monde*," he replied. "Quite far south of here. Much warmer. I think it would suit you very well."

"It sounds pleasant," Stratton agreed before turning back to Caroline again.

The saturnine form of Josiah Everett drew forward from the flock. He matched Michael's stride and cut his dark eyes sideways. "Teaching the earl a little of the local dialect, Wyverne?"

"Merely trying to be an accommodating host."

"My mother lived in Lancashire for a time. Had a rather salty tongue, she did."

"Ah."

"I think," Everett said, "that you've recommended an excellent location for your unexpected guest." And with a smile, he drew a thumb across his forehead in a mock salute.

So, at least one other person here knew that Michael had told a peer of the realm to go to hell. And that person approved.

Michael wished he had the knack for easy conversation, for this was the type of moment in which friendships were cemented. Instead, he returned the mock salute with a bob of his head that felt awkward and over-stiff, and when Everett turned to answer a young lady's question, Michael lengthened his stride to pull away. He was thankful for the distraction of movement. Working his body, tiring it out, always lessened his tension.

He was full enough of it now—needing a wife, wanting a woman who wouldn't marry him.

Caroline seemed happy here, didn't she? But he had said too much when he told her she looked as though she belonged. She wouldn't marry him; twice, she had said so. And so he couldn't talk to her with their former ease. He couldn't show her his deepest self again.

Damnation, she was so beautiful. It was a mistake having her here, for he would never shake his want of her as long as she was around. Even with Miss Cartwright nearby, he only wanted to follow Caroline. He wanted to unravel her pride, unwrap her from her pelisse, unbind her hair, unveil her body.

He wanted to understand her. How could she share her body with him, then act as though nothing had changed? As though he had never touched her at all?

He shivered, chilly spasms that had nothing to do with the temperature. In fact, his head felt as hot and sandy as though he had a fever. Still his feet moved down the road, his head nodded in response to the words he heard only dimly. Every speck of his attention went to pushing himself down the road.

Eventually he would reach journey's end, a place where everything felt like home again. Eventually.

Twenty

They reached Preston without much more conversation, and Michael turned the party loose on Fishergate Street. One of the city's main thoroughfares, it was well paved and bustling, with rows of stocky, neatly painted shops crammed together like tea sandwiches on a tray. For a city of middling size, it had more than its share of prosperous citizens, and pride twinged through Michael to see even Lord Stratton's eyes widen at the stretching street of ceaseless traffic.

The ladies of the party took their leave in pairs and trios, searching for milliners and drapers, while the gentlemen hunted booksellers and gunsmiths. Preston was, it seemed, the ideal size for Londoners: large enough that they could amuse themselves without boredom, yet small enough that they could remain confident in their own city's superiority.

Best of all, for this brief window of time, the guests were not Michael's responsibility. He could relax, catch his breath for the first time since Caroline had happened upon him that morning.

Well. Maybe. Just then, Caroline headed down

Fishergate with her friend, Lady Tallant, leaving Michael with a parting nod of significance that he could not interpret. *Don't botch this*, perhaps.

In another second, he understood why, for a voice sounded at his side. "It is noticeably warmer here than at your home, Wyverne."

He turned to see Miss Cartwright standing next to him. They were in an oasis of calm at one end of roiling Fishergate, standing at the edge of cobbled Winckley Street. The gardens of the city's wealthiest residents formed a lush, manicured boundary behind them.

"Yes," he confirmed. "We are closer to water here, and that moderates the chill, I believe."

She fixed her cool eyes on him and nodded her understanding. Quickly as that, the subject of the weather was disposed of.

As she seemed content simply to watch him, waiting for further explanation, Michael began to feel distinctly twitchy. He settled his feet, but within his boots, his toes tapped out their desire to begin pacing. "Ah… do you not care to shop, Miss Cartwright?"

"Indeed, no. I can shop when I return to London. Here, I have other interests."

Michael's shoulders tensed. Was Miss Cartwright flirting with him?

Certainly not. Miss Cartwright had a curious, logical mind, and she seemed as little inclined to casual flirtation as did Michael.

He flexed his shoulders, trying to loosen them, but his tailored coat had no give. "What are your interests?"

"The cotton mills, of course. Are they visible from

here?" She craned her neck as though the extra inch gained would lay out all of Lancashire before her eyes.

"Not from within town," he replied. "They are right on the river Ribble, for ease of transporting raw materials and finished goods."

"Ah, yes, that makes sense." She turned to face him again. "Could we tour one, do you think?"

"I have not made arrangements, but... well, it might be possible. Are you very interested in cotton mills?"

"Yes." She seated herself on a nearby wrought-iron bench, situated under a gas lamp for the convenience of wealthy loiterers. "I'm interested in factories of all types. Lancashire is best suited to coal mining and cloth making, I believe, and while I am here, it only makes sense to learn as much as I can about both. For example, I hope you will enlighten me about the methods used for mining coal on your lands."

"I—yes, I suppose I can do that. The Wyverne lands possess several good seams of coal."

"And coal prices are good this year. The cold weather, you know."

"Yes," Michael replied vaguely. He took a step toward the bench but decided to remain on his feet. Standing gave him more opportunities to shed tension, preventing it from collecting into a vise at his temples.

"You might take advantage of that fact to excavate more. Even so, your tenants could make a steadier income through employment in factories." Miss Cartwright looked up at Michael through undeniably long lashes. "Why have they not left off working the land or mines?"

"I cannot say."

"Cannot or will not?" Her eyes looked suddenly hard and calculating as a stockbroker's—an odd contrast to a rose-colored gown and a bonnet trimmed with pheasant feathers.

"*Cannot,*" he said. "I can speak only to the decisions I have made. I regard my land as a legacy, entrusted to my care only temporarily. I am honored to provide a living for those who care to make their home on it."

She shrugged and looked away down the street. "Well, as you're not taking particularly good care of your land, maybe it's time to try making money in a different way."

Michael took a reflexive half step backward, his boot twisting on a loose stone. He felt as though Miss Cartwright had shoved him. *No one* had ever spoken to him in such a fashion before: not his creditors, not Sanders, not even Caroline. Who were, as far as he knew, the only people who were aware of the full extent of his financial difficulties.

Surely Caroline had not told Miss Cartwright. Surely not. Not even to persuade her to come to the wilds of northern England and marry a madman.

His knees threatened to buckle, and he locked them, fighting against a reeling grayness at the corners of his vision. *Surely not,* his head pounded. The traffic on Fishergate receded into a blur of noise, and the gardens behind him seemed to mock him with their well-tended, well-groomed industrial wealth. He was a duke, one of the highest nobles in England, yet he could not convince his land to behave as these minor magnates of cotton and coal had done.

Miss Cartwright was looking at him in that

appraising manner again, and Michael struggled to find something sensible to say. "I..." He took refuge in a chilly stare down the length of his nose. "I did what I thought best. Naturally, I am aware that not all calculated risks pay off in the desired fashion."

Miss Cartwright—he was not sure of her Christian name or whether so crisp a female even had one—converted her expression into a smile, though it didn't touch her eyes. "Of course, the unseasonal cold has altered much. In a future year, you might see the yields for which you hoped."

The tone sounded condescending, not comforting. Michael folded his hands behind his back and inclined his head in a crisp acknowledgment.

He ought to draw her out further, for her purse was fuller than Midas's, her family's touch just as golden. But he didn't want her prying into his affairs anymore. So he shifted the subject to scientific innovation, a topic he thought they would both appreciate. "Do you note the pole behind you, Miss Cartwright?"

She turned. "A gas lamp?" Her features looked as pristine as a porcelain doll's as she followed the line of the tall pole up, up to its glass lantern of a top.

"Yes," Michael answered. "The city was lit by gas only last year. It was the first in the country, save London." Some devil possessed him to add, "I provided political encouragement and financial backing for the process."

As if this near stranger deserved proof that his enlightened schemes did not all go to waste, here was nine feet of tangible accomplishment.

Miss Cartwright looked up at him. "What good is it?"

"It provides a steady, clean-burning illumination at night."

She frowned. "Yes, I know how gaslight operates, and I am in agreement that it's a marvelous invention. But how does it benefit you? Why should you plow your own money into lighting Preston? Do you see a dividend?"

"I haven't yet, no." He was annoyed at the pang of embarrassment that followed this admission.

Miss Cartwright said, "Hmmm." That was all. Simply *hmmm*. And she pivoted on the bench and ran her gloved hand up the light post, then dropped it, rubbing together her fingertips as though she'd found it dirty.

And Michael knew she thought him mad.

Not in the way everyone else did; oh, no. She could understand his fascination with modern improvements, for she shared it. But to the brilliant counting machine of Miss Cartwright's mind, innovation for its own sake was madness. Innovation for the sake of profit, well, *that* was worthwhile.

Michael felt as though he'd been ground under the heel of her dainty little nankeen boot.

Then it got worse. "If we marry," Miss Cartwright said, turning back to Michael, "I shall insist on full control of the money I bring to the marriage. There will be no point in my settling your debts if you are only to throw good money after bad."

Michael knew two phrases that worked in almost every social occasion. As he looked at Miss Cartwright's lovely, severe face, he thought, *Deuced cold, isn't it?*

But he spoke the other. "I beg your pardon?"

She raised her eyebrows. "Our marriage? Lady Stratton notified me that you were interested in marrying, and I was amenable to the suggestion. I confess I was curious about where all the Wyverne money had gone, for I know the dukedom was flush with funds as recently as two generations ago."

Michael wished they were not having this conversation in a public setting. Or at all. "I am not required to satisfy the curiosity of those unconnected with my affairs." He donned the armor of his chilliest demeanor. "But I have invested in improvements that will yield great results in the long term, though they may not in the short."

"Quite a gamble, is it not?"

"I have never considered land a gamble."

She lifted her chin. "Do pardon my curiosity, Your Grace. I only seek to understand the terms of the investment I am considering."

There was no armor thick enough for a conversation such as this. Miss Cartwright was determined to joust, and Michael's heart pounded as though he saw the lance approaching.

"I understand you quite well, Miss Cartwright," he said crisply. "I too am considering the positive and negative aspects of a potential alliance."

"I was not aware you were in a position to dictate the terms of your marriage." She studied her gloves: delicate dove-gray kid, perfectly fitted to her hands.

"A duke is always in a position to dictate terms." This young woman might forget with whom she spoke, but he would remind her. Not even for

Wyverne would he allow this woman to look upon him as an unprofitable speculation.

"When excessive pride becomes involved," Miss Cartwright said, rising to her feet with long-legged grace, "I find it desirable to call a temporary halt to negotiations. If you'll excuse me, Your Grace? Thank you for a most enlightening conversation."

She retrieved her abigail from several feet away and strode off down Fishergate without a backward glance.

Michael let out a slow breath and allowed himself to sink onto the bench. He faced away from the street and focused his eyes on the gardens opposite, the tame slivers of nature that Preston's wealthy had permitted into their purview.

He would not turn to sift the crowds for the steadying calm of Caroline, who could read people as clearly as Michael could read the land.

An apt comparison, for Michael had misread the land this year, and it seemed Caroline had misread the marriage prospects with which she thought to match Michael. It was like that children's story with the three bears: Miss Weatherby had been too soft; Miss Meredith too hot. At first, Miss Cartwright had seemed just right, aiding him with the magic lantern show. But now he knew she was both too hard and too cold.

In other words, she was too similar to himself.

Whereas Caroline brought a spark into his life; she was the flint to his tinder. With her help, he had survived even the London season.

Well. A few weeks of it.

But she had turned him down twice. There was no

evidence to indicate that a third offer would be more acceptable. He had nothing she wanted, nothing but debt and solitude.

In children's fairy tales, the princess never refused the prince, did she? So how would this story end?

Perhaps he didn't yet know who the princess was.

He knew full well that for him, there might be no happily ever after. But he must ensure a happy ending for Wyverne, whatever the cost.

Twenty-one

After two hours in Preston, Caroline thought she had a fair idea of the life of a governess.

It had not begun that way. She had intended to shop with Emily, wanting to buy something that would make her feel beautiful again, even next to the engraving-sharp loveliness of Eleanor Cartwright. A gold necklace, maybe, or some frivolous, silky underthings to lie next to her skin and remind her that she was still a young woman, desired and desiring.

Though the thing she desired most was to listen to Michael's conversation with Miss Cartwright, to understand how that lady was able to captivate someone Caroline had not thought could be captivated.

Before she and Emily could do more than decide which shop to enter first, though, Caroline recalled her mission in relation to Lord Stratton. The man was as unwelcome as a fly in aspic, and she must remove him just as carefully so as to attract no embarrassing attention. She needed to find the earl, drag him to some sort of hotel, and see that he lodged there until he could be returned to London.

"I'm so sorry, Em," she sighed. "But it seems our plans to buy half the city in order to make me forget my woes must wait, for there's a woe I must deal with at once."

"Do you refer to a woe the shape of a ninepin, with a padded coat, answering to a name that rhymes with *flatten*?"

Caroline couldn't help but smile. "The very one. I'd love to flatten him for coming here without an invitation. But I'll try to be a touch more diplomatic and herd him into a hotel instead."

With a sorry wave, she left her friend in consultation with a milliner whose outrageous prices practically guaranteed a bustling shop.

She found Lord Stratton quickly, for his voice carried over the winding babble of the shoppers and gawkers on Fishergate. Almost as soon as Caroline heard him, she saw him; his beloved amber-headed cane swept the pavement clear of passersby in front of him, as though he wished not to have to share space with anyone.

When he saw Caroline approaching, he executed a neat swivel in the opposite direction.

Caroline made a leap for him and hooked an arm around his flailing cane. "A paltry attempt to escape, Stratton," she said through gritted teeth. "If *you* pretend to have forgotten our mission in Preston, *I* have not."

The next two hours were an excruciating exercise in patience and tact, as Caroline was required first, to physically maneuver a person who was both heavier than herself, most recalcitrant, and with few scruples about placing his hands on her person; second, to locate a hotel that his lordship would deign to enter, which necessitated a trudge eastward to the crossroads with a quiet street called Winckley; and third, to procure him accommodation when he refused steadfastly to speak for himself. The cursed man only folded his arms in determined silence before a succession of stiff-necked servants.

In her ear, he murmured, "You can't make me do anything I don't wish to. Nor can you make me stop doing something I enjoy."

"Maybe *I* cannot," she replied in a voice of false sweetness. "But I can make others do what I wish. And there are plenty of people in this town who are larger than both of us."

When a strapping manservant passed by in the lobby of the hotel, Caroline pressed a crown into his hand and asked him to assist her *dear* relation into the *best* room available, as she feared he was rather *simple*. "He's out of his wits from time to time, and I shouldn't like him to frighten any other guests. Could you ensure he remains in his room?"

A few ruthless waves of her lashes and wiggles of her chest, and the man was happy to oblige.

"Do have a pleasant journey back to London, Stratton," she said with a cheerful wave as the manservant hoisted the earl up the hotel stairs by an elbow.

He struggled, but in vain. "Not bloody likely."

"Now, now, you're speaking to a lady," grunted the manservant, restraining Stratton from another attempt at escape.

"Not bloody likely," the earl repeated.

Caroline rolled her eyes. "I shall have your trunks sent here from Callows so that you may have your own things about you until the time of your departure. What's yours is yours, isn't it? Just as what's mine is mine. I remember."

The look he shot her was pure murder. But in another second, he was dragged around the bend of the stairs.

Caroline stood still for one second, feeling as buoyant as a governess whose least-beloved charge has finally gone away to school. Then she shook off the annoyance that Stratton always roused in her, and she stepped out of the hotel into the silver sunlight of Preston.

She looked left and right, hoping to catch a glimpse of her friend. Emily loved to wear yellow, and as a result, she was easy to pick out in a crowd.

But Caroline's eyes caught first on a tall, dark-haired figure, folded up on a bench across the street from her. There was nothing unusual about his appearance, but he might as well have been dressed in cloth of gold and an ermine cape, so quickly did she notice him.

Her feet pattered over the pavement toward him.

"Michael," she called once she drew within a few yards. He was leaning forward, elbows on his thighs, studying his interlaced fingers. She could see the lines of his lean muscles through his breeches. *Ohhh*. She wanted to touch him.

He looked up at the sound of his name. Quickly, she wiped the lust-struck expression from her face.

"I've dispatched Stratton," she said.

His mouth curved. "You can't mean you've killed him."

She laughed. "Not this time, though I was tempted. I've installed him in a hotel under guard and made it quite clear that he was to return to London."

He nodded, then shifted to settle against the back of the ironwork bench. His arms spanned the top of it.

If she sat next to him, she would be within the span of his embrace. Practically.

Instead, she puttered around, swinging her gaze between the quiet, well-tended gardens and homes of the wealthy, the bustle of Fishergate, and the pole that stretched high and imperious behind Michael.

"Is that for gaslight?" No wonder he sat here. Gaslight would draw him as surely as it would a moth.

"Indeed." His mouth pressed into a flat line. "I have lately been informed that it is a marvelous innovation, but to be pursued only if one sees an immediate financial return."

"You sound distressed."

"I *beg* your pardon. I'm nothing of the sort." He looked down his nose at her. "I might be slightly fatigued, that is all."

His fingers began tapping on the stern metal of the bench; Caroline suppressed a smile. His body roiled with energy; it would ever betray his true feelings. "So, what is not distressing you?"

"Everything in the world is not distressing me, because I am not distressed."

"Excellent. So you find Miss Cartwright acceptable, then. Has she proposed to you yet?"

His back went rigid. "Has she—*what*?"

A gratifying reaction. "I asked you if she had proposed. Marriage, I mean, not some business affair. She knows you want a wife, and she is accustomed to making swift decisions. It's a habit she learned at her father's knee, I believe."

His mouth seemed to be getting flatter still; it allowed a single sentence to escape. "That's not a habit I expected in a wife."

"Why not? It's a trait you share."

His throat worked. "I am not yet certain whether I shall pursue Miss Cartwright. It may not be desirable that my life's mate reflect all my own qualities."

Not yet certain. After everything Caroline had invested. He rejected her aid and her choices, the purpose of this whole house party, as though they were no more significant than a bowl of soup that was not to his taste.

She noticed, detached, the way her skin heated as if slapped, then prickled with icy numbness. The blank before agony. Dimly, she felt surprise that a single phrase could matter so much.

And then feeling came rushing back, her ears roaring with all the noise of the crowds on Fishergate. She knew she must look as wrong as she felt. Michael had tilted his head in that curious way he had.

When she spoke, her voice was carefully quiet. "Your uncertainty surprises me."

He lifted his brows, imperious as a bust of Caesar. "Why need you concern yourself with my actions?" *After all, I am not concerned with yours* was the unvoiced second half of that sentence.

Caroline drew herself up to her full height and

peered down at him, taking advantage of her standing position to impress her point on his notice. "Because, *Your Grace*, my own reputation is on the line. On this house party, and on your engagement, depend my place in society as well as yours."

The bust of Caesar knit his brows. He did not understand.

She bit back a sigh. "You made a fool of me once before, Michael. Yes, it was long ago, but if you choose not to marry now, after I have publicly aided you, the *ton* will remember. Their respect will turn to mockery."

She hated even to say the words, true as she knew them to be. She had already lived through this once.

Her plan had begun so well: she would triumph over him, and herself, and the polite world. Not in any malicious way, but in a way that would give them all what they needed. Society would get its gossip about the change in the mad duke; Michael would win a rich dowry. And Caroline? She would come to understand him, and the means by which he had so long kept her fascinated.

Now, with every knot she untied, she snarled up two more. She must untie them all, though, and redeem herself. She must once again play matchmaker.

She could not remember when her heart had been in it less. How could it, when it was already spoken for?

Her hands clenched; Michael's eyes followed their movement. "So you want me to choose a wife to bolster your social consequence."

She frowned. "No, Michael. I want you to give the

selection of a duchess at least as much attention as you give to a magic-lantern slide of a steam locomotive that once ran for a few weeks in London. Because you need to know now, and for the rest of your life, that your whims affect others too. If you ruin your life, you'll lessen mine too."

"But you once told me, Caro, that I had not the power to ruin you." He captured her gaze with those tree-green eyes.

Neither blinked, neither moved, as they recalled the moment of their mutual ruination. Their bodies entwined, the breathless hours in which they both seemed to have found what they longed for. What they had always longed for.

How transient the fulfillment had been, yet how painfully lovely. The thought of it made the fine hairs on Caroline's arms prickle and rise, as though they sought his touch.

She could have sighed, or cried, or lied to him.

But she didn't. She stood straight and tall and alone, and she laid herself bare. "It seems you have more power over me than I realized."

She raised a hand, stared at it as though it belonged to a stranger. Then she took a fraught step closer to him and laid her hand on his chest with a gentle, rolling pressure.

"We've tied ourselves together, Michael, for better or worse."

For richer or poorer, in sickness and in health.

No, never that. She had made that clear.

Michael folded his arms, as though this would protect his heart. But it only thudded faster, wanting her to notice it. Wanting her to slip her hand under the shirt that lay over his chest, to stroke his skin.

Treacherous body. He should never have allowed it to waken to her touch.

He scooted back on the bench, freeing himself from her, then forced himself to his feet. His legs were disinclined to support him, and he circled behind the bench to lean against the iron-steady support of the gas lamp. Willing his heart to slow, *slow*, but his sullen flesh instead sent the pounding upward to his head.

He squinted, wishing the thump in his head would diminish along with his field of vision. "I am not being flighty in my choice of a wife. To the contrary, I hope to make a marriage that is both sensible and financially advantageous. And of course, I hope it is a happy union too."

Caroline's smile looked odd. Rather frozen.

He drew himself away from the support of the gas lamp, stepped closer to her again. The ironwork wall of the bench held them a decorous yard apart. "What is the matter?"

"Oh, nothing, nothing," she said through that frozen smile. "You brought up happiness, that is all, and I am merely sharing it. I am happy, Michael, that *you* should regard as worthy of mention such a nebulous, unscientific quality as happiness."

Michael's brow furrowed. "You are teasing me."

"Not at all." The smile melted away. When she spoke again, her voice was pure vinegar. "But are you quite certain of what you want in a wife? Are you absolutely sure—sure enough to stake your dukedom's solvency—that Miss Cartwright cannot make you happy? Because you certainly can make her so, simply by hauling out your magic lantern."

He wondered why her demeanor had changed so swiftly between sweet and sour. But since she assured him she was not, in fact, teasing him, he would give her a serious reply.

He considered before he spoke, letting the distant sun warm his thoughts to life. If the sky seemed endless in Lancashire, somehow the sun seemed farther away. Those who wished for a life of easy gain would be better off matching their mettle against a different part of the country.

"I do not know," he said, "whether I truly can make Miss Cartwright happy as a wife. But she might not look for happiness. I believe she is most concerned with the expansion of empire."

Caroline's brows lifted. "A characteristic that a duke with a taste for innovation ought to admire. Covet, even."

At the word *covet*, his veins rushed warm. Caroline could not possibly know the depth of covetousness a man could achieve when he pent up his physical urges for thirty-two years, then lavished them one single time on one wondrous woman. "You do not know what I covet."

"Oh, I think I do. Or I know what you *don't*. You did not care for the delicate sensibilities of Miss Weatherby or her mother, who dared take umbrage when you spoke the word *damn* in her presence. Yet you also did not care for Miss Meredith, who was too indelicate for your tastes." Her hands flexed. "Now you also reject Miss Cartwright, who is a wealthy orphan *and* who likes magic lanterns, and who would dutifully bear you an heir without being horrified by your own passions, nor bestirring them overmuch. And so," she concluded, sinking onto the bench, "I can only conclude that you covet solitude."

She looked away from him, for which he was grateful. She had flayed him with her logic. Terrible woman, to turn one of his own favorite weapons against him. And when she stripped from him all other possibilities, shields, armors, the only thing he had left was the naked truth.

"Not solitude," he said in a voice that was raw and new. "Only the right person."

He had invested himself in her, and now he had nothing left to give to another. She had bankrupted him, but it was his own fault. He should have remembered to trust only himself.

"Fine, fine." She splayed her hands in an I-give-up gesture. The movement drew his eye to the slim line of her wrist, the shape of her palm, the spread of her fingers and thumb.

She had run those fingers over the whole length of his body, palming his troubles and flicking them away with her every movement.

Only for a while, though. Only for a short while. She could not know the determination it took to overcome one's deepest faults or the rigid control used to manage the tensions, worries, burdens of a lifetime.

He had his pride: the pride of a man, and a duke, and a rejected lover. It was a pride of practically infinite dimensions. So he flung himself into its puffery and replied, "In time, I will come to terms with Miss Cartwright. She will benefit materially from the connections she will gain as a peeress. It is a most logical match."

Caroline's last speech seemed to have drained her. Rather than having the lushness of a rose in bloom, she was simply a slim blond woman with pretty features and elegant clothing, sitting carefully straight on a bench. No spark in her.

"I am sure you are right," she said in a colorless voice. "It will be the best of bargains. No compromises, only gain for both parties. I will do what I can to help you, though I do not believe you will require my help much longer." She smiled faintly. "We have not even used all six days that I thought I might require, have we?"

"I've lost count," Michael said through a throat that seemed crammed with cotton.

"I too." She sat, silent and still, for a moment, then added, "Miss Cartwright has as much pride as any woman I've ever known. Well, *almost* any woman." Her smile turned wry before vanishing. "I'll try to smooth her prickles and charm her a bit for you, since I do have that ability left to me, for now."

Her kindness rasped at him; he disliked the ease with which she turned her gifts to his benefit, to throw him at another woman. He thought about saying, *There's no need to tie yourself to me any more closely. I can manage this myself.*

"Do as you think best," he said at last. Letting her decide how close, or how far, she wanted him.

"You could survive on very few phrases." Caroline rose to her feet, smoothing her skirts. "*Do as you think best. I beg your pardon. Deuced cold, isn't it?*"

"*I am accustomed to doing what I like*," Michael shot back.

"That one's as true for you as it is for me," Caroline said. "Don't you think?"

He could only stare at her, stunned. Of *course* he didn't think that was true. His days were crammed with obligations. His pockets were empty. His house was overrun by strangers. And he would soon need to marry for the sake of everyone in his dukedom, except himself.

But he said none of this, only shook his head.

Caroline watched him for a few endless seconds, and something in her expression seemed to waver. Michael did not know whether it was anger or sorrow or merely exasperation.

Finally, she tilted up her chin with as much hauteur as any duchess, then marched away from him, slipping into the teeming crowds of the street.

Twenty-two

"Won't you join us, Wyverne?" Lord Tallant hefted a billiard mace in one hand and a cue in the other.

The party had returned to Callows in time for dinner; now the guests sought amusement again. Michael hoped the good-tempered earl had more of a knack for billiards than he did for cards. Quite well, he recalled the evening he'd spent at Tallant House, when the earl had been bested at whist less by the Weatherby women than by his own poor memory for cards.

At first, a refusal hovered on Michael's lips. A sheaf of papers as thick as his fist awaited his attention in his study, and he felt a nagging urge to look through them before he turned in for the night. Caroline's abrupt departure in Preston had left him in a spin of unsettlement, and he knew from long experience that the best way to calm himself was work. Work to the point of exhaustion.

But then he remembered, as surely as if Caroline had spoken the words in his ear: *you are the host*. He owed the guests his time, especially if he ever wanted the *ton* to trust him again.

And if he played along with this game, perhaps Caroline would hear of it—and then she would know she had judged him too hastily and too harshly.

"Thank you, Tallant," Michael said. "I believe I will."

The wood-paneled billiard room was stuffed with male guests, all imbibing either port or tobacco. After neglecting that sacred alcohol-based ritual the previous night, Michael was atoning.

"Your Grace?" A cue waved in Michael's face. "Will this one work for you?"

Michael offered the cue-giver a creaky smile. "Thank you… Hambleton."

He must have recalled the man's name accurately, because the curly-haired dandy colored over his absurdly high shirt points and bobbled back to the side of the billiard table with a series of shallow bows.

Michael swatted the cue into his right palm. Again, Caroline was right: a lofty title plus a leavening of kindness predisposed people to judge him more lightly.

The billiard room was in better order than many others at Callows, for its condition mattered greatly to its purpose. A desk, for example, worked as well whether polished to a high gloss or nicked to high heaven. But a billiard room must be well paneled and insulated, so that temperature and humidity would neither warp the table nor crack the ivories. It must be lit well, too, so a man could make his shot without being confounded by shadows.

The Callows billiard room, Michael realized, was something to be proud of. He knew this because the Londoners were not looking about themselves dubiously, as they had in almost every other room of his house. Instead, they were selecting cues in the deliberate way men used when trying to impress their skill upon their peers.

It was agreed that Hambleton, Tallant, and Everett would play the first game with Michael, while those who didn't wind up with a cue contented themselves with a bottle of something spirituous instead. The four players began as usual, by stringing for the lead.

When Michael stepped up to the table, he exhaled, squared his shoulders, aimed his cue. Stringing was simple, for it depended only on force, not on angle. All he need do was strike the ball hard enough to roll it to the cushion at the upper end of the table—which it reached, slowly, and settled against. He nodded his satisfaction and straightened.

And was faced with the other three players, looking like the horsemen of the apocalypse. Tallant's shock warred with his normally pleasant features; Hambleton had gone pale as death. Everett wore a pestilent grin.

"Fine shooting, Your Grace," he said. "I've never seen anyone string up as perfectly as that."

"Truly?" Michael looked at the cue in his hand, wondering if it had transformed into a snake to shock them all so. But no, it was nothing but a long stick of maple with a leather tip.

Oh. Maybe it was that. "You might find that the leather tips of these cues assist in your aim. They were first used by a Frenchman about a decade ago. I've been pleased with the results."

The three seemed to accept this answer, but they had less luck than Michael. Hambleton's ball was a foot shy; then Tallant's shot cracked against Hambleton's ball and sent it against the side cushion.

The earl peered at his cue, frowning, then shrugged. "Sorry about that," he said to Hambleton's storm cloud of a face.

Everett made a nice shot that finished only a few inches away from Michael's. He turned from the table, his dark face as full of wicked humor as ever. "That'd have been good enough in most games, Your Grace. I'm not sure it's the cues so much as the players wielding them."

Michael cleared his throat. "Yes, well, I've often heard that it's not so much the make of a cue as the way it's used." This bawdy joke went over with a gratifying amount of raucous laughter. It seemed a male audience liberally plied with spirits was quite ready to be amused.

This was rather a novelty. And rather… rather pleasant.

He realized now what Caroline had tried several times to tell him: that everyday pleasures enriched the business of life.

The other men collected around the table, watching as the game began in earnest. Michael started cautiously, giving up a hazard in order to take the measure of the other players.

They were much as he expected from their first shots. Everett was careful but no expert. He would never humiliate himself with a terrible shot, but he hadn't the eye for a great one. Hambleton was forceful and had a good mind for the angles, but his temper got in the way of his play, and he was as likely to be dreadful as spectacular. Tallant was a careless player, just as he was at cards. He biffed away at whatever ball was closest to him, whether the ivory cue or one of the red-painted object balls.

Michael's turn again. Now he knew the other players. He was prepared.

He bent, aimed. His mind mapped the angles needed, a web of lines arrowing over the table. With a dull *thup* of leather against ivory, the cue ball obediently rolled to one red ball, knocked it with a crisp crack, and sent it in a quick carom to the other red ball.

It was all over in a second. Michael stood and looked toward Everett.

The younger man shook his head. "You go again, Your Grace."

Ah, that was right. Michael rarely played a full game of billiards—with whom would he play?—though he enjoyed the geometric exercise of practicing angles. It relaxed him, freed his mind. Another way of managing the headaches when they began to gnaw.

He realized, as he bent and eyed the length of his cue again, that everyone in the room was staring at him. And he realized too that this didn't bother him a bit, because there were no continuous variables here. There was nothing to doubt. There was only a ball, a cue, and two targets to hit.

So he hit them again. And again. And again.

But he was the host, and he must not consider only himself. After his fourth successful shot, he looked up to Everett. "We can move on to another inning if you wish."

"If I wish?" Everett laid his cue against the wood-paneled

wall. "No, indeed, Your Grace. I should like to see how long your luck holds." Tallant seconded this notion.

"It's not luck," Michael replied. "It's geometry."

Hambleton pulled a face. "It comes to the same thing where I'm concerned."

"Nonsense," Michael said. "You've a natural eye. Apply geometry, and you will be the master of any table."

Hambleton looked unconvinced. "Can you demonstrate?"

All around the edges of the table, men bent down as though pulled by a drawstring, following the line of Michael's cue as he pointed it at the spots of contact on the walls, then laid it flat to show angles.

"Damnation," breathed a youthful-looking man with a halo of red curls. "I'd have paid more attention in mathematics class when I was up at school if I'd known it would help plump my pockets."

Michael's ears pricked. He had never considered using this particular talent to wager his way back to financial health. A brief, riotous vision flooded his mind: sharping his way through London, driving stakes high, gambling his way to fortune and freedom. Persuading a certain woman to his bed…

All impossible, of course, and not only because he had vowed to take no more financial risks.

"Curse me, but I can't get the feel of it," Hambleton grumbled. "I understand what you're saying, Wyverne, but it's easier said than done."

"Give it another try," Tallant said. "It's not as though we've bet money on the game. What have you to lose?"

"Why haven't we bet?" asked a man named Watkins, who was well into his port and had developed a slight hiccup. "I'll put twenty quid on the duke to make five more in a row."

"I'll take that bet," said Hambleton.

Puzzling. "You're betting money on my skill at billiards?"

"To be accurate, Hambleton's betting against you." Everett grinned. "But yes. How much faith do you have in your geometry, Wyverne?"

"Five in a row is the bet?" When Watkins and Hambleton nodded, Michael agreed. There was no need for faith, only for observation.

His eyes imagined the spiderweb of bumps and caroms needed, tracked the resolution of the shot back to its origin.

Smack. He hit the cue ball cleanly, and with a neat *click-clack*, it rolled into one red ball, then the other.

"There's one," he said over his shoulder.

Two, three, and four followed just as neatly. As he lined up his cue for the final shot, a sharp rap at the door interrupted him.

Caro.

His hand shook; quickly, he straightened up to cover the tremor. "Come."

It wasn't Caro who peeked in, though. It was her close friend Lady Tallant, who wrinkled her nose and fanned away the clouds of cigar smoke as she stepped into the room.

"Everything all right, Em?" Her husband detached himself from the human wall around the billiard table and stepped closer to the countess. She looked far too feminine for this room, her light yellow gown frothy against the dark wools and knits and suedes of the men's clothing.

"Yes, yes," she choked. "My goodness, this is more smoke than air. How can you all breathe?"

"Tobacco smoke is preservative," Tallant said. "At least, I think it is."

Michael suppressed a cough. "Might I help you in some way, Lady Tallant?"

"Yes, if you'll all accompany me," said the countess. "We ladies are tired of needlepointing the world and we desire a little male company. I grew alarmed when we hadn't seen or heard anything from you. Now I see that was a ridiculous fear, as you're all preserving your good health through pickling and smoking."

She peered into the gap around the billiard table left by her husband. "Billiards? Are you playing red winning or red losing?"

"Carambole," Michael replied.

The countess's eyes lighted. "May I join you?"

More than one man groaned. "I'll just… ah… be heading to the drawing room," said Lord Tallant, sidling toward the door of the billiard room. "Em, you'll come with me?"

"Indeed not." His lady wife picked up a discarded cue, tossed it a few inches into the air, and snapped it in a neat overhand catch. "I've just arrived. Why would I want to fuss with a needle and thread when I could play billiards?"

"I myself have a great fondness for needle and thread," Hambleton said. "If you'll all excuse me,

I'll just..." He followed Tallant to the doorway and vanished through it.

In quick succession, the other men followed, muttering various excuses. Everett was the last. He rapped his knuckles on the edge of the table as he left, muttering, "Good luck, Wyverne. She's the only person I've ever met who can shoot as well as you."

When the door clicked closed behind them, Michael turned to face Lady Tallant, half-mystified, half-annoyed. He had been constructing a framework of camaraderie, and she had smashed it with her impatience to get a bit of male company for the women of the party.

To his surprise, though, she grinned at him. "I must say, my ruse worked remarkably well." She laid the cue on the billiard table. "I have no real desire to play—unless you do, Your Grace."

"What ruse is this?" Lady Tallant was known to be devoted to her husband, so this was not a flirtation. It must therefore be...

"Caro," Lady Tallant finished his unspoken thought. "Yes, I thought it was time I talked to you about her in private."

"I cannot imagine what you could impart to me that would be inappropriate for others to hear."

The countess raised one eyebrow. She was quite skilled at that expression. "Since you've no idea what I'm going to impart, that makes perfect sense. Why not hear me out? And if you're comfortable with having others hear it, then I'll apologize for breaking up your cheery game and I'll send all the men back in."

Michael considered. "I'm sure that won't be necessary. I would, of course, be delighted to hear whatever you wish to tell me."

Her other eyebrow shot up to join its mate. "I'm not sure how delighted you'll be, but I am glad for your time."

Lady Tallant rolled the cue under light fingertips, back and forth on the table. Now that she had gained Michael's full attention, she seemed uncertain how to make best use of it.

"She's not who you think," she finally said. "Caro, I mean."

"Perhaps not." Michael kept his voice noncommittal as he held his cue up to his eye and stared down its straight length. "Though that depends on who I think she is. I am sure you are not implying that she has a false identity."

"I am, actually."

Michael's fingers slipped on the cue, catching it right before it clattered onto the billiard tabletop.

The countess smiled. "Not in the sense that she's… oh, a pirate, or anything like that. But she's not exactly who she appears to be, either."

"A countess who holds the polite world in the palm of her hand?" Michael raised his own eyebrows, setting the cue down with nerveless hands.

"She's that, but much more too. Because everything she is, she created herself."

Michael studied Lady Tallant's expression. Her pale face was earnest, even beseeching under its coiled crown of auburn hair. She didn't look as though she were trying to trick him.

He unbent. "Please sit, Lady Tallant, if you are so inclined. And please explain yourself further."

A bit brusque, but the countess smiled at him with the same unsinkable good humor her husband possessed, poising herself at the edge of a leather-upholstered chair that looked far too large and masculine for her slim form. Michael sank into a chair a few feet away.

"I have known Caroline for more than eleven years," she began, then gnawed on her lip.

"I too knew her long ago," he prompted.

"Yes, exactly." Lady Tallant took a deep breath. "I hope you will not be offended, Your Grace—"

"Wyverne," Michael corrected. "I assure you, Lady Tallant, I am never offended by the truth. Please put your mind at ease on that account."

His companion nodded. "Thank you. Caro and I debuted together, as you know. Though she had no fortune and was not of noble birth, she was irresistibly lovely and charming."

"Yes," Michael said drily. "I recall."

Lady Tallant shot him a sharp look. "Yes," she echoed. "Well, then, perhaps you recall how admired she was?"

"Yes."

"How many men courted her?"

"Yes."

"It's the same way now. The *ton* is much fuller of followers than leaders, and those followers all wanted to pursue the maiden that had been deemed the most brilliant diamond of the year."

"Yes." Every time he agreed, he felt diminished.

She could have anyone, you know. He propped himself up with elbows on his thighs, his body a rigid right triangle.

Lady Tallant pulled a long breath through her nose; then she let it out in a quick sigh. "They only wanted her until you left London, Wyverne. And then it all went to hell."

Michael snapped upright so quickly that his teeth clacked together. "I *beg* your pardon."

"It's quite true. You can't be caught embracing a woman in that way, then leave her without a proposal."

For an instant, he thought she was talking of his recent journey to London, and he almost said *I did propose.* But now: they were caught in the past.

How entwined it had become with the present.

"I can. Did." He knit his brows. "I did, but I… shouldn't have?" It was hard to recall exactly what had happened, in the long-ago flood of lust and dread. To complicate matters, his long-ill father had died shortly after Michael returned to Lancashire. Once he became Wyverne, he needed no excuse to keep his distance from London.

Lady Tallant grimaced. "I don't know. Things would be different now, to say the least, if you had not acted as you did." She offered a thin smile. "While you were in town, there was much gossip that Caroline Ward was going to trap herself the heir to a dukedom. Though a few rumors swirled about you—well, you were still an heir to a dukedom, and you seemed amenable to Caroline."

"Yes." Surely the understatement of the century.

"Especially after you two were discovered—"

"Yes, I know." He didn't like to think of it: a surrender to passion, a dip into madness. Recently it had happened again on a much greater scale.

"When you put about that your father was ill, everyone understood that you would need to leave for Lancashire. But you did not propose to Caroline, and you never came back."

"No." A new refrain at last. "There was nothing for me in London."

The countess winced. "That became quite clear. It was clear, too, that none of the gossip about your courtship was true. That you had meant nothing serious when you kissed Caroline. Most people thought you had seduced and abandoned her."

Michael could not suppress a bark of surprise. "Hardly a credit to me."

"No, but it didn't matter. As you weren't there, and as you were titled and a man, there was little outcry against you. Caroline was the one who suffered. Everyone who had admired her charm now remembered that she was a penniless country girl, and they saw her as an upstart. She was all but ruined. She *would* have been if the old Earl of Stratton hadn't taken a fancy to her."

"Yes..." The word was a sigh. He hadn't known any of this.

Oh, he had known they kissed—*God, what kisses*. He had been shocked by the force of them, undone by his own desire for her. Never had he imagined—but then there were so many eyes surrounding them, such laughter at their discovery, and what had been a private revelation turned into a mockery. Caroline had laughed too.

Maybe she had been laughing from glee, thinking he would propose. Or maybe she had simply been young and startled. Maybe she had not turned on him.

But he had turned on himself. When the crowd dispersed, taking Caroline with it, he had slipped into the walled garden behind Lady Applewood's mansion. And there, quite suddenly, he had gone mad. A fit of shaking, lost mindlessness that robbed him of all his hard-won security.

Soon afterward he had walled himself away in Lancashire. He had known he tightened the reins on his own control, allowing none of the fleshly distractions that had consumed his father and that he himself seemed vulnerable to.

At this distance in time, and in his beloved home, it was difficult to recall the urgency with which he had torn away from London.

It was still more difficult to recall how he had managed to stop kissing Caroline once he had ever started.

He had not known how greatly Caroline was affected. It simply had not occurred to him, inexperienced dolt that he had been at the age of twenty-one, that passionate kisses came with expectations. He had never held any expectations himself that a woman such as Caroline would want him.

Until, one day, she did.

Lady Tallant's story was a lens, focusing an image of Caroline that had blurred into incomprehension. Now he understood her essential sweetness, sometimes washed over with bitterness; her insistence, earlier today, on maintaining her reputation. Her love of people who made their own way in life. The clergyman's daughter had bought herself respectability by marrying an old nobleman, and who was Michael to say whether that was too high a price?

"I understand," he told Lady Tallant.

Instead of softening, she shook her head so vehemently that a loose hairpin fell onto her lap. "No, you can't possibly. You've never suffered as she has."

"You might be surprised. It's not precisely pleasant to be called mad." He tried to make a jest of it, but no one in the world knew how true and deep the pain of it ran.

"I am sure it is not, Your Grace. But as I said, you weren't in London. You didn't have to listen to the talk. It has taken great courage for Caro to reclaim her place in society, to lead it with kindness and never to take revenge on those who hurt her."

Michael nodded, unable to muster a yes.

Lady Tallant rose to her feet, and Michael popped from his own chair. "Thank you, my lady. I am very glad you have reposed your trust in me."

She smiled at him. "I would not have had I not thought you worthy of it." She nodded toward the door. "Or of Caro. I've never seen anyone come close to touching her heart. She's my dearest friend, but she has shields even I've never seen past. But with you… I hope. That's all."

I hope. It was better than *despite*.

Though he had wounded Caroline so long ago, she had offered to help him anyway. Yet whether she intended to or not, she had certainly taken a perfect revenge on him. She had captured him, mind and body, then sent him packing.

A dish served with all the coldness of eleven years' wait. Well, some wounds could last a lifetime. He knew this; he had lived this.

Lady Tallant spoke softly. "Shall I call the men back, Wyverne? Or is there something you might wish to discuss with Caro instead?"

Michael heard her only dimly; his mind was clicking all the pieces into place. He would make this right. He would fix this situation. It was long past time.

"Yes," he said, already pressing at the door handle. "Yes, I must speak with her right away."

Twenty-three

La fée verte. That was what the French called absinthe, wasn't it? Caroline had never tasted it herself, but she knew of its ability to contort the world. If the world already seemed contorted, maybe absinthe would set it to rights.

Unfortunately, there was nothing stronger than sherry in her glass, so she must make do. She had already drunk more than she ought, enough that everything seemed muddled.

Or perhaps it was already muddled, and that was why she had drunk too much.

The men had trudged into the drawing room like whipped puppies. Considering Emily hadn't accompanied them back from the billiard room, Caroline suspected that was exactly what they were. She knew her friend's skill with a cue.

Michael hadn't come in with them, though. This probably implied some sort of a Secret Plot on Emily's side.

Hambleton perched himself on the arm of her chair, teetering on the frail wood support. He positively reeked of Spanish cigars.

"How was billiards?" Caroline managed to ask.

"Fair enough." He opened and closed his mouth a few times, then added, "Some were fair. I was more than fair."

"I am sure you were, Hambleton. We both know of your gift for games, do we not?"

Everett had found himself a glass of something spirituous upon entering the drawing room. "I myself was rather abysmal," he admitted as he approached Caroline. He tugged a chair over to sit at her side. "I seem to be better suited to observation than participation. A hazard of my occupation, probably."

On this rare vacation from his employer, a capricious baron, Everett was quite frank about being on the hunt for amusement—though with limited coin, his greatest pleasure must lie in mockery. At least he was willing to turn his wit upon himself.

Now, Caroline wished he would turn it to others. The guests were scattered around the drawing room, indolent as cats in the sun. Their complacence stifled her. They were *all* accustomed to doing what they liked.

Just as she'd said to Michael, though her badge of courage had somehow become an insult. It was not as though she wanted anything particularly noble. Right now, she wanted nothing so much as to drown her winding thoughts in the bottom of her glass.

She tipped it up, emptied it again.

"Do allow me," said Hambleton. He collected her glass and scurried off to refill it, a puppy, fetching and carrying.

She could no longer enjoy the simple pleasure of

having a man do a favor for her without wondering… *why?* Michael had led her to question it, and this ruined the spun-sugar fantasy that she and her puppies felt any real regard for each other.

With Michael, she never had to wonder about motive. He gave her frankness and the freedom to be frank with him in return. These gifts were greater than she had realized.

"Here you are, Caro." Hambleton thrust a glass before her eyes, which took a bleary instant to snap into focus. Her face required another instant to take on the correct expression of flirtatious pleasure.

"Thank you, Hambleton. If I'm not careful, I shall end by becoming quite intoxicated, and that would never do."

"Oh, wouldn't it?" He leered, just as she'd known he would, and she smiled dutifully in return.

Surely it should not be so much work being ornamental. Or maybe she just hadn't the spirit for it tonight.

Fortunately, Emily banged back into the drawing room then, humming a little under her breath. She looked smug, which usually meant she had dispensed advice with a heavy hand.

And behind her… Michael. Marching swiftly as a soldier, his expression set and stubborn.

Caroline suddenly felt apprehensive, and she sat up a little straighter in her tapestry-covered chair. Hambleton stood at her side. They both stared as Michael strode over to loom before Caroline.

"You are mistaken in your assumptions," he said without preamble.

She could not fathom what he was talking about—or what could have made Emily look so pleased with herself, and Michael so *dis*pleased. "I beg your pardon, Wyverne." A phrase he knew well.

His nostrils flared. He looked a little wild, like that German composer. Beethoven, was it? The same tousled hair, raked by an agitated hand; the same strong blade of a nose. From his neck down, though, he was utterly English in his ducal uniform of snowy linens, dark coat, and a green brocade waistcoat the precise color of his eyes.

Which were, right now, narrowed at her. He seemed not even to note Hambleton standing at her side or Everett seated only a few feet away. "You, and the rest of society, have been under the misapprehension that I abandoned you eleven years ago. I assure you, I regret that you were nearly ruined."

The room went quiet at once.

"I beg your pardon," Caroline said again. Her voice sounded wrong, shaped by numb lips.

"Though my departure was swift, it had nothing to do with you," he continued, his hands folded behind his back. "In truth, I was eager to leave London for reasons of my own. When my father died shortly thereafter, I was unable to return. I had no notion that my own family affairs would affect your social standing."

Oh, God. *This*. This, after all these years. This, in the presence of a dozen and a half members of polite society. Thirty-six ears that collected gossip just as honeybees collected pollen. Like honey, the best gossip never lost its flavor.

Her eyes flicked to Emily, who looked as stunned as though feral pigs had just run into the drawing room. So this wasn't part of Emily's Secret Plan. A small blessing.

Caroline emitted a bell of a laugh. No matter if it rang a little false. "We need not discuss something that happened so long ago. Surely it's of little consequence now."

The taut silence of the room snapped into whispers. Caroline's skin disobeyed her careful discipline, though she did not know if her face had gone bone white or berry red. She tried desperately to send Michael a message with her eyes.

Stop. Talking. Now.

Naturally, he misinterpreted. "But I can see that you are upset. Caroline, I cannot allow you to hold me in disfavor after all this time."

"I do not, I promise." There, that sounded a little better. Some of the numb-slapped feeling was ebbing, and sensation was returning to her lips. "*We are all* in your drawing room, *are we not*? *Everyone who is here* must count you as a friend."

He looked at her a little oddly, not picking up on the reminder that others were scattered all around them.

He pressed a thumb against his temples, shutting his eyes. She tried again. "Wyverne, you look a trifle ill. Shall we check the stillroom for something to help your head?"

Not her most subtle segue, but when he opened his eyes again, something seemed to have cleared. "Very well," he accepted with a curt nod.

Caroline excused herself, her head high as she

crossed the wide drawing room. The old memories clawed at her exposed back as she trod the patterned carpet, aware of Michael's presence behind her, aware of the eyes on her and the whispers that roiled.

Just as they had eleven years ago. Damn the man. She had tried to warn him. No doubt Emily had tried too. But there was never any warning Michael, nor any warning *for* him. He was as purposeful and blunt as a club.

And a club could easily destroy the subtler weapons Caroline had honed. Charm and graciousness were too fine and fragile to stand up to such a beating.

As soon as they entered the corridor outside the drawing room, she reached past him to press the door shut, then rounded on him. "You dratted duke," she hissed. "You have humiliated me in front of others."

His head jerked. "I—"

"If you say 'I beg your pardon,' I will not be responsible for my actions."

"Already I do not comprehend your actions. You appear to be angry when I meant only to offer you an apology."

She yanked at his sleeve, pulling him further away from the drawing room door, then hissed, "An apology? Is that what it was? I couldn't tell, as I never heard the words 'I'm sorry' come out of your mouth. Instead, there was a lot of tosh about you abandoning me and my complete insignificance to you, which, considering the ancient vintage of those events, surely did not need to be brought up with such urgency in front of *all your guests*."

Her voice was rising again, and she shoved open

the nearest door and pressed Michael's surprised body through the doorway. She followed him and kicked the door closed behind her.

One of the inevitable Carcel lamps sat on the mantel, revealing the dim shapes of the room: chaise longue, flat-cushioned chair, a wallpaper that loomed dark in the low light. They were in the dizzy-patterned Chinese room. It seemed an age, rather than the span of a single day, since Caroline had lounged in here with Emily, talking of Michael as though she had all the time in the world to make something of him, or of herself.

Instead, he had unmade her in a few swift instants—just as he had so long ago, with a kiss that changed her life.

"You don't even know what you've done." She stumbled over to the chaise and sank onto it, heavy and dull.

"Maybe it wasn't the most articulate apology, but an apology is what I intended."

Michael threaded his way through the clutter of furniture with aggravating certainty and seated himself on the fragile chair Caroline had occupied that morning. It creaked a protest as he settled onto it, leaning toward her. "Your friend Lady Tallant let me know that you had suffered greatly during your debut season, eventually undergoing what was practically a forced marriage. As the author, if unknowingly, of your distress, I sought to make amends."

Caroline sank into a recline and covered her face with her hands. "This is too ridiculous," she said through her fingers, then allowed her hands to drop.

"I'm sure you meant well, and Emily did too. But I am also sure that Emily did not intend for you to profess your desire to undo an ancient humiliation."

"I—"

"Don't. Say. It."

He let out a surprised cough. "I was about to say, 'I cannot be sure of her intention, because she herself was unsure of your feelings.' That is all."

"I don't think either you or Emily wants to know my feelings right now." She pushed herself up to a seated position. "I don't even know if I can express them in words, since I've never collected the vocabulary of profanity that most gentlemen enjoy." She sighed into the silence. "But you wouldn't know what to do with feelings anyway, would you? So let me respond to your ridiculous theories."

"I—"

"I will kill you if you say it. I swear it."

Michael's brows knit. "You are in some distress."

"Very astute, Your Grace."

She could see his body snap straight, as though her sarcasm had sliced him. His face moved out of shadow and into the dim lamplight.

He looked wounded. Good. She was tired of being kind and gracious, especially with him. "You want the truth, Michael? You are sure you cannot be offended by it?"

"Offended? No. Not by the truth. It is an essential foundation for any relationship."

"Very well. Here is the truth: you have absolutely nothing to do with my social standing."

He opened his mouth, then pressed his lips together.

Caroline was sure another *I beg your pardon* had tried to slip out. "How is that possible?" he said instead.

"In the same way it is possible for a clergyman's daughter to become a countess. Michael, that was my doing, not yours."

"You cannot have wished to marry the late earl. Your friend told me it was a choice you made only to avoid social ruin."

She bit her lip, hard, to stay a quick reply. When she answered, her voice was as measured as any lover of science could wish. "That was my choice too, though. I could certainly have retreated from society if I wished for the quiet country existence my parents led during their lives. But I did not wish that. I am also the niece of a baronet, and I grew up in the pocket of his household. I wanted a life in the highest circles of society, and I chose a marriage that would give it to me."

She let this sink in, then added, "They were my choices, Michael. It was my choice to kiss you, and it was my choice to marry the late earl. I do not apologize for these choices, and there is certainly no need for you to."

"But the way that society cut you after I left—I did not know that until this evening. I would have made the situation right."

"By doing what? Rushing back to London and offering me marriage?" She batted the ridiculous suggestion away with a flick of her hand. "Nonsense. Here is all that happened when we were young: we talked; we kissed; you left. And what happened a few weeks ago? We talked, we… kissed… and again, you left."

This blunt recital echoed Michael's style: logical, clipped, emotionless. Caroline could not bear to describe the spell cast over her nineteen-year-old self by twilight conversation on a terrace, by the deep gaze of young Michael Layward, who seemed to look into her soul. She had felt he *knew* her, and his kiss was exhilarating, like being swept into a fairy story.

But such stories always ended. Caroline made no mention of the desolation she had felt when he left London without a word to her. So much had he preoccupied her every thought that she did not at once realize that new invitations were addressed only to her cousin, that whispers followed her down the street. Oh, she knew the power and pain of whispers; maybe that was why she was now so determined to abolish them when she could. Even for Michael.

Especially for Michael.

In those quiet long-ago days when she realized Michael was gone, so was the respect in which society had once held her. But what would be the purpose of bringing that up now? She had put those events behind her. She had remade herself, gilded and bright, and she wanted none of this pitying shadow from him.

Quietly, she added, "Perhaps you are chafing at being misunderstood. But it's done, Michael. Your departure was for the best. We would have matched even more ill eleven years ago than we would now. *Don't say it.*"

His mouth pressed shut over the inevitable *I beg your pardon.*

Oh, that mouth; it was a poem, with its full swoop and determined curve. But all it could utter was prose.

He had no heart, only a ledger in which he had now totted up an old equation that he could not solve.

"I do not think we match ill." His face was grave, tired. He looked as alone as Caroline felt.

"You have no inkling," she said. "You clearly think you mean well, but you're only indulging yourself at the expense of others."

"Indulging myself?" He let out a sharp sound that was not quite a laugh. "Madam, look around you. I'm hardly living in sinful comfort here." His fragile chair creaked alarmingly as he shifted his weight.

"I'm not talking of surrounding yourself with silks and pillows and expensive brandy. I'm talking of how you do as you like, heedless of how it affects others. You've done that to your tenants for years; you did it to me tonight. You never consider whether the end justifies the means you employ."

Michael stood in a whip-quick movement and began to pace the small room in short, choppy steps. He wound amidst the furniture, falling alternately into the light and shadow of the lamp.

Restless, always restless. She felt still more tired just watching him. It was like talking to a caged animal; all he knew was his own tumult, not the tumult he left behind.

"I will ignore," he said in a voice as clipped as his stride, "your inaccurate use of the universal 'never.' I assure you that the *means*, as you put it, preoccupy me constantly." He booted a puff of a footstool out of his path. "I simply do not always foresee the end. As you once said, I am not a Gypsy prognosticator."

"Fair enough. But what I mean is that you don't

consider the cost. You simply blunder ahead with whatever it is you want to do. Perhaps you felt a twinge of guilt when Emily told you how I had been scorned over a decade ago. But did you consider nothing else? Such as the fact that referring to an old humiliation creates a new one? You eased your conscience, but now eighteen people might be whispering about my scandalous ways."

His feet bumped up square against the edge of her chaise, and he stared down the length of it, finding her face.

At last she had his full attention, and she pressed on. "Or to draw a parallel to the land you love so much—did you never consider that if you had simply continued the methods of your father, you might never have bankrupted your dukedom? That all your planned innovation might be foolhardy? Yes, you enjoy it, but there you have it once more: it's self-indulgent. It pleases no one but you."

He sank slowly onto the end of the chaise, like an empty suit of clothes being dropped.

Caroline folded her legs to get them out of the way of his heedless body. He didn't look at her or speak, and she suddenly felt a piercing guilt of her own. She had struck too hard at him, maybe, repaying a minor wound with a mortal one.

He fixed his gaze on the clear light of the lamp on the mantel. "Is that what you truly think of me? That I never consider the cost?"

She took a breath. "How can I think anything else after the carelessness with which you have treated me? Or Wyverne? All the polite world knows your family used to be wealthy, and now you are not. The problems cannot all have begun with the terrible winter this year. They have no doubt been burgeoning for years."

"They have." His voice was quite calm, almost spiritless.

She forced down a treacherous urge to clasp his hand, to take it all back. He wanted the truth from her, and he deserved it. For reasons good and ill. "Let us leave the subject of your dukedom. It's none of my affair. But I must make you understand, Michael, how I have built my life."

The room felt cold and dark around her, and she struggled to muster her thoughts into a neat structure. "I chose to make myself a countess, even though I knew what it would cost. I took the gifts I had been granted—youth and beauty and a fair amount of wit—and I sold them as dearly as I could. Even before I met you, I never expected to marry for love. I wanted a different sort of life, and I considered that above all."

Mostly, she had—until heedless Michael had caught her eye. Her lips. Her heart. She had not even thought about his title, only about him.

"When you left London without a word, I set such foolishness behind me and returned to the business of catching a husband. Yes, the matter had become urgent due to the rumors that swirled about my loose morals. But fortunately—maybe due to those very rumors—I caught Stratton's eye almost at once. I traded my youth for his coin, and in return, we were kind to one other."

Kind. As good a word as any for the nine years she'd

spent nursemaiding, housekeeping, opening her legs. Whatever her husband required so that his final years would be pleasant. In his final decline, she spoon-fed him and read to him. She had comforted him, and in return, perhaps he had even loved her. Perhaps, had forty years not separated their ages, she might have come to love him too.

"He left me a life settlement and a house in London," she added. "Under the terms of our marriage settlement, the money stays with me, not the Stratton earldom, even if I remarry. Thus the constant attention of the puppies." A thought struck her. "Maybe you and I are not so different, after all, both selling ourselves in marriage. But I've already sold myself once, Michael. I won't do it again. I have earned the right to live for my own pleasure at last. And you insult me by offering an apology for the life I have built."

As he had promised, he did not look offended. After a long moment of scrutiny, he said, "I do understand what you are saying."

She blinked. "Truly?"

"Yes. But what I am not sure of is why."

"Why what?"

His dark brows knit. "Why do you value a life in high society? What is the purpose of it all? You have criticized me for finding little pleasure in life, but that is because of the demands of my dukedom. You've called me self-indulgent for submerging myself in those same demands, for meeting them as I judge best. You, though—you have constructed your life solely to fulfill your own desires. Yet I do not believe you find much enjoyment in it."

He might as well have smacked her across the face. Caroline felt his words as a blow, nauseating and swift, and she wadded herself more tightly against the arm of the chaise.

He leaned against the low back of the chaise. His long hands fidgeted as he formulated his next thought. "I know you want to be needed. And I know you do not particularly care for the attentions of your suitors. So I wonder why you criticize me for burdening myself with obligations that prevent my own happiness when you are doing the same. They merely take a different form."

He turned his head to look her in the eye, and she was fully aware of him not as a man, but a duke: powerful and cold and inexorable. "What is the purpose of this independence you're so determined to protect? What good is it if you use it only to spend time you don't enjoy with people you don't care for? How is that different from the years of your marriage?" Leaning closer, he brushed her cheek with a questing fingertip. "What do you really want, Caroline? Do you know?"

The air grew heavy, her breathing shallow. She was folded into the corner of the chaise, with nowhere to escape as he caged her with questions, with the span of his hand. Her legs trembled, and she was glad she was seated. These questions were too weighty to be borne.

Oh, she could tell he was affected too. His pupils were wide in the low light, his lips parted. His fingertip whispered over her face like a butterfly learning the shape of a new flower. Even now, she could slip into his arms and drug him with the passionate response of his own body.

She felt suddenly as if she were nineteen years old again, young and brash, being offered what she thought she wanted. But she had learned better with the passage of time. At nineteen, she had known that her fondest childhood wish—all the ices she could eat—would only sicken her. Now, at thirty, she knew that Michael was no better for her than too many desserts.

"I don't want this," she lied, satisfied when he pulled away from her in an instant.

He stood calmly, smoothing his clothes. His face was inscrutable as he made a bow to her. "If you figure out your answers, my lady, do tell me. But until then, I shall be looking for a wife."

He had already turned toward the door before she could unlock her tongue for a reply. "You won't be looking anywhere near me. I'll begin my journey home tomorrow."

Petulant, maybe. But who would care?

Slowly, he turned on the heel of his boot, then folded his hands behind his back. "*I beg your pardon*," he said with deliberate clarity. "We have three days left on our contract. I had not thought you unreliable."

"Of course you did. Everyone does," she said. "And it was only a verbal pact; it was hardly the Ten Commandments. I've organized a house party for you, and I've spent a night with you. Surely that's more than an adequate commitment of time."

He lifted a hand to his temple.

"And please," she added in a voice of chilly splendor, "do not think to come after me. I don't imagine we have anything more to say to each other, do you? Not after all this time."

He wouldn't follow; she knew that. He never did. She only hoped to hurt a bit less if she could pretend he stayed away at her wish, not his.

He let his hand fall to his side. "You once insisted I not gainsay a lady's request. Therefore, my lady, I shall leave you to your plans. If you require any assistance, you need only to ask." He turned to leave. With his hand on the door handle, he paused. "I wish you a safe journey home, Caro."

The door closed behind him far too quietly considering the finality of what had passed.

She had got her way, as always. She had chastised him, cut the tie between them, gathered all her dignity about her in preparation for a splendid exit.

So why did she feel like an empty shell? Her life was lovely on the outside, but there was nothing of substance within.

He was right, wasn't he? Damn the man.

Twenty-four

Caroline was not left alone very long.

Only a minute after Michael left her, she heard footsteps and the *crick* of the stubborn door handle. She sat up straight, smoothed her hair and gown. He was going to apologize? Fine, she would consider it.

It wasn't Michael who entered, though. It was Stratton.

She gaped at him for an instant. "Damnation, Stratton, what are you doing here? I thought you on your way to London by now."

"But we have unfinished business, Caro." He took a step toward her, promptly tripping over the leg of a fussy little marquetry table.

She was not too proud to enjoy the sight. "No, we do not. I cannot be clearer, Stratton, that I will not marry you." She shook her head. "How did you even get into the house? And why?"

He dropped into the tottery chair Michael had abandoned. It groaned and wobbled gratifyingly under his weight. "I came through a window in some deserted room full of tatty old furniture, then started checking each room for you. When I heard your voice in this one, I waited outside until the duke huffed out."

"Huffed?" Caroline wanted to sigh. "Stratton, that doesn't matter. Look, you cannot keep coming to a house to which you have not been invited. This is not sane behavior."

"Yes, it is. You wouldn't talk to me any other way, and you must hear me out. I have a proposition for you."

"I don't want to hear it."

He looked smug. "I think you do, for it involves that duke you're so fascinated with."

Her fingers went cold. He couldn't have overheard, could he? About her night with Michael? Their supposed contract?

He might have. Stratton would do anything to get her money—even, it seemed, cross the country and commit multiple acts of trespass.

"I'll hear you out," she granted, "though I may yet have you thrown out the window you came in through."

"Very well." He looked far too pleased for a man threatened with defenestration. "It's a simple proposition. I know you're helping Mad Michael find a wife, and it's not going well. There's talk about you."

"You have no idea," she murmured. Evidently, Stratton had missed the lovely little scene in which Michael rehumiliated her in front of her friends.

"It wouldn't take much to whip up the scandal rags further. Not only caricatures, but stories. Poems. Bawdy songs. The press needs someone to mock, and it might as well be Wyverne. What do you think his chances of finding a wife would be then? Why, he'd be fortunate if anyone would even speak to him. And what would be the effect on you for hitching your wagon to a madman?"

She refrained from telling him she'd had the same concern. "Your point?"

He shrugged his sloping shoulders; the chair groaned again. "I have plenty of influence with the newspapers. For my wife, I would keep out any items that might affect her or her friends. For someone who is only a relation by marriage, however..."

Why, the rat. She could cheerfully poison him.

"Publish and be damned," Caroline said. "I shan't marry you to prevent you blackmailing me. Wyverne and I have both dealt with rumors before."

"My point exactly." He smiled. "This is not the first time Wyverne duped you, made a fool of you. That doesn't speak well for your judgment, does it? Or for your importance. If he wants nothing to do with you—*again*—perhaps there's no reason anyone else should either." He reached for her sleeve, running his finger inside the cap of fabric. "Besides the obvious. I suppose even a madman such as Wyverne can appreciate your physical charms."

She slapped his fingers away. "How vulgar you are, Stratton. Not even a title can give you the air of a gentleman."

"Nor does yours make you a lady."

"It made me wealthy," she said, "which is more than you can say."

He recoiled at that hit, and she used his silence to think. The most distasteful bit of Stratton's plan—if she could choose only one—was his willingness to attack and blight Michael's good name only to punish Caroline. This could not be permitted.

Kicking her feet up onto the end of the chaise that Michael had recently vacated, she felt as though he'd left some of his logic behind. Her thoughts snicked into order, like a box full of magic lantern slides. Just as clearly, she saw what to do next.

She slipped a cool smile over her features. "Here's something else you cannot say, Stratton: that the young women of London care for your opinion. You may hold the papers, but I still hold sway over fashion. If you and I both try to lead, the women of London are much more likely to follow me than they are to attend to trash printed by a jumped-up cit of a journalist." Leaning back, she folded her arms behind her head in utter unconcern. "In fact, if you threaten me or propose to me again, *I* shall turn all the young women of society against *you*. No more shall I excuse your behavior for the sake of avoiding scandal."

"You are the one who will be embroiled in—"

"Bosh," she cut him off. "If you attack my reputation, or Wyverne's, I shall starve you in your hunger after money."

Stratton's smile crystallized.

In truth, she was not sure whether she had such influence. She had seen the power of the scandal rags to hurt Michael's reputation, the wariness with which even the fringes of society had once regarded him. And she had not forgotten the faces once turned away from her, or the chill of being pushed to the edge of society.

But she had once told Michael the importance of showing someone how to respond. So with a sweet smile, with an imperious lift of her chin borrowed from His Grace, the Duke of Wyverne, she displayed a confidence she did not feel. "If you play this game, Stratton, you will not win. No wealthy young woman will speak to you, much less consider placing her dowry in your hands. The more you try to ruin me, the less likely it is that you shall get what you want."

The earl jerked to his feet. "You'd like to think so."

"I would indeed. And I do."

His eyes flicked around as though hunting inspiration for a reply. "You think you've finished with me, but I know your weaknesses."

Yes, you do. "I doubt it."

Glaring, he said, "I shall think on this matter and speak more to you of it later."

She sat up again and inclined her head with regal disdain. "You may do that, Stratton. But mind you, come when I'm at home to callers. If I ever see you coming in through a window of my London house, I might be so startled that I cry for the Watch to come cuff you. And who do you think would be caricatured in the scandal rags then?"

With admirable grace, Stratton spun on one patent-shoed foot and exited the room. Caroline wondered for a moment how he would get out of the house without being discovered, then decided she didn't care. Soon enough, he would develop a repulsive new plan to entrap her, and she would be required to dwell on his schemes them.

For now, she had many things to think on besides

the dubious escape strategy of her idiotic relative. First, she had staked her reputation to help Michael. *Again.* She had once told Michael that if he persisted in his social eccentricity, he could drag her down by association. Today, he might have done just that, in the small segment of polite society that currently whispered in his drawing room.

Surely, though, there would be no lasting damage from this night. Surely she would be able to salvage something of her reputation for charm, for appeal, for desirability. Some of her devoted puppies were here, after all, along with her loyal friends Lord and Lady Tallant.

Even so, the idea of remaining in Michael's home another day sickened her. Because she had defended him to Stratton—would always defend him to anyone—and now she knew why.

Oh, she wouldn't dare call it love. With all her fortune, she couldn't afford love. But it leaned that way, precariously close. She could accept flowers or jewels from a man without being touched at all, but seldom did men offer her vulnerability. Never had one given her his virginity.

She prized those gifts, prized him. And she wanted so badly to believe he prized her in return. But he wasn't giving her anything else. His honesty came coupled with too much disdain for her way of life; his vulnerability, with no love.

Since she could not bear to be without that, it was better that she return to London. She had settled Stratton well enough; Michael and Miss Cartwright seemed sure to reach an understanding soon. No one needed Caroline anymore.

In the morning, she would make her excuses to the party. Possibly she could say she needed to visit her cousin, Frances Middlebrook, who lived just outside London.

Yes, that was a good idea. She would say she'd had word from Frances, and she must depart at once. Whether Emily assumed the hostess role or the house party dissolved, Caroline didn't care much.

She didn't have to care about anything, did she? She was accustomed to doing what she wanted to.

Even if she didn't know what that was anymore.

Twenty-five

London was never at its best in autumn. Much as Caroline loved the City, she was willing to admit that.

Four weeks had passed since she left Lancashire, narrow weeks of vivid silks cloaking bleak moods. The silks and the moods were equally of her choosing, for she had spent those weeks at the home of her dear friend and cousin Frances and Frances's husband, Henry. Henry was an artist by training, and he and Frances took students together. Consequently, their cottage was always full of bright paintings, some lovely, some lamentable.

It had been a comforting visit, friendly and familial. Caroline admired the life her old friend had built. But there was nothing so cozy waiting for Caroline herself. The man who had offered her the chance to be needed… well, he needed nothing from her except her money. Since Miss Cartwright would do as well in that regard, he might even be married to her already.

She wished them well. Somewhat.

As Caroline's carriage rolled up to her narrow Albemarle Street house, she saw no color in the world but gray. The sky dropped cold drizzle, ruffling and spraying behind the wheels as they rolled down muddy streets. Her stuccoed house appeared the dull color of an old bone.

A footman let down the carriage steps for her, then helped her hop down under the cover of an umbrella held by her watchful butler, Pollitt. She could not help but remember the time she rode home with Michael, when she had much, much more to look forward to than a solitary evening in a poorly lit house.

Her heart didn't seem to beat in time with the City's tonight. Maybe because she had been gone for so long, or maybe because she'd left her heart behind her.

Such reflections were not helping her mood either.

Under Pollitt's sheltering umbrella, she bustled up her front steps and inside the house. Once in her entry hall, things seemed a bit more cheerful. Her chandelier—not Venetian glass like Lady Kettleburn's, but lovely all the same—cast its hot little lights down on her, brightening the tiles of the floor and the plaster and paper on the walls.

She looked around as though she were a purchaser seeing it for the first time. Narrow, stretching steps. Glossy marble and clean white trim. Blue plaster and dentated moldings.

She had arranged this house to her liking, and here she would probably live out her life. Surely there was nothing so melancholy about that. She had been alone before. It was nothing she couldn't handle.

"I'm for bed, Pollitt," she sighed.

Tonight she was too tired. She would handle it in the morning.

In the morning, Caroline awoke with renewed purpose. There was no need to be lonely just because she had fallen in love with a stubborn man who was a stranger to all feelings but honor and duty.

She covered her face with a pillow, as though she could smother her own feelings. But it only made her recall his presence in her bed. It made her wish to breathe him in, his scent as clean and sharp as desire itself.

Damnable man.

He would be difficult to forget again—more difficult than ever before, because he was twined through her wholly, body and heart and mind. But forget him she would. Eventually. She just needed the right distraction.

She tossed the pillow aside and slid from her bed, then padded across her room and retrieved her heavy red banyan from her wardrobe. She shrugged into it as she crossed to her writing desk.

There, lined up next to her writing paper, was the penknife Michael had used to cut her corset strings.

Caroline shook off this reminder, which brought with it an unwelcome plummet of the stomach. She rang for her maid, ordered a bracing amount of coffee and toast, and set to work.

An hour later, the coffee and toast were gone, and she had scrawled and sealed a tidy pile of notes. She nodded her satisfaction. Now she only needed to get ready for her grand new plan.

At two o'clock that afternoon, Caroline Graves, the dowager Countess of Stratton, stood in her drawing room awaiting her callers. She had taken great care with her appearance. Her hair was a neatly coiled mass of honey-gold; her dress was elegant but demure, a Paris-green silk with a high waist, beaded bodice, and long sleeves trimmed with gold lace. With emeralds at her ears and around her throat, she knew she looked regal. Respectable. Ready to conquer.

When she heard a tread on the stair, she lifted her chin and smiled her brightest, most welcoming smile.

In the doorway appeared the fair head of Lady Kettleburn—wife to a much older baron, hostess of that fateful ball at which Michael and Caroline had discovered one another. Gowned in a silk of her favorite pale blue shade, the baroness looked as frosty as the weather. "How do you do, your ladyship?" The stiffness of her greeting was another icicle.

"Come, none of this formality." Caroline took the younger woman's hand. "As you're first to arrive, Lady Kettleburn, you must pick the best chair. I can tell you *not* to choose that spindly beech chair in the corner. It will positively reshape your spine."

The baroness permitted herself a small smile, and Caroline pressed her advantage. "I've heard that you are fond of a lemon tart, as am I. My cook is rather vain about her abilities with pastry. Won't you give one a try?"

Today Caroline had taken as much care with the room as with her own appearance. Instead of the customary hothouse blooms from her callers, every surface had been covered instead with eatables—trays of pastries, small sandwiches—all arrayed on her favorite Sheffield plate tea service. There was something very welcoming, she thought, about a groaning platter of food.

By the time Caroline had finished plying her first guest with confections and assuring the young lady she had selected the best chair, Lady Halliwell had arrived.

"Darling!" Caroline called. "You are wearing peach again. How lovely you look." Lady Halliwell was too round of feature for true beauty, but she was cheerful, which was quite as good. Caroline did not exaggerate the effect on that lady's appearance; the light color warmed Lady Halliwell's hair and brought a lovely rose into her cheeks. As this new guest beamed and air-kissed Caroline's cheek in greeting, Caroline marveled at the ability of a simple compliment to make not only one person happier, but two.

One after another, women arrived, filling the drawing room not with the booted feet and raucous laughter of suitors, but with demure low voices and the costly click of bugled trim on lacquered furniture.

This was Caroline's grand plan: she would rediscover the joys of friendship. As much as possible, she would surround herself with kind and delightful people. In time, they might assuage her feeling of loss as substitute suitors never could.

For Michael was right; her puppy suitors brought her no real pleasure. Instead, there was a pleasure in being needed within the scope of a drawing room. Keeping conversation flowing, introducing new acquaintances, making sure every lady had her favorite sweet and beverage. If Caroline made sure they had a wonderful time, they would come back. They would invite her to their homes too. And eventually, she might end with friends. Not just friendly acquaintances, but people who truly cared about Caroline herself, as Lady Tallant did.

Well, about Caroline and about her cook's lemon tarts.

If there was some initial awkwardness between nodding acquaintances as the drawing room filled, cup after cup of sweetened tea and a few amusing anecdotes about the rigors of travel to and from Lancashire helped to honey over any rough spots.

"And then," Caroline concluded, leaning forward with just the right air of intimacy, "the innkeeper *let the coachman into my room*, as though we were… well, you know." She rolled her eyes dramatically, and Augusta Meredith giggled. Even Lady Kettleburn pressed her lips together to smother a laugh.

Jovial Lady Applewood chuckled. "It wouldn't be such a bad thing if the coachman was good-looking, would it? You being a widow, I mean, rather than an unmarried girl." Again, she laughed. "Do you all want to hear a story that will *really* curl your hair?"

The fifteen minutes allotted for a visit of mere courtesy were long past, Caroline noticed. Yet her guests made no move to go, as the marchioness began a bawdy tale about the France of forty years earlier, in which she had slipped away from her mother to explore Paris and found herself, a maiden, alone in the Moulin Rouge.

"I surely would have been ruined," Lady Applewood continued, her plump bosom jiggling within the velvet casing of her gown. "But for Wyverne, that is." She pressed a hand to her heart and allowed herself a soft sigh.

Caroline's own heart flipped. "Wyverne?" Just in time, she remembered to lift her brows in an expression of mild curiosity.

"Oh, yes." The older woman winked broadly at the room. "Not the present duke, of course, but his father. Such a libertine, he was, and so handsome! Wyverne saved me from ruin that day and brought me safely back to my mother. When we were back in London, though, Wyverne and I met often, and we never quite shook the topic of my ruination." Her cheeks grew pink under their powder.

Caroline laughed along with the others, but a question pressed at her lips. She was grateful to Miss Meredith for asking it first. "The present duke isn't much like his father, then?" Under her copper hair, Miss Meredith blushed.

"He's the fair spit of his father in face and form." Lady Applewood's hands fluttered, fanning herself. "My, yes—both such handsome devils. But young Wyverne is much more serious-minded, not nearly the ladies' man the old duke was."

"Oh, I don't know about that." Lady Kettleburn leaned in as though ready to impart a secret to the whole room. "Wasn't he hunting himself a wife with your help, Caro?"

All eyes turned to Caroline. Her mouth dried under the sudden scrutiny, but she tossed off a careless laugh. "Yes, that's right. But it's hardly improper to search for a wife, is it?"

"Did he marry, then?" The baroness cocked her proud head.

"If he hasn't yet, he will soon." Caroline smiled with frozen lips. "An heiress to an industrial fortune who shares his interest in modern improvements. They'll deal well together, I am sure."

"He was growing you a special flower, wasn't he?" Lady Halliwell clasped her plump hands together over her peach-clad bosom, her starry eyes wide.

"That didn't work out, I'm sorry to say. It couldn't survive in London." An apt summation of their entire relationship.

But if Michael could not survive in London, she would. She hid a throb of anguish under a smile, offering a plate around. "More lemon tarts?" Pastry never failed to divert a conversation, and her guests swooped on the sweets.

Just as Caroline settled herself in her chair again, she heard the tread of approaching footsteps on the stairs.

"Expecting someone else, Caro?" Lady Applewood raised her eyebrows. "If that's Lady Tallant, I shall have to scold her for being late. She shan't get a lemon tart."

Caroline's brow furrowed. "It can't be Lady Tallant. She's not yet back in London."

Darling Emily, to remain at Callows for the rest of the house party, serving as hostess for Michael's guests. She had sent Caroline a letter to that effect during Caroline's visit to her cousin Frances, though the letter had been irritatingly short on further details—just a simple "things are progressing as planned," and a reassurance that Caroline need not worry herself.

And a request for the date of Caroline's return to London.

Caroline had sent Emily the date and her thanks. And she *had* worried—but not enough to return to Lancashire.

No, she had been sent packing as surely as Stratton had, though at least she'd been permitted to set the time of her departure herself. When a man told one he was determined to sell himself in marriage, there was no more reason to stay with him, or to hope for anything to be different.

"That sounds like the tread of boots," said Augusta Meredith. "A *man* would not intrude on our time together, would he?" Bless the girl, she looked eager.

Caroline realized in a flash who it must be. *Stratton*. Stratton, who would see a roomful of women to harass. Perhaps he meant to begin some rumor before a crowd.

There was no help for it; she would simply have to murder him.

"If you'll pardon me," she said to the room at large. She rose to her feet and sidled toward the fireplace, where she could easily lay her hand on the poker.

Not that she would *really* kill him. But if she waved a poker at him, he would surely retreat. And then she'd have to smooth things over with her roomful of startled guests.

She would need a lot more lemon tarts for that. Drat.

She waited for the door to open, her hand hovering in readiness over the poker.

Her butler, Pollitt, poked his narrow head into the room. Caroline deflated, sagging against the carved marble of the chimneypiece.

"My lady, a gentleman wishes an audience. I told him you were not at home to male callers, but he was most insistent."

"Throw him out the window," Caroline muttered. The ever-tactful butler pretended not to hear her. "Very well, Pollitt. Show him in. Between the lot of us, surely we can dispose of him." She looked around the room with a we're-all-in-this-together smile, bracing herself with her guests' friendly expressions.

A swift drumbeat of boots up the stairs, and the door was flung open again. *Stratton*, she was ready to say.

But it was not Stratton. It was Michael.

And he looked furious.

Twenty-six

LADY APPLEWOOD GAVE A TRANSPORTED SIGH. Augusta Meredith blushed again. Caroline froze.

She was standing in the middle of a roomful of women, all set to tongue-lash Stratton, and in came Michael instead. Michael, whom she hadn't seen for a month.

Michael, who looked... oh, so delicious. So dear and unexpected and familiar and sudden that she had to lock her knees so they wouldn't wobble.

"Your Grace," Caroline murmured. Somehow she felt her way back to her chair and sank into it.

She had forgotten nothing of him since she last saw him, yet she gulped in every detail of his appearance now. His hair was a bit longer, disheveled as though he had been running his fingers through it. His skin was more tanned, no doubt from hours outside. His clothing was scrupulously fashionable, though. A tailored coat stretching over those broad shoulders; white linens intensifying the olive of his tan, the green of his eyes, the darkness of his hair. He looked mysterious and stalwart, a wild creature trapped in superfine and starched linen.

He also looked as though he was ready to knock heads together.

He nodded curtly at her, at the roomful of women. "Ladies," he said by way of greeting. "Lady Stratton, I need to speak with you." He folded his hands behind his back and glared, as though waiting for the world to obey him.

"Please do so, then, Your Grace." She smiled prettily. "I am at home to callers, as you see, and quite willing to entertain another."

"Yes, I do see that." The heel of one boot ground into the vine-patterned carpet. "Very well. I suppose this is of a rather public nature, at that."

He pulled a creased paper from the tail pocket of his coat and handed it to Caroline.

She recognized it at once as a caricature from the latest issue of London's favorite scandal sheet, *The Wagging Tongue*. A tawdry drawing depicted Michael, wild-haired and wild-eyed, clothing askew, prostrating himself at the feet of a young lady. She was waving a good-bye, holding the arm of a smug-faced man shaped suspiciously like a ninepin.

I shall be Ruined If You leave Me My Dear, said the prostrate caricature through a frothing mouth.

I shall Be Ruined if I Stay with you Mad Michael, quoth the young woman.

The ninepin-shaped man had the cherubic face of Stratton, with an unmistakable leer. *This Ruin shall be the Making of Me*, he spoke behind the cover of his hand.

"How vulgar." Caroline handed the caricature back to Michael. "I am sorry for it, Your Grace. I had not realized you were still a target of the press."

To her surprise, his mouth pressed into an expression of unwilling humor. "I will probably always be a target, but that is not why I show this to you. Rather, I ask you to note that your relative has eloped with the bride you chose for me."

Every china cup in the room clinked into its saucer; then followed a sharp silence. Rather like their confrontation in the Callows drawing room—only this time, the humiliation was not Caroline's, but Michael's.

As always, she yearned to offer comfort. "Again, I am sorry. Defenestration is far too good for Stratton."

She gestured around the room, to indicate to everyone that no, nothing scandalous was occurring, and they might as well all take part in this conversation. "A few minutes ago, Your Grace, we were discussing your interest in finding a wife. You must be disappointed by this… unexpected development." That sounded more diplomatic than *Stratton's contemptible act of betrayal.* "But I assure you of my continued friendship, as I am sure all these ladies do. I shall try to help undo the wrong done to you, and perhaps others will too."

Caroline caught Lady Applewood's eye, knowing the marchioness would nod eagerly. That lady's fondness for the late duke would certainly lead her to assist his son.

And where a marchioness and countess led, the rest of the drawing room followed, just as Caroline had hoped. The whispers that followed seemed sympathetic rather than furtive; Michael had become the wronged party, to be pitied rather than censured.

But, contrary man, he had no use for pity. He held up a hand to silence the room, then pressed it to his temple. "That is not necessary." He shut his eyes for a moment. "I have allowed others to choose for me long enough. Rather, my lady, I have called to inform you that I shall choose for myself from this point forward."

Were it not for the high back of the chair in which she sat, Caroline rather thought she would have collapsed. So, he had come all this way to reject her help. To again prove to the world that he had no use for her.

Mindful of the room full of women taking in her every word, she said only, "Of course, Your Grace. That is to be expected. I wish you all the best."

She held out her hand to shake his in farewell, wondering how quickly he would leave and how long before she might clear the drawing room of her other callers. The fewer witnesses to her unraveling self-possession, the better.

Lowering his hand from where it pressed at his temple, he took her fingers in his. Instead of releasing them after a correct second, he pressed them. "You are mistaken in your assumptions," he murmured. In his eyes was a wicked gleam.

Caroline's face went hot. "I… what? What do you assume that I assume?" How articulate.

"I have already made my own choice. Would you have me announce it now?"

She tugged her fingers free from his, then folded her hands primly in her lap. "You may do as you like, Your Grace."

"Of course I may," he muttered. "I'm a dratted duke. Did you not say so once?"

She managed a tight little smile. "I said a lot of things."

His brows lifted. "You are certain about this? All right, then."

With a deep breath, a settling of his feet on the carpet, he turned to the room at large. Behind his back, Caroline saw his fingers lace bloodlessly tight, though his voice was cool and steady. "Ladies, I intend to propose marriage to Lady Stratton."

He turned to Caroline with an expression as bland as though he'd stated that the weather was to be found outside, or that Lancashire lay to the north of London.

Caroline froze. Again, he spoke the words she craved. And again, she could not fathom what motivated him to propose marriage. She wanted, in equal parts, to throw herself into his arms and to chuck a vase at his head.

She cracked through the icy chill and forced herself to stand. "Let us discuss the matter later, Your Grace."

"Nonsense." The bubbling voice of Lady Applewood rang out. "It's past time we leave you to your conversation, Caro dear." The marchioness rose to her full, miniscule height. "We have far outstayed our welcome, but only because we've had such a delightful time. Isn't that so, my dears?"

She waited until the other women chorused their assent before adding, "Such a lovely afternoon. You *will* have us over again, won't you, Caro? And I *must* get your receipt for lemon tarts. My cook can't hold a candle to yours. Wyverne, it is a *pleasure* to see you."

"Thank you, Lady Applewood," Caroline fumbled.

"I would be delighted to have you call again. I shall send out notes to you all."

"You need have no doubt that I shall accept." And with another wink, that cheerful lady made her way to the door.

Michael's eyes widened as the marchioness passed behind him, and Caroline feared very much that Lady Applewood had patted him on the bum.

That delectable arse. Caroline had told him of its wonders.

One by one, the other women made their good-byes, with curious glances or knowing smiles. What they thought they knew, Caroline couldn't imagine, but she met everyone's farewell with a gracious reply; she parried every glance with a smile. She promised the receipt for lemon tarts to no fewer than four people, and when they all left, she was satisfied that they had been well enough amused to come again.

She'd made a beginning at making friends. She had a winking ally in Lady Applewood. And now she was alone with His Grace, the Duke of Incomprehensibility. Again, he pressed at his temple; his mouth made a dash between two parentheses of stern creases.

"You look quite melodramatic," Caroline said. "Are you well?"

"You keep me in unbearable suspense, Caro."

She sank into her chair again. "Do sit, Michael, and tell me what has brought you here. If your motivations are the same as previously—namely, that you wish for my money—my answer must be the same as well. Simply because Miss Cartwright has run off with Stratton does not mean I will consent to fill her role."

She was rather impressed by her ability to construct a complete sentence over the pitiful heavings of thwarted hope.

"You wish to understand my motivations?" Michael creased the thin paper of the caricature with great deliberation, his face an unreadable composition of angles. He drew up a chair near Caroline and folded his long body into it. "They are the purest. But I must explain everything, or you won't believe me."

He sank back in his chair. His eyes closed, and Caroline could see purple shadows beneath them. He had been sleeping poorly again. So, everything was just as it had always been: his burden of responsibility, his impatience.

The way her heart pounded, wishing he would care for it.

His eyes opened to regard her. "The name, *Mad Michael.*" He waved the folded caricature as gingerly as he would a dead mouse, then slipped it back into a pocket with as much distaste. "It's why I came to London eleven years ago, and also why I left so quickly. You see, I wanted to prove my reputation wrong, but I ended by proving quite the opposite. Since my youth, I've been thought eccentric. I was sent home from school for tinkering and solitude, and at that time, I suppose, my father turned against me."

A pause succeeded this speech, so long that Caroline finally said, "I am sorry to hear it. But is that all?"

Michael's head snapped back. "Is that *all*? It was enough to blight years of my life."

"I don't mean to belittle the experience," Caroline hurried to explain. "But from what I've heard of your father, he was flighty and dissipated. I should rather regard any criticism from him as a mark in your favor."

Michael let out a startled laugh. "I had not regarded the situation in that light."

"It's how I choose to regard it."

He slanted a look at her. "Thank you for that. I assume, then, you have heard a few rumors about my father."

"More than a few. I know he had a taste for female company."

"That and any other expensive amusement you can think of. Drinking, gambling, horses, mistresses, and... well. You understand. After my birth, my mother was quiet and sad, and she soon dwindled away. My father was then free to leave Lancashire—and me—behind, living a profligate life in London and the great cities of Europe, at least until war closed the Continent to him. He scarcely gave a thought to his dukedom beyond the rent deposits into his accounts, and when those began to decrease, he borrowed to make up the difference. His charm was always enough to convince the polite world that Wyverne was as sound as ever."

"Ah." Caroline knew full well the ability of a bloated charm to hide a lonely truth.

Michael's voice turned hollow. "In temperament, I was as different from him as one could imagine. On those rare occasions he returned to Callows, he communicated his—let us call it disappointment. He could not understand why a future duke would waste time with books and tinkering when the world was full of feasts and drink and wenches."

"Then he was a fool." A vivid picture sprang into

Caroline's imagination: a dark-haired boy bent over a magic lantern; a brash and bitter man with grass-green eyes fuming behind him.

Michael gripped the arms of his chair tightly. "Maybe I should defend his memory, but I cannot. He returned to Lancashire permanently, to live in the dukedom to which he had laid waste, only when he developed the French disease."

Syphilis. Caroline shivered despite her long sleeves. "How dreadful." She had heard horrid tales of that disease, eating away its victims from the inside out, driving them to physical and mental ruin.

"It was, rather," Michael said with a touch of black humor. "In his decline, I believe my father went mad himself. He admitted none of his own wrongs, instead raving about the numerous ways in which I had disgraced him."

A muscle twitched in his jaw. "I tried to be a good son—a good man—to prove I would make a good duke. And so I traveled to London, but once I arrived, I knew not what to do. There was nothing I could build. No one I could help. I hated being the object of any curiosity, certain as I was that I was being judged by society and found wanting."

His shoulders hunched; then he forced them square. "In the City, I made myself circulate in polite society, though dreadful headaches began to plague me. Still, I walked the narrow edge of propriety; I never took refuge in the laudanum or fleshpots to which my father became enslaved. But when I met you, I forgot my careful vows. You were so different from anyone I had met. Full of delight, kind and friendly, beautiful inside and out. You were… irresistible."

Her hand drifted up to touch her lips; the memory of their stolen long-ago kisses seemed to press hot on her mouth. "I found you irresistible too."

Irresistible enough to follow him about from ball to ball, to drift onto the terrace at Lady Applewood's house and surrender her dignity into his strong hands. Heedless of her reputation, of anything but her fascination with that harsh, beautiful man. "Yet how irresistible could you truly have found me, Michael? We were caught in an embrace, yet you left. For eleven years, I heard nothing from you."

"I heartily regret that." He grimaced. "Yet even now, I do not know what I ought to have done instead. You have called the idea of a proposal ludicrous, and—"

"Never mind that," Caroline said. "Please. I was impolite."

"Perhaps, but you were honest. At twenty-one, I was a fool. I did not know what to do, and I had a fit of panic. It felt like madness, the madness I had never quite accepted I possessed."

"Panic? Such as the… episode… you had in my bedchamber?"

"The only two such I have ever had," he confirmed. "I became distressed at my own loss of control, and I left London at once with my father's ill health as an excuse. Much to my surprise, he did soon succumb to his ailment. So then I was Wyverne."

"And you had no need of London then," she

murmured. "You told me you left nothing behind that you cared for."

"That was not strictly truthful. But my time in London, far from being a triumph, became a humiliation. I was relieved to take on the responsibilities of a dukedom—not only to protect it and save it from ruin, but to prove to myself that I could do something right in a world with which I'd always felt out of step. I wanted to be a better duke than my father ever imagined, or ever was himself.

"The only problem was the force of my desire for you. It had proved to me that perhaps I wasn't so different from him as I thought, that lust was strong enough to overpower reason, and that I must bottle it tightly and control it if I were to serve my dukedom well."

"You *have* served it well." And the last time she'd seen Michael, she'd accused him of wrecking Wyverne for his own amusement when the deed had been his father's. "I should not have doubted you."

Even so, she was not sure what he meant by telling her all this or what he truly wanted from her. Was it an apology? An excuse? Or a long-delayed atonement?

"I have tried my best," he said. "I have given my dukedom my whole self, wholeheartedly. I have become accustomed to ignoring untidy emotion in favor of logic and work."

"I know you have." He had unlocked all his secrets for her now. At last, she understood him, understood the unique snap and tug of desire and duty that shaped him.

Why she had once thought this would make her stop loving him, she couldn't fathom.

His hand lifted to his temple, then fell to his lap. "As a wise woman once told me, I have made my dukedom my whole life. And in doing so, I have made it more burdensome. I have stripped the pleasure from existence."

Caroline's heart thumped. "Are you referring to me as a wise woman? I must write this in my journal."

He lifted his brows.

"Yes, I'm teasing you," she said.

He smiled. "I thought you were. And here is what else I think: that I have denied myself much that would make the burdens of life lighter. You are right, that I should not ask anyone to share a life I do not enjoy.

"In truth, I do enjoy it. I am honored to be a duke, to provide employment for my tenants and care for the land. But I don't want to be *only* a duke."

"What do you want?" Her breath caught on the question. When he had asked it of her, she had no answer.

"I want to marry you."

Twenty-seven

Somehow, Caroline kept her features serene. "I can't accept. I just cannot. I will not marry you for money."

"I'm not asking you for any such thing."

He stood, began to pace. "When you confronted me at Callows, I cannot deny that your opinion of me wounded me. You saw my efforts to save my dukedom as signs of failing in my character."

"I'm so sorry."

"Given time to parse your words," he continued, feet still marking a neat series of steps, "I realized that you were correct in some respects. Namely, that I was using the methods I preferred—and *only* those—to try to pull Wyverne back to solvency. I invested too much in untried innovation and not enough in the old ways that had worked for so long. I gave too much to Wyverne's future but not enough to its present."

He halted, turned on one heel to face Caroline. She felt very small as he looked down at her, magnificent and proud. "I'm not saying that the old ways will work forever, Caro. Times are changing. But I realized if I pursued only steam power and irrigation, I was fighting the land, and my tenants would soon be driven from it into the factories Miss Cartwright loves so dearly.

"Some of them might choose that life after all," he mused. "But anyone who wants to stay shall have the means to make a good life. You see, in excavating one of the canals, we found a new seam of coal."

Caroline felt a step behind. "Coal? But you've always known you had coal on your land."

Michael sank back into his chair. "Yes, but it's never been worth the trouble to ship it off the estate before. Coal may be plentiful in Lancashire and needed in London, but the cost won't bear transporting it overland." His mouth tugged up on one side. "I owe a bit of thanks to Miss Cartwright. She was determined to understand my financial status, and she inquired in such detail into the coal reserves that I ordered some more exploration and found that a known seam of coal extends into my network of irrigation canals."

"But if the cost won't bear transporting it, as you said?"

"Not overland. But by water, it will. Because of the cold weather, coal prices are high in the cities this year. If my canals are widened and graded, they will take on enough water for transport. And then the coal can be shipped: water to water, canal to river to sea."

Caroline's head felt very full. "Your canals." She choked out a laugh. "Incredible. Your canals have saved you after all."

"My canals and the long winter. But eventually the weather will thaw and the sun will come out. If the price of coal drops again, then the canals can be used for bringing fields back to life. And if I am blessed beyond deserving, then all of my plans will bear fruit."

"Your creditors have stopped dogging you, then?"

"Indeed they have. It is amazing what wonders may be worked by the promise of a steady income from a known commodity. As soon as I arrived in London, I met with Weatherby and the other bankers and laid out my plans. They were satisfied enough by my sanity and my reason," he said drily. "Bringing Wyverne out of debt will not happen in a year, or even in a decade. But perhaps not much longer than that. It *will* happen."

"So you don't need to marry for money anymore," she said faintly.

"I do not." His face was solemn. "And I know that you *would* not. The last time we spoke, in the Chinese room at Callows, you stated that you considered our acquaintance at an end and that I had nothing more to hope for. I was prepared to cut all ties with you."

"I'm sorry," she blurted again. So much to apologize for; so much that had gone wrong.

"Do not apologize. Or rather, I will apologize too. We both spoke harshly, and I'm sorry for my part in that." A faint smile touched his lips. "Then an unlikely source retrieved my hope. Stratton."

"Stratton did something helpful? I can scarcely credit it."

"Unintentionally, I assure you. He found me just after he left you in the Chinese room. I had thought him on his way back to London, so I was not precisely pleased to see him again. I was pleased, though, by what he had to say."

He leaned forward, holding her gaze. "He was adamant that I go to you, for the sake of your reputation, and convince you to cease your matchmaking efforts on my behalf. He was in a rage over the fact that you showed more loyalty to me, a near stranger, than you did to him, your own kin by marriage."

"I would show more loyalty to a hatstand than I would to Stratton."

"And that hatstand would deserve it more, I'm sure. Regardless, I gathered that you had defended me, spoken warmly about me—and that you'd somehow angered Stratton. This, I thought, was all promising evidence that you weren't so set against me as you had indicated."

"I was only hurt, Michael. I was never set against you."

"So I hoped." His fingers flexed, then stilled. "So I hoped."

Though gray and chilly as ever outside, the drawing room seemed to warm. "Perhaps Stratton isn't completely worthless after all," Caroline said.

"That will be for his wife to determine and to deal with. Fortunate Miss Cartwright—that is, the new Lady Stratton. I gather she could not resist the idea of leading a nobleman about by golden reins."

"No, I imagine not." Caroline wanted to sigh. "Stratton cares for money above all else; he will not underestimate her worth. I believe he will make her a devoted husband."

Miss Cartwright had been willing to sell herself—or to be more accurate, to buy Stratton. But such devotion, based on pounds and pence, held no value for

Caroline. She wanted a devotion that was difficult to earn, from someone who was reluctant to trust. Someone strong enough to venture across a nation alone and strong enough to admit his faults.

Strong enough to match her love? Hope trembled like a hummingbird, caged.

"So. Now you know the full truth of it," Michael said. "Why I acted as I did eleven years ago, why I have become the man I am now. I have a cold, run-down dukedom and a backbreaking quiver of responsibilities. I know you love London, and you have many friends here. I can't offer you that sort of elegance or ease. I'm stubborn and proud, and I don't make decisions lightly. I say the wrong thing much more often than not."

"Yes, I know all of that." She tilted her head. "Is a declaration lurking somewhere within this recital, or are you trying to make me boot you out the window?"

With a dry laugh, he said, "I'm not making a very good case for myself, am I? Perhaps I cannot. But I will never be quit of you, Caro, even if you're quit of me. It's not in me. I love you."

"You love me." She had wanted to hear it so long and expected to hear it so little, that the sounds hardly made sense in her ears. "You love me?"

"I do. I offer you my heart. I don't know if you've any need for it. But if you'll allow me the three days that were left on our old contract, I'll try to convince you of my feelings."

Slowly, Caroline shook her head, as a sweet bubble of joy filled her. "I won't listen to you because of that silly contract, Michael. I cannot be bought. Only given." She allowed herself a moment of tantalizing silence, to study the look on his face. He had stilled, every muscle and fiber waiting for more.

"You're a brilliant man," she continued, "and yet you overlooked something quite obvious. Michael, I never wanted anything from you but love. Not eleven years ago, when I had nothing to offer you but my heart. Not now, either. I turned down your proposals because I didn't want to be courted for my money. I wanted to be courted for… well, *me*. I wanted to be needed."

He was blinking rather more often than usual. "I did tell you you'd be needed if you were a duchess."

"Oh, hang your tenants." She bounded to her feet, her whole body humming discordantly. "Not literally, of course. But don't you see the difference? I can't marry to help nebulous legions. I'm far too selfish for that. The tenants of your dukedom don't care who your duchess is; any woman would do as well."

"No one could do as well as you."

She smiled. "Ah, that—that's what I wanted to hear."

"It's true."

"It's proof of your faith in me," she replied. "Faith, and a kind view of me despite my shallowness and flaws."

"You are the kind one. One of the kindest people I have ever known." He reached out, caught her hand in his long fingers, and tugged her until she was within inches of him. One more tug, and she lost her balance and sank onto his lap.

Strong arms wrapped around her, and his chin snugged into the angle of her neck and shoulder. "I had not understood how you could take me to your bed but decline to marry me. Fool that I was, I thought you had cheapened the experience when you really refused to set a price on it."

"Yes," was all she could manage. His cheeks, chin moved against her skin with his every word. She was aware of his mouth, so near her skin—that mouth that had devoured her own, that had kissed her body.

He pulled in a deep breath. "Do you accept my proposal, then?"

"You haven't proposed."

"Haven't—" Michael leaned back, goggling at her. "Caro, I have proposed to you three times."

"No, only twice before today, and those proposals were all logic and transaction. As for today, you said you *intended* to propose, but you haven't actually said the words. I would have remembered."

"I see." A smile played on his lips. "I must do the thing properly, then. If you'll rise?"

He pressed her to her feet, then slid from the chair and dropped to one knee. He took her hand in his own roughened one. "You will not be offended by the truth?"

She looked down at him, this kneeling duke, with his odd, deliberate ways. There was simply no one else like him, and she loved him for that. "I might. But I want it anyway."

He worked shaking fingers between hers, then gave a sharp nod. "Here it is. Eleven years ago, you married an old man who wanted to cheer his last years with a nubile young wife. I have no expectation of dying soon, so I am quite prepared to see you grow haggard and fat over the forthcoming decades."

A crack of laughter burst from her throat; his mouth creased in a barely suppressed smile as he added, "My finances are adequate without the aid of your fortune. And—forgive me for mentioning it—but my bloodline is more noble than yours too."

"This is hardly a litany of praise."

"It's the truth. And so is this: that there is only one remaining reason for me to offer you marriage. I love you." His grip about her fingers tightened. "For many years, I had no talent for using my heart, and so I never bothered with it—until you entered my life and showed me the pleasurable bits of life that I was missing. How much sweeter is work when there is someone to play with at day's end. How a small kindness can grow to touch everyone around it. Everything is better with you near."

The walls around her heart were weak now, indeed. "I want to believe you. So much. But I know your nature is solitary. How can I be sure you won't tire of me and toss me aside like a Carcel lamp?"

"I would *never* toss aside a Carcel lamp."

She couldn't help but laugh.

"But, Caro, such a comparison does not do you justice. You are far more precious than any work of human hands. I don't trust easily, yet I trusted you with my future when we met on that terrace—and I have long wished that my future would include you. I hope that you, in turn, can trust that I am yours: heart and mind, body and soul." Eyes never leaving hers, he brushed his lips over the back of her hand. A whisper of a kiss—a promise. More, more to come. More.

She tugged him to his feet, then wrapped her arms

around him as though she could pull him into her heart. "You dear, dratted, wonderful man. I love you dearly. And I would be honored to marry you."

He let out such a deep breath that for an instant he seemed boneless in her arms. "I am delighted to hear it. I wanted you to agree, very much."

"I would have agreed weeks ago had you asked for my heart instead of my fortune. But if Stratton convinced you that I might care for you, why have you waited so long to come?"

His gaze sidled away. "I have found that it takes twenty-one days of conscious effort to form or break a new habit."

"Am I a habit, then? I'm not sure whether that's a compliment."

"Not a habit, but a hope. After our last conversation, I realized I could never convince you to marry me unless I could save my dukedom without your money. I also realized that, even with a houseful of guests, I missed you. And even with twenty-one days of hard work and planning, you were always on my mind. As a promise unfulfilled or..."

"Or a hope," she repeated. "Yes. I hoped too."

"In those weeks, I could not get out of the habit of loving you. I didn't even want to try. I cursed every day that it took me to travel south from Lancashire. Then, when I arrived in London, I blessed the scandal rags, for they showed me that Stratton and Miss Cartwright had neatly removed themselves from our concern. I hoped that if you knew I didn't want anyone else—that I never had—"

Again, she laughed. "You should have begun your

proposal with all this, instead of that business about me growing haggard and fat."

With a deep sigh, he pressed a kiss against the side of her neck. "I told you I always say the wrong thing. Yet you agreed to marry me anyway. I suppose you really do love me."

"Just as you are. Yes. I suppose I really do." She tightened her arms around him.

And with that, he kissed her. A kiss of sweet hope, of passionate promise. His mouth firm on hers, hands laced around her waist.

More kissing followed, not just the neck, but the lips, every part of the face. Hands slid, stroked. Caroline's limbs began to weaken from lust.

Joy welled up in her, pure and elemental. "I do."

Against her cheek, she felt the flex of his throat, tight over a choked swallow. His skin was warm, his cheek just barely stubble-scratchy. "I hope you will marry me very soon, Caro. I cannot do without you: I told you I never decide anything lightly."

"Very soon," she agreed. "And you shall not do without me. Come to my bedchamber and we'll practice for our wedding night."

"A lady's request," Michael said, "should not be gainsaid."

"How well you have learned the lessons of society—and in fewer than six events too. Shall we credit my talents or yours?"

"Both," he said. "We could only accomplish so much together."

"I know we have all night," Caroline said as she pushed closed the door to her bedchamber. "But there's no reason why we should not get started right away, is there?"

"You want me to cut your corset strings again?" Strong hands slid around her waist and tugged her into the solid wall of his body.

"Do whatever you want to." She pressed herself more closely against the support of his chest, belly, the ridge of his cock. "As long as you do it to me."

His hands roamed over her back, teasing open the buttons at the back of her bodice. When he worked free the last button, he caught her gaze. His jaw was set in tight control, but his eyes showed his true feelings. Warm in the low lamplight of her bedchamber—still an Argand lamp; how had she not remedied that?—they looked so intently at her that they seemed to strip her bare in every way. The pupils were dilated, as though he must drink in the sight of her more fully. His lashes were sooty shadows every time he blinked.

How she loved him, this stubborn, loyal, determined man.

"This might be an excellent time to mention," he said conversationally, "that I've devised a new area of study recently."

"Does it have anything to do with removing your clothes?"

He gave her a tiny, wicked smile. "With yours, actually. If you'll permit?"

Hooking a fingertip under the loosened edge of her bodice, he worked it down her shoulders, arms, torso. The silk slid, heavy and slow, into a puddle of rich fabric.

Michael bent and coaxed Caroline's feet free, then laid the green gown carefully over the back of a chair. "I should hate for it to be spoiled," he said as he turned back to her. "It's the only one I've ever seen that comes close to matching your eyes."

She melted.

Liquid, she allowed him to free her from her corset and shift, crouch to tug her garters from her legs and roll down her stockings. His hands were roughened, but his touch was gentle. Under his touch, every cell in her body fired into heated life. But he avoided her center of pleasure, her belly, her breasts. As he unfolded to his full height again, tugging at his cravat, she felt positively molten.

"Show me what you've been studying," she said. "Show me." And with swift, determined tugs, she hurried him through his own disrobing.

Never had he smiled so much, this carefully coiled man. Never had he seemed so playful, so joyous, so wickedly delighted.

The undressing seemed to go much more quickly this time. Uncertainty had vanished; now they both knew what came next, what they wanted, what they felt. His hot tongue found the hollow behind her ear lobe, just as he kicked free from the last of his clothing. Caroline shivered and clutched for him, and they toppled onto her coverlet in a tangle of bare limbs.

Michael made up for the swiftness with which they undressed by stroking Caroline's body slowly. "Not everything I study is confined to theory," he murmured, running the point of his tongue between her breasts before settling next to her. Raised on one elbow, his left hand played over her. "Some of it can be translated quite well into practice. For example, if I've figured this correctly, you ought to enjoy this very much."

His head bent, teeth grazing her earlobe, just as his hand slipped over her breast and tugged lightly at the nipple.

"Ummm." She swallowed. "Do that again."

"Are you certain? Or would you rather I try something new?" His mouth replaced his fingers around her nipple, pulling hot and wet, sending liquid heat to her core. Those wicked fingers slipped down again, finding where she grew slick, and one, then two slid within her, filling her—almost perfect but teasingly different.

"You see," he said between licks and tugs at the nipple, "touching two points of pleasure at once more than doubles the sensation." His fingers slipped in her wetness, painting ecstasy through her body.

"How did you learn this? This couldn't… couldn't be from a book." Caroline's voice was unsteady, smoky from the fire within her.

"No." He rested his head flat on her chest, short hair teasing her sensitive skin. "It's billiards: identify the right angle for hitting two targets."

"Billiards?" She had to laugh. "That is absurd. You're very pleased with yourself, aren't you?"

"Not as pleased as you're going to be."

Caroline ran trembling hands over Michael's back,

pulling him atop her. He raised himself up on steady arms, caught her eye, and grinned again. "If one understands the capabilities of the equipment, one can calculate the preferred angle of thrust." With a sleek movement of his hips, he slid into her. His eyes closed, and a shudder ran through his long body. "God, Caro."

He swallowed heavily before wrenching his eyes open and adding, "And the correct amount of force."

Caroline's toes curled. "This is all most logical," she said in a husky voice.

"Logic is simply a means to an end," Michael said. "The purpose is to make you scream with pleasure."

"My dear future husband, I am a great admirer of your theories." She wrenched herself up to press hungry lips against his. Then she curled back onto the bed and tugged at his hips, sinking him deeper and deeper within her. "Everything's better with you, Michael."

"It will get better still." He sank onto his forearms and cradled her in his embrace. "For we have a lifetime to practice."

At last, he began to move, and he was right, the clever man. He found the spots that made her quiver; he teased them until she cried out, aching and full and needy. The angle, the thrust, the force... he filled her with pleasure until every barrier came down. Oh, she could never have imagined the sharp joy of this *making love*, melding the physical intimacy with emotional closeness just as deep. Never before had her heart and mind and body been so joined for one purpose.

"Together," she gasped, and he unleashed himself within her.

That was the last word either of them spoke for some time.

Epilogue

Caroline Graves, the dowager Lady Stratton, was married to the Duke of Wyverne just as a bleak autumn gave way to a bitter winter. Those members of society who had remained in London agreed that it was a most unlikely pairing: such a sociable creature wedding that solitary, eccentric duke.

At least, that is what the polite world said at first.

The newly married pair remained in London through the end of the year, as His Grace met with seemingly everyone in the financial heart of the City. There was, it seemed, no topic under the sun that did not interest him, from coal to shipping to agriculture. A rumor even flitted that he was considering development of a new type of railroad track, perhaps one of wrought iron, smelted in the inexhaustible coal-fired furnaces of Lancashire.

This idea would have seemed quite mad indeed, but for two things: Her Grace, whose opinions were sacrosanct, seemed convinced of her husband's good sense. And His Grace *did* behave fairly normally whenever the pair were out in public.

True, His Grace tended to hold his wife's arm in a very determined grip. He was never seen to dance with any other lady. The pair never lingered long at a mad crush of a ball. But as they were always gracious, the polite world was at last forced to conclude that they were besotted with one another.

It was charming, of course, but hardly worth gossiping about.

When Their Graces departed London for Lancashire at the beginning of 1817, the impression of their marriage as a love match was confirmed. Dear Caro was known to adore City life, but the mad duke and the madly attractive duchess had made Persephone's bargain: half the year spent up north and half in London. The new Duchess of Wyverne was, one heard, just as well loved in Lancashire as she was in the bosom of the polite world.

This was charming, of course. But hardly worth gossiping about.

In fact, news of the doings of Wyverne and his devoted bride garnered very little prurient interest from those in London, though the Marchioness of Applewood was seen several times to grow misty-eyed when someone mentioned the newlywed couple in passing.

By the time they returned to London for the season the following spring, the future duke—or perhaps a darling daughter—was expected. And His Grace had grown Her Grace a scrawny little red flower with which they both seemed delighted. Coquelicot, they called it.

They also professed themselves remarkably fond of billiards.

Author's Note

The year 1816 is sometimes nicknamed "the year without a summer." Across most of the Northern Hemisphere, temperatures were far colder than the average. In Lancashire, home to Michael's fictional dukedom, July 1816 is the coldest July recorded in more than two hundred years of weather record-keeping.

Modern climatologists think this odd weather was caused at least in part by the massive 1815 eruption of an Indonesian volcano, Tambora. Over the months that its ash cloud spread through the atmosphere, sunlight was blocked from reaching and warming the earth. Across Western Europe—especially in France, still reeling from military losses—agricultural failures and food shortages were common.

Apart from its unusual chilliness in 1816, Lancashire was a wonderful home for a Regency gadget guy such as Michael. As he informs Miss Cartwright, Preston was the first city to benefit from gas lighting besides London. Pioneers in the textile trade also hailed from Lancashire, introducing innovations like the flying shuttle, the spinning frame, and the spinning jenny to England's mills.

As for Michael's supposed madness: he has social anxiety, not that he would admit it. (He is, after all, a dratted duke.) Anxiety can manifest as headaches and—in the case of Michael's fateful London encounters with Caroline—panic attacks. His stern control is an attempt to manage this condition, as is his isolation—which can actually increase anxiety and certainly didn't do his reputation any good. To talk him through his concerns, Caroline uses the not-yet-invented methods of cognitive behavioral therapy, which to a social creature such as herself seem merely like common sense.

One last note: near the end of the book, Caroline tells Stratton, "Publish and be damned." She anticipates the Duke of Wellington, who, according to legend, made that response to a blackmail threat in 1824. Caroline has little else in common with the Iron Duke, but they share a confidence in their own reputations.

Read on for a sneak preview of

Secrets of a Scandalous Heiress

Theresa Romain

From Sourcebooks Casablanca

One

March 1817

Most people hoped to spot familiar faces in a crowded ballroom. Augusta Meredith prayed to see only strangers.

For nearly a week, her prayers had been granted. In winter's waning days, the *ton* kept its distance from Bath. The resort city's fashionable years were in the past, and so it was to be avoided in favor of the rural delights of hunting or the sophisticated pleasures of London.

Not that Augusta had ever been part of the *ton*. But like a moth before an ever-closed window, she had fluttered around its fringes long enough that someone might recognize her.

Thus far, though, the crowds in Bath's Upper Rooms presented her only with strangers. Merchants and cits and hangers-on. A lower social class; exactly the sort of person Augusta knew best. Exactly who she was. In Bath, she didn't have to pretend to be someone else.

The ballroom yawned high and stretched long, a

giant of a structure. Larger than any ballroom Augusta had seen in London, it was just as crowded, with slowly churning waves of people. But there was one great difference: here Augusta inhabited the center, not the edge.

"Mrs. Flowers, m'dear!"

The voice floated above the din in the high-ceilinged room, and Augusta turned toward it. "Mrs. Flowers!" The call came again; this time, the shouting man waved his arms too.

Augusta returned his wave with a graceful flicker of her fan, then flipped it open to hide her grin.

Well. Maybe she did pretend to be someone else, at that.

The shouting man was heavyset and young, probably less than her own twenty-five years. Every time he had spoken with Augusta, he had been tipsy; since she'd forgotten his name, she had mentally dubbed him Hiccuper. He shouldered toward her, making slow progress through the crowd. The pale-walled, elaborately plastered ballroom stretched high and long, yet babbling voices and dancing figures filled it brim-full, bouncing from the barrel-vaulted ceiling, raining from the wrought-iron faced walkway across the room's end.

Oh, Bath was a city of carefully calculated comforts, from the regimented hours for bathing and taking the mineral waters to the location of the nightly assemblies. Everything was orchestrated to bring strangers together in harmony. And through this sort of artificial harmony, Augusta would slip into the escape she craved.

Hiccuper had almost reached her; no doubt he intended to escort her into the winding figures of the dance. When the steps brought them together, he would leer at her breasts; when the dance was over, he might try to persuade her to accompany him home.

All part of what she planned when she wrote a false name in Bath's social registry—the Pump Room's guest book. By writing "Mrs. John Flowers" instead of "Miss Augusta Meredith," she became a widow instead of an unmarried woman, shedding the social manacles of an heiress who drew her fortune from trade.

And she didn't intend to carry out her plan with someone like Hiccuper. Augusta Meredith might not hope for better, but Mrs. Flowers could.

Hiccuper was still feet away, swept into a conversation with friends, when another voice spoke in her ear. "Mrs. Flowers, what good fortune to encounter you here in Bath. Do you know, you greatly resemble a young lady of my acquaintance."

A male voice. A *familiar* male voice.

Damn, damn. Her luck had just run out.

Still hiding behind her fan, Augusta turned toward the voice. From its cursed tone of humor, she knew it to belong to Josiah Everett—and here he stood, plainly dressed, handsome, and full of wicked glee. The worst sort of person she could have encountered: one who knew her too well to be fooled by her lie, but not well enough to take part in it.

"Mr. Everett." She forced a smile. "How unexpectedly delightful to see you. I would have expected you to remain in London for business reasons."

Like Augusta, Everett orbited society at a distance and had a few friends among the *beau monde*'s permissive fringes. Although of respectable birth, his means were straitened. He worked for his bread, serving as Baron Sutcliffe's man of business.

This much, Augusta knew from a house party to which they had both been invited the previous autumn. She knew little else about him.

"I almost believe your delight to be sincere." Everett bowed. "At the present, a particular errand requires my attention in Bath. But what of you, Mrs. Flowers? Your name tells me you have been recently married. Permit me to congratulate you."

Was that amusement in his dark eyes? Probably. Hmph. He always looked amused.

"Oh, I am not married at present, Mr. Everett." A true statement in itself. She fluttered her fan, an elaborate affair of lace and ivory and painted silk, before her bosom. Earlier this evening, a certain Mr. Rowe had informed her the gesture looked sultry.

As though a woman with hair the color of a persimmon could ever truly be sultry. With unfashionably bright red hair—there was no point in calling it auburn—and no birth to recommend her, Augusta had grown used to enticing men with her figure instead.

Everett refused to be enticed; he only folded his arms in his plain black coat. "Dear me. Ought I instead to offer condolences? Has Mr. Flowers departed this earth?"

Augusta snapped her fan closed. "Is there something you require of me, sir?"

"Only a confirmation." Everett's dark features held a sardonic expression. "My condolences, then. I did suspect you to be a *widow*"—he paused over this final word—"since half the men in this ballroom are singing your praises."

"Only half?" She arched a brow. "How sad. My popularity is declining."

Everett's smile grew. "I haven't been present very long. It might be more."

"And what are these men saying of me?"

He lifted his gaze to a chandelier, one of five elaborate gilt affairs that lit the stretching room and cast down as much heat as they did light. Outside, night hung like dark velvet over the clerestory windows. "I believe," he drawled, "that someone said your bosom could launch a thousand ships. That seems a bit much to ask of a bosom, though. It is not a dockyard."

"Certainly not for you," she muttered. It was, however, her best feature. Her indigo silk's low-cut bodice was trimmed in gold cord and lace, a fashion flattering to a young woman with more curves than elegance.

"Perhaps I shouldn't have told you what I'd overheard." Everett was looking at her again, dark brows slightly lifted as though he were challenging her. "Then again, if you're a widow, you can handle a bit of scandalous talk."

"Mrs. Flowers!" Hiccuper had pushed his way through the crowd at last, panting boozily. "Mrs. Flowers, m'dear."

"Ah, Mr..." She covered her uncertainty over his name with a titter. "How good to see you."

"You must dance with me, Mrs. Flowers. They're

forming a cotillion." The heavyset man leaned closer, the odor of perspiration and cheap sherry as sharp as a slap. When he breathed out, setting the curls at Augusta's ears into a dance, she went stiff.

Avoiding Everett's gaze, she simpered, "I'm sorry, dear sir, but I've just agreed to dance with this gentleman." She waved her fan in Everett's direction with languid disinterest, hoping he had manners enough not to give the lie to her words.

Indeed, Everett spoke up at once. "So sorry, *dear sir,* but perhaps you may have a later dance. Mrs. Flowers, shall we take our places in the set?" He held out a gray-gloved hand.

With a parting wave, she left a surprised Hiccuper behind and joined Everett in pressing through the crowd. "Thank you for covering my little falsehood—"

"One of several."

"—but," she added in a slightly louder tone, "you don't really have to dance with me. I could develop an urgent requirement for tea. Or a rest."

"I certainly *do* need to dance with you, if that's the sort of man who follows you around discussing your bosom." Everett frowned back at Hiccuper. "Your *dear sir* smelled as though he hadn't washed for a week. Has he bothered you before?"

"No. No one bothers me."

Everett slanted a sideways look at her, then set his jaw.

It was a rather nice jaw, clean and strong. As though his veins carried Mediterranean blood, his skin was a dark olive and his hair black and faintly curling. Within his gray gloves, his hands had a firm, pleasant grip.

How unfortunate that such a fine form belonged to such an unnerving man, with such a pestilent wit.

Though at the moment, his usual expression of humor had settled into solemn lines. "It is, of course, your business if you want to throw away your time on men who compare you to a dockyard."

"*You* were the one who made that comparison." She tried to tug her fingers from his grasp, but an elderly man with grizzled side-whiskers jostled against them just then. To steady her, Everett drew her closer against his side. Augusta took a startled breath; she caught a faint, spicy scent. Sandalwood?

Again, he looked at her sidelong. "Yes, well. I certainly wouldn't deny you could find better company than me. Though at least I wash every day. That's something, I suppose."

"That's something," she repeated. Under the guise of stumbling against his arm, then catching her breath in the crowd, she inhaled again. *Yes.* Sandalwood. A faraway scent, as unusual as it was masculine. Because it had to be imported from afar, from sultry corners of the world like India or Hawai'i, the golden oil was costly.

As the heiress to a cosmetics fortune, Augusta knew fragrances as well as most women knew fashion. Sandalwood was an unusual choice for any Englishman, much less one of limited means.

Well. She had just learned something else about Josiah Everett: he was a man of at least one surprise.

Maybe he would hold one more, if she could persuade him. Rising to her toes, she whispered in his ear, "Mr. Everett. How can I convince you to keep my secret?"

Encountering Augusta Meredith was not the first surprise that had befallen Joss since his arrival in Bath three days before, though it was certainly more pleasant than the ones that had preceded it.

Hearing Augusta Meredith referred to as "Mrs. Flowers"? Another surprise; this one, less pleasant. For a dreadful swooping moment he thought she had finally got herself married off.

But no: it seemed the name and the widowhood were equally fictitious, part of some plan of hers. As, no doubt, was her warm breath in his ear. Her husky whisper. The faint floral scent she wore, so delicate and sweet he could almost taste it.

How can I convince you to keep my secret?

He ought to require no convincing at all; he ought simply to do a lady's bidding. But as he knew quite well, secrets came at a great price. That was, after all, why he was in Bath to begin with.

"At the moment, my dear Mrs. Flowers, you need do nothing but dance with me." He drew her to one side of a set. Throughout the enormous ballroom, couples were grouping, four by four, into the squares of the cotillion.

Joss hoped he remembered the steps. He hadn't danced since he was a half-grown boy, filling in the sets with maids and servants to help his second cousin, Lord Sutcliffe, learn the figures he'd need to move in high society.

How many years had Joss spent helping Sutcliffe with figures? Though he was only thirty-one, it seemed the task of a lifetime. Now, though, they were figures of a different sort: amounts of money, curves of women.

But soon that would all be done, Joss's long servitude at an end. If he could get a few damned people to speak with him. So far, "Mrs. Flowers" was the only person who had given him more than a curious glance, or a dismissive one. And though her smile had been polite, he was fortunate her eyes were incapable of firing bullets.

He had hoped the fluctuations of Bath society, always bidding *bonjour* and *adieu* to travelers, would allow him to conduct his business more efficiently than in London. But no; even here, gazes skated over him. Maybe because of his dark complexion or the plainness of his clothing. To them, Joss did not appear as though he had anything to offer.

At least he made a better dance partner than an unwashed sot.

He looked down at Miss Meredith, standing to his right, impatient and fidgety under her lush tangle of red curls threaded with amber beads. Her bosom—which might not truly launch a thousand ships, but which was certainly worthy of a flotilla—rose and fell with fascinating force within her purple silk gown. Maybe she intended to befuddle him into agreement with her pneumatic talents.

He was quite willing to let her try. "Take hands, my dear widow."

With a filthy look quickly turned angelic, she let him draw her into the small circle of their dance.

"I wonder at your grimaces, Mrs. Flowers," he murmured, sliding over the smooth wooden floor in some semblance of the correct balances and steps and *chassés*. "*You* invited *me* to dance, after all. Is not this cotillion the fulfillment of your ambition?"

Her light brown eyes opened wide, but a retort was arrested by the movement of the dance: the four women stepped inward, forming a cross with their joined hands. After they completed their steps and turns, the men did the same. Joss's three companions bore a familiar look of determined concentration; one man was actually counting the steps to himself.

Bath in miniature: a polite grouping of strangers thrust into close proximity. Unwilling to give offense, but unsure whether they ought to have anything to do with one another. Yet the people, like the ballroom walls, were plastered and painted. Hoping to impress.

He was no different, was he? Except that plaster and paint were beyond his means. He had only ever seen the *ton* from the outside. Peering out from the corner of a ballroom, or down from a balcony's dizzying height. This feeling of being melted and mixed into a crowd was unfamiliar and, thus, not entirely pleasant.

Miss Meredith had only a moment to hiss in his ear before the dance dragged them apart again. "I do find you preferable to being pawed by a drunkard."

"You honor me. As I am not intoxicated, may I be permitted to paw you instead?"

Stepping, sliding, hopping again. This dance was not conducive to conversation. And Joss much preferred boots to the ridiculous glossy shoes required by Bath's Master of Ceremonies at these formal assemblies. It was so difficult to find his footing in this sort of place.

When they next passed one another, she gave him

a truly lovely smile. "You are welcome to try it and see what happens. Are you fond of all your fingers?"

"Indeed I am, my dear Widow Flower, so I shan't put a hand on you except as part of this dance. You deserve every courtesy, having married and buried a husband since we last met—when was it?"

"In Lancashire. Last autumn." She frowned. "At the Duke of Wyverne's house party."

"No doubt you are right," he said lightly. As though he couldn't remember the exact dates in September, or the bright shade of her hair under the cold northern sky.

A violin wandered out of tune; with a sweet rebuke, an oboe called it back. Joss stepped forward into the cross with the other men. Now the chain, in which his feet were supposed to do something intricate while he and Miss Meredith held hands. He settled for taking her fingers and shuffling back and forth just enough not to smack into the other dancers.

"As I said before, you have my condolences for your recent bereavement," he added mercilessly. "This festivity must be an attempt to kick away your mourning. Though it is a bit soon, if—"

"It's all a lie, all right?" she whispered. "Now stop. Talking. You know I'm not a widow."

Her sudden frankness surprised him into silence, as did the hard expression that crossed her soft features.

For a moment they simply shuffled gracelessly, hands clasped and bodies a breath apart. The pale swell of her flotilla-launching breasts, the fiery glints of her hair under the chandelier-light, had him wishing she were a widow in truth.

But she was a maiden. A *lying* maiden. And two generations of family scandal had taught Joss that, though lies might be permissible, dallying with maidens was not.

"I know you are not," he said in a voice touched with regret. "I'd love to lie about who I am. I simply didn't think of it."

"If only you had, then we would be on equal footing. As it is, my reputation is in your hands."

"Mrs. Flowers, every time a woman dances with a man, her reputation is in his hands. That is why it is such an honor when a lady agrees to dance with a man."

"But I asked you to dance," she said. "Or if we are to be accurate, I informed you that you were to dance with me."

"Then I suppose *my* reputation is in *your* hands."

She looked at him with some surprise; then the dance separated them. There ensued an interminable winding and stepping and crossing, until finally the orchestra's sawing dwindled away. As Miss Meredith applauded with the other dancers, Joss caught her elbow and steered her to the edge of the room.

The crush was slightly less here. When Joss glared at a dandy seated on a small bench, the fellow scrambled away and Joss handed his partner into the seat. "Do tell me, Mrs. Flowers," he said as he looked down at her, "how have you passed off this new identity?"

A fan dangled from one wrist; she caught it up in her other hand and began teasing it open. It bore a painting of some curly headed Greek-looking youth, with white draperies and tiny wings and puffed-out cheeks.

"Zephyr," she said, noticing Joss's gaze. "The god

of the west wind. An apt decoration for a fan, don't you think?" She waved it at him, and a welcome eddy of cool air brushed his features.

Joss ignored this attempt at diversion, lifting his brows.

She snapped the fan closed. "Very well. I'm visiting Bath in company with the Countess of Tallant. She was at the Duke of Wyverne's house party too, if you remember?"

"Yes, certainly." The young auburn-haired countess and her doting husband shared unshakable good humor, though the lady was considerably more talented at billiards than the earl.

"Lady Tallant is"—Miss Meredith paused—"not well. She's here to take the waters and doesn't plan to mix much in society. So I was tasked with visiting the Pump Room after we arrived, to sign our names in the guest book and meet the Master of Ceremonies and whatnot. I took the opportunity to…not be me anymore."

"You are still you," Joss reminded her. "You simply called yourself something different. Why Mrs. Flowers, by the way?"

She coughed. "I saw a vase of flowers in one corner as I was introducing myself, and that was that."

"To think, if the Master of Ceremonies had made your introduction in a different room, Bath might now be admiring the charms of Mrs. Roman Statue."

Her attempt at a frown was a dreadful failure; in a moment, it flipped into a smile and a low chuckle. The sound was throaty and knowing, entirely different from the feathery giggle she had used with the portly drunkard who had tried to seize her for a dance.

That had been a maiden's laugh. This? This was the chuckle of a woman who liked the company of a man.

Only when her laugh fell silent, the smile vanishing, did Joss realize he had been staring at her in some wonder.

"So you'll keep my secret?" she asked in a brittle voice.

"That depends on why you possess a secret in the first place." Though his brows were getting tired from all the lifting, he kept the blasé expression on his face. "Why are you posing as a widow, Miss Meredith? Are you in some danger?"

Her features crumpled; then she straightened her shoulders. "Not at all." She looked up at him, and her smile almost reached her brandy-gold eyes. "It's as simple as this, Mr. Everett. I require a lover."

Acknowledgments

Thanks to my husband, who critiques pages, listens to me mumble about story ideas, and puts our young daughter to bed every night so I can squeeze in a little more writing. And thanks to Amanda, who does the first two of those things with great cheer, even though she has kids of her own to put to bed.

On the Sourcebooks team, deep gratitude to Deb Werksman, Susie Benton, Danielle Dresser, and the folks in art and marketing. To Paige Wheeler, always a marvelous advocate. And dear readers, my thanks to you for finding my books.

And finally, thanks to my friends and family—especially my parents. They've both worked in the field of mental health since before I was a wee glimmer, and their expertise has inspired and informed this story.

Also, they gave me my first books. So really, this is all their doing.

About the Author

Historical romance author Theresa Romain pursued an impractical education that allowed her to read everything she could get her hands on. She then worked for universities and libraries, where she got to read even more. Eventually she started writing too. *To Charm a Naughty Countess* is the second book in the Regency Matchmaker trilogy. Theresa lives with her family in the Midwest.

Between a Rake and a Hard Place

by Connie Mason and Mia Marlowe

Lady Serena's list of forbidden pleasures

Attend an exclusively male club.

Smoke a cigar.

Have a fortune told by gypsies.

Dance the scandalous waltz.

Sir Jonah Sharp thinks Lady Serena Osbourne will be just like any other debutante, and seducing her will be one of the easiest services he's ever done for the Crown. Then he catches her wearing trousers and a mustache in his gentleman's club and she demands he teach her to smoke a cigar. But what will truly be Jonah's undoing is finding out he's an item on her list too, which makes him determined to bring her all the forbidden pleasure she can handle.

"Shimmers with romance… Well-rounded characters and effortless plotting make this installment the best in the series."—*Publishers Weekly*

For more Connie Mason and Mia Marlowe, visit:

www.sourcebooks.com

Much Ado About Jack

by Christy English

How to become London's most notorious widow:

1. Vow to NEVER re-marry

2. Own your own ship and become fabulously wealthy

3. Wear the latest risqué fashions in your signature color

4. Do NOT have a liaison at the Prince Regent's palace with a naval captain whose broad shoulders and green eyes make you forget Rule #1

Angelique Beauchamp, the widowed Countess of Devereaux, has been twice burned by love, and she is certain that no man will ever touch her heart again. But that doesn't mean she can't indulge a little—and it would be hard to find a more perfect dalliance than the dashing Captain James Montgomery.

After a brief but torrid affair, James tries to forget Angelique and his undeniable thirst for more. The luscious lady was quite clear that their liaison was temporary. But for the first time, the lure of the sea isn't powerful enough to keep him away…

Praise for ***How to Tame a Willful Wife*****:**

"Refreshingly honest and passionate."—*Publishers Weekly*

For more Christy English, visit:

www.sourcebooks.com

What the Groom Wants

by Jade Lee

USA Today Bestselling Author

An honest love...

Radley Lyncott has been in love with Wendy Drew as long as he can remember. When he went to sea, she was too young to court. Now that he's returned to take up his Welsh title, he is appalled to find that debt has ruined the Drew family, and—even worse—Wendy is being courted by another man.

Or a dangerous attraction?

Family comes first for seamstress Wendy Drew, who is forced to settle her brother's debt by working nights at a notorious gambling den. But her double life hasn't gone unnoticed—she has captivated none other than Demon Damon, a nefarious rake who understands Wendy's darkest desires and is hell-bent on luring her into his arms.

Praise for Jade Lee:

"Lee has a definite flair for creating engaging characters..."—*Booklist Online*

"Ms. Lee is a wonderful storyteller. I cannot wait to see what she has in store for her readers next."—*My Book Addiction Reviews*

For more Jade Lee, visit:

www.sourcebooks.com